Praise for William Shaw

A Song from Dead Lips nominated for a Barry Award
and named Best Crime of 2013, *Evening Standard*

A Book of Scars shortlisted for the CWA Historical Dagger and
named Crime Book of the Year, *Sunday Times*

The Birdwatcher longlisted for Theakstons Crime Novel
of the Year

'The most gripping book I've read in years. William Shaw is,
quite simply, an **outstanding storyteller**'   Peter May

'William Shaw is a **superb flowing writer**, both of police procedure and personal relations, and perhaps England's most adept
at using dialogue (as distinct from description) to propel his
always intelligent stories'   *The Times*

'The kind of writing – silky, seductive, unobtrusive – that carries
one along. I picked the book up to get a taste of it and an hour
later was still reading this **clever, absorbing** police procedural'
          Literary Review

'An **astoundingly good** crime novel'   Elly Griffiths

'A first-rate police thriller set amidst the seamy underside of the
Swinging Sixties . . . the totemic year of '68 **will never seem
the same** again'   C. J. Sansom

'Superb crime novels . . . combines nostalgic period detail with
an **emotional intensity** found only in the very best crime
fiction'   *Sunday Times*

William Shaw was born in Newton Abbot, Devon, grew up in Nigeria and lived for sixteen years in Hackney. He has been shortlisted for the CWA Historical Dagger, longlisted for the Theakstons Crime Novel of the Year and nominated for a Barry Award. A regular at festivals, Shaw organises panel talks and CWA events across the south east. He lives in Brighton.

Sign up for his newsletter at williamshaw.com
🆃 @william1shaw

BREEN & TOZER INVESTIGATIONS

A Song from Dead Lips
A House of Knives
A Book of Scars
Sympathy for the Devil

ALEXANDRA CUPIDI SERIES

Salt Lane

The Birdwatcher

SYMPATHY FOR THE DEVIL

William Shaw

riverrun

First published in Great Britain in 2017 by riverrun
This paperback edition published in 2018 by

riverrun

An imprint of

Quercus Editions Limited
Carmelite House
50 Victoria Embankment
London EC4Y 0DZ

An Hachette UK company

A CIP catalogue record for this book is available
from the British Library.

PB ISBN 978 1 78429 728 2
EBOOK ISBN 978 1 78429 725 1

10 9 8 7 6 5 4 3 2

Typeset by CC Book Production

Printed and bound in Great Britain by Clays Ltd, St Ives plc

For Susannah

ONE

Alone, the young man floats in water, his body still on this summer night, long platinum hair flowing around his head. The pool is heated. The water is warm. He wears only a multicoloured swimming suit and four large rings on his fingers.

A gentle mist rises from the water into the dark air.

It is approaching midnight; moths fuss around the blaring bulbs that light the way to his home, a red-tiled sixteenth-century farmhouse that squats like a toad crouching in the rolling hills on the edges of the Weald. The garden is lush, though a little unkempt now. The high hedges need cutting; the shrubs have outgrown their beds.

This is the house of a rich young man; a rock star.

A trail of wet footprints leads along the stone path towards the building. Through an open bedroom window on the first floor, comes the sound of a telephone. The metallic trill is interrupted by a woman's voice; 'Hello? Oh hi. No. I don't know where Brian is. Brian?'

1

It is his young pretty girlfriend. She calls from the room above. There is no answer.

'He's in the pool, I think. Yeah. I'm fine. Just hanging around, you know?' A sing-song voice with a slight Swedish accent. 'Brian? He's kind of stoned, I guess. Am I stoned? A little bit.' A giggle.

Another woman, blonde, emerges from the house while the other still talks. She is beautiful too, because this is a house where lovely women come and go. Even though the star is fading for the man in the pool, the women still come. He is a rock guitarist. Right now, there is nothing cooler. Often there are parties and loud music played on reel-to-reel tape recorders through massive loudspeakers.

The neighbours who live in the lanes around here are nervous; they are trying to keep up with the times, to be tolerant of the youngsters who arrive in cars and taxis, in Bentleys and on motorbikes, but these rich young people are changing their quiet hillside. On the nights where the music and shouting and revving engines continue late into the night, the locals lie awake in bed unable to sleep.

Tonight, though, is quiet. The rock star has been drinking and taking pills. No more than usual. Less, probably, in fact. He is tired and worn, weary of everything. The buttons of his shirts strain at the belly; his trousers are too tight. His band don't want him any more. Sometimes he cries and hugs the women who come here.

Though there is a Rolls-Royce sitting in the garage, undriven for weeks, he has spent all his money. He's never been sure where it all came from; now he doesn't understand where it's all gone.

The building work on the second living room is unfinished and the builders are asking for payment.

The woman approaches the pool looking for towels. Men just leave them lying anywhere. They expect the women to clear up after them. It's not fair.

She can hear the rock star's girlfriend upstairs, still talking on the phone. For a second, she wonders where the young man who owns the house has gone. She looks around. The pool is so silent; the water is still, lights from the house moving gently across the surface.

Besides a discarded towel and the empty glass of brandy sitting by the side of the pool, the place seems deserted. She picks up the towel and looks around again.

And sees him.

Under the water, he hangs, arms splayed out, inches from the bottom of the pool. He is like a diver in mid arc, except he is still, and beneath the surface, not above it. She looks harder. At first she thinks he's playing, but the water is too still.

Time seems to slow.

She runs back up the path and shouts and screams below the open bedroom window. It seems so long before anyone hears her.

And so much longer before the police finally arrive and see the body, skin like white rubber, pale and cooling, laid on the limestone paving at the pool's side.

'Bloody hell,' says a sergeant, tired at the end of his shift. It will be a long night.

Neighbours sit up in bed, unable to sleep again for the noise. But it will be much quieter here now, at least.

TWO

London; a summer evening.

Though she didn't live here, the middle-aged woman had her own key to the house; she let herself in. She was smartly dressed, a dab of Yardley on her décolletage. Looking at her, nobody would guess what her job was. That's the way she preferred it. None of her neighbours knew. She liked to imagine they assumed she was some rich bohemian living off her inheritance. They would be shocked if they knew.

Today was Friday. She was annoyed because she had left it too late to go to the bank and they all closed at three and wouldn't open again until Monday morning. It was OK. Lena would advance her a tenner to tide her over, but she didn't like to borrow. She was a professional.

She pressed the lift button and waited for the whirr of machinery. There was no sound.

It was one of the rickety, old-fashioned ones, with a criss-cross metal scissor gate. She tried the 'Up' button again, and once more.

'Hell.'

'Broken.' A voice behind her made her jump.

She turned. Mr Payne, the old man from Flat 1, was at his door. He seemed to lurk there, waiting for someone to talk to.

'Hasn't been working all day.'

'Hell's bells.' Now, every time a customer rang the doorbell she would have to traipse down two floors, and all the way back up again. With her knees.

'You'll have to stay down here with me.'

'Get lost.' She smiled at him. 'You pervert.' Pathetic, the way she enjoyed flirting with men more as each year passed, even the ones old enough to be her father. Once, she had lived off her looks. She looked up the steep stairs.

In younger days, when she had been slimmer and the cigarettes had not coated her lungs, two flights would have been easy, but she found on this summer evening, she was sweating by the time she reached the second floor.

She knocked on the door, as she always did, but opened it with her key.

'Hello? Only me,' she sing-songed, as she always did, but today there was no answer.

'Lena?'

The rest of the house was ordinary. The stairwell was drab. It was only when you went through the front door to Lena's flat that everything changed.

She didn't like her employer much, but she had to admit it; she had a kind of genius.

Pink. Everywhere. The walls, the curtains, even the lampshades, were a rich girlish colour. The carpet, at least, was white.

5

The beanbag, a shocking lime green. There was a framed picture of The Beatles on the wall, not as they were now, bearded, dissolute and immersed in Eastern philosophies, but when they were still neat, uncomplicated and joyful, and when every teenager loved them.

Everything had been picked with care. The pop group grinned, wearing pink shirts and ties and holding red roses. Other less famous stars surrounded them, some cut out from *Rave* and *Jackie* and stuck up with Sellotape, others framed and signed in black pen. Across the world, teenage walls looked like this now. Lena had invested in the place.

It was perfect, down to the collection of dolls and gollywogs, lined up on a bookshelf, which Florence hated. It wasn't just their unclosing stare that was creepy.

She looked around her and sighed. Most days Lena tidied up for herself. But there were rare times when she finished late and crawled into her bed, exhausted. Last night must have been one of them.

The teddy bear was on the floor, face down. The ashtray was full of cigarette ends, there were half-empty glasses on the table and an empty champagne bottle on the carpet.

Today was a Friday; the busiest night of the week. The first clients would arrive soon, after work. Everything had to be ready.

'Lena?' she called.

Still no answer.

Strange. She must have gone out. Florence checked her watch. The first customer would be here in half an hour.

She stuck out her tongue, threw open the window to get last night's stink of smoke, alcohol and whatever else out of the room. She picked up the stuffed toy, wrinkling her nose at him, plumped the sofa cushions, and then sat him in his usual place.

Someone had been using the record player and had not put the records back in their sleeves. There was a disc on the turntable and a single just lying on the carpet: 'Sugar, Sugar' by The Archies.

Lena was not normally this slovenly, but someone had been having a nice time. It looked that way, anyway. Who was the last one in yesterday? The man who always brought children's toys. Florence shuddered. So it wouldn't have been a social occasion. And though she went out to parties sometimes with the in-crowd, Lena never had friends over. In fact, she doubted Lena had any friends. If she did, she never talked about them.

The single rose in a vase had shed onto the polished wood, next to the bottle. She picked up the loose yellow petals and scrunched them hard in her hand until the colour stained her skin. The bowl of sherbet lemons had been spilled on the floor too. Someone had trodden one into the white carpet. Florence knelt down and started to pick pieces out of the pile.

She had almost all the bits, cupping them in her left hand, when the black phone began ringing. Lena had two telephones. The ivory one for personal, and the black one for business. This was the business phone.

Florence sighed and straightened, painfully. She was too old to be scrabbling around on her knees. She brushed the broken sweet off her hand into the litter bin under the mock Louis Quinze desk, then picked up the handset.

'Julie Teenager's apartment.' Her posh voice.

Many of the men were hesitant on the phone. You had to be

patient with them; try and make them think all this stuff was normal, else you'd scare them off. This one wasn't shy though. She recognised his voice; one of the regulars. It was one of the men who called himself Smith. There were a few. This was the large one, the married man who bit the nails of his left hand. She opened the appointment book.

'Sorry, Mr Smith. Nine o'clock is all booked up, I'm afraid.'

In the appointment book, each week had two pages, split into five days. Sundays to Wednesdays, Lena didn't work. The remaining three days were divided into four two-hour slots, starting at 5 p.m. and ending at 1 a.m.

'You're usually Thursdays, aren't you? We had been expecting you. Nothing the matter I hope? Is eleven tonight too late?'

Yes, eleven was too late, Mr Smith said, sounding annoyed. He had to be on the train home by then.

'Oh, what a shame, Mr Smith,' said Florence. 'Julie will be ever so disappointed. She always looks forward to your visits.' She smiled as she talked to him; a good impression was always important. 'Perhaps you would like to make a date for next week?'

She entered his name into the appointment book, closed it and looked around her, sighed.

The bedroom was worse. The bed was unmade, the ashtray spilled onto the carpet and Lena had left knickers on the floor. She was normally such a good girl, too. The school uniform, at least, was folded up neatly on the chair.

She put the dirty knickers into the bin and was about to close the bedside cabinet drawer, which was half open, when she saw a handful of pound notes stuffed in there. Honestly. Careless.

Florence peeled off ten. She shouldn't have to be doing this work anyway.

Then she looked at her watch. It was twenty to five already. Where did all the time go? And, for that matter, where was Lena? She went back and checked the appointment book. Her first customer was due at five. Another regular. Another Mr Smith. This one was an elderly gentleman, rich and well-connected, but a poor tipper, like all his sort.

She took the empty bottle downstairs with the rubbish and paused on the first floor to catch her breath. The students in Flat 3 had left their door open to let the air circulate. Peeking through the door, she spied a young girl, dressed in only a red T-shirt and a small pair of knickers, standing in the living room smoking a cigarette. It was the pretty one. All the boys who shared the apartment would be in love with her. She scowled and set off up the next flight.

She left the bathroom till last. She was surprised to notice blood in the toilet. It lay as a layer in the curve at the bottom of the bowl, vivid against the white. Unusual. It wasn't Lena's period. She knew that for a fact. They didn't work when it was.

She peered at the red blood for a while, frowning, then flushed the cistern. She looked at her watch again. Where the hell was she?

At five, exactly, the bell rang. The flat was tidy at least. But Lena was still not back.

The man arrived, panting from the climb, and sat on the couch next to the enormous teddy bear. He had brought a present, wrapped in white paper and tied with a big red ribbon. 'Would you like a cup of tea while you wait?' Florence asked him, looking at the red against the white and starting to feel as if something was not right. 'Or something stronger perhaps?'

'Bloody lift,' he said, catching his breath. 'Not working.'

Maybe it was a good thing Lena wasn't here. The man didn't look like he'd survive an hour with Julie Teenager anyway.

THREE

It was Saturday morning; Detective Sergeant Cathal Breen of the Metropolitan Police's D Division had just put on the first pair of jeans he had ever owned when the doorbell rang.

He opened the door only a little way. Elfie was standing on the doorstep, holding a cake. 'It's just so sad,' she said.

'What is?' called his girlfriend Helen from the living room.

In front of her pregnant belly, the young woman Elfie, who lived upstairs from them, held out the hot cake tin. 'This is. Look at it. I made it for us to take to the concert, but it's rubbish.'

Their neighbour was wearing a brightly printed muslin dress that you could see her underwear through. And oven gloves. 'Do you have icing sugar? I was thinking I could fill in the dip with it. Aren't you two ready yet? No point being late. We'll never get in.' She looked down. 'New trousers, Paddy?'

Cathal Breen's father had been Irish. Cathal had never asked to be called Paddy but the name had stuck. He looked down at his jeans. He was a policeman, unused to trousers without

11

creases; in the Met, only the Drug Squad wore jeans. 'Seriously. What do you think?' he asked. 'Are they OK?'

'Icing sugar?' called Helen from the living room. 'Will ordinary sugar do?'

Breen was never sure whether his girlfriend Helen was just winding Elfie up, or she genuinely didn't know this stuff. Elfie pushed past him into his flat where Helen was sitting in Breen's armchair eating biscuits straight from the packet.

Though they were both due in the next few weeks, Elfie's bump was huge; Helen's looked ridiculously small. They were both pregnant. Obviously he was glad the two women had become such close friends; he worked long hours. Who wouldn't be glad? It was convenient that Helen had company when he was on duty. But while Helen was a former policewoman, Elfie had never worked in her life. She was a hippie who lived with a man who drove an ancient sports car, who had some job in advertising in Soho. There were days when he wished he could spend more time with Helen, on her own.

'It's carrot cake,' said Elfie. 'I made real lemonade too. For the picnic.'

Helen spat biscuit crumbs. 'You can't make cake out of carrots.'

'You're not even dressed yet, Hel. We've got to get there in plenty of time because it'll be super-crammed and we'll probably have to walk from Oxford Circus.'

'We'll just push our way to the front,' said Helen. 'Make way. Two pregnant ladies.'

They laughed. Sergeant Cathal Breen stood there listening to the two women, still looking down at his new pair of trousers.

They weren't very flared at all, really, but he worried that they looked stupid on a man his age. Jeans were for young people. They'd look fine on Helen because she was eight years his junior. He'd bought a pair of dark glasses too.

'What do you think of the trousers, Elfie?'

'Do you like them, Paddy?'

'That wasn't what I asked.'

'Just be yourself, for once, Paddy. Not "The Man". Just be who you want to be. Come on, Hel. We'll miss it if you don't come now.'

He scowled at her, but she was right. The world was changing; he should change too. He would go to a rock concert. He would enjoy himself. It would be great, wouldn't it?

'Anyway, we can't leave yet. We're waiting for Amy,' said Helen, stretching the skin at the bottom of her left eye as she put mascara on in the mirror. Amy was another girl friend. Breen had grown up motherless, raised by his Irish father. All his working life had been around men. Now, it seemed, he was surrounded by women. He was not used to it.

'Is she coming with us?'

'Course.'

Amy arrived in a white men's collarless shirt and denim shorts. 'Where from?' demanded Elfie.

'Portobello Market. Second-hand.'

'You are so cool,' said Elfie. 'Seriously cool.'

Amy kept her hair short and wore her eye make-up thick. Where Breen's girlfriend Helen was angular and lanky-limbed, Amy was round-faced and her skin shone; she could pass for a model, even in a dead man's shirt.

As they walked to the bus stop, Breen tried the dark glasses on and ran his hand through his hair. It was getting too long. He should have it cut.

At Tottenham Court Road, from the top deck of the bus, they started to notice the change. It wasn't the usual Saturday crowd with prams and bags.

From all around, the young people were gathering. They carried backpacks, blankets and guitars slung over shoulders. The men wore T-shirts or had their shirts hanging out of the trousers. There was paisley, tartan, leather, embroidered sheepskin. A woman walked barefoot, not caring how dirty she became. On the news they'd shown hundreds of them sleeping overnight in the park so that they could keep a space at the front of the stage.

At Bourne and Hollingsworth, the crowd of shoppers parted. Two men, dressed in black and wearing Nazi helmets, strode west towards Hyde Park. People stared. The men pretended not to notice.

Elfie and Helen were at the front of the bus; he was sitting with Amy, just behind them, with Elfie's hamper, full of sandwiches, cake and thermoses, on his lap.

'I bet you don't even like the Stones,' said Amy.

'Loathe them,' said Breen. 'The drummer's OK, suppose.'

'I adore them,' said Amy. 'They're beautiful.'

At Oxford Circus they got off the bus and started to walk through the throng; the closer they got, the thicker the crowd became.

Ahead of them, someone was blowing bubbles. Against the blue sky, they drifted above the heads of the hippies. Amy took the Super 8 movie camera she carried everywhere out of her bag and pointed it at them.

As she filmed them, beautiful people posed and pouted, laughed and waved.

'Christ,' Breen said aloud as they crossed Park Lane. As far as he could see, there were people. Some were sitting on the grass, some were perched in the branches of the trees, some were handing out pamphlets, others playing guitar or dancing.

There was a war going on; old versus young. Here the young were winning. Other places, not so much. Last year the Soviet tanks had moved into Czechoslovakia. In Poland, they had come down hard on the student strikes. There had been concerts here in the park before, but nothing anywhere near as big as this.

'Go on, say it,' said Helen.

'No. It's great,' he said.

She grinned at him. To be fair, it wasn't that he resented young people having fun, just because his generation had never had anything like it; it was that so many people in one place made him nervous.

Helen understood that. She reached out and took his hand. *Keep calm. You're not a copper today.* He squeezed her hand back. Wherever Elfie and Amy saw peace and transcendence, he saw potential for crime and disaster. That's what the job did to you. Helen would know what he had been thinking, because she had been a policewoman too, once, working alongside him before she became pregnant.

And then the thick, oily scent came. People were smoking drugs; it was blatant.

'You're not on duty,' said Helen. 'Leave it.'

15

'Didn't say anything.'

'What are you two lovers whispering about?' said Elfie.

'Nothing.'

It's why Amy's boyfriend John Carmichael wouldn't come, even though Amy had asked him to. He was Drug Squad, jeans and all.

A uniformed copper was trying to keep people out of the road. He grinned. 'Hiya, Sarge.'

Breen recognised a young thick-necked constable from D Division, working overtime. 'What are you doing here, with this bloody lot, Sarge?'

For a second, Breen felt like a schoolboy caught bunking off. He was about to speak when Helen raised her finger to her lips and looked from left to right. 'Shh. He's undercover.'

'God, sir. Sorry. Didn't realise.'

'Carry on, Constable,' said Breen, and winked at him.

Helen was giggling; she looked around for Elfie who had disappeared into the crowd. Breen spotted her beckoning to them. 'Over here!'

She was holding hands with a big man who wore a baseball jacket and Michael Caine glasses. Like Breen, he was older than most people around him. With his free hand he was rubbing her large belly. 'How long till the baby, Elfie?'

Elfie grinned. 'This is Tom,' she announced loudly enough for everyone to hear. 'Tom Keylock. He works with the Stones.'

'Don't tell everybody. Christ sake, woman. Can't stop though, Elfie. I'm mad bloody busy.'

'Can you get us somewhere where we can see it properly, Tom? This is my best friend Hel. She's pregnant too. Please, Tom.'

'Bloody hell,' said Tom. 'Always the bloody chancer, Elfie.'

'Please, Tom. Pretty please?'

He rolled his eyes and grinned. 'Come on then, girls.'

Now Elfie was tugging Helen through the crowd, past loud activists with manifestos, and earnest hippies sitting cross-legged on the grass, past young women in cut-off jeans, revelling in the easy power of beauty, past the saucer-eyed man giggling to himself, towards the stage at the middle of the park.

The Hell's Angels were doing security. A young, pale-haired biker was turning people away from the back-stage area. Only a few, presumably those who knew some secret password, were admitted. It was funny, thought Breen, how a generation that hated the police so unthinkingly let these swastika'd bullies take their place. Helen must have noticed the look on Breen's face because she said, 'Don't. OK?'

'I didn't say anything.'

'They're cool,' Tom insisted to the man on security, and the Hell's Angel stood aside, moving as slowly as he could, as if to show his contempt for anyone so straight.

They had made it into a small, fenced area by the side of the stage. Elfie laid out the blanket and opened the basket. 'Ta-da!' she said. 'Best seat in the house.'

'Got to run,' said Tom, kissing Elfie on the cheek. 'Be good, darling. Love to Klaus.' Elfie's boyfriend.

Breen was holding out his hand to say thank you to the man when Elfie asked, 'What about Brian? Were you there?'

Tom's smile vanished. 'Not when it happened. No.'

'They're saying he committed suicide.'

17

'Got to go,' Tom said again, quietly, and pulled away.

'You can't actually see the band from here,' Helen was complaining as she tried to peer past a palm tree that had been placed by the improvised stairs up to the temporary stage.

Elfie didn't seem to hear. 'I think it's sad,' she said.

'Are you still on about the cake?' asked Helen.

'No. Brian Jones.'

'He drowned,' said Helen. 'That's what it said in yesterday's paper.'

'Never believe what you read in the papers,' said Elfie, opening a bottle of beer and passing it to Breen. 'Everybody is saying he was distraught because they'd kicked him out of the Stones. It was his group, after all.'

A band started playing on stage, but it wasn't the one most people had come to see. Nobody paid them much attention.

'Didn't your boyfriend arrest Brian Jones last year?' said Helen.

'Did he?' said Amy. 'Nothing would surprise me.'

Breen shook his head. 'It was before his time.' John Carmichael was Breen's oldest friend; they had been at school together, signed up for the force together. 'That was long before he joined the Drug Squad. He was still working with me on D Division.'

'Bloody shut up, you,' whispered Elfie. 'If they find out you're a copper I'll never live it down.'

'What happened to "Just be yourself, Paddy"?' said Breen.

'Just don't be a policeman, OK? I don't know why you're here. You don't even like rock music. First time I ever met you was when you called through our letter box telling us to turn down our moronic racket,' said Elfie.

Helen laughed. Breen smiled at her. 'It was loud.'

'Nothing like this!' She pointed at the massive stacks of speakers, piled on scaffolding in front of the stage.

'He's a dinosaur,' said Helen. 'He still wears a string vest. At least John doesn't wear old man clothes.'

Amy wrinkled her nose.

'What's wrong?'

'I think we're splitting up, me and John.'

'No,' said Helen.

'He never asks me out any more. Every time we're supposed to meet he calls up with some excuse.'

'He's a policeman. You know how it is.'

Amy lifted her camera again and held it to her eye, looking through it, though she didn't press the shutter release. 'I don't care,' she said.

From behind the barrier, people stared at them in the enclosure, trying to work out if they were celebrities or not. It was a strange feeling. Elfie was clearly enjoying it, flinging her arms around Helen as someone from the crowd photographed them.

It was a free concert and it looked like everyone in London who was under thirty was there. Just ordinary people, having fun. What was wrong with that? thought Breen.

'I bet he's here somewhere,' said Helen, looking around. 'Big John. Sniffing around with his Drug Squad mates. They can't resist something like this.'

'It's his job,' said Breen.

'Be ironic if he arrested onc of us,' said Elfie.

'It wouldn't be the first time,' said Amy, with a sad smile. 'That's how we met. He busted our cinema.'

Elfie thought this was hilarious, even though she'd heard the

19

story before. Amy worked at the Imperial in Portobello Road where the air at the late night screenings was often thick with pot smoke.

'He hates the Stones. Only likes bloody jazz. Like Cathal. Anyway, who's saying what about Brian Jones?' asked Helen.

'What if he was killed?' said Elfie.

'Who?'

'Brian Jones. Tom worked with Brian. He says they kicked him out of the band. What if . . .'

'Don't talk rubbish,' said Helen.

Elfie was handing out sandwiches. She'd made dozens. 'I'm not the only one saying it, Hel. Bloody hell. Don't look. It's Keith bloody Moon.'

Helen turned. 'Where?'

'I bloody love him.'

They watched Keith Moon passing around a bottle of wine which people were swigging from, until a man carrying four large cardboard boxes, one piled on top of the other, blocked their view. The boxes seemed to be extraordinarily light from the way he carried them. With the help of a lanky man in a cotton shirt, he stacked them up by the side of the enclosure, ten feet away from them.

Tom Keylock returned. 'That them?' he was asking. 'Sure they're still alive?'

'Don't ask me. Open them and find out. Where do they want them?'

'Put them on stage when they go on.'

Helen called over, 'What's in them?'

'Butterflies.'

'Butterflies?'

'Don't ask me,' said Tom.

Elfie had spotted someone else she recognised in the crowd. 'Hey, come and join us,' she called, waving at a dreamy young girl with long dark hair. The girl looked up, smiled shyly, gave a little wave back, then looked down again.

'Who's that?'

'She's going out with Eric Clapton,' said Elfie.

'Never,' said Amy. 'She doesn't look old enough.'

'Seventeen,' said Elfie.

'How old's he?'

'I don't know.'

'Look,' said Helen, suddenly excited. Dropping her food, she pushed herself up off the grass.

A little way off, a crowd of photographers were snapping eagerly. A couple of men were walking towards the stage. Both were dressed in long, untucked shirts. The one with the blue shirt paused to sign a piece of paper for someone.

'I can't believe I'm backstage with the Rolling bloody Stones,' said Helen, grinning like a teenager.

'It's their new guitarist,' said Elfie. 'The one who replaced Brian . . .'

Amy's movie camera was whirring as she focused it on the newcomers.

'The other one,' said Breen, nodding towards the gaunt-faced young man with long dark hair and big sunglasses. 'I came across him a couple of times.'

'You did?' squealed Elfie. 'Keith Richards?'

'Yes. Met him through work.'

21

Elfie's face fell. 'Don't say you bloody arrested him too?'

'Keep your voice down,' said Breen. 'You don't want everyone knowing I'm a copper, do you?'

He was aware of Helen grabbing hold of him. She was suddenly pale. 'What's wrong?'

'Stood up too quickly,' she said. 'A bit dizzy, that's all.'

She slumped back down again, leaning over into her lap. He dropped to his knees beside her.

When the Rolling Stones came on she was still sitting down, feeling lousy, while Elfie and Amy danced and hooted at the group they couldn't quite see. The air was full of pale butterflies struggling to take wing, and landing on their clothes.

In the taxi home to Stoke Newington, Helen placed a hand over the bulge. 'Sorry, Cathal.'

'I wasn't really enjoying it, anyway. Not my thing, really.'

'Yes you were,' she said. 'For once. You were actually having fun.'

'Just being out with you, you know.'

'Don't,' she said. 'I wanted to see it. I really did. I love the Stones. They're fantastic.'

He put his arms around her and she didn't move away. He was glad. He liked being able to look after her. Even if they hadn't planned it that way, she was pregnant with his child. It was the summer of 1969, the sun was shining, and he was happier than he could ever remember being.

FOUR

When he woke, Helen was already padding around in the hallway between their rooms.

She insisted on sleeping in the spare bedroom, even though he'd offered to buy a bigger bed that they could both share.

'Felt sick,' she said. She still looked pale from yesterday.

'I'll make a cup of tea.'

She walked over and followed him into the kitchen, lighting a cigarette. 'What am I supposed to do? I'm not used to not working. It's driving me nuts.'

'It's Sunday,' he said. 'You don't have to do anything.'

'I've worked all my life, on the farm or as a copper.' Farm girl; still had the Devon accent. He had grown fond of it.

'I don't understand why you think you have to, that's all. I'm earning enough.'

She just blew out smoke right at him. 'La la la,' she said.

It was going to be a bright sunny day. They should go out, walking in Clissold Park; it would be full of families. Boys would be playing with kites. Instead, she picked up her Arthur Hailey and started reading, ignoring him. She was still on the couch, a thin Japanese dressing gown covering her naked body, chewing on her tongue as she turned the pages, when the phone rang.

'It'll be your mother,' said Breen. Mrs Tozer usually called on Sunday mornings; telephone rates were cheaper. 'News from the farm. The price of milk.'

'Don't,' she said.

'Want me to get it?' She didn't move from he couch, so he picked up the phone.

'Sorry, Paddy. I know it's a day off, and all.'

It wasn't Mrs Tozer, calling from Devon. Behind the crackle and echo, the voice was Detective Inspector Creamer's; his boss.

'I told them I'd put one of my very best men on it,' he was saying in a jovial voice. 'Do you mind?'

'Creamer?' mouthed Helen. He nodded. Helen rolled her eyes.

Anyone else, it would be an order. But Creamer treated him almost like an equal. *Do you mind?* Like it was an invitation to an inconvenient dinner party. Creamer was the new boss, nervous around his more experienced sergeant.

'What does he want?' mouthed Helen.

Breen put his hand over the receiver. 'A murder,' he said.

On the pad he always kept near the phone, Breen scribbled down the address.

He covered the phone again. 'I can stay if you like. Someone else could do it.'

'No,' said Helen. 'You go.'

'Tied up, I'm afraid,' Creamer was saying. 'Prior obligation.

24

But I'm sure you'll be fine.' It would be something at the golf course, or a Rotary thing. 'Say the word and I'll have a car on its way.'

Breen put the phone down and said, 'I can still cancel if you like.'

'Who?' Helen laid her book on her chest and reached for another cigarette.

He knew what she meant. 'A woman,' he said. 'Young.' As if that would excuse him leaving her on his day off.

She nodded; she, of all people, would understand. The murder of a young woman. 'Other details?'

He shook his head. 'Not yet.'

Only last year, Helen had been a probationer in CID. She had wanted to stay on, but it hadn't worked out

'Can't be helped.'

'No. Fine. You go.'

He picked out a blue, flat-end, knitted tie and leaned in to the mirror in his bedroom to adjust it. When he made it back into the small living room in his summer suit and brogues, her nose was stuck back into her book, so close that he couldn't see her face.

'Bye, then,' he said when he heard the car arrive outside. She didn't answer.

The young driver was having difficulty trying to turn the large Zephyr in the small Stoke Newington cul-de-sac. It didn't help that Elfie's boyfriend's black MG was parked at an angle, one wheel on the pavement, boot jutting out over the cobbles. Breen got in.

'Sergeant Cathal Breen?' the driver said, flustered.

'It's pronounced *Ca-hal*.'

'Sorry.'

Most people just called him Paddy, anyway. A few children were attempting cricket on the wide pavements of Kingsland Road, but mostly the streets were empty. The shops and cinemas were all shut. Only the parks were open.

They turned into Old Street, heading towards Clerkenwell.

'It's Mint, isn't it?'

'Yes, sir.'

He should have made an excuse and stayed with Helen. Creamer could have found someone else. He looked at the driver clutching the wheel, a thin gold ring on the third finger of his left hand.

'Married, Mint?'

'I am, actually. Three years.' His hair was thick and wiry, parted on one side. Breen noticed a small gold crucifix in his lapel too.

'Kids?'

'Two.'

He could only be about 22 or 23; but coppers married young.

'What are they doing today?'

'Sunday lunch at the church, sir.'

'Church?'

'Sir.' Mint had the keenness of a man who had just transferred to CID. 'You're not supposed to call me "sir", you know,' said Breen.

'Sorry . . . Sarge.'

He drove badly, startled by other drivers, braking too hard, gripping the wheel so that his knuckles whitened.

★

From the outside, it was one of the smarter houses in Harewood Avenue; five storeys tall, brick and painted pale-cream stucco. Other buildings looked shabbier. Soon they would pull these old terraces down and replace them with newer, smarter buildings.

There were two police cars outside, and the usual small crowd of onlookers were craning to see past the constable at the front door who was muttering at them.

'Top floor,' he told Breen. The sun was already high; the constable held a handkerchief to wipe the sweat from his neck.

'Doctor here yet?'

The constable shook his head. 'Have to take the stairs. Lift isn't working.'

'Want me to stay with the car?' asked Mint.

'What good are you there?' said Breen. 'Follow me.'

Mint brightened. 'Yes, sir.'

Breen paused. 'Keep your eyes open. Make notes. Lots and lots of notes. Don't touch anything unless I tell you to.'

The stairs were built around the lift shaft. Breen took them in twos, all the way, Mint trotting behind him.

On the top landing, two beat coppers, one comically tall, the other squat, were peering up a ladder. Next to them was an elderly man in a brown housecoat who wore wire-frame glasses. As he reached the top landing he saw the legs of a fourth man on the ladder.

'What's going on?' he said.

'That CID?' called the man down the ladder.

'Where's the victim?'

'Up here. Bloody hell.'

'Do we know who she is?'

'Flat six,' said the man in the brown housecoat quietly. 'Miss Bobienski.'

Breen asked the man to spell it, and wrote it in his notebook. 'Russian?'

'Polish.'

'You found her?'

The man in the brown housecoat nodded. 'Rats,' he said. 'I heard them upstairs. Went to put poison down. Saw her there. Horrible. Poor woman.'

He was the building's caretaker, Breen guessed. He looked at the door behind him. There was a number eight on the door. Flat 6 would be the floor below.

The head of the policeman who had been up the ladder emerged from the rectangle opening. 'I mean. Bloody hell,' he said.

'Go on,' said the tall copper, yanking the torch out of the other copper's hand. 'My turn.'

'Get out of it,' Breen ordered. 'Now.'

Grumbling, the policeman stood aside. 'Has anyone else been up there?' Breen asked the caretaker.

'Just me and them guys.'

'Did either of you disturb the body?'

'Not likely,' the policeman said.

The caretaker shook his head. 'Excuse me, please. No smoking on the landing.' He was looking at the shorter of the coppers who was pulling out a packet of cigarettes.

'Hellfire,' muttered the constable. 'What is this? Buckingham Palace?'

'House rule,' said the caretaker. He spoke in a slight European accent. German perhaps?

Breen took the torch from the disgruntled policeman and went up the ladder himself.

The first thing he noticed was that it was a high loft with room enough to stand in; there were boxes stacked neatly towards the eaves and a pile of old metal bedsteads leaned against one of the chimney breasts. A wooden walkway made from old doors laid across the rafters ran from the hatch towards the lift mechanism which protruded through the floor.

He shone the torch at it, knowing that what he was about to see would not be pleasant.

She was lying, her back arched, over some machinery at the top of the lift, so that her head tipped backwards towards Breen.

Her teeth, slightly parted, were white in the torchlight. The eyes were gone; dark red hollows were all that remained. Her lips too. The rats had chewed away the soft tissue from between her nose and the top of her chin.

FIVE

Breen closed his eyes for a second, then opened them again. He could look at this stuff; it was his job.

He moved the torch down again, playing the light onto the boards between the opening and the lift. He thought for a minute, staring at the dead woman, then called down, 'Is there any other way to get into the loft, apart from this hatch?'

'No,' said the caretaker.

'So if anyone needed to work on the lift they'd have to come up through here.'

'Right.'

'You sure about that?'

'Yes, sir.'

'Mint?'

'Sir?'

He climbed down the ladder and handed the torch to him. 'Your turn. Just look. Tell me what you see.'

Mint turned his head from side to side. 'Me?'

'Up you go.'

Mint scrambled up the rungs.

'Have a good look around,' said Breen. 'Take your time.'

Apart from the scratching of Breen's pencil on his notebook, there was silence for a while. The tall constable peered over. 'Are you drawing?'

'Yes,' said Breen, not looking up.

'Is that her?' the copper asked.

From memory, he was sketching what remained of her face; the angle of her head.

'Jesus fuck,' said the constable.

'Told you,' said the one who had been up the ladder. 'No eyes.'

'Shouldn't we take a closer look at the body?' called Mint from above.

'Not till the photographer's been. I don't want to disturb anything until it's recorded.'

'She's beyond help, either way,' said the policeman, peering at Breen's notebook. 'Not bad, though. The drawing I mean. If I could draw like that I wouldn't be doing this. I'd be selling it along Green Park.'

Mint finally descended the ladder, his face white.

'Oi, smiler!' one of the coppers said to the caretaker. 'Fetch a bucket. I think junior here's about to bring up his breakfast.'

'Will you be OK?' asked Breen.

Mint nodded, but said nothing. With his pencil and notebook in his right hand he reached up and fingered the crucifix on his lapel. You always remembered the ones like this. However hard you tried, you'd never get them out of your mind. They would be with you all your life.

'What did you notice?' asked Breen.

'Notice? She was . . .' He tailed off.

'Dead?' whispered one of the local coppers, with a quiet snigger.

'Hush,' snapped Breen.

''Scuse me for breathing,' muttered the man.

'A young woman has been killed.'

'Sorry, guv.'

'Mint?'

'Um. I couldn't really see, Sarge.'

'How do you think she ended up there?'

Mint frowned. 'I guess somebody put her there.'

'How?'

'Carried her, I suppose?'

'Go up. Look again. Tell me what you see.'

Mint took a breath. He was heading back up the ladder, shakily this time, just as the pathologist arrived, panting. It was Wellington; he recognised Breen and scowled. 'Where is it?' he said.

'*She*. In the loft,' said Breen, pointing upwards.

'Let me at her, then.' Wellington was dressed in a dark wool suit, too heavy for the weather. 'I've a lunch at two.'

'I don't want anyone to go near her until the photographer's been,' said Breen.

'Naturally, but the sooner I get at her the better,' said Wellington.

'I need a photograph of the scene. He's on his way.'

'Oh, for pity's sake,' said the doctor.

Mint came halfway down the ladder, eyes wide.

'Well?'

'She must have been put on top of the lift on another floor.'

'Good,' said Breen. 'What made you think that?'

He came back down and dug into his jacket for his notebook. 'There would have been steps in the dust if somebody had taken her up there this way.'

'Write it down, then.'

'What is this? Sunday school?' Wellington took a pipe out of his pocket and put it in his mouth.

'No smoking on the landing,' said the caretaker.

'I'll smoke where I bloody like.' Wellington shook a box of matches. 'Just let me get on with my job, Paddy.'

'When did the lift stop working?' Breen asked the caretaker.

'Friday morning, probably,' he said.

'Probably?'

'I don't use it. But I clean it in the mornings. It wasn't functioning.'

'She's probably been dead three days, Wellington. Another hour won't hurt.'

'Not her I was thinking about. Another hour? Bloody hell, Paddy.' He looked at his watch.

'Is there somewhere we can talk?' Breen said to the caretaker.

The caretaker eyed Wellington holding a match above the bowl of his pipe but said nothing. He nodded towards Flat 7 on the other side of the landing.

'Come with me,' Breen said to Mint.

It wasn't a flat, it was a bed-sitting room, with an old sofa covered in blankets next to a gas fire and facing an old black-and-white TV. There was a curtain across the room, blocking most of the light from the windows; Breen guessed the man's bed was on the other side of it. Bookshelves were filled with boxes of all sizes – old cardboard shoeboxes, wooden cigar boxes, biscuit tins, tobacco tins – all full of doorknobs, sash weights, screws, hinges and the other paraphernalia of an odd-jobs man. His name was Benjamin Haas, he said, and he had worked here since shortly after the war.

'She was a working girl,' he said, shrugging. He filled a kettle from the sink and put it on a small gas hob.

'A prostitute?'

'If you like,' he said. 'A hard-working girl.' He had a mid-European accent. 'Always paid her rent. Always polite.'

'Friends, relations?'

'Only a maid.'

'Name?'

'I know only her first name, Florence. Maybe that's her real name. Maybe it isn't. It is not my job to ask.'

'So you don't have an address for her?' Spooning tea into a large brown pot, Haas shook his head.

'What about the lift. What was wrong with it?'

'The electric motor is finished. The repair man coming. But he doesn't come yet.'

'It was definitely out of action on Friday morning, you say.'

The body was on top of a lift in an open shaft; it would have been visible if the elevator car had descended.

'Did she have a boyfriend? Husband?'

Again, he shook his head. 'I don't think so.'

'Pimp?'

'No no no. She wasn't one of those girls. You don't understand.'

'What about any arguments? Any falling out? Did you have any problems with her?'

'Only pop music. She plays pop music a lot. And loud. Terrible music.' He smiled. 'Bang bang bang. Yeah yeah yeah.'

Breen looked around the room. There were dusty hardback books piled on the floor.

'You live here on your own?'

He put a tray on a stool; the teapot, three white mugs, a box of sugar cubes and a half-pint bottle of milk. Then he waved his arm around the room and smiled. 'Obviously.'

'You liked Miss –' Breen checked the name in his notebook – 'Bobienski, though.'

'She is half my age. Was,' said Haas.

'Are you Polish, too?'

'Austrian,' said Haas. 'As a rule, I dislike the Poles. After all, they, as a rule, dislike Jews, so I dislike them, but I liked her. She was different. She had . . . *Charakter*.'

'Character.'

'Yes.' He poured three cups of tea.

'Had she been here long?'

'Only two years.' The man rubbed his lips and then scratched at his arm.

Mint, who had been silent all this time, leaned forward and took his tea. Breen left his. 'She was a prostitute,' Breen said.

'We do what we have to do,' said Haas. He waved his hand around him. 'In Austria, I used to be a cello player in the Philharmonic Orchestra. Now I fix taps that drip.'

'You maintained the lift?'

'That . . . no. Too *kompliziert*.'

'Did she have regular customers?'

'Of course. She was a pretty girl.'

'Would you recognise them?'

'Men do not visit prostitutes in order to be recognised. In the evenings, I stay in my room and listen to the radio.'

Breen wondered if the guardedness of his answers came from being an outsider, from speaking a second language, or something more.

'Did she pay her rent on time?'

'I am just the caretaker. But I have never heard any complaints from the landlord.'

'You might tell him that it's an offence under the Sexual Offences Act to let out premises as a brothel.'

Haas shrugged. 'So? Maybe close down all the hotels here also.'

'Who else lives in the building?'

Four of the flats were empty, said the caretaker. One was awaiting a new tenant. One contained an elderly couple who had been away on holiday since the end of June. One of the basement flats housed a French family who returned home every summer. The husband worked in a restaurant. The other was being used to store furniture. 'On the first floor there are four students, from the University of London. Below that, Mr Payne,' he said.

'What does he do?'

'Old man,' said Haas. 'He is retired.'

Breen turned to Mint on the sofa next to him. 'Do you have any questions?'

'Me?' Mint sat clutching his tea, blushing under his thick dark hair.

'For example, when Haas last saw Miss . . .'

'Bobienski,' said the caretaker. 'On Thursday. Her pipes were making noises. She asked me to fix them.'

'Were you aware of men coming to visit that evening. On Thursday?' asked Breen.

'As I say, I make it my job not to be aware of these things,' he said.

Mint finally opened his mouth to speak. 'So can you account for your movements between Thursday night and . . .'

'Saturday morning?' suggested Breen.

'Yes,' said Mint. 'Can you account for your movements between Thursday night and Saturday morning?'

'Of course I can,' said Haas. 'I was here. I went to the shops to buy food and some hardware. I came home. I listened to the radio. They played organ music by Couperin.'

'And Friday?'

'Maybe I went to Bloom's. For lunch.'

Breen said, 'Blooms? In Whitechapel? That's the other side of London. Just for lunch?'

'I like the food. It's what my mother used to make.' It was a kosher restaurant; all the Brick Lane Jews ate there.

'Who did you eat with?' said Mint.

'Alone.' He shrugged.

Breen said, 'You went all the way to the East End to eat a meal on your own?'

'It is a very nice meal,' said Haas simply.

'What about Saturday? You were here all day?'

'Of course.'

'And in the evening?'

'They played Handel, I think.'

'What?'

'On the radio. Zadok the Priest.'

'So you have no alibi?' said Mint.

'I do not know that word,' said the caretaker, looking at Breen for an explanation.

'My colleague means that we only have your word for it – because you were alone.'

Haas shrugged, looked away. 'Ah. *Alibi*. I understand. Yes. You have only my word.' He stood and turned his back to them.

Outside, the photographer had arrived, a large man, grumbling about having to lift his lights up the stairs. 'About bloody time,' said Wellington.

Breen and Mint followed the caretaker down to the floor below.

'Crikey,' was the first thing Mint said when he saw the pinkness of the room. They stood on the white carpet, looking around the room, gazing at the artifice of it. There was a pile of *Jackie* magazines on the table. The giant teddy bear sat on the sofa, as if watching them.

The Beatles smiled.

'And how old was she?' asked Breen.

'I don't know. No no no. This was all theatre business.'

'Theatre business?'

'*Täuschung*. Illusion. Her job. She was not a child. She was a woman.'

'I don't understand.'

There was a small kitchenette to the right of the front door; a large main room, and two bedrooms. The first bedroom was the bigger of the two. Like the living room, almost everything in it was pink, including the bedsheets. It was a double bed, with a Union Jack bedcover and a yellow cloth rabbit placed on top of the pillows.

There were toys on the floor. A doll's house. A pink Dansette record player. All over the bedroom walls were more photographs of pop stars, stuck with Sellotape. Breen recognised some of them: The Kinks, The Who, Mary Hopkin, The Monkees.

'She pretended,' said Haas. 'Swinging London. You know?'

Among the photographs, Breen noticed the picture of a soft-faced young man with bright white hair. He was clutching a guitar. The photo was signed in black felt pen. 'Best wishes.' The signature was indecipherable.

'Who's that?' he asked Mint.

'It's that dead bloke, Sarge,' he said. 'In the papers.'

There was a dressing table artfully scattered with bottles of colourful nail varnish and make-up.

'And this was her bedroom?'

Breen pulled a handkerchief from his pocket, put it around the wardrobe door handle to open it.

'No. This was where she worked. Her own bedroom was across the corridor.

One half was full of ordinary clothes, a mac, a cocktail dress. The other side was full of what appeared to be costumes.

There were three school uniforms and a pink flouncy thing with ruffles, several brightly patterned miniskirts, tops with stripes and polka dots, and two pairs of bright, patent-leather thigh-length boots.

'She was a specialist,' said Haas. 'She knew how much you English men liked young girls. That was the name she used. Julie Teenager. She was quite well known, I believe. A pop star.'

'Julie Teenager?'

'And you didn't have any problem with that? In your house?' asked Mint.

'It is not my house,' he said flatly.

'Must have cost a bit to rent this place,' said Breen.

'Nineteen pounds ten a week,' said Haas.

Mint raised his eyebrows. It was a lot for a flat in London, especially around here; Breen paid less than a quarter of that, but that was in Stoke Newington. 'She must have been earning a whack, then,' said Mint.

'I never asked her.'

'You have the key to this flat. When you didn't see her, did you let yourself in?'

'No. Miss Bobienski's maid Florence knocked on my door on Friday night to ask if I had seen her. She was worried. She had heard nothing from her. There were men coming.'

'Customers.'

'Exactly.'

'But she didn't report anything to the police?'

Haas smiled. 'Obviously not. The police do not always treat people like her well, perhaps.'

'So the maid had a key too?'

The caretaker nodded.

'Friday night? And the lift was definitely not working then?'

'As I have said.'

'She dressed up as a teenager?' asked Mint. 'For men?' He looked shocked.

'She looked younger than she was, I think,' said Haas.

They crossed the corridor. In contrast to the other frivolous rooms, this was monastic. A small space, with a single high window that faced out onto the back of the building, a colour television and a shelf full of novels. On her dressing table here, a small family photograph taken at some smart event.

Breen picked it up. A couple with a young boy and an infant. The man wore an RAF uniform and held the hand of the young boy dressed in a stiff suit. The woman wore a hat with a single feather in it and clutched the baby in her arms. It looked like it had been taken during the war. He stared at it for a second.

'She never talked about them,' said Haas, before Breen'd even asked the question. 'It is a tragedy, now you see the family. He fought Nazis, you see?'

'Yes.'

'Royal Air Force.' Haas stood stiffly alongside him as Breen flicked open the clips on the back of the wooden frame and took out the photograph.

On the landing, Wellington looked ostentatiously at his gold wristwatch, still waiting for the photographer to finish his work, as Breen appeared out of the dead woman's flat. Breen ignored him, shouting up through the hatch to the cameraman. 'Get photographs of her rooms too, OK?' Then he turned back to the caretaker. 'What about the lift?'

'I think the engine is broken. It's old.'

Breen grasped the scissor gate and shook it; the metal rattled.

'Careful,' said the caretaker.

'Why?'

'It's old, that's all.'

Breen pulled the gate open. She would be lying above him now.

'What if the lift wasn't here? Could I open this door?'

'You're not supposed to be able to. For safety.'

'Are you sure?'

'No. I'm not sure. It's old,' said the man. 'It is not safe. I don't like it. I tell the landlord we need to close it down. He does nothing. That's why he is rich and I am poor.'

Breen led him to the floor below. The gate there was shut. You could see through to the other side of the square spiral stairway, the brown wood banister descending at an angle, dust on the untouched ledge beyond.

He shook the scissor gate again. It was locked. He thought for a minute, then reached into his trouser pocket and pulled out a penknife and opened the blade. He manoeuvred it into the joint at the side and pushed the blunt edge against the clasp that hooked into the side of the door. A small movement and the lock sprang free. Breen slid back the mechanism. 'Is it supposed to do that?' he asked.

'It's old. I said it already,' said the caretaker.

In front of him, the lift shaft was empty. Grabbing the side of the door frame, he peered downwards. There was some litter, dropped onto the floor at the bottom; old cigarette packets, sweet wrappers. Then he looked up, towards the underside of the lift above.

'Where's the machinery? The motor that makes the lift work? Can I see it?'

'Downstairs,' said Haas.

They descended two more floors. There were two small flats in the basement. Between them there was a third door. Haas pushed it open and went inside.

Everything about the lift was ancient. It must have been installed between the wars. Breen squatted down, peered at the electric motor, looking for signs that it had been tampered with. He could see nothing obvious, but he was not the practical man his father had been. His father had been a builder, an Irish immigrant who had discouraged his son to have any interest in his trade in the hope that he would better himself. By which he had not meant becoming a policeman.

'The engineer says he is coming tomorrow,' said Haas. 'Maybe the next day.'

'He can't touch it until we've looked at it.'

'How long will that take?'

'I'll let you know,' said Breen. On the way out he said, 'Is this door usually unlocked?'

Haas shrugged. 'No. There is nothing valuable here. Some tools. Nothing much.'

Breen strode up to the ground floor, then down again, and back up, counting stairs. Mint trotted silently behind him. After making a couple more notes, he walked out into sunlight where an ambulance waited outside to collect her body.

The young men from the new C Department had arrived with their briefcase bags of equipment, powders and brushes, tape measures and scalpels. Most of the men Breen knew in CID resented this new intrusion of science into the job. They'd managed fine without it before.

Outside, London was looking grubby and ordinary. The huge trees were still, leaves heavy above them in the quiet of a Sunday afternoon.

SIX

When he got home at six, Helen was still sitting in his father's old armchair; there was no sign that she had moved. The ashtray contained eight partly smoked cigarettes; it looked as if she had had a couple of puffs from each then put them out.

'Well?' she said.

He went to the fridge and pulled out a bottle of Bass and opened it, then returned to the living room and sat down.

'A prostitute. She called herself Julie Teenager.'

'Was she pretty? They love it when it's a pretty girl.'

'Not pretty any more,' said Breen.

She nodded. 'Grim?'

'Yep.'

'Sorry,' she said. She picked at her nails. 'One of her clients?'

'Too early, really.'

Reaching over to the coffee table, she lifted up her packet of cigarettes to light another. 'Go on.'

'What?'

'What are the details?'

'Give me a minute. I just got in. Have you eaten anything?'

'Toast. Loads. I was starving.'

'You can't just eat toast all day.'

She shrugged, sucked on her cigarette. 'I can. I didn't even know there were brothels in Harewood Avenue.'

He left her in the living room and went to cook an omelette with pieces of bacon and some chives that he'd bought the day before, after they'd got back from Hyde Park.

'It wasn't a brothel. She was a specialist. She dressed up as a teenager,' Breen called from the kitchen. 'School uniforms. Pop music. Everything.'

'That's horrible.'

When he'd finished, he cut the omelette into two, took it into the living room and put it down on the dining table. He watched her picking out the green bits, like she always did, and covering the rest with tomato sauce.

'How old was she?'

'I'm not sure. I think probably mid-twenties.'

A little older than Helen herself. 'And was she raped?'

Helen was always direct; unlike the men Breen worked with, she didn't find it hard to talk about these things.

He put down his fork. He wasn't so hungry. 'I don't know. I don't think so. She was in an ordinary dress. She still had everything on.'

'Dressed for work?'

'Actually, that's a good point.'

'What sort of dress?'

'You know . . . Just a dress. Like something you'd wear.'

'I don't wear dresses.'

'Yes you do.'

'Only 'cause I'm pregnant.'

He sighed. 'Like something you'd wear if you did wear dresses.'

'So not exactly dressed for work, then.'

'I suppose not.'

'How was she killed?'

'Head injury, Wellington said.'

'You had him, today?'

'Yes.'

'That man's an idiot,' she said, dolloping more ketchup onto her plate.

'He's probably right, though. You could see from the state of her.'

She nodded thoughtfully. 'So, what? It was in her home?'

'I'm not sure where she was assaulted yet. Possibly in her flat, yes, or somewhere nearby. Her body was dumped on top of the lift. I don't think that was where she was killed. She's been missing for at least two days, probably three, but nobody reported her. And then the caretaker found her.'

'How the hell did she get there?'

'I'm not sure.' He held out his plate to her.

She scraped his half-eaten omelette onto the remains of hers and dug her fork into it. 'Her pimp?'

'She worked with a maid. I'm trying to track her down.'

'Ask the women police in D Division. Maybe they'll know. Specially if it was so close to the station.'

'Really?'

'We know all that stuff that goes on; the stuff you blokes never notice. They're saying they're going to merge us into the rest of the Met now. All that's going to change. They'll make us more like you lot.' Breen noticed that she still used the first person, even though she wasn't a copper any more. 'I think they'll lose something, to be honest. We'll just be annoying old farts like you.'

It was Sunday night; there was nothing on television. At nine Helen got up and said, 'I'm tired.'

'You haven't done anything all day.'

'I know. It's bloody exhausting,' she said, without smiling. Another half-smoked cigarette had burned out in the ashtray, leaving a curl of grey ash.

He listened to her in the bathroom preparing for bed. She closed the bedroom door behind her without saying goodnight.

He woke, sweating, short of breath, filled by a sense that his arms and legs were tied. He lay still, too terrified to move them, in case he was right.

It took almost a minute before he summoned the will to reach out his arm and switch on the light. He blinked in the sudden brightness.

He looked down. His pyjamas had ridden up. The scars were still pink on his stomach.

The one thing that was OK about her sleeping in a separate room was that she didn't know about this. He had thought that these episodes were going away; he hadn't had one for two or three weeks.

It was the sight of the dead woman, of course.

When the photographer had gone, he had ascended the ladder again to watch as Wellington had carried out his duties. Her back had been arched over the machinery at the top of the lift, both hands splayed above her head. In the darkness her eyes had looked heavily made up; that and the deep curl of her hair and the soft, child-like curves of her face had made her look a little like Clara Bow, until Wellington had shone his torch on the absence of her eyeballs. Red, dark holes.

He sat on his bed, unable to get back to sleep for thinking about her. If she had been dumped there, how had it been done? Had it been planned, or had it been an act of panic? She was small; child-like. She had traded on that. She would have been easy to lift. Anyone could have managed it.

A door opened; a light came on outside. Helen was awake too. He looked at his watch. Just gone three in the morning.

'Helen?' he said.

She peered round the door to his bedroom, holding a glass of water in one hand and another paperback in the other. 'It's like trying to sleep with a two-bar electric fire strapped to your stomach.'

He moved aside, shifted the pillows and patted the bed beside him. 'I couldn't get that woman out of my head,' he said, though that hadn't been what woke him.

'Me neither.'

When Helen had been a teenager, her own sister had been murdered and left in a ditch in Devon. It was why she had wanted to escape to London and become a policewoman in the first place.

In the end, it had been Breen who had tracked down her

sister's killer, not before he had murdered again; the scars were a reminder he had almost killed Breen too.

At some point he noticed it was light outside. When he looked at Helen, she had fallen asleep, her book on the mound below her small breasts, its spine cracked.

He tried to get back to sleep himself, but she had somehow slid across the bed and he found himself perched on the edge. In the end he got up and sat, snoozing, in the armchair in the living room for an hour until it was time to get up to go to work.

When he tiptoed into the bedroom Helen was snoring gently. She was still fast asleep when he left into the bright morning light. This is what he did. He found out who killed people. He had done it before. He had done it for Helen.

It was a terrible world; it was a sunny day. Though his father may have wanted better for him, there was no other job in the world, he thought, that he should be doing.

SEVEN

When Breen had arrived at D Division, the CID room at Marylebone had been comfortable. The solid old wooden desks must
have been there since the 1930s; no one had painted the place
in years. Nicotine had yellowed the ceiling and walls. It had
been lived in; manly.

Creamer had changed all that. He had sent all the old furniture
to the tip, replacing it with neat, steel-framed tables with easy-
to-clean Formica tops. There were new, lightweight typewriters
that were small enough to be put away in drawers, and the latest
beige telephones that the new secretary, Miss Rasper, could pass
calls through to at the press of a button.

Instead of the heavy old desks, filled with long-forgotten files,
old tobacco tins, broken pencil sharpeners, knives removed
from teenagers and unanswered correspondence, each officer
now only had two slim drawers in which to keep all their
belongings.

Outdated manuals on roadcraft and criminal law had been

binned. The walls had been stripped of all the old pictures and newspaper cuttings and repainted a bright, clean white.

The dark old floorboards, worn down by generations of officers' boots, were now covered with blue linoleum.

But however modern Creamer had tried to make the room, the old Victorian station, with its old metal windows and stone sills, still asserted itself. There was an annoying buzz on the new phone lines that no one from the GPO could seem to fix. The lino was already dotted with black cigarette burns.

'Sorry, Paddy. Bit tied up, yesterday. All OK?' Creamer looked around for an ashtray for his cigar.

Breen put down the handset he had just been talking on. 'Sir?'

'Yesterday. Harewood Avenue. Everything under control?'

'Fine, sir.'

'Good man.' He smiled, tapped on his cigar, then placed it in his mouth again while waiting for the men to settle. Monday's buzz of conversation was always a little louder than other days'. They had weekend stories to swap, the films they'd seen, the cricket they'd lost at, the girls they had gone with. The men sat on desks, reluctant to start the day's work.

'Right. Order, boys. Order,' Creamer shouted eventually.

The chatter died. Men turned. The day began.

'Well, Breen?'

Breen walked to the front of the office, where everyone could see him, his back to the secretary's desk, and pulled open a brown folder and held up a single black-and-white 10-by-8. 'Lena Bobienski, twenty-six. A prostitute. Murdered, we think, between Thursday night and Friday morning.'

They crowded in, stared at the photograph. Breen raised it so everybody could see.

'Oof,' muttered Jones, the youngest constable on the team.

'Rats,' explained Breen. 'She was a professional. Earning a decent amount of money for her line of work, by the look of it.'

'Got any photos?' asked Jones.

'Pervert,' said another.

'Toms have photographs, don't they?' protested Jones. 'To advertise their line of work. Nobody's going to recognise her looking like that.'

'Fair point,' said Creamer.

Jones beamed, keen to prove he was just as good as Mint, the bright new boy.

'A client, I suppose?' asked Creamer.

'The pathologist's preliminary report indicates that she was assaulted before the fatal blow. There is serious bruising on the face and abdomen.' This morning, he had spoken to Wellington who was still bad-tempered about missing his lunch yesterday.

Wellington would be detailing each bruise now. In the next day or so he would send a more detailed report, but this was all they had to go on, so far.

'He thinks she would have been conscious during the initial assault, which suggests anger, or sadism, or both. We don't have an accurate time of death yet.'

All eyes were on him.

'Weapon?'

'All we have up to this point is blunt instrument. Wellington reckons a bottle, perhaps. I think it's relevant that she was dumped in the building. I reckon whoever put her in that position knew she wouldn't be found till after he got away.'

He reached in the folder and pulled out another photo. 'She was discovered on top of the lift. The caretaker says it was out of order on Friday morning. But it was clearly working at the time when her body was put on the roof of the elevator compartment. I believe that means that someone killed her late on Thursday night or at some point early the next day, placed her body in that position, then raised the lift to the top floor, so the body would have been concealed. Either the lift then chose that moment to break down, or the killer then disabled the lift somehow. I don't know how yet. But that way he could get down the stairs and out of the building.'

'So someone who knew the place?'

It was Mint who had spoken. Breen turned to him and said, 'Exactly. I'm pretty sure that's who we're looking for. So it's a question of timing. Precisely when did the lift break down? So far, no one remembers. I've asked C Department if they have an engineer who could look at the mechanism. We know it was at least forty-eight hours before the body was discovered. If the lift was deliberately broken, so that she was concealed in the loft –' he picked out another photograph of the body taken from the attic entrance – 'then was the killer playing for time? Else he'd have just left her in her flat, assuming that's where he killed her.'

'One of the residents, then. Or her johns. Someone who knew his way around,' suggested Mint.

'Yes. Or the maid. According to Haas, the prostitute worked with a maid, who arrived on Friday night, and let herself in to the dead woman's apartment. But as far as we know, she didn't report Bobienski to the police as missing. That would have given her ample time to clean up the scene of crime.'

'But the maid went to the caretaker and asked if he'd seen her,' said Mint. Then his eyes widened. 'Oh . . .'

'Exactly,' said Breen. 'We can't rule her out. She may have been covering for the fact that she needed to return to the place to tidy it up after the event. It's crucial we find her. As for the johns . . .' Breen heard the door opening behind him, but ignored it. 'Her clientele were not the usual lot. Her speciality was dressing up as a little girl. So we're looking for a type of man.'

He looked up. Something unusual was happening. CID men were predictable. They made lewd jokes whenever there was an opportunity, but nobody had responded to the cue. Instead, the men in front of him were standing up straight.

'Morning, sir,' said Creamer. 'To what do we owe the . . . ?'

Breen turned. Behind him was Superintendet McPhail, arms behind his back and chest puffed out. He had entered the room without announcing himself. A six-footer in his boots, bristle-chinned even in the morning, McPhail had been an infantryman in the war and stood like he was still enlisted.

'Doing the rounds,' said McPhail quietly. 'Doing the rounds. Carry on. Don't stop for me.'

'Tea, sir?' said Creamer. 'Miss Rasper, make the Superintendent a cup of tea.' The new secretary was another of Creamer's innovations; a prim-looking woman who smoked Park Drives and who typed at an astonishing speed.

'I don't want tea, Inspector Creamer. Ignore me, men. I'm just watching.'

55

'Of course. Carry on, Paddy,' Creamer said. 'You were saying?'

Breen nodded. 'Constable Mint and myself will be interviewing the residents this morning. We'll also be trying to build a list of Miss Bobienski's clients. If, as we think, it was somebody who knew both Miss Bobienski and the building, it may have been a regular.'

'Get on to Vice Squad,' Creamer said. 'Find out if they know anything.'

'Paddy's already asked me to do that,' volunteered one of the men.

'And the local beat constables,' said Creamer, eager to put on a show for the boss. 'See if the local shift sergeant can help you there.'

Breen had just been doing that, too, ten minutes before; he had the list of names of the beat men. But, out of kindness to Creamer, he said, 'Right away, sir.'

'Door to door,' Creamer went on. 'Records of any local deviants. That sort of thing.'

Breen picked up his pad and tried to look interested, for Creamer's sake.

'Any significant leads?' asked McPhail quietly.

'Too early,' said Creamer.

'Can we keep this out of the press, sir?' asked Breen. 'There's a small article in today's *Standard*, but it doesn't have a name. If news gets out, it may scare the customers off, sir. If we're going to find out who her clients were, it'll help if we can rule out any who turn up . . .'

'Good thinking. I'll square that with Scotland Yard.' McPhail wasn't the sort of officer who thought much of the press at the best of times. 'Anything else?'

Nobody spoke.

'Keep me informed with this one. I want to know what goes on.'

'Absolutely,' said Creamer. 'I'll do it personally.'

'I'm sure you will,' said McPhail quietly. He turned on the shiny leather of his soles and left.

'And this,' said Breen, pulling out the photograph he had taken from Lena Bobienski's bedside. 'Her father was a Polish refugee, by the look of it. Joined the RAF. We'll need to track down the family.'

He was pleased with the way things went. Creamer had barely interfered. The investigation was already taking a shape of a kind. There were clear suspects, even if their identities were not yet known. Unlike some cases, where you found yourself performing the routine tasks of detection with little sense that they would lead anywhere, this felt like it was in motion already. Some cases were simple. The guilty were easy to find. Maybe this would be one of those.

As he walked down the stairs towards the back of the station, he whistled. At the door he realised it was a pop song he had heard Helen playing in her room.

It was a short walk to Harewood Avenue. Breen walked fast, Mint a pace behind him.

'What was McPhail doing?' Mint asked.

'What do you mean?'

'Sticking his nose in. At the meeting. I've never seen him do that before.'

Breen considered. 'Just checking up, that's all. Why shouldn't he? It's his station.'

But afterwards, as they rounded the corner into the street, he realised it was a perfectly reasonable question. Why had McPhail appeared so interested in this particular case? It was unusual. He wondered if the confidence he'd felt earlier would see the day out.

EIGHT

The forensic crime scene men had worked late into Sunday night. Their Commer van was still outside the house.

'I wanted to say, Sarge. About the caretaker,' said Mint.

'What about him?'

'Did you notice? He looked suspicious when I asked if he had an alibi for the weekend.'

'Suspicious?'

'Sort of . . . shifty. I've been reading up on psychology.'

'Psychology. Really?'

'Yes, Sarge. And I've just got quite a good knack with people, telling if they're dissembling. There are signs. They call it "Pinocchio's nose". The things people can't help doing when they lie. They hesitate. Or they keep moving all the time. Or hold their hand in front of their face, like this.' Mint demonstrated.

'Is that so?'

'The caretaker was avoiding our eyes. That's a classic sign of lying.'

'Was he really?' said Breen.

'Yes. I noticed it. It's an indication that he's concealing something.'

They went into the house. The post had arrived. The caretaker had left the letters in a pile on a small table by the door. Breen leafed through them to see if there was anything there for Miss Bobienski, but there wasn't.

'Of course,' said Breen, 'it could also be a sign that he's a Jewish refugee who is nervous around policemen, especially when they ask him to prove that he didn't commit a crime.'

'Obviously, yes.' Mint blinked furiously. 'It could be that, too.'

Instead of going up to Bobienski's flat, Breen led the way down the stairs. A technician Breen had met on a couple of other jobs was in the basement shining a torch on the lift's motor.

'Anything?' asked Breen.

The man straightened up. He held a small screwdriver in one hand and had a smudge of grease on his cheek. 'Haven't taken it apart yet,' he said. 'But smell it.'

'What?'

'Go on.'

Breen bent down and sniffed. 'Burning,' he said.

'Electric motor. Load of old crap. Could have burned out any time, anyway, I 'spect.'

'Fluke, you mean? That the lift is stuck where nobody is going to see the dead body. It's not likely, is it?'

The man shrugged. 'Can't see anything, that's all. And something this old could just break, ask me.'

'Could someone have jammed it somehow?'

'Course.'

'Jammed the lift itself, so the motor burned out?'

'Not so likely, but I'll have a look,' said the man. 'You never know.'

Aside from Haas the caretaker's and the dead woman's, only two of the remaining flats were currently being used. It was a Monday; Breen would have expected the residents to be out at work, but both flats were occupied.

There were students on the first floor; Breen sent Mint up to interview them. He knocked on the door of the ground-floor flat but no one answered. Breen went to knock again, but Haas said, 'Give him time. He's old.'

The man who finally opened the door was dressed in greasy trousers and a woollen waistcoat that was unravelling at the hem. He had the urinous smell the old sometimes have.

'You had better come in,' the old man said, after Breen had introduced himself. 'Did I hear anything out of the ordinary? I'm afraid not. Would you like tea?'

'I don't really drink it.'

He said his name was Payne. Breen followed him cautiously. Piles of books all but blocked the hallway. They had to walk as close as possible to the opposite side to avoid kicking them over. When Breen entered the living room, an entire wall was filled with bookshelves bending under the weight of what they carried. Wherever there was room at the front of a shelf, more had been piled, obscuring the ones behind. A smaller free-standing bookshelf, equally crammed, jostled for space with a tiny dining table. Even the floor was a maze; there were narrow pathways between the teetering mountains.

'Something else? I have whisky.'

'I'm fine,' said Breen. 'You knew her, Miss Bobienski?'

The old man reached out a hand into the air and felt for one of the dining chairs. It was only at that moment that Breen realised he could see nothing. Payne was blind. If he had been a suspect before, he was not one now.

'I didn't like her much,' Payne said. 'She didn't like me, either. She's dead now and I'm sorry for that. Sit down, sit down.'

The only seat left that did not have books on it was a dusty old armchair, whose springs sang as Breen lowered himself onto it.

'Did you ever see any of her clients?' Breen asked, and regretted the question immediately. 'Or hear them?'

'I'd bump into them, sometimes, coming in the front door. But if you're asking if I have any idea who would have killed her, I have none at all. A hazard of her profession, I suppose.'

Breen noticed a long yellow toenail pointing through a hole in Payne's left woollen slipper.

'Did you ever hear any of their names?'

Mr Payne giggled. 'They were not the kind of men who gave their names.'

'You said you didn't like her. Did you know her?'

'She was perfectly civil. But she didn't like old people, I could tell. She always tried to avoid me. Old people revolted her. "An aged man is but a paltry thing".'

'There was a woman who worked with Miss Bobienski.'

'The delicious Florence. The procuress. Her,' he said, 'I liked. She has always been kind to me. Sometimes the men brought the unfortunate young girl chocolates. She never ate them, of course. I think she was terrified of putting on the slightest bit of weight. Looking like a half-starved adolescent boy, it's such a popular look with the girls these days, don't you think? Or so I'm told. I'm more of a Rubens man, myself. Florence would sneak the chocolates down to me. I adore chocolates. I would happily scoff the lot.'

'Do you know Florence's last name? Or her address?'

'I haven't the faintest idea. I'm sorry. I never asked her. I considered inviting her for dinner, but I'm not much of a cook and what would she be wanting to go out with me for?'

'Never mind.'

'She teased me, in a nice way. "Imagine me naked, Mr Payne. I could be right now, for all you know." I don't see very well at all, you see. Would you like to see a painting of her? She gave it to me as a joke, I suppose.'

'A painting of her?'

'She is an artist's model. In the evening, she used to help Miss Julie take her clothes off. In the morning she used to remove her own.' Mr Payne stood and made his way to the bedroom at the back of the flat.

It was a small dark room with a single bed, covered in a worn eiderdown. As with the living room, its floor was piled with books. Payne switched on the light. 'There,' he said.

Above the bed hung an oil painting of a fleshy, middle-aged woman lying on a couch draped with a white sheet. One leg was raised slightly, the other dangled off the sofa; she was presenting herself for the world to see. Her pale breasts spilled sideways. Whoever painted it, thought Breen, had captured the woman's solidity and the strange way in which light falls on bare skin.

'One of the painters who did her in the buff gave it to her.

63

She didn't like it much. She thought it was a little too rude for her own collection. So she gave it to me.'

She was round-faced; in a splash of pink, the painter had captured broken veins on her cheek. 'Is it a good likeness?'

'Haven't the foggiest,' said Payne. 'I think that's why she enjoyed giving me it. She knew I wouldn't be able to see it properly. She found that amusing. So did I. There she is in her altogether and I can't see it at all. I wish I could. She used to tell people I kept a naked picture of her in my boudoir. I don't suppose I'll see her any more.'

'Did she get along with Miss Bobienski?'

'The tart? I doubt it. There was something in the girl that was easy to dislike. It was purely a business arrangement between the two of them.'

'Did they argue or fight?'

The man hesitated. 'No. No. Not like that. Florence was feisty, but . . . no, not like that. No.'

'You don't sound certain.'

'Of course I'm certain.'

'She has not been seen since Friday.'

The man's hands were trembling gently as he stood by the door of his bedroom. 'I don't suppose there is any particular need for her to be here now, is there?' he said and looked away, unseeing.

'I have to speak to her. Do you remember which art schools she modelled for?'

The man shook his head. 'I don't think it can have been far away,' he said, switching the bedroom light off again.

★

Breen went up two flights of stairs and pushed open Bobienski's door. 'Hello?'

'In here.'

Two men were working in the pink bathroom.

'Anything?'

'Nothing. Doesn't even look like a crime scene, being honest. That or someone cleaned the place up.'

Breen sat on the side of the bath and watched them. One of them opened the bathroom cabinet and started going through the pots of cream and bottles of pills.

It took him a second to realise the phone was ringing. All three men looked at each other, then Breen leaped up and launched himself out of the room, down the corridor.

He picked up the handset and held it to his ear, saying nothing.

'Hello?' A man's voice.

Breen said nothing.

'Julie? You there? Julie?'

'Julie's out,' said Breen eventually. 'May I take a message?'

The other phone slammed straight down. Hearing a man's voice instead of Julie's or the maid's would have unsettled him. Breen stood there holding the handset; it had only been a few words, not enough to get an impression of who he had been talking to, beyond the fact that the man was well-spoken, probably middle-aged.

'Rang off?' said one of the forensics team.

'Has the phone rung before?'

The man shook his head. Breen thought. As the week progressed, customers would be calling up to make appointments, but they would be expecting a woman's voice.

'Should get someone down at the local GPO,' said the man. 'Monitor the line at the exchange. If you can keep them talking for a minute someone can note down the switching settings and you'll have their number.'

Breen put the handset down and stood a while, thinking.

The door of the first-floor flat above Payne was already half open. Breen pushed at it and called, 'Hello?'

'In here, Sarge.' Mint's voice came from down the hallway.

The living-room ceiling was hung with what looked like a huge tie-dyed sheet in red and orange and purple. It draped downwards to head height in the centre of the room. Breen realised that it was a parachute. Light from a single bulb above it cast a coloured haze on the room.

Mint was there, sitting on a beanbag, clutching a cup of tea which he put down as Breen entered the room. 'Sarge,' he said, struggling to stand.

The four students were crammed onto a single sofa opposite Mint. 'Hi,' said a girl dressed in denim dungarees. The others nodded but stayed silent.

'They say they knew her, Sarge,' said Mint, lowering himself back on the beanbag again. 'I checked their alibis. They were together all weekend.'

'Well, that doesn't make them very good alibis, does it?'

'But we were,' protested one of the girls.

Breen looked around for somewhere to sit. There were large cushions propped against the opposite wall but if he sat on them, he'd be even closer to the floor than Mint. He remained standing.

'She was a cool lady,' said the one in dungarees. She seemed to be the leader, the one others deferred to. The others nodded some more, looking sombre.

'So, you knew her well, Miss . . . ?'

'I'm Lulu. Yeah. We were just telling your, um, colleague. Pretty well.'

Breen looked around the flat. They had taken up the carpets and the boards were bare, with just an old Afghan rug lying under a tea chest that served as a coffee table. Sitting in the middle of it, in a large white enamel jug, was a bunch of yellow roses.

'When was the last time you talked to her?'

They looked at each other. 'Don't know really.' The window at the front of the flat was crowded with spider plants, hanging in a maze of macramé holders.

'Did you speak in the last week?'

'Last week? Not really. No.'

'But you knew her pretty well, you said?'

The others started talking now too. 'Well, I wouldn't say that well.' One nudged the other.

'What about visitors?'

The two men both had thin beards; they glanced at each other and smiled. One giggled.

'What?' demanded Breen.

'I mean. Her visitors,' the man who had sniggered said. 'They were, like, old men.'

'Stop it,' said Lulu. 'She's dead.'

'I don't know how she could put up with it,' said the second girl, looking away.

'She was a prostitute,' said Breen. 'That's how she put up with it.'

'When you think about it,' said Lulu, 'she was fucking the system. That's what I always said.'

Cautiously, the other three nodded.

'What does that actually mean?' asked Breen.

'Taking money from the rich men. That's what she was doing. I think she was brave,' said Lulu.

'Yeah. But old men,' said the other girl.

'Would you remember any of them?' Breen asked.

None of them spoke.

'Did you see a middle-aged woman going up to the flat?'

The four of them looked blank.

'Her name was Florence. She worked with Miss Bobienski.'

They shook their heads. 'They were men. Men in suits. Dirty old men.'

'How old?' asked Breen.

'Some as old as my dad,' said one of the young men. 'Like, forty, fifty.'

Breen was in his early thirties. They would probably think him old too, he thought. 'Would you know them if you saw them again?'

The young man who had spoken hesitated. 'I'm not sure. I don't know.'

'What about their voices?' Breen asked.

The young man looked blank. 'I don't know.'

'They didn't speak,' said Lulu. 'Of course they didn't. They were ashamed.'

'So you didn't notice anything special about them?'

'They were just men.'

'What do you think they were ashamed of?' asked Breen.

'Cheating,' said one of the boys. 'They wouldn't want their wives to find out.'

Lulu shook her head. 'They were ashamed because they were part of the hegemonic elite, yet a woman half their age had this power over them.'

'It wasn't like that,' said one of the boys, grinning nervously. 'They were paying her.'

And the four started arguing. They had such strong opinions of why these men came to visit the prostitute upstairs, Breen thought, yet none of them had observed anything about their appearance. The self-absorption of their generation made them poor witnesses. So far, an old man who couldn't see, a caretaker who appeared to do his best not to notice, and four young people who didn't look.

'You're here for the summer?' he asked.

They nodded. It was the academic holiday.

'You're not planning to go anywhere, are you?'

'Why? Are we suspects?' said the one called Lulu.

'Of course you are,' said Breen. 'Until we rule you out.'

'But the constable just said . . . We have alibis.'

'Only for each other,' said Breen.

They looked at each other, shocked. 'Do we need a lawyer?'

Breen smiled, leaned down onto the tea chest and wrote a number on a page on his notebook, tore it out and handed it to the girl called Lulu. 'If you think of anything at all that might identify one of the men, or if you see anyone you don't recognise coming to the building, call me, OK?'

She took it and nodded. It did no harm to scare them a little. They would be keen to demonstrate it wasn't them, at least.

'Anything unusual you notice, let me know. OK?' As he put the pen back into his briefcase, he noticed a yellow petal on the plywood of the tea chest and frowned. There had been a single dying rose in a vase in Miss Bobienski's flat, he remembered.

'Where are the roses from?'

The girl who wasn't Lulu said, 'Bob gave them to Lulu because he fancies her.'

One of the two boys squirmed; he must have been Bob. 'Stupid,' said Lulu. 'I don't believe in relationships. That's a fascist kick.'

'I think it's lovely,' said the girl. 'You should be grateful.'

'Where did you get them?'

The boy looked more uncomfortable still. 'Found them,' he said.

'You said you bought them,' said Lulu.

He shook his head and said again, 'Found them.'

'Where?' asked Breen.

'Outside,' Bob said. 'Someone left them outside the front door.'

'When?'

'I don't know. They were there this morning.'

'So you picked up someone else's flowers and gave them to Lulu? That's pathetic,' said the girl.

'Was there a note?'

'Shit. They were meant for the prostitute. That's disgusting,' said the girl.

'No,' said the boy. 'I swear. There wasn't anything. I'd have left them if there was.'

'I don't want them in my flat,' said the girl.

Lulu sounded more amused. 'He brings me a dead whore's flowers. It's so Baudelaire. Or Verlaine.'

'She's dead anyway,' the boy was protesting.

Breen left them bickering, Mint following behind. 'Sorry, Sarge, only they said they knew her. I did take notes of their alibis if you want to see.'

On the way downstairs, Breen met the technician coming the other way. 'I've got something you might like to see,' he said.

Mint followed Breen into the small dark room behind the lift. The technician had unbolted the electric motor from its housing and then removed the case.

'The windings have shorted out,' he said. 'Look.'

He pointed to a bundle of copper wires, blackened and tangled.

'Are you saying it's an accident?' said Breen.

'Nope. I think you may have been on to something. Look at this.' And he picked up the motor's metal case and handed it to Breen. It was surprisingly heavy. The engine's housing was old, green-painted metal. As he held it, the technician pointed to a hole – a vent presumably. The surface on one side of it was blackened.

'What?' said Breen.

The technician took the casing back off him and replaced it over the motor's rotors. The burn was directly over the ruined copper.

'So someone shorted it out deliberately?'

'I'd say.'

'What? Stuck a piece of metal in there?'

'Something like that. Lucky he didn't blow his bloody hand off.'

'Or someone who knew what he was doing?'

The technician nodded thoughtfully.

Haas appeared as the man was unscrewing the whole engine from its mounting.

'What is happening?'

'This is evidence,' said the technician.

'Evidence of what?' said Haas. 'How will the lift work if there is no apparatus?'

'Do you keep any tools down here, Haas?' Breen said.

'Behind you. A hammer. Sometimes I have to hit the engine. The rotors become stuck, you understand.'

'What about a piece of metal, about this thick?' asked the technician.

'A screwdriver? What you want it for, mister? Don't you have your own?' Haas looked around the shelf where the hammer lay. 'Should be a screwdriver here. Somebody has taken it, I expect.'

They were back on the pavement outside when the girl from the flat – the one that wasn't Lulu – came down the stairs barefoot, carrying the jug of roses. She stepped into the London street. There was a grey metal dustbin at the top of the steps down into the basement area. She lifted the lid and threw the flowers inside.

NINE

At the stroke of one o'clock, one of the sergeants said, 'Who's coming to the Crown? Paddy?'

Breen was back at the Marylebone station, making calls. 'Give me a minute,' he said.

'Where's Minty?'

'He said he had something to do,' said Breen, cupping the mouthpiece of the phone. He was holding for a man from the Ministry of Defence who had gone to consult a card index in some distant Whitehall room.

Miss Rasper answered her phone. 'CID?' Then called out, 'There's a young lady downstairs for you, Sergeant Breen.'

'Young lady. Oi, oi!'

Another voice was speaking in his ear. 'Got him. Flying Officer Jan Bobienski. 303 Squadron. Spitfires, mostly. Hurricanes too.'

'Is he still alive?'

The man at the other end of the phone talked slowly, enunciating each syllable as if words were precious. '303 Squadron disbanded in 1946. According to this, he was demobbed. No other record.'

'Pension?'

'I haven't got those precise details here. I can look if you like. Last address was in Gloucestershire, but that's no longer current. There doesn't appear to be anything else.'

'Do you have any contacts from anyone else who would have flown with him?'

A sigh. 'I shall ask around.'

Downstairs, Helen Tozer was sitting on the old wooden bench inside the front door.

'First time I've been here since I left,' she said.

'Missing it?'

'This hole?' She looked around. 'More than I ever thought I would, as it happens,' she said. 'Brought you lunch.' There was a raffia shopping bag beside her.

'Lunch?'

'Why not?'

The other CID men came down the stairs, chatting and laughing. Creamer had joined them; he was the type who liked to have a drink with the men, whether the men wanted him there or not.

Seeing Breen talking to Helen, he barged past the others. 'Is this your good lady, Paddy?' Creamer beamed, holding out his hand. 'Will you be joining us?'

'Helen's just brought me some lunch,' said Breen, butting in, taking her arm to help her stand. 'Maybe I'll join you later, sir.'

They walked out into the grey London summer. 'What if I wanted to go to the pub?' said Helen. 'Like the old days.'

'Troublemaker,' he said.

'Can't hold it down, anyway,' she said. 'But I miss it. I thought I was going to die on the bus. There was a woman going on and on about Judy Garland. She said she couldn't stop crying. Saying how she was going to miss her.'

'You never make lunch when I'm at home.'

'Don't get any ideas. It was just too hot to stay in the flat. And Elfie made a meat loaf. It was her idea for me to bring it, really. I just made the sandwiches.' She stopped on the pavement and caught her breath. 'My back hurts. I just want the little bastard out now.'

'It doesn't have to be a bastard.'

'I didn't mean that kind of bastard.'

They crossed the Outer Circle into Regent's Park and found a space on the bank next to the boating lake. Helen had brought an old tweed blanket from her room; it had been his father's. She laid it out on the thin grass and sat on it. Nearby a couple of young women from an office were trying to sunbathe in short summer skirts hitched up to their knickers, Dr Scholl sandals kicked off bare feet.

'I feel ugly,' said Helen, glaring at their thinness.

'I think you're beautiful.'

'Shut up and eat so you can be as fat as I am.' She handed him a slice of meatloaf and unwrapped a tinfoil parcel of sandwiches. 'Oh,' she said, pulling a battered magazine out of the bag. 'And you might want to take a look at this. Elfie found it. I thought you'd want to see it.'

Breen took it from her. It wasn't a normal magazine, but one of the new alternative ones, amateurishly laid out, like *Private*

Eye or *International Times*. This one was called *OZ*. The cover was a grotesque cartoon of a bare-skinned black woman with absurdly fat lips and huge red nipples. 'Fingerlickin' Good', it read.

Breen turned the cover back on itself so people wouldn't be able to see what he was reading, but found he was looking at a page with a photo of a naked woman instead. 'PUSSYCATS. A BRAND NEW SERIES OF FIVE SUPERB FEMALE PHOTOS. 10/-.'

'Is this magazine even legal?' he said.

'Oh shut up.'

He turned to the front pages. There was an article by Andy Warhol, then another by an American called Malcolm X and a review of a band named MC5. Everything seemed to be printed in orange and pink; it hurt to even look at it.

'Why would she think I'd be interested in this?'

She snatched it off him and flicked through he pages until she came to a page called 'Spike File'. 'Look.'

Under a cartoon of a dead body, pierced by a thick spike, was a column full of tittle-tattle and paranoia. The first item was a self-righteous tirade, complaining about the magazine's own printers who had refused to take material because of complaints about obscenity and references to drugs. The second reviewed *Revolution for the Hell of It*, telling readers it was 'the most important book to leap from the Underground'.

And finally there was a short paragraph:

So it turns out there is a hooker called Janey Teenager working in London (not that we have need of her services!!). I'm told

Janey is no teenager at all (longer in tooth), but all the same, very popular with a lot of what used to be known as The Establishment. Remember them? Youth is a commodity these days. An illusion to be bartered along with HIPNESS AND COOL. Don't knock it. Capitalism is a tool, just like any other.

'Janey?'

'They got the name wrong. But it's her, isn't it? Klaus said he'd heard of her too.' Klaus was the father of her baby. 'She did some modelling too. It turns out she was quite the celebrity. Ham sandwich?'

'Elfie found it? How did she know that I was working on this case?'

'I told her about it, course.'

'It's work, Helen. You're not supposed to be talking about it to anyone.'

'I'm only trying to help.'

Breen took the sandwich. It was about two inches thick on one side and barely half an inch on the other. He started on the thinner edge.

'Maybe I can ask around?' said Helen.

'Maybe.' He picked up the copy of *OZ*.

'Don't sound so enthusiastic. Do those pictures of naked girls interest you?'

'No. Of course not. I was just looking. It's my job.'

'Liar,' she said.

'. . . Looking for the address of where it's published.'

'Notting Hill. I already looked.'

'Where?'

She pointed to the name of a street in W8, written in tiny letters on the inside cover. 'Want to go there? I could come with you. Act as your interpreter. You'd need that.'

He put down the magazine. She was lighting a cigarette. 'You've hardly eaten anything,' he said.

'Well? What if I come with you?'

There was a man dressed in white shorts and a tennis shirt running along the path. People stopped, stared. Nobody ran anywhere in London unless they were after a bus. The man was muscular and fair-haired, but as he approached, Breen saw he looked older than he had done at a distance. 'I bet he's American,' said Helen.

'You know I'd like you to, Helen, but you can't come with me. You're not a policewoman any more.'

She looked away. 'I knew you'd say that,' she said. 'You're so . . . boring.'

And she re-wrapped her own half-eaten sandwich in the tinfoil and returned it to the raffia bag.

'I know you were trying to help,' he said.

'Yeah, yeah,' she said. 'Do it your way.'

They sat in silence for a while. A small fat boy in school shorts was throwing large chunks of bread at a pigeon. Each time the bird hopped towards one of the pieces the boy would throw another, attempting to hit it.

The constable was sitting on the bench where Helen had been when he got back to the station.

'Paddy Breen?' He stood. 'You wanted to see me.'

Breen must have looked puzzled. The man added, 'My beat

includes Harewood Avenue. I was just about to go on, only the gaffer said I had to see you first.'

He was one of the tough old ones, late forties, face veined with red, either from being outside too much, or at the bar too long; one who walked the slow gait of a copper keen not to wear their shoe leather too hard.

'Come on up.'

When the constable reached the CID office he looked around at the newly decorated walls. 'My, my. Changed a bit in here, hasn't it? Fancy nancy. You'll be getting lace curtains next.'

'Miss Rasper? Do you have a second to make Constable . . .'

'Jenks,' said the constable.

'Constable Jenks here a cup of tea?'

Miss Rasper looked up. 'Can't you manage that yourself, Sergeant Breen?'

Breen hesitated long enough. She pushed back her chair and stood. 'Fine then,' she said curtly. 'How do you like it, Constable Jenks?'

'Time of the month?' Jenks said aloud when Rasper had left the room.

'Don't think she has periods,' muttered one of the constables.

Breen pulled up one of the plastic chairs to his desk and motioned Jenks to sit in it. The constable ambled across the room.

'Lovely flowers, an' all,' he said. 'Does the cup of tea come with a paper doily?'

On his desk was a vase of chrysanthemums. Breen stared for a second. 'Why has someone put flowers here?' asked Breen looking round.

'Don't you like them?'; 'Prefer pansies, Paddy?' All the usual.

But before he could say anything, Miss Rasper returned from the kitchen with a single mug of tea. 'They're mine, actually. The very nice Constable Mint here bought them for me. Unfortunately, I suffer from hay fever, so I cannot have them near me.'

Young Constable Mint blushed. 'I didn't exactly buy them for you, Miss Rasper.'

'I'm wounded,' said Miss Rasper, feeding paper into her typewriter.

'No,' said Mint, blushing more. 'I didn't mean . . .'

Miss Rasper didn't smile, just started clacking away at the keys.

'And you, a happily married man,' said Breen, and this time he thought he saw a twitch in Rasper's lips.

'I bought them as part of the investigation,' said Mint.

'For your sergeant. That's nice,' said Constable Jenks. 'I see how it is round here.'

'After you left I stopped at a few of the local florists,' Mint told Breen. 'I wanted to ask if anyone had bought yellow roses off them early this morning. Most don't do yellow roses, but the one outside Warren Street did. I thought I'd ask if he saw anything this morning. Old bloke there said he'd only talk to me if I paid for something, so I did.'

'He bloody did see something,' said Jenks. 'He bloody saw you coming for one.' A big laugh.

'I was hoping I could claim them on expenses,' he said.

'Expenses? Lah-di-dah.'

'Well?' said Breen. 'Did he tell you anything of interest?'

'Man said he didn't know. His son would have been there this morning. I should come back another day.'

'I feel used,' muttered Miss Rasper.

Breen sat at his desk; there was a note on it in Rasper's handwriting: *Squadron Leader Zygmunt Wojcik*, and an address in West London. When he looked up, he noticed Jenks was frowning at the vase of flowers, so he grabbed it and put it on Mint's desk on the far side of the room, saying, 'Give them to your wife.'

When he returned, he said to Jenks, 'You're aware of the murder of the prostitute Lena Bobienski?'

'Course.'

'Did you know her?'

Jenks shook his head. 'Never seen her, personally. Not until they took her body out.'

'But you knew she was operating a business from that address?'

The constable nodded. 'A business. You could say that.'

'How?'

The constable blinked. 'Well it's obvious. Anywhere you see men coming and going in taxis after closing time is either a gentlemen's club or something else. And I don't think it was a gentlemen's club, exactly.'

The best beat coppers had built years of experience; they learned the fingerprint of each individual street they walked, developing a skill for understanding what normal was, looking for anything that didn't fit. The overdue tax disc on a car, the milk bottle left on the doorstep.

'Would you recognise any of the men who went in or out?'

Jenks looked down at his shiny black boots. 'That's where it's more difficult.'

81

'Because?'

Again, there was a fraction of hesitation. 'I don't know. Just maybe didn't pay attention because they weren't no trouble.'

'Really? Well, it looks like one of them was trouble. She's dead.'

'It's a busy beat, you know it is.'

Breen picked up a pencil and flipped it in his hand. 'Really? You didn't notice who was going in and out?'

The man looked around the room, avoiding Breen's gaze. 'We get all sorts, you know. Sorry, Sergeant.'

'Maybe I should have a word with your boss. Tell him you might need glasses. Or maybe that you're getting too old for it.'

'You do that,' said Jenks, evenly. 'Tell him I need a nice cushy job like yours. With flowers and everything.'

Breen had been hoping for more, but CID just rubbed some coppers up the wrong way. Constable Jenks stood, picked up the cup and drained what was left in it. 'You used to be down the Louise in the old days. I don't see you in there.'

'My girlfriend is pregnant,' said Breen. 'I don't go out so much.'

A small frown from the copper at the word 'girlfriend'. 'You should do,' said the constable, slowly. 'Show your face.'

Breen sat there for a while after Jenks left, flicking his pencil into the air, wondering what the copper had meant. Vice Squad at Scotland Yard had said they didn't have a file on either Julie Teenager or Lena Bobienski. He had spoken to the women police, as Helen had suggested, but they had not been any more useful. They had all heard about Julie Teenager but none of them had ever met her. Because she was never any trouble, they said. The optimism of the morning was running thin.

The office was so much quieter than it used to be. The lino muted the clatter of boots and the modern typewriters were delicate compared to the big iron monsters that Inspector Creamer had thrown out. Even the new phones seemed to ring less urgently. Nobody was allowed to play the radio any more. He had never liked the idiotic chatter and the pop songs, but now he missed the noise. The silence made it hard to think.

TEN

A little after four, Constable Mint returned from the *OZ* offices, with another copy of the magazine held between finger and thumb. 'I think they take drugs, too,' he said.

'Well?'

The constable opened his notebook. 'Firstly, it wasn't exactly an office. It was just a flat, really.' He looked up.

'Go on.'

'I encountered a woman there. She assumed I was there as part of a police raid. When I asked what she thought I'd be raiding them for, she said . . .' He turned the page. '*Take your pick.*'

Jones looked up from his desk and laughed.

Mint continued. 'The said woman refused to give her name and she said the editor was in Morocco, but the person who'd written the article about Julie Teenager was a man called Felix. She said he sold advertising for the magazine. However, she declined to give me his last name or address because . . .' He turned the page again. 'She said I was a pig.'

Even Miss Rasper was laughing now. Mint squirmed.

'Carry on,' said Breen.

'Is this OK?'

'It's excellent,' said Breen. 'Don't leave anything out.'

Mint turned another page in his notebook. One of the sergeants stood, walked over to Mint's desk and picked up the copy of *OZ*. On the cover there was a cartoon of Mickey Mouse; Mickey was sticking out his tongue. Resting on it was a big, round pill. The sergeant flicked through it and whistled.

Mint continued. 'Said woman offered me some free products and I warned her against bribing a policeman.'

'What products?'

'Some . . . cream. From one of their advertisers.'

'*Magnaphall*,' read the sergeant. '*A sound and successful way of improving virility and increasing the size of the male organ*. That the cream she gave you, Minty?' He put the magazine down on Miss Rasper's desk. 'Here you go, love. Show that to your boyfriend.'

Miss Rasper rolled her eyes.

'She didn't give it to me,' said Mint. 'I wouldn't take it.'

'On account of how you don't need it.'

'As a policeman, I don't accept gifts from members of the public.'

'Quite right,' said Breen. 'What about this man . . . Felix?'

'As I said. She refused to give me his contact details. I suggested that we would return with a warrant to search the premises.'

'I don't think we'd go that far,' said Breen.

'Oh. Right.' He reached into his wallet. 'I have a receipt for the magazine,' he said. 'Three shillings.'

Miss Rasper held up the copy and read, '*Advertising. Contact Felix Dennis on 727-8456.*'

'Oh,' said Mint.

Constable Jones snatched the magazine back from Miss Rasper and looked at it. 'She's right. It's there in black and white.'

'It's OK. You did well,' said Breen, writing down the number and reaching for the phone.

'How do they get away printing this crap? They got one thing right though,' said Jones. 'There's an article here saying the Drug Squad are bent.' He looked up and grinned.

Monday evening, there was no one in the flat when he got home, but he heard the music playing upstairs.

Elfie smiled when she saw him standing at the door with his briefcase. She had a smear of tomato puree on her face and was holding a whisk. He smelt chicken. 'I'm cooking dinner,' she said. 'Come and join us.'

Helen was in Elfie's living room, sitting on the floor, surrounded by album sleeves and tape boxes. Elfie's boyfriend had a sophisticated modern hi-fi with a big Ferguson reel-to-reel machine, massive speakers in wooden cases, separate record player, the works.

He bent down to kiss her, then sniffed. 'Is that pot?'

'Bog off,' she said.

He took out the copy of *OZ* Mint had bought and tossed it towards her. She took it. 'Subscriber now, are you? So, what did you find out?'

'Nothing yet. I've arranged to meet the journalist who wrote it.'

'Felix?'

'How did you know?'

She shrugged. 'Aren't you going to say thank you?'

Elfie appeared with half a bottle of wine. Her eyes seemed red and puffy, like she had been crying.

'Wine? Is everything all right?' he asked.

'Why wouldn't it be?' She handed Breen a glass without asking if he wanted to drink or not. Nobody in the East End drank wine apart from Elfie and her boyfriend, especially on a Monday.

'I'm trying a new recipe,' said Elfie. 'Chicken Pilaff.'

'I'll definitely need wine,' he said.

'Don't be horrid.'

'Anyway. What if I called Felix up?' said Helen. 'Ask to meet him.'

'You can't just do that,' he said.

'Why not?'

'It's a murder investigation.'

'Exactly,' she said going to the thick pile of LPs that leaned against the wall. He opened his mouth to say something, but didn't. It was best not to argue with her when she was like this.

'What about her customers?' she was asking. 'The dirty old men.'

'We're still trying to track down her maid. The GPO are going to monitor the line at the exchange.'

She added a single to a stack on the turntable stand and switched it from 33 to 45. 'You should put me in the flat,' she said. 'Pretend to be a tart for you.' She laughed, low and loud.

'Not with your accent,' he said.

'What's wrong with my bloody accent?'

Living in London had done nothing to soften the Devonshire in her voice. He left her listening to something with wailing guitars on it and joined Elfie in the kitchen. She had recently painted the walls bright orange and all the kitchen's wooden chairs in glossy green.

'Need a hand?'

'The recipe says walnuts but I don't have any. D'you think peanuts will do?'

'What's this?'

'Yoghurt.'

He dipped his finger in and sucked it. It was surprisingly tart. He was about to try it again when Elfie slapped his wrist.

'Where's Klaus?'

'Oh. You know. He works.'

'Are you OK?' he asked.

She didn't answer; instead she dipped a fork into the rice to test it. 'Fuck. Burned my tongue.'

Breen took the fork from her and tried the rice himself. It was overcooked. He took it off the gas to drain it.

They sat at a pine dining table in Elfie's crowded kitchen, eating from mismatched crockery. Helen had put some music on and turned it up next door so they could listen while they ate. Breen's father would have hated it. When he had been growing up, alone with his dad, eating had always been a silent affair. His dad never even switched the radio on.

'What if,' said Elfie, pushing the food around her plate with a fork, 'someone had Brian Jones killed?'

Helen laughed, spraying rice across the table. 'Why would someone kill him?'

'Just saying. I mean, what if someone did? To get him out of the band. Klaus thinks so.'

'He was out of the band already,' said Helen.

'Brian Jones was a drug addict,' said Breen, putting down his fork. 'Drug addicts don't need people to kill them.' He had had some wine and was a little drunk.

'Not everyone who takes drugs is an addict,' said Helen.

'No, but Brian Jones was. Drug Squad arrested him last year—'

'Pilcher arresting anyone doesn't prove anything. He planted dope on Lennon,' said Helen.

'Planted dope?' said Breen. 'When did you start calling drugs "dope"?'

Elfie laughed.

Breen went back to his food. Elfie's cooking was unreliable. Sometimes it tasted terrible, but tonight it tasted good – in spite of the rice. Having grown up in the war, when food was meagre and basic, having chicken in a rich, spiced sauce and drinking wine was like pretending he was middle class for a moment.

He looked up. Helen had only eaten a tiny amount. 'It's not fair. I've got nowhere to put it,' she said. 'I used to eat twice as much as him.' She nodded at Breen. Breen grinned back at her.

A fork clattered to the floor. Elfie stood abruptly, pushing back her chair and walking out of the room so fast she was almost running.

'Is she all right?'

'Klaus is having it off with another girl,' Helen whispered.

Klaus: Elfie's cool, posh, long-haired boyfriend, who wore velvet jackets and flares and who had brought her here to live and have his babies. Breen looked towards the kitchen and said, 'Should you go and . . . ?'

'Elfie only found out yesterday. The cow he's having sex with called her and told her she was sleeping with him. Elfie told me all about it when I got back from seeing you today. Apparently this girl he's fucking is a model for *Vogue*. When she asked Klaus if it was true, he told her that monogamy is bourgeois.' She reached out for an ashtray. 'Unlike being an advertising copy writer, which is a revolutionary act.'

'What is she going to do?'

'She's in love with him,' she said, as if that explained it all.

Breen lifted his glass of wine and finished it.

On the doorstep, Elfie acted as if nothing had happened. 'So lovely. I feel so good having you around. We should just knock a staircase through from the basement,' she said, laughing. 'You're my best friends, now, you two.'

Back downstairs, Helen said, 'She'd be better off without him. He's a prick.'

'I thought you liked him?'

'I'm stuffed,' said Helen. She was wearing a plain, blue dress. Standing in the middle of the living room she pulled it over her head and stood in white knickers and tan bra. 'I've got boobs,' she said, as if surprised. 'Look.'

He looked. They had grown along with the bump.

'Something else,' said Breen. 'The street the prostitute was murdered in. The local beat copper says he didn't notice anyone going in and out of Julie Teenager's flat.'

'Didn't notice?'

'I know. I thought it was weird.'

She was still standing with one hand under each bosom, testing them for weight. 'You know why, though, don't you?'

'Why?'

'Because a copper was shagging her. Or one of his mates. What's the betting? How close is it to your station? Not far is it? Bet it's one of yours.'

'You think?'

'Bet you anything,' she said. Then she looked up from her own chest. 'Are you staring at my boobs?'

'Sort of.'

'I used to put socks in my bra, when I was a kid. Now look.'

She stood, pale-skinned and bony-legged.

A day gone and there had been no progress in the case. In spite of what he had said to Mint, in terms of the residents of the house, the only person who was a possible suspect was Haas the caretaker. That left the prostitute's maid and the clients, but they had no leads on either.

'What if you and I sleep in the same bed tonight?' he said. 'If that's not too bourgeois.'

'Are my bosoms getting you all bothered?'

'No. I mean. Well, they're supposed to, aren't they? But I meant just for company.'

She hesitated, but then said, 'I would, but it's too hot,' and padded to the bathroom on her own. Listening to the sound of water running, he picked up the dress and held it for a minute, then hung it over the back of a dining chair.

ELEVEN

On the phone, Wellington complained. 'I am busy.'

'So am I,' said Breen.

'You're a pain in the bloody arse.'

Breen was at his desk. It was now Tuesday morning, forty-_
eight hours since the body had been discovered; no significant
progress had been made. 'I need to know the time of death. I
think it's going to be crucial to the investigation.'

'And I will call you when I know anything.'

'Just a preliminary idea would be useful.'

There was a sigh. 'Body temperature is no good. She'd been
dead too long. You know how we normally find out the time of
death from a cold corpse? I stick as needle in its eye. Checking
the amount of potassium in the aqueous fluid is the best way
to determine how long a body has been deceased. Only even a
plod like you might have noticed, she didn't have any bloody
eyeballs, so there's not an awful lot to go on, Sergeant. I'll be
investigating her organs and will let you know. On paper she

could have been killed any time between Thursday and Saturday morning. Which is what I told you yesterday. Will that be all?'

Wellington didn't wait for an answer. Breen was left holding the phone. 'Bollocks,' he said.

'Temper, temper,' said Constable Jones, not looking up. 'Oi. Where are you going, Sarge? Creamer said there's a nine-thirty meeting.'

Breen walked faster, letting the door swing behind him.

It was easy to see which one Felix was; he had long black hair and a beard.

They sat at a small table, each with a coffee in front of them. Felix had his black.

'She said absolutely point blank no. I told her I'd pay her like I was a punter and all she had to do was talk, we didn't even have to have sex.'

'Generous of you.'

'I know. But she wasn't interested. I called her up because I'd seen her put an advert in *Private Eye*. I said you don't have to waste money on that. We'll give you free publicity. She said no.'

Breen sat at the small table with an espresso in front of him. Felix talked fast and unstoppably.

'I didn't understand it at first. I told her it was a great story. Perfect for *OZ*. There's a young Australian lady called Germaine on our magazine, I said, who writes about sex all the time, she's amazing; she'd love to meet you. She could write all about you. Make you a huge star. It would be amazing. She was perfectly polite, don't get me wrong, but she turned it down. See? Don't you think that's relevant?'

They were at the 91 in Charlotte Street. It was a rough place, but unlike everywhere else nearby that served instant, this cafe had an elderly but serviceable Gaggia. For Breen, growing up in post-war London, the thunk and hiss of these Italian machines had represented the new world, a long way away from the uniformity of English tea and toast and rationed margarine. He respected anyone who drank his coffee black.

'She turned down free publicity. See? That's got to be a clue, hasn't it?'

'Not necessarily,' Breen said.

Felix ignored him. 'She was gorgeous, by the way. Did I mention that? Very, very fuckable. Sort of petite and flat-chested which made her look younger than she was. And I thought she was fantastic. Germaine says the English like that gamine look that Twiggy has because actually they really want to have sex with little boys. I think she has a point.'

George, the cafe's owner, leaned over them to wipe their table clean. He was a Maltese man with a razor-scarred face. The artists and lowlifes who crowded here assumed he was a villain of some sort, though Breen had never heard of him being involved in trouble. He was a sweet, mild-tempered man, but the bohemians, who came here for George as much as the coffee, liked a hint of misbehaviour.

Breen interrupted Felix to thank George, but Felix didn't stop. 'All she wanted to do was book an advert. Thing is, she was kind of famous already, wasn't she?'

'Was she?'

'Oh God, yeah. You'd see her at parties. She was on the scene. Everyone knew who she was. I told her she should go to New

York. They'd have loved her there. All that Andy Warhol, you know?'

'Not much, no,' said Breen.

'Awful American artist but some great music around him. You heard of Nico? No? I had seen Julie Teenager before at a party too, I realise. At the Pheasantry.'

Breen shook his head.

'You don't know it? It's a commune in the King's Road. Eric Clapton's there. He shares it with a couple of the Australians from the magazine. It's sort of a crash pad. There was some American rock 'n' roll manager guy who hired Julie Teenager for the night to dangle her on his arm. It was kind of ugly, but I can remember thinking how fucking beautiful she was even then. The thing is, Julie Teenager was a genius, I found that really interesting. She'd have all these rich, middle-aged men's tongues hanging out. As a business proposition it was pure gold. All your generation have that anger. "How come we didn't have all this when we were growing up?" It's like, however powerful they are, they can never have it? You see? It builds up in them when they see the girls in short skirts, screaming at pop stars. It makes them so jealous. That's what she was exploiting.'

He picked up his coffee but didn't bring it to his lips, put it down and started talking again.

'So she's a mover. Was a mover I mean, poor girl. You know why this country is crap compared to America? We have no innovators. All we have is old industries that are dying. All we have is fucking trade unions. Old men holding on to what they've got. A generation knows that it's missing the boat. All the schoolgirls screaming at DJs and pop stars. There's Eric

95

Clapton boning some teenager, and you know what? They're bloody jealous. She saw a business opportunity in that. She gave them a chance to have it, if they were willing to pay to pretend to be young. It's the revolution as commercial opportunity. And that's exactly what *OZ* is too. If England is a nation of shopkeepers, how do you revolt? You take over the whole fucking shop.' He stopped talking and looked past Breen, a flicker of anxiety on his face, as if he had spotted someone he didn't want to meet.

'You said we're angry,' prompted Breen.

'Well, yes. You're angry. All your life you did the right thing and look at you.'

'Who says I did the right thing?'

'Sorry. Got carried away. You're a cop. Course you don't. But all the other buttoned-down men.'

Breen wondered if Felix was on drugs, he talked so much. And there was that twitch in the eyes again. Breen checked his watch. There was a morning meeting. He would be late. He picked up the small cup and savoured the taste. 'So you think one of her clients was so angry he killed her?'

'Fuck, no. You are completely missing the point. She's feeding on their anger. They're not angry at her. The opposite.'

'What then?'

Felix lifted a briefcase onto the wooden cafe table. Breen was surprised. Felix was the first hippie Breen had ever seen who carried one.

'Look. Think about it. She didn't take my money. I was even offering her free advertising. So?'

'So?' said Breen. But he was leaning forward now, interested.

'Don't you get it? Either she's earning a fortune already and doesn't need it or she has something to hide. Don't you think?'

'Don't you think, what? I don't understand.'

'Do I have to spell it out? That she must have been having sex with someone really important. I mean really big important, you know? Otherwise why would she want to keep it quiet? And why would someone want to keep her quiet?' He looked from side to side. 'How much can I trust you?'

'I'm a policeman.'

'My point exactly,' said Felix.

'Trust me about what?'

'You're not the first person who's been looking for me about her since she died.'

'Who else?' asked Breen.

'There's a bird been calling me. And I think I'm being followed.'

'Who by?'

'I'm not sure. I just catch people looking at me out of the corner of my eye.'

Breen frowned. 'Did you question her about it? Did you discuss who her really important clients would be?'

'No. I only figured it out afterwards.'

Breen looked at Felix and thought of Elfie and what she said last night about the Rolling Stone being murdered. This generation's sense of self-importance meant that they believed themselves to be the centre of everything. They could only understand misfortune and chance as conspiracies against them.

'Wouldn't it be more likely that she didn't advertise because

97

she was just worried about becoming too public? Being too famous might scare away her clients.'

Felix opened the briefcase and took out an old brown envelope, then pulled a photo out. 'She wasn't that scared being looked at. Look.'

It was a black-and-white of Lena, taken in a photo studio. Wearing a crocheted dress, she was sitting on a TV that was on, legs apart, either side of the screen. The television was showing some pop group. Under the dress she appeared to be naked. Breen could see her nipples through the wool. Her eyes were wide and her mouth a round 'O' shape.

'Fabulous, isn't it?' said Felix. 'Just fucking fabulous. Apparently she sold these to her . . . you know, clients. J. Walter Thompson couldn't have done it better. You've got to admit it. She knew exactly who she was teasing. All just a bit old-fashioned, the page-boy haircut and the make-up. Sort of 1967. But actually, that was spot on, because her clientele are a bit old-fashioned. They wouldn't want to see Marianne Faithful with a half-melted Mars bar. That would be too scary, wouldn't it?'

Breen had no idea what he was talking about.

'So she clearly wasn't worried about being too public. She was in business. But don't you find it interesting she didn't want to be interviewed? She didn't want anybody asking her about the details of what she was doing.'

He studied the photograph. 'Can I keep this?'

'See what I mean? Tasty, isn't she?'

'Just because she didn't want to do an interview for your magazine doesn't mean anything. Maybe she didn't like the juvenile tone.'

Felix giggled. 'We're very proud of it, that juvenile tone. Maybe you're right. I don't know. But admit it, you'd like to have fucked her, wouldn't you?'

'She's dead, Felix. I saw her body. I wouldn't want to have sex with her, no.'

Felix's eyes widened. 'Did you? See her body, I mean.'

'Of course. I'm a policeman.'

'Christ. Poor girl. Sorry. I'm an idiot. I just get carried away.' He stopped. 'Don't look behind you now,' he whispered.

'There's nothing necessarily suspicious about a prostitute not wanting to be interviewed by the press. Why would men pay money to her to sleep with her if they thought she was going to talk about it to journalists? All men who use prostitutes are men who have secrets.'

'Right behind you. Woman with short hair. She's watching me. If they weren't so bad at it, it would be laughable. A cop, what do you reckon?'

'Are you on drugs?'

'You don't have to believe me. We have the fuzz round all the time. Our phones are tapped. You can hear the click every time you pick up.' He lowered his voice. 'I swear. The woman on the table next to us has been listening in to our conversation.'

'Right,' said Breen.

'Every time I look up, she pretends to look away. It's hilarious. Don't look now,' he said. 'I'll tell you when.'

Breen rolled his eyes.

'Believe what you like. I think Lena was mixed up in something. OK. She's lighting a cigarette. Look now.'

Finally Breen turned. The young woman waved a cloud of smoke away from her and smiled at Breen.

'See?' said Felix.

'Fancy meeting you here,' said Breen.

'I know,' said Helen. 'What a coincidence.'

'Oh,' said Felix.

'This is the woman who's been following you?'

'Yes. Do you know each other?'

Helen held her bump. 'Just a little.'

'Christ. I thought – Well, I mean, it's not just her. All sorts of people have followed me.'

'Right.'

'You must be Felix,' she said, holding out the hand without a cigarette in it.

He shook it. 'How do you know my name?'

'Felix is just going,' said Breen.

'Am I?' said the young man.

'Here's a funny thing, Helen. Felix thought you were tailing him. He thinks he's being followed.'

'How do you know I wasn't following you?' said Helen. 'Just because you're being paranoid doesn't mean they're not out to . . . you know.'

'Tell me about it,' said Felix. 'We have the Vice Squad after us.' He turned to Breen. 'If you see them, tell them our next issue is going to be for homosexuals. Going to drive them nuts.'

'I thought your mag was all naked hippie women,' said Helen.

'Sexual liberation.' Felix grinned. 'That's what we represent. Homosexual. Bi. Polyamorous. We don't care.'

'So, you a homo?' Helen asked.

'Me? Not me, no. God, no. But we see our mission as to blow away all those repressed Victorian attitudes to sex.'

'Hear that, Paddy? Paddy here's repressed, aren't you?'

'Very. Thank you for meeting me, Mr Dennis,' he said, leading him to the door. 'I'll be in touch if I need anything else . . .'

After Felix had gone, she said, 'Quite nice-looking too. Shame you're not allowed to grow a beard, Cathal.' She tapped cigarette ash into the small tin ashtray on her table. 'So?'

'So,' he said. 'How did you know to find me in here?'

'Intuition.'

He raised an eyebrow.

'And it was in your notebook.'

'You've been looking through my police notebooks?'

'A little. I couldn't sleep. I'm sorry.'

He paid for the coffee, looked at his watch again. 'It's not the notebook I mind,' he said.

She looked down at the Formica tabletop. 'You don't under-stand how boring it is for me.'

'You've got Elfie.'

'She's nuts. And she's depressed about Klaus. All she wants to bloody do is cook. And clean things.'

He was about to say something, but before he could, she looked up. 'So. What did he say?'

'I thought you could hear it all.'

'Some of it. He thinks that she was killed because of something she knew about one of the men she was sleeping with. It was someone trying to shut her up. Do you think that's possible?'

'Of course it's possible,' said Breen. 'But it's not likely.' He checked his watch again. 'This was hardly an assassination; she was beaten badly before she was killed. That makes it look much more like anger. A spur-of-the-moment beating that got out of hand, maybe.'

'Rather than just a reasonable, ordinary beating,' Helen said.

Breen ignored her. 'And let's face it, that would fit. Her whole operation was a tease. Even he was saying that. She was pretending to be a schoolgirl.'

'So she deserved it, you mean?'

'I'm late, Helen. I have to go. There's a meeting,' he said.

'Yeah.'

He leaned forward to kiss her but her head was back down as she tapped her cigarette into the small red tin ashtray. So he straightened and walked out, looking back to see if she turned to watch him go, but her back was still towards him.

TWELVE

The meeting was already underway when he got back to the station. Creamer tapped his watch as Breen hung his jacket on the back of his chair, but he said nothing.

'I assumed it was one of these two,' Mint was saying. He had found an *A–Z* fold-out map of London, pinned it on the wall and marked out art schools in a red pen. There were 'X's as far west as St Martin's and as far south as Chelsea. He was pointing to two locations that were within walking distance of Miss Bobienski's flat. 'I phoned them up but neither had anyone called Florence or Florrie working for them as a model.'

Breen gazed at the map, saying nothing. When it came to his turn to speak he repeated what Wellington had told him earlier that morning, discussed how he had been attempting to track down information about the victim's family, but left out Felix Dennis's conspiracy theories.

The meeting petered out. Creamer returned to his office and

closed the door. There was a sense that little progress had been made since the day before.

Mint lingered in front of his map. 'But we have no suspects. Not actual people.'

'Sometimes it's like that.'

'I mean, we can't just let whoever it was get away with it, can we?'

Breen turned to look at him. 'Sometimes they do get away with it.'

'That's awful,' said Mint.

They stood there, side by side, looking at the map.

'She's using a pseudonym,' said Breen.

'What?'

'The madam. That's why you couldn't find her. She won't be using the name Florence. In prostitution, nobody uses their real name.'

'I'm so thick,' said Mint.

The Slade was in Fitzrovia, closest to Lena's flat, but Heatherley's was in George Street, closer to the police station. Breen had always wanted to go to art school but his father had discouraged him. 'Go back to the flower shop you found yesterday,' he said. 'See if the man who runs it is back.'

'Right,' said Mint, eager again. He was scrambling in his desk for a notebook as Breen left the room.

A BOAC 707, on its way to London Airport, roared overhead.

Breen was sitting in the back garden of a semi-detached house in Whitton. Pink roses fringed the suburban lawn, and the air was full of the scent of freshly mown grass.

Zygmunt Wojcik was in his mid-fifties. He was lean, wore a neat American-style tennis shirt and pressed trousers, but had a drinker's eyes. 'Jan Bobienski,' he said, 'was an idiot.'

'Be nice, Ziggy,' said the plump woman who was putting tea on the table. Wojcik's wife was English. She spooned sugar into her husband's cup.

'He was stupid,' he said, squinting into the sunlight.

'What do you mean, stupid?'

'A pretty good pilot though. He got eight German planes. Mostly Dorniers. I got ten.'

'The Battle of Britain?'

'Of course. We Poles won it for you, you know? Our pilots had experience fighting Germans. Yours had none. Never was so much owed by so many to so few. But you never paid us back. You wouldn't even let us march in the Victory parades because you didn't want to offend your new friend, comrade Stalin.'

He looked up into the sky. Already another airliner was following the last.

'That really wasn't fair, was it, dear?' said Mrs Wojcik.

'Where is he now, then?' asked Breen.

'Dead, of course. Bobienski went back to Poland after the war with the rest of the idiots from our government-in-exile. Come home, they said. Come home. Everything will be fine. Some of us did. I told them not to.' The Pole gulped his tea down in one. A bumblebee hummed at the grass around their feet. 'I was right. Stalin shot them or sent them to rot in the gulags.'

'Terrible really,' said Mrs Wojcik. 'After all they'd been through already.'

'Idiots,' said Wojcik. 'Stalin didn't want anyone who knew

how to fight for the freedom of Poland. The sort who fought for the Polish people. Why would he? We were dangerous men.'

'Yes,' said Mrs Wojcik, with a smile at her husband. 'They were.'

Wojcik looked away towards the end of the garden and scowled. 'I told Jan Bobienski, he was a fool to even think about it.'

'So he would have been sent to a prison camp?'

'Who knows? I never heard from him again. He disappeared. All of them disappeared. Everyone who went back.' Without explanation he got up and walked stiffly to the bottom of the garden, waving his arms. Breen watched him, thinking at first this was some strange expression of grief.

'It's the butterflies,' explained Mrs Wojcik. 'This year they're bad. They're ruining the cabbages.'

Breen reached inside his briefcase and pulled out the small photograph he had found by Lena Bobienski's bed, the couple with the boy and the young baby, and handed it to Mrs Wojcik. She raised her hand to her mouth and gasped. 'Ziggy. Come and look at this. He has a photo of Jan.'

'I don't want to see it.'

'Jan and his family. Before they went back to Poland.'

Wojcik stopped shooing the butterflies off his plants but stayed at the bottom of the garden, away from the table.

'Come, Ziggy dear. The policeman brought it for us to look at.'

Eventually, Wojcik walked back towards them, snatched the photograph, looked at it for a long time, stony-faced. 'Idiots,' he said eventually.

'What was her name? Cathy, I think. They married a little before us, didn't they, Ziggy?'

Her husband grunted, put the picture down on the garden table, then returned to the vegetable patch.

'He doesn't like to talk about it all,' she said, picking up the photo again. 'It was a wild time. Most of them didn't have girl-friends. Not steady ones, anyway. Nobody knew how long they were going to live, you see? I got along OK with Cathy, but she was a bit younger than me. The little boy's name was Stefan, I think. I don't recall a baby.'

'Her name may have been Lena, I think,' said Breen.

She shook her head. 'I don't remember.'

'What happened to his wife?'

'He took her to Poland with him, I think. They all ended up in those ruddy gulags, like Ziggy said.'

'The children as well?'

'Probably,' said Mrs Wojcik. 'It was awful. But there was so much horror going on after the war, all the refugees everywhere, nobody really said anything about it.'

'No,' shouted her husband from the end of the garden. 'Not the girl.'

'What, dear?'

'Not the girl. She was sick with tuberculosis. She stayed in England, with the Krysia family.'

'I don't remember that.'

'I remember it. I told them not to go. Bobienski was supposed to send for her when she was cured, but he never did. How could he? By then he had disappeared.'

'The baby's name was Lena?'

'Lena and Stefan, yes,' he said.

'So her family left but she stayed in England?'

107

'After the war, all sorts of people disappeared,' the man said. 'Fuck off. Fuck off,' he shouted, apparently at the butterflies, though Breen was not sure. 'I think they took her in. We look after each other.'

'More tea?' said Mrs Wojcik, though he hadn't touched his first cup at all.

Afterwards, Mrs Wojcik saw Breen to the door. 'Sorry about Ziggy. He doesn't like to talk about everything that happened after the war. He was very disappointed in Mr Attlee, after all they had done. Well, we all were. The war was his time. It's all been a little hard for him, afterwards.'

Breen shook her hand, politely, and she closed the door behind him. He sat in the car for a while, looking at the photograph of the mother and father and their two children. Old history. He had still been a boy when the war had ended.

That afternoon, he walked from the police station to the Slade. London in the summer was beautiful. Everyone seemed to move a little more slowly, to lift their eyes off the grey pavements and look at the world around them.

The Slade was on one side of a leafy quadrangle, a large, pale university building decorated with absurd Corinthian columns. At this time of year, with the students away, Breen's footsteps echoed in empty corridors.

'Know what? I bet you she's the old bird who's been modelling for one of our Summer School courses,' suggested an eager man with big round glasses and a brightly checked suit. 'Come,' he said.

He led Breen into a studio, a large, white-painted hangar of a room, where stood dozens of half-finished sculptures, some made of clay, others plaster of Paris. Wire frames poked through the incomplete pieces. The man in the checked suit looked around until he found one in clay; a standing nude whose face was half finished.

'Ta-da! Is it her?' The man's voice boomed in the empty room. 'I bet it is. One of the old school. All the young ones disrobe for tuppence these days, but they're useless. Can't sit still.'

Breen peered at the clay. The face in Mr Payne's painting had been fleshy and round; this face appeared to show the bones beneath the skin. He was comparing a likeness with a likeness, not the real thing; he could not be sure.

'Or this one? Same model. Different student.'

It was the breasts that were not right. 'It's not her,' he said. This woman was flat-chested; Florence's bosoms had been large, drooping down her chest. He shook his head.

'Frankly, I'm disappointed. I was so looking forward to this old girl being a murderer.'

'I didn't say she was,' said Breen.

'I shall pretend she is, all the same,' said the man, showing him to the door.

Breen walked west, towards the second of the art schools. It was the third day of the case. Mint's anxiety was justified. If there wasn't some kind of breakthrough now this could easily become one of those investigations that rolled quietly along for months. She had been a prostitute. There were no colleagues or relations to urge the police onwards, and nobody to shame them when they didn't produce results.

When he arrived at Heatherley's he checked his map to be

sure he was in the right place. This was not such a grand affair as the Slade. From the outside it looked more like a workshop.

He knocked. No one answered the door, so he opened it. Sitting at a small desk in a small room to the right of the entrance hall was a young man in a hand-knitted sleeveless jumper and a T-shirt doing a crossword puzzle in a newspaper.

'Didn't you hear me knock?' said Breen.

'Yes, but most people just come in anyway,' said the man.

'I'm looking for a woman who models here,' said Breen pushing his warrant card under his nose. The young man, skinny, with wire-framed glasses, looked up.

'We have all sorts of models,' said the man.

'Do you have a list?'

'Somewhere, I suppose.'

'A middle-aged woman. It's important.'

The man shrugged. 'I wouldn't know. I'm just on the front desk. They let us off some of our fees if we help out. Hey. You can't just walk in there.'

Breen had left the small room, returned to the hallway and pulled open two dark swing doors. As they opened, the aroma of linseed and turpentine made him pause.

'It's private. If you wait in the front office I'll see if I can find someone to help show you round.'

Breen ignored him, pushing open the door of the first room he came to. It was empty. Easels circled around a chaise longue. The walls were covered with paintings of still lifes and nudes, some framed and hung, others propped against the edges, half finished. The floor was rich with colour from spilled paint.

He looked at the pictures. This was not a fashionable art

school full of daring new painters like Peter Blake and David Hockney. Or Andy Warhol, even. This was clearly not the Slade, either. These were old-fashioned, painterly works, the sort that still made it into the older, dimly lit Bond Street galleries, not the new trendy new ones like Robert Fraser's or Kasmin's.

Back in the corridor, he heard voices. There must be students upstairs.

He made his way up and found a room full of artists. The reinforced glass, though covered in pigeon shit and dirt, still bathed the rooms with even north light. Under it, a young man stood, one leg in front of the other, arms crossed, completely naked. He was an athlete of some kind; his stomach was even, muscled, and shone, as if oiled. There was something deliberately cocky about the way he turned his head a few degrees to look at Breen, eyebrows raised slightly, as if daring Breen to stare. Surrounding him, the students paused, brushes in mid-air and they, too, looked at Breen.

'Sorry,' he said and was about to close the door when he saw her.

It was a painting, propped on the opposite wall. Florence was reclining in the same pose as in the picture he had seen in Mr Payne's bedroom, but in this version the light was vaguer, kinder to her older flesh. He walked across the room to look at it. It was good. The pale pinks and blues of her skin were delicate without being hesitant. He wished he could have learned to paint like that.

He pointed at the picture and said, 'What's this woman's name?'

The tutor, an elderly man in half-moon glasses said, 'No talking.'

'What is her name?'

'I beg your pardon?'

'The model?'

'Next door,' the tutor said, irritated at the interruption.

Breen closed the door behind him and moved down the corridor.

THIRTEEN

After a couple of days when nothing happens, sometimes, you have a stroke of luck.

It was her; the woman called Florence. And if she was the murderer, she would not find running away easy. Like the man in the last room, she was naked but for a wisp of silk that covered one breast, leaving the other bare. Unlike the man in the previous room, she didn't look up as he entered.

'You're late,' said a squat, round woman in a blue boiler suit smudged with colour. 'Hurry up.' She pointed to an easel at the far side of the room.

'I'm not—'

'No talking,' she snapped. 'We work in silence.'

He paused for a moment, considered pulling out his warrant card to explain himself. But there was no need to embarrass the woman, and besides, he found it useful to observe a suspect. So he walked across the room and stood in front of the easel. There was an empty canvas already on it, and, placed on a low table, a small wooden box, a dirty cloth, a bottle of turps, another of linseed oil, some charcoal and a tin filled with brushes of all sizes.

His place was towards the back of the room. From where he stood he could see a few other half-completed pictures. A young woman with straight fair hair in front of him, slightly to his right, turned and gave him a small, welcoming smile. She was working with a palette knife on a thick layer of paint.

He picked up charcoal and started to sketch a rough outline of Florence. The easel was not in the best position. He had a view that was side on, slightly towards her back. Her hands were in her lap, so her arms obscured the folds of her belly and breasts.

He tried to remember what little he knew. It was about how the light fell on skin, and how that skin absorbed or reflected it. To paint was to learn how to see it, then how to re-create a drama of seeing. He opened up the box, and looked at the names on the tubes: *Payne's Grey, Sap Green, French Ultramarine*. He grinned, like a child opening chocolates.

The woman in the boiler suit was watching him disapprovingly.

She clapped her hands once. 'Work,' she said.

When he had roughed out a shape, he picked up the Orange Ochre and began mixing it with a little white and started laying a foundation, but on the canvas it looked too dark. He mixed more white.

He had learned, as a boy, playing with paints and pencils, the importance of working decisively. With oils you could revise and overpaint, but the strokes needed to convey a real sense of intention.

That said, he had always been better at drawing than painting. Breen had bought all his equipment with money from paper rounds and Saturday jobs, though he'd never been able to afford materials this good. His father, who had struggled to establish himself in the building business when he had arrived in London from Ireland, had never encouraged him to paint; he had wanted to protect him from disappointment.

Growing in confidence now, Breen added more colour, pleased with what he was achieving. The weight of the woman sitting in the chair had begun to transfer itself onto his canvas.

He paused as the tutor moved to stand behind the pretty, fair-haired woman who was obviously struggling; her version of the nude model was disproportionate and flat. The tutor harrumphed, took the woman's brush from her hands, dipped it onto her palette and added a simple highlight to her canvas in one stroke. 'There,' she said.

'Thank you,' said the woman, peering at the transformation. 'Why didn't I see that?'

'Because you don't feel anything,' said the woman.

Breen turned to his own painting again and worked on it harder. He squinted at the model, noticing for the first time a kind of rich purple in her skin, beneath the pallid surface. He searched his colours to find a way to represent it, working animatedly.

A dollop of paint fell on his brogues. Taking the rag, he bent to wipe it off and when he straightened he realised that the stocky tutor was now standing at his picture, leaning forward and scrutinising it.

He stood, watching her examine his work, saying nothing.

The painting was still in its early stages, but he was pleased at how much had come back to him.

'Where did you say you trained?' she said finally.

'Just at school.'

'God save us,' she said, quietly. 'And have you painted much since?'

'No,' said Breen.

She turned and walked away.

'Well?' he called after her.

She stopped and said, 'You have no technique at all. You're wasting your money here. Come back when you're ready. Class is over now.' She clapped loudly.

The model picked up a cotton dressing gown and wrapped herself in it, taking a packet of cigarettes from the pocket.

The painter with the long blonde hair was looking at Breen sympathetically. 'Mind if I look?' she said.

'Go ahead. It's appalling, apparently.'

She stood next to him and looked at the vivid shapes he'd made on the canvas. 'Don't worry. She's like that with everyone. Even the ones with some talent. I have none, obviously, but I just love doing it.' She was smiling at him. 'I don't think yours is that bad at all, actually. Jolly sight better than mine, that's for sure.'

The students had started cleaning their brushes. He did the same.

'A few of us go for a drink afterwards. Would you like to join us?' she said, but he didn't have time to answer, because the model had put on her dress and was heading for the exit.

'Excuse me,' he called. Florence was already at the door. He dropped his brush, ran after her and caught up with her in the corridor, laying his hand on her shoulder.

She turned, cigarette still in hand. 'I need to talk to you,' he said. 'About Miss Bobienski.'

'Oh,' she said, as the students who had just been painting her pushed past them. He scrutinised her face.

'You're Florence, aren't you?'

'No.'

'I know you are.'

'Not here I'm not, anyway,' she said. 'What's this about?'

'I'm a policeman.'

'If I'd known you were a copper I'd have had you thrown out of there.'

'I apologise.'

'For someone who's just spent forty minutes staring at my naked fanny without asking permission, you're suddenly very sensitive.'

'I didn't interrupt because I didn't think these people would want to know that you also work as a prostitute's madam.'

'I'm a maid, not a madam. It's completely different.'

One of the students who had been watching this exchange, big-eyed, said, 'Is he bothering you?'

'This is an art school. If anything, working as a maid gives me a certain cachet. Did my body excite you, officer?'

'Not particularly.'

She laughed; a rich, phlegmy cigarette-smoker's laugh. 'I have nothing to say to you.'

'I'll have to arrest you then.'

She lowered her eyes. 'She's dead, isn't she?'

'Yes. How did you know?'

'There was nothing in the papers, but I've seen the police at her flat. It's not hard to work it out. I knew something was wrong.' She looked up again, meeting Breen's eye. 'I called her, but nobody answered. So I knew why the police were there. Was it bad? I'd like to know.'

'You should have come forward. We've wasted time looking for you.'

'What? So you can arrest me?'

'That depends on what you've done.'

'I see,' she said.

'What should I call you? Florence?'

'You can call me Mrs Caulk,' she said, descending the stairs. 'How did you find me, then?'

'Mr Payne showed me your painting. So I've seen you naked already.'

'And still you come back for more?' Another deep, rumbling laugh. 'Poor Mr Payne. How is he? You've talked to him? I bet he loves all the coppers coming and going. He's lonely.'

He followed after her. They walked out into the brightness of George Street.

'Why didn't you contact the police when you suspected Miss Bobienski was dead?'

'Why do you think? I've been busy,' she said, looking down again.

He stared at her some more. Was she hiding something, or was it just her profession's usual reluctance to talk to policemen that made her so evasive? 'When did you last see Miss Bobienski?'

She set off again, walking back the way he'd come. 'Thursday night. I'm busy now as a matter of fact.'

'So let's continue this conversation at the police station.'

'Are you going to be boring?' she said.

'Very. Unless you talk to me now. You're the last person we know of who saw her alive. And you're a suspect, obviously.'

'Do I have to?'

'Do I have to make you?'

She stopped walking and scrutinised him. 'What I really want,' she said, 'is an ice cream.'

'Follow me,' he said.

They walked down George Street towards an Italian restaurant that Breen knew. The owner emerged from the kitchen to shake his hand. 'What flavour do you want?' asked Breen.

'Strawberry,' said Mrs Caulk.

'*Fragola*,' said the man.

He returned two minutes later with two ice-cream cones. 'No money,' he said.

Breen pulled out a ten-shilling note. 'People might think you're bribing me.'

'I am trying,' said the restaurateur, laughing.

They sat on a bench in the sunshine in Manchester Square watching the crowd of girls who stood outside EMI Records.

'Yes. I suppose I should have come to see you,' said Mrs Caulk. 'Poor Lena. Was it bad?'

'I can't tell you.'

She nodded. 'I'll be honest. I didn't like her much, really.'

'How long had you known her?'

'Lena hired me about ten months ago,' said Mrs Caulk. 'She said she needed a maid. I wasn't looking for new work, but the money was good, so . . .'

'She dressed up as a teenager.'

'Everything is about being young these days. Everybody wants to be young. She understood that.'

'I saw her clothes.'

She stuck out her tongue and ran it slowly up the side of her ice cream. 'Oh God. This is the 1960s. Youth is everywhere. Some people, like you . . . I can see you looking at those young girls.' She nodded towards the EMI building. 'Some of them are young enough to be your daughter.'

'I'm a policeman. It's what we do. We look.'

She took another lick and said, 'The policemen I have dealings with don't usually stop at just looking.'

'It's nothing I'm interested in.'

'I expect you're a poof, then,' she said.

'Definitely not.'

'Don't get all huffy with me. There's nothing wrong with poofs. They're the most honest men I know. They've owned up to what they really want, at least. Plenty of men never do.'

'And what do men really want?' he asked.

She was down to the cone already. She crunched through it loudly. 'Power. To have it or to lose it. Some men like being spanked. They like being dominated. Others like to dominate. The men who used to come to Julie, they would have sex with those girls there if they could. They're the ones who like that kind of power. Understand power and you can be rich.'

Breen looked at the lovestruck teenagers across the road who spent their time mooning around outside recording studios, or some pop star's flat in Montague Square.

'What sort of men want to have sex with those girls over there?' she asked.

'Perverts, I suppose?'

' "Pervert". What does that even mean?' she said. 'Do my job for long enough and you'll come to realise that all men are perverts.'

'I'm a policeman. I think everyone's a criminal.'

She laughed, briefly. 'Careful,' she said. 'It's about to drip on your trousers. Don't want any embarrassing stains, do we?'

Vanilla ice cream was trickling down his hand. He walked to a bin and threw away his half-eaten cone, then wiped his hand with a handkerchief. As he did so, he watched a taxi arrive outside the record company. A doorman emerged to shoo the girls away. Some were cool and leggy in miniskirts, others dressed as if they didn't care, in old leather jackets and boots. They hooted at the doorman; in return he shouted something back at them, but they didn't budge.

'They don't look that easy to dominate, to me,' said Breen.

She laughed again, but then stopped just as abruptly. 'You're right. They're not. They're not like I was when I was their age. When I was a teenager I did what I was told. Mostly, at least. But that just makes them more desirable, doesn't it?'

'She pretended to be like that?' He nodded towards the girls.

'I've been a maid for a lot of women,' she said. 'Never one like her. She was a piece of work, I tell you. I mean, nothing against her. But she had an act. It was good. She didn't mind turning it on to get what she wanted. I respected that. Didn't like it, though.'

'What sort of act?'

'I thought it was a bit creepy, being honest, all that teenager thing. She always used to get the gentlemen to buy her presents. This little-girl show. "Promise me you'll get me it?" She'd order them to bring her singles. Or clothes. Or chocolates. Jewellery. Underwear. She knew that would embarrass them. Just like a selfish little modern girl, really. It was this big performance and they lapped it up. She knew that they were all a bit frightened of little girls like that.'

'She teased them?'

'It's what they came back for. They all bought presents. Like good little boys.'

'So they were regulars?'

'Mostly.'

'How many?'

'Thirteen. No, twelve. They paid well. It's all she needed. They were her sugar daddies. That was the ones she wanted. Regulars who came back. She cultivated the ones who she could control.'

'So they might have been angry at her because of the way she manipulated them?'

'Of course. It's always dangerous. That's why you have a maid outside. If you can afford it.' She reached inside her shoulder bag and pulled out a cigarette, offering Breen one. 'But I wasn't there when it happened.'

'Tell me about Thursday night.'

'She worked three nights a week. Thursday, Friday and Saturday. Thursday she only had a couple of appointments.'

'Was there anything different about that night?'

'Not really. I remember she was a bit irritated that Zapata didn't tip.'

'His name was Zapata?'

She laughed. 'Don't be stupid. I called him Zapata because he had a silly moustache. His first name is Torquil, I think, but none of them ever give their real names.'

'So he left?'

'Yes. Then at eleven it was Mr Bites-His-Nails.'

'Another regular? Someone who bites his nails . . .'

'Yes. But only on his left hand which I thought was strange. Like I said, she only has regulars. This wasn't a walk-in business. It was specialist. These were big payers.'

'Were you there when Mr . . . Nails left?'

'Obviously. That's my job. To stay till they're finished. That's what I'm paid for. That was how it worked. That was why it was odd when I came and she'd been entertaining after I'd gone. The place was a tip.'

'It was? It was tidy when I first saw it.'

'Because I'd cleaned it up. I got there on Friday and the room was a mess. Someone must have come around later.'

'A boyfriend?'

'I doubt it. She didn't have one. Not as far as I knew. She wasn't like that. For someone whose job it was to look like she was enjoying herself, she never had any real fun. Not for herself, anyway. Besides, it's not unusual for working girls not to have boyfriends. If they do, the boys either want them to stop working, or they're cheeky bastards who want some of the money.'

'Tell me exactly what the room looked like when you found it. What was different to normal?'

'There was a champagne bottle on the floor, for starters. A couple of glasses. Cushions had been knocked about a bit. The bed wasn't made.'

'So it was someone she knew who'd been drinking with her?'

'It certainly looked like it.'

'And someone she'd gone to bed with?'

'Not necessarily. She usually tidied up her bed sometime after the clients had been. Sometimes she left it to the morning. Maybe she hadn't done that before . . .'

'So you washed the glasses and threw away the bottle?'

'I dropped it in the bin on the way out.'

Blunt instrument, thought Breen.

'Do you remember? Was the lift working on Thursday night?'

'It wasn't on Friday, that's for sure. But I think it was fine the day before. In fact, yes. I remember Mr Bites-His-Nails taking it down. He was a little drunk. He took a while closing the lift door. It's one of those gates, and unless you close it properly, it doesn't work.'

She finished her cigarette and stubbed it out on the pavement.

'You realise you tidied up a crime scene? There might have been fingerprints.'

'Oh,' she said. 'I wasn't to know.'

The leaves of the plane tree moved slowly in a breeze. 'Do you make up names for all the men?'

'Do I get protection?'

'Why would you need it?'

'Well, somebody did something to Lena, didn't they? Because I'm not giving you anyone's name unless you can guarantee my safety.'

'You have their names?'

'Not their real names, mostly. It's like Zapata. I keep notes in my diary. A list of the johns. I was always careful.'

'What about financial records?'

'They all paid in cash, so there were no cheques. We didn't accept them. You can always cancel a cheque after. Once they get home to their wives the poor little boys are ashamed of what they've done. If I talk to you, how are you going to guarantee my safety?'

'Were any of them ever violent with Miss Bobienski?'

'Other girls I've worked with, they've been attacked. Some men like to be rough. That's why I keep all the names, as much detail as I can. It's part of the job. But nobody touched Lena. Except . . . well, obviously they did in the end, didn't they?' Her hands shook a little, as she said it, but her face showed no emotion.

The square was filling up with office workers taking a lunch break. Men with their jackets off; women in dark glasses. They unwrapped packets of sandwiches and pulled out flasks, sitting on the grass.

'So let me get this straight. The men call up to make appointments?'

'That's right.'

'Did they speak to Lena, or to you?'

'She preferred it that they called in the evenings when I was working there. Thursday to Saturday. She didn't like to be the one taking the calls and discussing fees. It didn't fit with her little-girl act. And that way I knew all her appointments, see?'

'I'll need that diary you talked about.'

'I don't really think so,' said Mrs Caulk. 'It's personal.'

'It was business, you said.'

'What if I don't want to?'

'Why wouldn't you want to help catch someone who killed the woman you worked with?'

'What's in it for me?'

'I don't prosecute you for living off immoral earnings.'

'You're such a bloody policeman, you know that?' She sat for a while, a dark look on her face, then opened her shoulder bag, lifted out her purse, then pulled out a desk diary. 'I always carry it with me. Force of habit.' She held it out. 'I want it back.'

'It's evidence.'

'Copy it out then. But that's mine.'

It was a well-thumbed black book with '1969' in silver on the cover. Breen flicked through the pages. The bottom of Lena's working days was ruled off into several sections. There were names written into each slot. Some were simple enough. Bill. Harry. Mr Jones. Others looked like they had been more obviously made up. Vincent Price; Fingers.

'Vincent Price?' he said, looking up.

'If they didn't give their name, either she'd make one up for them or I would, so we'd both know who it was. He's a regular. He looks a bit like Vincent Price, that's all. That's not going to help you much.'

He turned to Thursday, 3 July. Just as she said, there were two names. 7 p.m. Zapata. 11 p.m. Bites-His-Nails. It was a neat, businesslike, if slightly unconventional record.

'You didn't like her, though, did you?' he said.

She shook her head. 'I can't lie. There was not much of her

to like. She worked. She did the Julie Teenager act and she was very good at it. But a little ruthless, even for my taste.'

'How so?'

'It was a job, that was all. And maybe she could be a bit cruel, too. There was one man. Public school. Oxbridge.'

'He told you this?'

'They don't have to. You can tell. The way they talk and dress. All buttoned up and shy. It's like they're fighting to catch up with the modern world. Like you.'

'You don't know anything about me,' said Breen.

'You'd be surprised. That haircut. Those shoes. Working-class boy made good. The way you look at those girls.'

'Anyway,' he said.

'This one called himself Ronnie, and in his case I think that probably was his real name. No surname though. He was only young. Married. Children too, I think. He always took his ring off but you could see the mark on his finger. Some of our johns are just playing a game. Others fall in love. It's bad when that happens. God, he fell in love. And she played him. She made him buy presents. Little things, but quite expensive.'

'She blackmailed him?'

'Oh no. It wasn't like that. It was funny, some of it. She'd asked for jewellery or something, and he turned up with this piece of antique jet – a necklace. It looked like he'd inherited it from a maiden aunt. Lena burst into tears like she was some disappointed teenager. Fake tears of course. I don't think anything real ever made her cry. But she did it so well it was creepy. He came back next week with this Andrew Grima ring.'

He must have looked blank.

'Grima, for pity's sake,' she said. 'He does all Princess Margaret's stuff. Has a shop in Jermyn Street. You've honestly never heard of him?'

'How do you spell it?'

She grabbed his notebook and wrote down the name. 'It was a pretty thing. A bit gaudy, perhaps. Something like that would have cost at least sixty quid. Imagine. God knows what Ronnie's family were living off. And when I asked to see the ring later, she told me she didn't have it any more.' She looked at him then added, 'I bet she just flogged it.'

'When was this?'

''Bout a month ago.' She grabbed the diary off him and scanned the pages. 'There,' she said, pointing to a date in May.

He took it back from her and looked at the page. Ronnie. 9 p.m. 16 May. A Friday. 'So it could have been him?'

'It could have been any of them.'

He turned back through the days. Ronnie's previous appointment had been the weekend before. He pointed at the entry: 'So that's when he offered her the necklace?'

'Yes. It must have been.'

'Did she ever talk about her family?' he asked.

'Yes, I asked about it once. I think her father was a big war hero. She never really talked about him, though. It was only business.'

'What about this coming weekend?' He flicked forward a few pages.

'Quiet, so far. They only tend to book a week in advance. And of course, this weekend I wasn't there to take anything. I think there's a couple on Thursday, though.'

He turned the page again. 'Thursday, seven p.m. Vincent Price.'

'There you go. Always pays in single pound notes.'

'Nine p.m. Mr Smith.'

'I know. So predictable. Shall we walk? I've been sitting still all morning while people like you paint me. I get stiff.'

They stood and walked back in the direction of Baker Street, towards the police station. The pavements were crowded with tourists. Americans seemed to be everywhere, these days, talking loudly, cameras around their necks.

'So on the Friday, did the men who had made appointments arrive?'

'Why? Because if they turned up, they probably didn't do it?'

'I'm asking.' He was always cautious of giving witnesses too much detail; she was right, though. Only the murderer would have known that Lena Bobienski was dead.

'The first appointment arrived.'

'Mr Smith?' Breen read from the diary.

'Yes. His real name was Leonard as far as I know. But I left after that. There wasn't much point staying on if she wasn't there.'

He looked down. The next appointment was for a man named Jones.

'Smith. Jones, you know how it is,' she said. The 11 p.m. slot was taken by a man known as Spanky.

'So you don't know if either of these men came to see her?'

She shook her head. There was an old man with a white scarf around his neck, crooning 'Three Coins in a Fountain' on the street corner outside the post office. Breen pulled out a sixpence and dropped it in the man's hat.

'What was driving her to do what she did?'

'Driving her to do it? Nice girls don't fuck for money?'

She said the word deliberately loudly. The busker stopped mid-line, wolf-whistled, then picked his tune back up. 'Men always think that. They think there must be some dark reason for a woman to go on the game.' She walked on. 'They can't think a woman would do anything because she just wants to make cash from gullible men.'

'What about Lena?'

'She earned a lot of money. She was the most successful girl I've ever worked with. Ever. But maybe you're right. There was something dark in there, but I could never really put my finger on what.'

'We're going to have to eliminate all the men in this book,' said Breen. 'You're going to have to go in to Lena's flat, the day after tomorrow, just like you always did.'

It would be best not to tell her that they would also be monitoring the calls at the exchange.

'Are you paying me for this? I've lost my job, you know.'

'No. I am hoping you'll do it because you want to find out who killed your employer.'

She sighed. 'It's not my business any more. I don't want to get mixed up in it.'

'Well in that case, I'll arrest you now.'

'It's not exactly a choice, is it?'

At the police station steps, he stopped. 'Will you come in? I'll get someone to go through this diary with you.'

'Wouldn't be surprised if I recognise one or two of your colleagues. And not from them arresting me, either.'

They went past the front desk and into the main corridor. Mint came clattering down the stairs. 'Sarge. About the flower shop—'

'Not now, Constable. This is Mrs Caulk, Constable Mint.'

'Oh,' said Mint, realising who Breen meant. 'You found her. Is she under arrest?'

Mrs Caulk looked him up and down. 'What a very nice young man,' she said.

'He's married,' said Breen.

'They usually are.'

Breen handed Mint her desk diary and said, 'Come with me.'

There was a small room on the ground floor that they sometimes used for interviews. He looked in. It was empty, though it stank of sweat and cigarettes. Mrs Caulk wrinkled her nose as she entered.

'Constable Mint. Mrs Caulk is a suspect, but we have no grounds on which to arrest her at this time.'

'Well, that's a mercy,' said Mrs Caulk.

'I'd like you to fetch Mrs Caulk here a nice cup of tea—'

'Just one sugar,' she interrupted. 'Tiny bit of milk. Do you have any biscuits?'

'. . . then come back here and go through her diary with her, and make a note of every name in there. Description, habits, any clues as to what they did for a living, or where they lived, married, single. She's going to give us enough so we can find every man in the book, right?'

'Oh Christ. We're going to be all bloody night,' said Mrs Caulk.

Mint flicked through the diary. 'What, sir? All that's in here?'

Breen pointed at Mrs Caulk's head. 'The best bits are in there.'

'Just me, Sarge?' he said.

'Just you, Constable. Big job. You ever heard of a jeweller called Andrew Grima, Mint?'

'No, Sarge.'

Mrs Caulk sat down at the chair and took out her packet of No. 6's. 'And bring me an ashtray, will you, lovely?'

'One thing. The man who bought the ring. What name did he give again?'

'Just Ronnie.'

'No last name?'

She shook her head.

'Mint?' he said. 'Can you have it on my desk, first thing in the morning?'

'Yes, sir!' he said.

'Mrs Caulk. You're not planning on going anywhere over the next couple of weeks, are you?'

'My villa in the South of France.'

'Not funny,' said Breen. 'We will need you around.'

'So. Will I be getting protection or not? What with me giving you all this information?'

'I somehow doubt you need it.'

She snorted and rolled her eyes, but she remained seated in the interview room. All the same, he waited until Mint had returned with a mug of tea and an ashtray before he left her, just in case she changed her mind.

FOURTEEN

He walked all the way to Piccadilly whistling the tune the accordionist had played. It was summer. He had found the maid. He was feeling good.

It turned out there were several jewellers in Jermyn Street but Grima's was easy to find. The others were discreet and Dickensian. The shop was in a modern concrete building, one of those that had taken advantage of what the Nazis had destroyed. The frontage was deliberately at odds with its neighbours, and was covered in huge, raw chunks of cut slate that left small windows into which you could peer to see the trays of gaudy rings.

Breen, who had never worn such things himself, looked. This was jewellery for the international jet set, all gold, diamonds and big colourful stones, sculpted into ostentatious swirls and asymmetrical shapes. They were large and contemporary.

The man behind the counter was dressed in a flowered shirt with long lapels and wore a silver chain around his neck. 'In May, you say?'

Breen said, 'Yes. The ring was given as a gift on 16 May. I think it was bought sometime in the previous week.'

'And you only have the name Ronnie?' The man returned with an invoice book and flicked through the pages. 'Oh yes. Poor Ronald.'

'You remember him?'

'Oh goodness, yes. And he chose two rings. One very ordinary and one quite nice one. And he asked for two receipts. Let me get the copies.'

He disappeared through a door next to a perspex spiral staircase and returned a minute later with two sheets of paper. They were carbon duplicates. One was made out to a Ronald Russell at an address in Upper Addison Gardens, Shepherd's Bush; the other was left blank.

'Why two receipts?'

'Why do you think?'

One was made out for seven guineas, the other for sixty. 'One was bought for his wife?'

'Precisely,' said the young man.

'And the other one wasn't?'

'It happens from time to time. A man with a guilty conscience. One for the glamour girl, another for the little lady. A rather simple ten-pound ring with a tourmaline setting, very sweet actually, and this somewhat more gorgeous one with tanzanite and diamonds for –' he lowered his voice – 'his mistress, one presumes. I remember he asked specifically for separate receipts. Tsk, tsk, tsk.' The shop assistant grinned. 'Not that I would know anything about that sort of behaviour.'

134

'Do you have a picture of the rings, or anything that I can use to identify them?'

The man smiled. 'I'll show you the ring itself, if you like.' He took a set of keys from a drawer and went to the front of the shop, opening the back of the glass window display.

He pulled out a box. The setting was a curved triangle of some purple stone that glittered in the light; one side was crusted with tiny diamonds.

'Spectacular, isn't it?' said the man. 'Absolutely exquisite, don't you think?'

'This is a copy?'

'No. This was a one-off. It's the exact same ring.' The man curled his lips. 'She brought it in two weeks ago. That's why I remembered. We gave her the refund, of course. She had her receipt, after all.' He laughed. Breen's eye lit on another, simpler ring. A twist of gold, with two green gems, one at each end. 'Poor Ronald. I think she rather took him for a ride.'

'Ronald's fine,' said Breen. 'She's the one you should feel sorry for.'

And the man's face fell as Breen picked up the ring he had spotted and held it up to the light. 'Tourmaline,' said the shop assistant. 'A bit like the other one he purchased, as a matter of fact. Pretty, isn't it?' he said, a little less certainly than before.

Rather than catch the bus, he took the long way back, detouring through Soho, fingering the box in the pocket of his lightweight summer mac.

He had never bought anything like it before; he had never had anybody to buy something like this for.

He felt young; and the whole city around felt young. Taxis were honking their horns as smooth young men on mopeds weaved around them shouting insults back at the drivers.

This is where he and Carmichael had spent their teenage years, sneaking to Moka on Frith Street and drinking so much espresso they didn't sleep for twenty-four hours, or searching for Dizzy Gillespie discs in Berwick Street.

In Soho Square he went into a phone box and started flicking through the telephone directory. He was there: *Mr & Mrs R. Russell. Notting Hill.* Why not? he thought.

A woman answered. A thin, posh voice. 'Yes, this is Mrs Russell.'

'Is Mr Russell at home?'

'He's not back from work yet. He'll be en route, I hope. I'm expecting him at six-thirty. Should I mention who called?'

'Oh no,' said Breen, smiling to himself. 'I want to surprise him.'

'Are you a friend?' she was asking as he put down the phone.

He pushed the door open. The roses in Soho Square were pale and heavily scented, sweetening the exhaust-fumed air.

But instead of leaving the box, he let the door close, and dialled another number. 'Guess where I am?' he said.

Sergeant John Carmichael said, 'Hackney Hospital. In the maternity ward.'

'Bit early for that, John. Soho Square. Fancy a drink?'

When they were younger, Soho was full of gangsters, foreigners and film stars. The movie companies had their offices here. One summer night they had slept on the grass here under their coats, and woken to find the American film star Barbara

Payton, sitting a bench ten yards away, drunk and shivering. She said she had been at a party and now she wanted to go home but she'd lost her handbag. Carmichael had wrapped his overcoat around her and together they put her in a taxi, gave the driver a pound, and told him to take her to Claridge's, where she said she was staying. She told Carmichael he was adorable. The coat had been Carmichael's pride and joy, cashmere, Italian-tailored; when Breen and Carmichael went to the hotel to get it back the next day, the manager insisted there was no guest called Barbara Payton and threw them both out.

'Never too early for that, Paddy. The York Minster?'

'I was thinking The Louise.'

'Slumming it with the rest of us?'

Soho still seemed like the centre of the world, to Cathal Breen. The women here were beautiful. Long dresses were back in. Miniskirts were out. The cooler girls stalked the streets in long flowing garments, dark glasses poised at the ends of their noses.

The shops had closed by the time he passed through the less glamorous location of Great Titchfield Street, and the restaurants were opening.

The Louise had only been open half an hour by the time he arrived but it was already packed with men from the afternoon shift. They drank before returning home to their wives and families, or to their section houses, in which drink was not allowed. It was a coppers' pub; if you didn't like that, you didn't come in.

When he'd first moved to D Division, Breen had come here all the time; it's what coppers did. When his father had become ill he'd spent his free time looking after him and he'd lost the habit of drinking in pubs.

He hadn't missed it. The truth was, The Louise was a dump. The gloss-paint walls made them easier to wipe clean, but they made the place feel too bright. Hung crookedly above the optics, there was an old picture of the Queen, taken around the time of her coronation, and below it a sign that read: *We do NOT take cheques.*

Breen looked around. Jenks was at the bar, talking loudly with a couple of constables. He had changed out of his uniform and was dressed in a check sports jacket that looked a size too big for him.

As Breen approached, he held up an empty glass. 'Don't mind if I do,' he said. 'Pint of best.'

You didn't come to The Louise except to drink, so he ordered a lager and took out a cigarette. Breen was a careful man. He smoked five a day; he checked the nicks he made with his thumbnail on his packet. This would be number four.

'I'll have one, too,' said Jenks, reaching to take one of Breen's cigarettes. 'Got your man yet?'

'Early days,' said Breen.

The barman put down Jenks's beer, splashing some onto the bar. The copper picked the glass up carefully and sucked a quick inch from the top. 'Empty the piss sack,' he said.

'Right,' said Breen.

Breen followed the older constable to the toilets. Despite the sign that said *No Cigarette Butts*, the white trough was always full of dog-ends that flowed down to the end and blocked the drain. Yellow liquid threatened to lap over the edge onto the floor.

There was a constable already there, splashing noisily.

'Right, Jenksy?' another man called.

Jenks unzipped his fly and started urinating next to him. Breen stood by the sink, waiting. When the other policeman had gone, Breen said, 'What was it you couldn't tell me, back in the CID office?'

'You guessed, then?'

'Even a shit copper like you would have an idea who was going in and out of a knocking shop.'

Jenks snorted. 'Fuck off.'

'What then?' said Breen. 'Were you using the knocking shop yourself?'

'What would a handsome man like me be needing a tom for? No.' With his head, he beckoned Breen over. Breen edged closer. 'We got told to look the other way. Told to avoid patrols down that street. Big hush-hush.'

'To not police Harewood Avenue at all?'

'Leave it off the beat after dark. That's right.'

'Why was that?'

'Don't know. All I was told was to keep shtum.'

The door banged open. 'Oi, oi,' said a constable. 'What are you doing, Jenksy? Showing Paddy the size of your doo-dah?'

'Jealous, aren't you, Paddy?' said Jenks.

The man stood the other side of Breen. Jenks had finally finished and was buttoning up his flies. Breen followed him as he moved to the tiny sink. 'Who told you to look the other way?' Breen said quietly.

Jenks jerked his eyes towards the constable at the urinal. He didn't want to talk when there was someone else in the room.

When he'd finished washing, Jenks wiped his hand on the grubby towel hanging on the wall. Breen waited for the other man to leave.

'This isn't Hampstead Heath bogs, Jenksy.'

'Fuck right off,' said Jenks.

'Keep your hair on,' said the man.

When he'd gone, Breen asked, 'Who warned you off?'

'Your boss.'

'Creamer?'

'No. Higher.'

'McPhail?'

The door slammed open again and the noise of pub chatter filled the small Gents' toilet. Another copper came in, weaving his way across the concrete floor. Before Jenks turned to leave he gave Breen the slightest of nods.

When Breen emerged back into the public bar, Carmichael was there, a pint of lager in one hand and a cigarillo in the other.

'Paddy fucking Breen,' he shouted.

People were crowded round Carmichael; they didn't see so much of him now he was in C1, the Serious Crime Squad at Scotland Yard. He still came back every now and then to catch up on the gossip.

'Old times' sake,' said Carmichael, grinning. Until last autumn, before he'd left to join the Drug Squad, he had worked in D Division with Breen. This had been his local. He had continued coming here long after Breen had stopped. 'Another?'

'Jesus, John. You look terrible,' said Breen.

'Thanks,' said Carmichael. 'You're no less ugly, neither. How's Hel?'

'Fine,' said Breen. 'Thriving.'

'Really?'

'Why wouldn't she be? What about Amy?'

His face softened. 'Not so great. We argue all the time.'

'Nothing changed, then.'

Amy complained that Carmichael was always too busy with work and was threatening to chuck him because of it.

'She's nuts. She's always filming stuff. She ever show you it? The other day I watched about an hour of it. Felt longer. Couldn't make head nor tail of it, really. But she was so, you know, intense about it. You're on this prostitute case?'

'How do you hear that?' said Breen.

'I hear everything, me,' said Carmichael, and belched gently. 'Any joy?'

'Yes. I think so.'

Carmichael nodded. 'Good. Get the bastard. Coming together?'

'My hunch is, it can only be a handful of people. I've got a lead on them now.'

'Good. Good,' Carmichael said, and slurped an inch out of his pint.

'Why do you want to know?'

Carmichael rolled his cigarillo between his fingers. 'So I can tell you how it should be done. Like always.'

'Did you hear anything about that Rolling Stone who died last week?'

'Stupid prat,' said Carmichael.

'It was drugs?'

141

'Should have seen the look on Pilcher's face. I thought he was going to cry. He'd wanted to nail him once and for all.'

Sergeant Pilcher was Carmichael's colleague in the Drug Squad; a copper who liked to see his picture in the papers. There were rumours he had a bingo card of pop stars he had his eyes on, and crossed them off, one by one.

'You know how he likes all the pretty ones,' said Carmichael. 'Brian Jones got off lightly last time Pilcher busted him. Pilcher hated that. Wanted to get him back for it. Told the magistrate he was cleaning up his act. But they never do, do they?'

'Elfie's going round saying there's more to it. There's not, is there?'

'Doubt it. I hate the Rolling Stones,' he said. 'Fake blues crap.'

'She thinks something went on between the group and Brian Jones.'

Carmichael shrugged. 'I heard they keep some poor company. Drug addicts, the Soho gang crowd from the Flamingo, you know, a few of the Krays' old mates. They love all that. Makes them feel tough. But it's all show. Nothing to it. They're nice boys. Good families.'

'Know a man called Tom who works with them? Big guy? Glasses?'

'Exactly what I mean. Tom Keylock? God, yeah, I know him. Likes a drink. Doesn't mind throwing the odd punch. Talks shit but he's OK. Pussycat in real life.'

Over Carmichael's shoulder, Breen saw Jenks opening the door to leave the pub. On the doorstep he caught Breen's eye, raised a finger to his lips, then left.

'You'll be thinking of moving, then, when the baby's due?' Carmichael was saying. 'Don't know why you don't move into a police flat. Save a ton of money.'

'Can you imagine Helen in police flats? She'd hate it.'

Carmichael lived in a police section house. He preferred to spend his pay packet going out on the town. 'Serious, though. You two OK? You and Helen?' he said, draining his glass.

'Why wouldn't we be?'

'Because, you know. With the baby coming.'

'Look.' Breen dug inside his mac pocket and pulled out the ring box.

'Jesus, Paddy.' Carmichael's eyes went wide.

'Will she like it?' asked Breen.

'Will she bloody like it! Course she'll like it,' said Carmichael. 'She's a bloody girl, isn't she? Everybody! Look at this.'

'Shut up, John.'

'Paddy here's going to bloody propose. To an ex-copper.'

John was roaring now. 'Get the fuckin' drinks in, will you, you buggers. My best friend's going to bloody get married.'

People were turning now, grinning at Breen, raising their glasses. 'What you drinking, mate? You'll bloody need it.'

Breen stood in the crowded bar for a while, while people shook his hand and slapped his back until he'd had enough of it and said, quietly, 'Excuse me, I've got to make a call.'

'Tell the new wife you're working late, eh?' Big laugh.

There was a payphone on the wall at the far end of the bar. Breen put in a shilling and dialled the number he had found in the directory. After a few rings, a woman answered.

'Is that Mrs Russell?'

'Yes. Who's calling?' There was a radio on in the background playing something bright and cheerful.

'I'm looking for a Ronald Russell.'

'You phoned earlier, didn't you? I'm afraid my husband is still out,' she said. 'May I take a message?'

'Will he be in later?'

'I can't hear. There's a lot of noise where you are.'

Breen repeated the question, louder this time.

'I'm not sure,' she said. 'He called to say he will be working late.'

'Does he often work late?' Breen asked.

There was a shriller tone in her voice when she said, 'Just who is this?'

On the bus home Breen dozed, head against the window, and almost missed the stop at Stoke Newington. What Jenks had said to him was going round in his head. Why had beat officers been told not to patrol Harewood Avenue? What had been going on there that they hadn't wanted ordinary policemen to notice?

His head felt heavy and dull with alcohol.

FIFTEEN

When he arrived home, Helen was cooking, which was nice, but he knew better than to make anything of it. Instead, he stood behind her, leaned forward and kissed her on the cheek, smiling.

'Are you drunk?' she said.

'Bit.'

'You stink of beer, Cathal Breen.'

'I met John Carmichael.'

'Did you ask him why he's pissing off Amy by never turning up when they have a date?'

'Not really.'

'What do you talk about, then?'

He sniffed. 'What is it?'

'Rice casserole. I thought I'd take a leaf out of Elfie's book. It was in a magazine.'

Breen resisted the temptation to peer into the pot, and maybe make a few suggestions to improve the dish. Helen cooking was rare enough. His mother had died young; for as long as he could remember he had cooked for himself and his father. It was a change to have a woman doing this for him.

'Look on the table,' she said. There was a copy of the *Daily Express* there. The headline was: 'COLOUR: WHAT BRITAIN REALLY FEELS'. Next to that: 'Would YOU like immigrant neighbours?'

'Not that,' said Helen. 'Inside.'

He turned the pages. On page 7 he saw it: 'BRIAN JONES (AFTER DRINK AND DRUGS) IGNORED SWIM WARNING FROM NURSE'.

It was the report of the coroner's inquest. A pretty woman who had been with him that night had told the coroner that the pop star was drunk and had taken some black pill called Durophet.

He read to the bottom. '*Verdict: misadventure.*'

She put the pan down and said, 'I'm not even hungry. Maybe I'll have some later.'

He lifted the lid.

'Elfie thinks it's a cover-up.'

'A cover-up of what?' said Breen.

'Go on,' she said. 'Taste it.'

He did so. 'It's nice,' he said. 'Lovely.'

'Really?'

'Maybe a bit of salt?'

'You hate it, don't you?'

'No. Really. It's fine.'

'I got you a bottle of beer if you like, too. Only you've prob-ably had enough.' She took one out of the fridge and poured it for him, while he ladled some of the casserole onto a plate and sat down. He ate another forkful. It was glutinous and stuck to the roof of his mouth and he was grateful for the beer to wash it down with.

'You don't have to finish it,' she said. 'It's OK.'

He put down his cutlery. 'It's quite filling, though.'

She slumped her shoulders. 'I'm rubbish at this, aren't I?'

'You're not used to it, that's all,' he said.

He turned back a page and started reading a short article. 'SPY EXCHANGE MAY GO AHEAD SOON.' Two Soviet spies, the Krogers, were to be exchanged for a British lecturer called Gerald Brooke.

'But it would be pretty easy, wouldn't it?' Helen said. 'Drowning someone who was already stoned and making it look like an accident.'

'What's got into you?'

'Wouldn't it, though?'

'I don't know. Maybe. But who would want him dead? He was on drugs all the time, anyway, John said.'

'"John said",' she mimicked.

'It's his job to know things like that,' said Breen.

'The Drug Squad don't know anything,' she said.

'That's why they need someone like John. He's a great copper.'

'You're drunk, Cathal Breen.'

She took the paper away from him and turned back to the article about the dead pop star. In the photo, a man who was described as Brian Jones's builder was clutching the witness, a voguish young woman in dark glasses who was trying to hide her face with her large floppy hat.

'You don't really believe Elfie, though, do you?' said Breen.

It wasn't that he didn't think that you could cover up a murder. He thought about Jenks again and felt suddenly uneasy.

'Of course not.' Helen took his plate away from him. 'I'm not doing the washing-up though,' she said.

He fingered the ring box in his trouser pocket. Now would not be the time to give it to her. She was right. He was drunk. He should go to bed.

Cathal Breen rose early, thirsty.

It was light by five. Helen was still asleep. He tucked the ring box into his sock drawer, made himself a coffee, drank it quickly, then let himself out quietly.

Morning was a good time to travel, because though not all the routes were running yet, the buses that were were still half empty. The only other person on top of the 76 was a nurse coming home after a night shift.

London looked magnificent in low summer light. Behind St Paul's, the cranes from where they were building the new skyscrapers of the Barbican caught the sunlight. The city was remaking itself again.

He got off at the Aldwych and took another bus towards Notting Hill and, clutching his *A–Z*, found the Russells' house easily: a large, white, four-storey Georgian mansion set back from the road.

Around him curtains were being drawn. There was the whine of a milk float. A milkman got out, left one pint at the Russells' door and returned with an empty.

One pint. No children. The paperboy staggered up each path with a huge canvas bag. Russell took *The Times* and the

Telegraph. Two girls marched sullenly, hand in hand, up the pavement.

Mr Russell emerged out of his front door at a quarter past eight. He called, 'Goodbye darling,' before he pulled it to behind him, and walked, whistling, down the short pathway. He was dressed in a grey summer suit, carried a black case and looked about the same age as Breen.

Breen fell into step with him as he strode north towards the main road. Russell sped up; Breen kept pace.

'Mr Russell?'

The whistling stopped. The man turned and looked.

'I'm a policeman. I would like a word with you.'

'I beg your pardon?'

'Marylebone CID,' he said.

Russell looked confused.

'About Julie Teenager.'

Russell turned his head. There was a brief moment in which, when caught unawares, a suspect's face could tell you a lot. That glance could have been a man looking for an escape route, calculating whether he could outrun Breen, or it could have simply been the panic of a man assumed to be respectable by his neighbours, anxious they might see him talking to a policeman.

'I'm Detective Sergeant Cathal Breen,' he said quietly. 'I'm here to ask you some questions.'

The look was one of shock, but that didn't necessarily signify much. All men who visited prostitutes believed they could keep that life separate.

Briefcase in one hand, Russell looked down at his watch. 'I'm going to be late,' he said.

'That's a shame, but you'll have to think of an excuse. Because I need to talk to you.' Breen was quiet but firm.

'Yes. But . . .'

'I can see you at home, then, if you prefer.'

'It's just it's not awfully convenient now.'

'Then I shall have to be inconvenient, Mr Russell.' He took Mr Russell by the elbow and led him up the street. At Shepherd's Bush there was a small cafe called Florian's run by a young West Indian man who wore knitted sleeveless jumpers. Breen ordered himself a coffee and bacon and eggs.

'Pepper sauce?' asked the man.

'Do you recommend it?'

'Always.'

'Nothing for me,' said Russell, when Breen asked him what he wanted.

'Sit down then,' said Breen. 'Come on. None of your friends are going to see you in here. I'm sure this isn't the kind of place they go.'

Russell looked at his watch, then sat; Breen took the mismatched chair opposite.

'How often have you used the services of Julie Teenager?' Breen asked.

Russell was a neatly dressed man; suit and tie, hair fashionably slightly over his ears, but nothing too showy. 'What makes you think I ever did?'

Breen breathed out. 'I can always call on you at home and continue this conversation in front of your wife, if you prefer.'

The man stared at the wooden table and said, 'She is a bit of fun, that's all.'

'She offered sexual services for money,' said Breen.

Another pause, then a cautious, 'Yes.'

'How did you find out about her?'

'I can't remember.'

'I'm sure you can,' said Breen.

He looked away. 'Probably a men's magazine. She advertises.'

'*Groovy young girl seeks rich older man*?'

'I suppose you think it's all very foolish,' said Russell.

The West Indian put a single coffee down in front of Breen.

Breen said, 'How long have you been doing it?'

'Three . . . four months.'

'That all?'

'Maybe a little longer. Probably, yes. I'm not sure.'

Breen said, 'What do you do with her?'

The man looked startled. 'What do you think I do with her?'

'Tell me.'

He leaned forward a little and whispered. 'She is a prostitute, for God's sake.'

'There are plenty of prostitutes. What makes her special?'

The cafe owner raised his eyebrows and took a step back from the table.

'She is innocent. Almost child-like. Not like other prostitutes.'

'You often slept with prostitutes?'

'No. I mean . . . Not like what I imagine prostitutes to be. She is . . . sweet, I suppose. Just like a little girl.'

'She was twenty-six.'

'Was?'

'She is dead.'

'Christ. No. Fuck.' His reaction seemed genuine enough. 'How?'

'Did you know she was twenty-six?'

'I thought she was younger. How did she die?'

Breen ignored his question. 'Did she tell you she was younger?'

'I suppose she did, yes.'

'And you like to have sex with little girls?'

'Are you enjoying this? I presume she was killed, yes? Poor Julie.'

Breen took a sip from his coffee. Not as bad as he had imagined it would be. 'You liked her because she pretended to be a little girl.'

'It was a play-act, of course. I knew that. Jesus. This is horrible.'

'What was the attraction?'

'The same as it always is. You know.'

'Not really, no. I would like you to explain.'

Breen was reminded of arriving at school as a young boy; he had grown up in a house with no women. His mother had died when he was young; he had no sisters. His father raised him alone. He had been amazed to discover how much boys talked about sex in the playground. Imaginary sex was easy for them to talk about, he quickly realised; it was the reality they were coy about.

'But it wasn't a play-act, was it?' he continued. 'You bought her a ring.'

He looked shocked. 'How did you know that?'

Breen reached into his briefcase and brought out the two receipts.

'She asked me for it,' he said. 'She liked to get presents.'

'Is that all? She asks you for a ring worth sixty guineas and you just buy it for her? And then give her the receipt.'

'Yes,' he said. 'That's all.'

'This one was for your wife, I suppose.' He showed the second receipt.

'Oh my Christ. You're not actually going to tell her any of this, are you?' asked Russell.

'Why shouldn't I?'

Russell looked like he was going to be sick. An ordinary-looking man, the kind you passed in the street without thinking twice about him.

'Right,' Breen said. 'What about her other clients?'

'She said they didn't mean anything to her.'

'But you did, naturally?'

'I suppose you think I'm a silly arse?' said Russell.

'Did she ever tell you anything about them?'

Russell shook his head. She had created a drama in which every client was the star; of course she hadn't let any of her customers see each other. That would have spoiled the illusion. Which meant that Mrs Caulk was the only person who saw all the men who visited Lena Bobienski.

'When did you see her last?'

'A couple of weeks ago, I suppose.'

'You must have been very angry at her, asking you to buy her expensive jewellery, when it was all a big play-act.'

'I wasn't angry at her. I bought it for her willingly. Look here, I had nothing to do with her death.'

'I would have been angry.'

'I know it was just a game. I'm not entirely stupid.'

The bacon and egg arrived with a red pepper sauce in a small pot. He tried a little with his little finger. It was searingly hot.

'Like it?' said the cafe owner.

He placed a small dollop in the centre of the yolk and cut into it.

'Where do you work?'

'I'm a journalist. Foreign Correspondent.'

'With an expertise in Polish affairs.'

'Ha ha,' said Russell drily. 'I'm a Soviet specialist, actually.'

'Who for?'

'The *Sunday Times*.'

'You knew she was Polish, then?'

Russell coloured. 'Of course.'

'She talked about it?'

'Only once, as a matter of fact. She told me about her father. Obviously knowing I was knowledgeable about that kind of thing. She hated the Russians. She said they had murdered her parents. Things happened after the war. Terrible things.'

'Where were you at the weekend, Mr Russell? From Thursday night until Sunday morning?'

The pink left his cheeks. 'Is that when it happened?'

'Please answer, Mr Russell.'

'Thursday night I was at home.'

'From when?'

'From about seven, it must have been, when I got back from work. I had Friday off.'

Mrs Caulk had left Miss Bobienski late on Thursday evening.

'And your wife can confirm that?'

154

'Oh, bloody hell. Will you have to ask her?'

Breen picked up a paper napkin and wiped his chin. 'Of course,' he said.

'Can't you trust me?'

'The word of an Englishman?'

'It's difficult.'

'Not as difficult as it was for Lena Bobienski. I need an alibi.'

Russell put his head in his hands and sat there for a while. Breen noticed he hadn't seemed surprised when he had used her real name.

'Everything OK?' asked the West Indian.

'I think he may have drunk too much last night.'

'Pepper sauce. It's good for headaches,' said the man.

'I believe you,' said Breen.

Russell looked up. 'Wait. What if someone else could tell you? My brother-in-law was there. He can confirm I was there all evening. We had dinner that night. I remember.'

'Your brother-in-law? Won't that be a little awkward?'

'He's a man, at least. Couldn't you just say it's a confidential matter? I mean, you don't actually have to tell him why you want to know, do you?'

'He would need to confirm you came home and stayed there,' said Breen.

'He will. I promise. Because I was.'

'OK. What about the next day?'

'At ten in the morning, we left for my mother-in-law's. Every year she holds a garden party in the Cotswolds. It's a big family do. We drove out there and I was there all weekend. So was my brother-in-law. He'll tell you.'

Breen added a bit of bacon to the egg and put it in his mouth. It was delicious. The spiciness of the sweet, hot sauce cut through the fogginess that had surrounded him since he had woken. 'It's good,' he said. 'Sure you don't want some?'

Russell shook his head. Breen took his time. He was enjoying the food. 'Good,' he said, holding up his cup to the cafe owner. The man just shrugged.

Russell looked at his watch again. 'I should call the office if this is going to take much longer. I would never have harmed her,' he said. 'You have to understand that.' He reached into his pocket and pulled out a pen, then a business card, and wrote on it. 'This is my brother-in-law's telephone number. I'll tell him to expect your call.'

'There are rumours that the Soviets have a moon mission planned. Do you think they're true?' asked Breen.

'Are you checking me out?'

'I'm just interested, that's all.' In days, the Americans were going to land on the moon themselves.

Russell relaxed a little. 'Why are the Americans landing on the moon?'

'Because they can?'

'It's theatre. They will beam pictures from space to show how superior they are to the Soviets. It's Hollywood. Then ask yourself whether the Soviets would share those priorities. Of course they wouldn't. They are secret-keepers. And Brezhnev is a militarist. He's more concerned about responding to the Allied missile threat than a theatrical gesture. I've stood in Red Square as the tanks roll past on May Day. That's the only kind of theatre Brezhnev is interested in. And the Soviet economy is growing at three per cent a year. Soon he will have more missiles than the Americans. There's an arms race and the Soviets are winning. Doesn't that concern you?'

'I'll call your brother-in-law this afternoon,' Breen said.

'What will you say?'

'I'll think of something.' Breen sighed. 'Don't worry. I won't tell him.' Breen stood.

He paid the cafe owner and left a shilling tip. By the time he turned round, Russell had gone.

SIXTEEN

And, catching the 27 bus back into town, he was still in the office before anyone else had arrived.

It was a good time to get things done, so he sat at his desk and wrote up notes of his meetings with Mrs Caulk and Ronald Russell. Tracking down the Krysia family had not been hard. The woman who had adopted Lena now lived in Warwickshire. 'Lena left home at seventeen,' she said, her Polish accent almost indecipherable on the phone. 'Never sends a Christmas card. Nothing. Never grateful.'

She had had no contact with her since Lena had left home to find work in London. 'I expect nothing,' she said. 'But a Christmas card would be nice. Is she in trouble?'

Mint was next in, panting from taking the stairs in twos.

'Oh. You're here already,' he said, disappointed.

Briefcases were not common in CID, but Breen noticed that Mint had somehow acquired one. It was brown leather, similar to Breen's, but newer and cheaper-looking. He lifted it and clicked it open.

'Here,' he said, pulling out a folder. Breen took it and removed several sheets of paper carefully bound with a green-string treasury tag.

'How was she?'

'Exhausting,' said Mint.

'Really?'

'I mean, as a talker,' he flustered.

Breen looked at the first page. He had given a label to each of the men, Mr A, Mr B, Mr C and so on, up to the letter L. Every label had a short paragraph after it. The notes were, he had to admit, excellent.

Mr A was described as 'around 6 foot two. Sweaty. Gold wedding ring. Bites nails of left hand but not right.' The attention to detail was good. Mr A was a regular: 'Thursdays only 11 p.m.' Mrs Caulk had good eyes. Mr C, who dyed his hair and wore Viyella shirts, had 'ink-stained fingers'.

Breen flicked through it. Some were almost comic. For instance, Mr E insisted on Miss Bobienski showering before he arrived and applying Johnson's Baby Oil to her body. Vincent Price was there. He was Mr J, who, as Mrs Caulk had said the day before, paid in single pound notes. He also had, Mint had typed, 'a chipped tooth'.

Others were more disturbing. Under Mr F, Mint had written 'Rubber wear'. Mr K 'Buys Bobienski children's toys. Wendy doll and doll's house furniture.' Mr H, who was 'early 30s', 'asked if he could spank L. Refused.' Breen tried to imagine the expression on Mint's face as Mrs Caulk told him that.

Mr H had also asked if he could take photographs. When Miss Bobienski had forbidden it, he had attempted to smuggle a camera in ('Kodak Instamatic'). Miss Bobienski had confiscated it and fined him £50 on top of her usual fee; obediently, he had paid up.

Other details were more prosaic. Mr B was a foreigner who brought wine. Mrs Caulk described him as 'Slavic' and 'a looker, but a bit on the thin side'. Mr G usually arrived with flowers on each visit. 'Expensive clothes,' Caulk had noted, though he wore ankle boots and double-breasted suits which she had thought was an unpleasant combination. Mr G, Mint had written, 'is nice but emotional, arrives at short notice after work, sometimes drunk. Often cries.'

Mr D was at the top of the second page: 'Ronnie'. It was clearly the same man he had seen this morning. So D, at least, was Ronald Russell. Caulk had included the detail of the Andrew Grima ring and added, 'Definitely married. Dyspeptic. A bit of an intellectual.'

Mint hovered by Breen's desk. 'Well?' he said.

'It's good,' nodded Breen. 'Very good.'

Mint grinned. 'Want tea, Sarge?'

'No.' Breen was engrossed in reading the file. 'What is the red dot?' On the top right-hand corner of D's sheet, Mint had added a small red circular sticker.

'When I asked Mrs Caulk which ones she thought were more likely to have a temper, or capable of doing something bad, she picked four.'

Breen flicked through them. She had identified B, D, G and L.

'But that's only her say-so, though,' he added. 'She said any of them could have been.'

'Very good,' said Breen.

Only Mr F, who had called himself 'Jones', and L had let slip what they did for a living. Mr F was a chartered surveyor; L was a car dealer, and Mint had added, with no intended humour, 'specialising in Bristols'.

Breen took out fifteen sheets of typing paper. 'Got a felt tip pen?' he asked.

Mint found one in his desk and passed it to Breen. He labelled them 'A' to 'L', and headed the thirteenth sheet 'Haas'.

'So it could be him?' said Mint.

'Logically, yes, it's possible.'

Then, in pen, he started filling in all the key details on each sheet. He was still doing that when Creamer arrived. 'Meeting, OK, Paddy?'

'Yes, sir. Give me ten minutes.'

'Righto.'

On the fourteenth, he wrote 'Florence Caulk'.

'Really? A woman?' said Mint.

'Gut feeling says it's not her. But you have to keep an open mind.' Mint peered at sheet 'D' and said, 'How did you find his name already?'

'The ring. I went to the shop.'

At the bottom, Breen had written 'Claims to have alibi but needs checking'.

The map Mint had worked on yesterday was pinned onto the partition wall of Creamer's office. Breen took it down and started replacing it with the sheets of paper with drawing pins he'd borrowed from Miss Rasper. By the time he'd put the fourth sheet up it was clear they hadn't enough space. 'Help me with

161

this desk,' he ordered Mint, and they moved it back two feet so that they could get at more of the wall.

He added a new sheet: 'Weapon'. On it he wrote: 'Champagne bottle?'

'Florence Caulk said she'd tidied a bottle away on the Friday when she arrived,' explained Breen.

When they'd finished, Breen, Mint and Miss Rasper stood looking.

'One of them, is it?' said Miss Rasper.

'I think so,' said Breen.

'Well, I hope you catch the bastard,' she said. And the office went silent for a second, because in the weeks she had been here, nobody had ever heard her use a profanity before.

When Creamer rounded the corner and saw the collection of sheets of paper, he exclaimed, 'Oh, very good. Very good indeed.'

'What about my desk?' grumbled the detective whose desk Breen had pushed aside, but no one was listening.

Creamer inspected each page, one by one.

'Was this your work, Sergeant Breen?'

'Constable Mint, sir. He interviewed the prostitute's maid.'

'This is exactly what I've been talking about. A team-based approach.'

Mint looked down at his shiny black shoes, embarrassed. Behind Creamer's back, one of the CID men flicked him a V-sign.

'You can rule the woman out, though. I spoke to Dr Wellington just now. From the angle and force of the blow that killed her he is convinced we are dealing with a man.' The rest of the men had gathered round now. Creamer pulled a pen from inside his jacket, turned and put a cross on Mrs Caulk's sheet. 'From the position and nature of the fatal impact, Dr Wellington believes that the victim was probably beaten from the front by someone who was able to lift the weapon above her head –' he lifted his arm and brought it down – 'so before receiving a further traumatic hit to the back of the head, from the same blunt instrument that would have almost certainly been the cause of death. But the bruises were not well developed, which suggests that she was killed soon after the beating started.'

Creamer looked around at his men, his hand still gripping an imaginary weapon, clearly enjoying the attention. 'Anything else we can use to rule any of these out?'

'Timing?' suggested someone.

'Wellington is still having difficulties ascertaining the time of death, however, so we are still left with a window of up to two days, unfortunately.'

'One day,' said Breen, 'if we accept that it was the killer who deliberately disabled the lift.'

They stared at the sheets some more.

'When will we be able to search the place?' asked Creamer.

'The forensics men should be finished any time,' said Breen. 'So as soon as we get the call through about that, we can get in.'

'Right. So. How do we track these fellows down?' said Creamer. 'Details, details, details. Where do they work?'

'I was thinking Mr C might be a printer. He had inky fingers. Or a clerk of some sort,' said Mint.

'Some kind of desk job?'

'Doesn't exactly narrow it down.'

'Mr A's short fingernails on the left hand might make him a musician,' said Breen. 'Violin. Or guitar.'

'Nice,' said Creamer. 'But not a lot of use. London is full of them.'

They stared at the wall. 'Mr J paid in single pound notes,' came Miss Rasper's voice from behind them. 'I'll bet he worked behind a till.' They turned and stared at her a second. She had joined them again, peering at the wall.

'Good,' said Creamer finally. 'Anything else?'

'One thing I forgot,' said Mint quietly. 'I didn't put it on the list.'

'What?'

Everybody looked at him.

'Right before she was going, Mrs Caulk said maybe we know who it is already.'

'What?'

'Exactly,' said Mint. 'I asked her why she said that. She was a bit coy at first, like she didn't want to say. So I pressed her and said we'd have to keep her in if there was something we thought she wasn't telling. I'm not sure. We could do that, couldn't we? Withholding evidence?'

'What are you talking about, Constable?' said Creamer.

'Well. In the end, after I said we could arrest her, she said she thinks one of them was a copper.'

There were a few seconds' silence.

'I don't understand,' said Inspector Creamer.

'When Miss Bobienski said she was going to advertise in *Private Eye*, Caulk advised her against it. Said it might attract the attention of the Vice Squad. Miss Bobienski just laughed at her and said she had a friend who could sort all that out.'

'A policeman?'

'That's what she thought Miss Bobienski meant, yes.'

'You mean, one of the victim's . . . customers . . . may have been a policeman?'

Breen turned back to the sheets of paper. 'Which one?'

'She didn't know. Miss Bobienski never told her which one. Only that one was a copper.'

'I don't understand,' said Inspector Creamer.

'Sure she wasn't just trying to wind you up?'

'No, sir,' said Mint.

'Ah,' said Creamer, looking down at his shoes.

'I know it's not good, one of ours visiting a prostitute,' said Mint, looking around the room, puzzled. 'But it might be useful, no? Whoever he was, I mean . . . Perhaps he can tell us something, if we can track him down? Maybe we can figure out who it is?'

There was a heaviness in the room; nobody spoke.

'Just thinking aloud,' said Mint.

'OK, everybody, back to work,' said Creamer quietly. 'That report you gave to Sergeant Breen,' he said to Mint. 'I'll take that, please.'

Breen took the sheaf of papers off his desk and handed it to the inspector who retreated to his office, closing the door behind him; through the glass you could hear him talking on the phone.

Miss Rasper's electric typewriter sprang noisily back to life.

'What just happened?' said Mint.

Constable Jones said, 'Don't you get it, teacher's pet?'

'What?'

'Are you thick?' Jones sneered; he enjoyed having someone to pick on. Until Mint had arrived, Jones had been the junior officer around here. 'Why do you think McPhail was interested in this case, all of a sudden?'

The typing stopped again.

'You don't think it was him?' said Mint.

Jones burst out laughing. 'That would be something, wouldn't it?'

Miss Rasper pursed her lips.

Breen said, 'If it's a copper, a senior copper especially, that would explain why they're keeping an eye on us, why McPhail was so interested. And why the beat coppers were warned off.'

'What?'

'I had a whisper that the beat coppers were warned off Harewood Avenue after dark.'

One of the men whistled.

'Exactly.'

'Unfortunate.'

'One of ours? I mean, it's just around the bloody corner, isn't it?'

'Something that won't look good in the papers,' said Breen. 'Right now the boss will be phoning McPhail to let him know what you've turned up. Don't expect a medal.'

'And don't be surprised if our lot doesn't get pulled off the case, neither,' added Jones.

Mint looked shocked. 'Really?'

'Take a car. Go and find Mrs Caulk. If she's not at Heatherley's, check her flat. Bring her back in,' Breen said. He looked at his watch. 'We'll need to talk to her again.'

'Sorry, Sarge,' said Mint, looking down at his desk. 'I mean, I just thought. Do you think that's why they took the beat officers off the street? They wouldn't do that, would they? Not to protect a copper.'

Breen didn't answer, though he had been thinking the same. 'Before you go. Was that the only copy of that report, Mint?' he asked.

'No. I've got a carbon.' Mint dug inside his new briefcase, drew out a second folder and handed it to Breen. He leaned towards him and whispered, 'What if they are protecting somebody big, though? A senior policeman.'

'We don't know anything,' said Breen.

'Admit it, though. It's what you're thinking.'

But Breen was already on the telephone. Mint turned away, looking troubled. Ronald Russell's brother-in-law was a civil servant at the Ministry of Agriculture. An officious switchboard operator demanded to know the nature of his business. Then, when he was finally put through, the brother-in-law demanded in a taut voice, 'Why do you need to know?'

Like his brother-in-law, he probably imagined policemen as people you only called on when someone had stolen your antiques.

Breen resisted the urge to tell him that he was calling because his sister's husband had been sleeping with a prostitute who had been murdered; instead, he just said, 'Nothing major. Just routine. One of those boring things we policemen have to do.'

'Ronnie's not in any bother, is he?'

'Oh no. I just need to confirm that he was at your mother's last weekend.'

'Yes he was. What is this about?' People always wanted to know. It was natural curiosity.

'Don't worry; it's just paperwork. It's all we ever do, these days. We're having to check the details of several people simply to rule them out. You were with him from Thursday night?'

'As a matter of fact, I was.'

'And you travelled together to . . .'

'The Cotswolds. My mother's house.'

Breen swivelled his chair around to face the wall behind him. 'And he was at home all Thursday night, and at your mother's house for the entire weekend?'

'Yes.'

'Thank you.'

'Is that it?'

'I'll need you to sign a statement to that effect. I'll send a man round. That's all right, isn't it?'

'I suppose so, yes.'

Breen replaced the phone and phoned the forensics team at Scotland Yard.

'Harewood Avenue?' said the man. 'We finished there yesterday.'

Breen blinked. 'Why didn't you let me know?'

'Sorry, mate.'

Breen put down the receiver. The brightness of the morning seemed to have vanished. Before he left the room, he peered through the glass door into Creamer's office. The inspector was still talking on the phone to someone, a worried frown on his shiny round face. He wondered if it was McPhail on the other end of the line.

Breen reached Harewood Avenue a little before eleven. Now that the forensic team had left, there was no longer a policeman stationed on the front door.

Breen had no key yet. The forensics team were supposed to have passed it on, so he rang the doorbell until Haas the caretaker appeared. 'Welcome, welcome,' the man said, and beckoned him in with an exaggerated swing of the arm. 'In and out. In and out. I thought I had got my house back, but I suppose you also want to look upstairs again.'

'The lift fixed yet?' asked Breen.

Haas shook his head. 'Your policemen took away the *Elektromotor*. How can it work?'

Breen trudged up the stairs back up to Bobienski's flat.

At the second-floor landing, Breen paused and asked, 'What time did the other policemen leave?'

'Which other policemen?'

'The science team from Scotland Yard.'

'About four yesterday. The other ones have just gone.'

Breen put his foot on the first step of the next run and then stopped. 'The other ones?'

Haas paused. 'Maybe half an hour since. Other ones. I don't ask. They had a card. Like your one.'

Breen climbed faster now. Haas took his time, ascending slowly.

'Were they in uniform? Or like me?'

'Like you,' said Haas, following up the stairs, panting slightly. 'Only not so much talking talking talking all the time.'

'They came after the others had gone?'

'Yes yes. This morning. Early.'

'Did you recognise them? Had they been here before?'

'I don't know. So many people coming in and out, in and out.'

The caretaker stood outside Bobienski's flat, with his large bundle of keys, searching for the right one, hands trembling gently. When he eventually found it and pushed open the door, the first thing he said was, '*Scheisse.*'

Feathers swirled into the air, disturbed by the draught. Fine dust caught the sunlight. The floor was littered with horsehair, tugged out of sofas and chairs. Pillows had been emptied. The pink curtains had been shredded, their linings slit open. Scattered across the carpet were the contents of the desk's drawers – pens, ink, old magazines.

Everything had been searched. The Bakelite covers had been unscrewed from electrical sockets; the screws lay strewn next to them.

Somebody had methodically, thoroughly, gone through the rooms, looking for something.

'Your people, they make a fucking mess,' said Haas, looking around.

Breen said nothing. Creamer's pride would be stung because whoever had done this had not even bothered telling anyone at D Division CID. His, too, he realised, looking at the armchair, tossed onto its side, hessian torn off the base.

The large teddy bear sat on the floor, flock guts spilling out of it onto the carpet.

SEVENTEEN

In the bathroom, Haas wrung his hands. 'Are you paying for this?'

The hardboard panel at the side of the bath had been torn off, exposing the dusty space underneath.

'There was no need. If they told me what they wanted, I would have found my tools. *Unnötig*, all this destruction. They are *Schläger*. Like thugs.'

Breen looked at him. The man's arms were trembling gently. He would have seen things like this before, thought Breen, in Austria.

In Lena Bobienski's small bedroom, the rug had been moved and a floorboard taken up. Under it was a small metal tin, also open.

'Anything there?'

'Empty,' said Breen.

Breen had hoped to be here first. The flat had already been cleaned once by Mrs Caulk, but now everything had been disturbed a second time. Whoever it was had beaten them to it.

Breen examined the floorboard. The nails had been removed to make the wood easy to lift. Mint was right. It had been a hiding place; but what had Bobienski kept here?

'Did you know this was here?'

'No no.'

'The people who did this. Did they leave a card?' asked Breen. 'Anything to tell you which department they were in?'

'No,' said Haas.

'You just left them the key and let them get on with it?'

'That's what they said for me to do. I don't interfere.'

'So what were they looking for?' Breen looked at the man. People only tore the place apart this way if they were searching for something specific.

'Why would I know that?'

They would be hunting for exactly what Breen had hoped to find, he supposed. A list of names, perhaps. He sat down onto the edge of Lena Bobienski's small, spartan single bed. The mattress had been sliced diagonally from top to bottom.

'What happens when you find what you're looking for?' said Breen.

'Why are you asking me?' Haas looked wary.

'Look around. If you've found it, why would you carry on looking?'

'Oh,' he said. 'You mean . . . they didn't find it? Whatever it is they were looking for?'

'Maybe,' said Breen. 'Or maybe they weren't actually looking for it as much as making sure it wasn't here.'

'I don't understand.'

'No. Neither do I,' said Breen, standing.

They went back to the living room. Haas left the flat and returned with a long-handled dustpan and broom. Breen kicked through a pile of loose feathers, scattering them upwards into the air. 'When did these people arrive?' he asked

'Maybe nine o'clock,' Haas said. 'Maybe half past.'

That was before Mint had told the meeting that one of their suspects might be a policeman. So the flat hadn't been cleaned on McPhail's orders, because of Mint's discovery, at least. Yet whoever had done it had been professional and methodical.

Haas swept feathers; each time he tried to catch them, more seemed to escape the bristles of the broom, flying upwards into the air, hanging in the sunlight. Breen watched him work, frustrated at his inability to make the room any tidier than it was when he started.

On the way out, Breen paused, then knocked on Mr Payne's door.

'Oh, it's you,' Payne said. 'Come to look at my dirty picture again?'

'Some men came here earlier today. They searched Miss Bobienski's flat. Did you hear them come in?'

'Do you think I'm the kind of man who spends his days listening to who comes and goes?'

'Yes.'

Mr Payne giggled.

'Did you hear any names? Anything that might give a clue who they were?'

Payne shook his head. 'They said very little, as a matter of fact. Benjamin the caretaker let them in. I didn't hear what they said. Normally you lot never shut up. Everything's quiet here now. I can barely sleep, it's so silent.'

Breen hesitated by the door.

'What do you mean? You could hear what went on in Miss Bobienski's flat?'

Payne laughed. 'People have such fanciful notions of the blind. I don't hear any better than you do. No, I just meant the comings and goings. I was used to them. Cars turning up here all times of night.'

'I don't suppose you'd recognise any of them, the cars?'

'What, from the delicate purr of their engines? Don't be ridiculous.'

'No. Sorry.' Breen turned to go.

'There was one, though, used to keep his motor running while he waited. He came several times a week.'

'Someone had his driver bring him here and wait in the car?'

'I know. Kept the fellow up hours. Made of money, those men.'

'A taxi?'

'No. Not one of those sort of rough motors. A car. Always the same car. He played the radio too, all bloody night. Awful pop music.'

Since they'd set up Radio 1, the pirate stations had mostly disappeared from the dial, but Radio Luxembourg still broadcast until three in the morning. Sometimes when he couldn't sleep he could hear its chirpy sounds coming from the transistor in Helen's room.

'The same man?'

'I don't know. The same driver, at least.'

174

'Bringing the same person?'

'Maybe. I don't know.'

Haas was waiting by the door to show him out. 'Mr Payne mentioned a driver who waited outside with the engine running.'

Haas shrugged. 'I'm upstairs. Top floor. I don't hear anything.'

'Do you have a car, Mr Haas?'

Haas laughed, like the idea would be ridiculous. 'I can't even drive. Why should I be wanting a car?'

Breen walked out onto the pavement feeling exhausted. What had seemed simple was becoming more complicated, more obscure. He took his time, walking back to the station. He had thinking to do before he talked to Mrs Caulk again.

She would be waiting at the station now; but it would be good to make her feel a little nervous.

He walked past the station and took a right down Charlotte Street, to the 91, where he ordered a double espresso and smoked a cigarette.

'Where did you get those scars, George?'

George frowned. 'I don't like to say.'

The cigarette tasted dry and stale on his tongue.

'You look unhappy, sir.'

'Do I, George?'

'Like you ate something bad.'

Breen nodded. 'That's about it.'

In less than two weeks, a man would walk on the moon. The Met were living in a different century.

He was ready to meet Florence Caulk, but Florence Caulk was not at the police station.

Mint stood when he entered the CID room, looking like a dog waiting for its master to return, eyes wide. 'She's gone, Sarge.'

'Gone? Mrs Caulk?'

'Cleared out. I went to her flat, like you said. She didn't answer so I was worried. Remember she was concerned about her safety? I was thinking something might have happened.'

'How do you know she's gone?'

'Found a concierge who let me in to her place. She'd cleared out in a hurry, I reckon. The drawers were open. Bed not slept in.'

'You sure?'

'Yes. Not taken in the milk nor anything.'

Breen sat at his desk, put his head in his hands. Their crime scene had been erased; now their main witness had disappeared.

Mint looked shocked.

Breen didn't look up. 'Did you speak to any neighbours? Did anyone see her going?'

'Yes, Sarge. I mean, no. Nobody saw her going or nothing.'

'You think she went last night? After you'd interviewed her?'

'You reckon she knew something she wasn't telling?'

Breen didn't move, head still down. She had been a suspect; he should have been more careful. She had been nervous about something, after all. This was his fault. She mustn't be allowed to get away. 'Circulate her description. Ports and the airports. If you don't know the procedure, get Jones or someone to help you. We need to knock on all the doors at her block.'

Mint picked up the phone. 'What about you, Sarge? Anything?'

Breen lifted his head and said, 'Somebody has cleaned out

Bobienski's place. I don't know who.'

'What do you mean, "cleaned out"?'

Whoever had searched the prostitute's flat had done a thorough job. They had come equipped with knives, jemmies and screwdrivers, to make sure that either they found what they were looking for or at least no one else did.

'C1, Sarge? Scotland Yard?'

'That's the thing. I don't know. Whichever department it was didn't bother to tell us about it, anyway.'

'I mean,' said Mint, 'that's out of order. They should have followed procedure. We're the ones supposed to be investigating this, aren't we?'

It was a possibility. He called up Carmichael. The Drug Squad were part of C1. If someone from Serious Crime was investigating it, Carmichael would have heard.

'What's up, Paddy? You a father yet?'

'John, this is important. Is anyone from C1 investigating the murder of Lena Bobienski?'

'That's yours, isn't it? Why would C1 be looking into it?'

'I'm not sure. Possibly because one of the suspects might be a policeman.'

Breen heard Carmichael put his hand over the receiver and shout, 'Shut up, will you. I'm trying to talk on the phone . . . Why would you think that, Paddy?'

'There's a witness who says that there was a copper who slept with her.'

'No, Paddy. Haven't heard a peep.'

Mint was watching his face as he talked, and when Breen put down the phone and shook his head, he said, 'But if it wasn't

Scotland Yard, who was it?'

It took a minute, but Breen could see the thought arrive on Mint's face. His mouth fell open. He came closer to Breen's desk, as if worried about saying it out loud. 'Sarge? What if it's the policeman we're looking for? What if it's him cleaned out the flat, so there's no evidence?'

'Yes. What if.'

'That couldn't happen though, could it?'

'Couldn't it?' said Breen looking at him.

Mint looked horrified. 'Yes. But. Even if it could, they couldn't get away with something like that. Could they?'

'Of course they can't,' said Breen wearily. It had been a bad day. 'If they could, that would mean that someone in the Met was corrupt, wouldn't it?'

Mint stamped his foot. 'Don't patronise me.'

After the bang of boot on floor, there was a sudden hush in the CID room as everyone stopped and looked at Mint, now red-faced, standing by Breen's desk. Like Breen, they were shocked by the junior policeman's sudden burst of anger.

When he got home there was still a light under Helen's door and he could hear music, so he opened it and went to sit on Helen's bed in his father's old bedroom. 'I was almost asleep,' she complained.

'Sorry. The radio was on.'

'It helps me sleep . . . Doesn't matter,' she said, sitting up on her elbows. She looked dark-eyed. 'Have you got a cigarette? Elfie says she's given up.'

'I think you may have been right,' he said, pulling a packet from his jacket.

'Don't sound so surprised. What am I right about this time?'

'When you said you thought a policeman was sleeping with the prostitute.'

She was awake now. 'Knew there was something funny about it,' she said.

'Don't sound so pleased.'

She sucked on the cigarette. 'What's the betting Scotland Yard try and muscle in now?' she said, though she couldn't stop smiling to herself because she'd been right.

'I know,' he said. 'If they haven't already.'

'What do you mean?'

'Nothing.'

He sat by her, running his hand over the mound of her belly, feeling the tightness of skin and the shape beneath it until she pushed his hand away. 'Don't,' she said.

When she was halfway through the cigarette she handed it to him. 'Everything tastes funny. Even fags.'

He stubbed it out for her and switched off the light, then turned the radio down and sat there with her as some singers chanted 'Baby Come Back', and a DJ played chirpy jingles about 'going with 208' until her breathing slowed and he was sure she was asleep. He sat in the darkness.

Florence Caulk had vanished. He had been careless.

EIGHTEEN

On the Thursday morning after the murder, he knew it would be a long day, so he made sandwiches from salt beef, mustard and pickled gherkins that he bought from one of the Jewish shops on Kingsland Road, wrapped them in brown paper and set off for work.

On the way to the station he stopped off at the Euston telephone exchange to meet the technical officer, who assured him that yes, all the paperwork had been completed and there would be someone there tracing calls to Lena Bobienski's phone for the next three days.

So when he arrived at work, everyone was already in; behind her desk, Miss Rasper beckoned him to come closer, then whispered, 'McPhail is in with Creamer.' Then, a little louder: 'Inspector Creamer would like to see you.'

Maybe not such a long day, after all, thought Breen. Perhaps Helen was right again. Was C Division being taken off the case?

The door to Creamer's office opened. 'Ah. Breen,' said Creamer, pale and unsmiling. 'A word, please.'

Breen walked towards him through a silent room, conscious of the stares of other officers.

'Close the door.'

There were two chairs in Inspector Creamer's room: one behind the desk, another facing it. That chair was already occupied by Superintendent McPhail.

'Sir?'

McPhail turned his head to look up and acknowledge Breen. The room was small, so Breen found himself standing next to McPhail's chair, looking down at the seated man.

Creamer sat. 'Question. Can you account for your movements after leaving the office yesterday, Paddy? Superintendent McPhail would like to know.'

Breen was puzzled. 'What's happening?'

He noticed Creamer's hands were shaking slightly. Why? Was it anger? He looked back at McPhail's face to try and understand. Had there been an argument between them? But McPhail was calm, expressionless.

'Well?' Creamer said.

'I was working, of course. On the Bobienski murder.'

'Specifically, where were you and what were you doing?'

Breen turned to Superintendent McPhail. 'Do you know who searched the premises at Harewood Avenue yesterday? Was it you, sir?'

'Please do not interrupt,' said Creamer. 'I was asking you a question. Superintendent McPhail needs to know everyone you talked to after leaving the office yesterday morning.'

Breen glanced from Creamer to McPhail and back again. 'Why?'

'Bloody hell, Paddy. Please. Just tell me.'

'I went to Miss Bobienski's apartment; I spoke to the caretaker and to one of the residents, a Mr Payne. After that . . . I walked about a little. Then I came back here.'

'Walked about a little? What were you doing?'

'I was thinking.'

'Thinking?' said Creamer.

'Why not? We have a large number of potential suspects. I wanted to think about ways we could eliminate them.' Breen looked around. Creamer had put up photographs of himself: as a cadet at Hendon in 1948; one with the Duke of Edinburgh. Another of him in a dress suit, standing next to the Hollywood actor Stewart Granger; the star had a neat white handkerchief in his jacket pocket and a slightly confused look on his face, as if he didn't quite know what he was doing next to this middle-ranking copper at some social event. 'So I went for a coffee in order to think, then I came back here to speak to the team.'

'So you spoke to nobody else?'

'Obviously I spoke to people. What is all this about, please?'

'Who else did you discuss the case with?' asked Creamer.

McPhail opened his mouth, finally, still not turning to look at Breen. 'A reporter from the *Mirror* called Scotland Yard last night,' he said. 'He wanted confirmation that we were investigating one of our own for the murder of Lena Bobienski. What we want to know is: who told the journalist?'

This was not what he had been expecting. 'Are we investigating one of our own for the murder of Lena Bobienski?' asked Breen. 'Is there something I don't know about?'

'Answer the question, Paddy?'

'So someone went to the press and you think it was me?'

Superintendent McPhail finally looked around and said calmly, 'Did you?'

Breen looked at McPhail; he returned the gaze evenly. 'No, sir,' said Breen simply. 'What makes you think I would have?'

'Well, someone did,' said Creamer. 'And, logically, because we were the ones investigating the case . . .'

McPhail ignored him. 'So who else was aware that we believed a policeman was on the list of Miss Bobienski's customers? Though Inspector Creamer assures me that no one in his department would dream of talking to the press, he would, of course, not want to see any flaws in his own department.' He looked contemptuously at Creamer as he spoke. 'And we know that only a handful of people would have known about your new theory about there being a policeman in the list of suspects. It is only a theory, I take it? Had you discussed it with that woman you live with, for example?'

'That woman that I live with?'

'Inspector Creamer tells me your common-law wife is a former constable. Miss Tozer. According to files I've just looked at, she was a suspect in a previous murder inquiry. Did you discuss the case with her?'

'Are we more concerned that a policeman, possibly a senior policeman, is on the suspect list for the murder of a prostitute, or about whether the press find out?' Breen said.

McPhail was calm. 'Please answer the question.'

'Yes. I discussed the case briefly with my girlfriend. She is interested in what I do. We talked about the case last night before I went to bed. No, she didn't call up a reporter and tell them.'

'You're sure of that?'

'Of course, sir.'

'But she was aware that a witness had alleged that a policeman may have been one of Miss Bobienski's clients?'

'Yes,' said Breen. 'While we're at it, permission to ask a question. I believe some men searched the building yesterday. You may be able to help me, sir. What were they looking for?'

For the first time, Breen saw a flicker of uncertainty in McPhail's face. 'Our men?'

It wasn't uncommon that the Met's left hand didn't know what its right one was doing; it could have been a mix-up. But Carmichael had already told Breen that it wasn't C1. Was McPhail pretending he didn't know who had searched Bobienski's place?

'After the forensics team had packed up, somebody else came in yesterday and tore the place apart,' Breen said. 'They identified themselves to the caretaker as policemen. I have no idea who they were. So unless they share what they found with me, a crime scene that had already been tampered with once has now been totally destroyed. Unless someone was deliberately trying to make sure it was destroyed.'

McPhail said nothing.

Sensing his advantage, Breen pressed on. 'I'm not sure how we're supposed to make any progress if another department barges in. And if there is another department involved, why do you assume it was D Division who went to the press?'

McPhail looked increasingly less certain of himself. Creamer sat up a little in his chair.

'And what about the prostitute's maid, Mrs Caulk?' continued Breen. 'She was the one who alerted us to there being a copper on Bobienski's list. She is a key witness. And she has gone missing.'

'Missing, you say?'

'She appears to have absconded.'

'She sounds to me more like a suspect than a witness.'

'Maybe.'

'And you let her get away?' McPhail said, accusingly.

Breen didn't answer.

'So *she* could have gone to the papers?' said Creamer hopefully.

McPhail said nothing.

Creamer relaxed a little. 'You can rest assured that we shall look into this, sir.'

'Are they publishing the story?' Breen said.

'No.'

'Why not?'

'A certain Chief Super at Scotland Yard told the journalist it was not in the public interest and would prejudice an investigation. He was not happy about being disturbed at home, you understand. But we're going to find out who did this and if it's a copper, they better start looking for another job.' McPhail stood, picking his cap off Creamer's desk. 'And do you have any idea who this supposed policeman who has been having sex with a prostitute may be?'

Did McPhail know the answer to that question already? Was

185

he playing some kind of game with him? 'We don't know, that either, sir.'

'You don't really know much, do you?'

'No, sir. However, we're working hard on trying to find that out, sir.'

McPhail made a face like he'd just eaten something sour. 'It's to your advantage that I believe in taking a copper's word for something, even when the evidence points in the other direction. It's the kind of thing that holds us apart from the mob,' he said. 'But if I get so much as a sniff that it was you who went running to the papers because you thought your toes were being trodden on, I'll dismiss you without a second thought.'

'Understood, sir,' said Breen.

'The Yard don't like it when they have to lean on the press to kill an article. Right now they would love nothing better than to run a dirty story on the police. In days gone by, they had respect for the institutions of state. All that is changing. Right now, it's like we're in a game of catch with the newspapers. We have three chances. Once you've used them up, you've nowhere left to hide. One day soon, the press are going to turn up something really nasty on us and we'll have no lives left. And then the trouble is going to really start. Think about it.' He glared down at Creamer. 'Everything we respect will go. Do we really want a police force which is run by the newspapers? There are a lot of naive people out there who imagine that if everybody just knew the whole truth, things will be better. There are some things it's better not to know. But the way things are, these people are getting the upper hand. And believe me, when it starts to come down around here, there's going to be one almighty mess.'

It was the longest speech he'd ever heard McPhail give.

'So D Divison is more interested in protecting the reputation of the police than investigating a murder in which a policeman might, at best, be a witness, sir?'

'Sergeant Breen!' said Creamer. 'Enough.'

'Don't caricature what we're doing here, Sergeant,' said McPhail. 'If the Met loses its reputation it will have nothing. Without respect, there can be no authority.' He looked hard at Breen.

'In the meantime, sir –' Breen returned his stare – 'perhaps if you have some information about the identity of the policeman who paid for Miss Bobienski's services, you could share it.'

'Why would you expect me to know that?' asked McPhail blankly. 'However, if you find out, I will expect you to tell me before anyone else. Especially the fourth estate. I'm sure we all understand the importance of protecting the reputation of the firm. Good morning.'

Creamer and Breen saluted, and McPhail stepped out of the office into the main CID room.

'Wait a minute, sir.'

Without waiting to be excused by Creamer, Breen left the office. McPhail paused by the CID-room door that led out onto the stairwell. 'What now?'

'Question, sir. Why did you tell beat policemen to avoid Harewood Avenue?'

McPhail frowned.

'Is it true? You told them to skip it from their patrols.'

'Who did you hear that from?' he demanded.

'Can't say, sir,' Breen said. 'It would be squealing.'

'Don't mock me, Sergeant,' McPhail said, quietly. His head was lit by a shaft of sunlight in the dark stairwell.

'No, sir. But if it was something relating to Lena Bobienski, we should know.'

'I am not at liberty to tell you, and you will proceed as best you can with the resources you have.'

'You see, I had assumed it was Scotland Yard that were treading all over this case, but I'm beginning to think maybe I'm wrong. Because I called C1 and asked them, and they didn't know anything about it. Or anything about who searched Miss Bobienski's flat yesterday. Which makes me wonder.'

'As I said, I am not at liberty to discuss it with you, and I would appreciate you not asking me again.'

'It's just that there's a limit to how much we can find out, sir.'

In the shaft of light, dust swirled around him. 'I don't like whiners, Sergeant Breen.' McPhail pursed his lips. He seemed to be thinking.

'Does what you know have anything to do with our inquiry about an officer?'

'I have said before, I am not at liberty to tell you that.'

'If it's not C1, do you know which department they were from, sir?'

McPhail didn't answer directly; he simply said: 'That's not your business. In the meantime I expect you to proceed as best you can. And if I find out who has talked to the press, I will seriously fuck up their career for ever.' McPhail was already walking out of the light and up the stone steps. 'OK?'

★

When he returned to the CID room, Miss Rasper looked up from her typewriter and whispered, 'So? What was all that about?'

'Someone went to the press last night,' answered Breen, loud enough for everyone in the room to hear. 'About the Bobienski case. Leaked that a policeman might be among the suspects.'

At the back of the room, Constable Jones whistled.

'McPhail thinks it might be someone from D Division.'

The room was full of resentful muttering. 'No one from our lot would dare snitch on another copper, would they? Doesn't deserve to be on the firm.'

Out of the corner of his eye, Breen was suddenly conscious of the eager-faced Mint, with his nylon shirts and gold crucifix, staring hard at his desk. Breen considered for a minute, then approached his desk. 'Constable Mint?'

'Sarge?' Mint looked up anxiously; miserably.

'Anything on Mrs Caulk?'

'Possible sighting of a woman of that description getting on the ferry at Ramsgate. Nothing else.'

'Get out and look for her then.'

'What? Now? Where?'

'Use your initiative,' Breen snapped. 'Ask around. Interview the neighbours. And find a minute to call up your wife and let her know you're going to be working late.'

'Tonight, sir?'

'Yes. Tonight. It would have been a working night for Lena Bobienski. We're going to see who turns up. We can put some faces to these names. And I'm guessing that anyone who turns up doesn't know she's dead. Is tonight a problem?'

'My wife goes to a women's social. I usually look after the kids.'

'I don't care.' Breen raised his voice. 'You're going to have to tell her you're working. Get out there. Now. Quick.'

Mint looked stung.

Breen looked down at his desk. 'Get a bloody move on.'

Across the room Miss Rasper looked up from her work and frowned. Breen was not normally like this. He was the polite one. But Breen wanted Mint out of the office before anyone started to ask questions about who it was who had tried to leak the story to the press.

'Oh, and Mint.' Mint was just picking up his mac. 'Get into her flat. Find out what she's taken. See if she's left an address book or anything that might tell us where she's gone.'

'I don't have a key, sir.'

'Just bloody go.'

Miss Rasper's glance had turned to glare. 'By the way, Sergeant Breen,' she called across the room. 'You have something on your shirt.'

Breen looked down and saw a streak of yellow down his pale blue button-down shirt. It was the mustard from when he had made the sandwiches that morning. It would have been there through his meeting with McPhail. He sighed and went to the Gents, removed his shirt and ran it under a cold tap.

A constable he didn't recognise came in and stared for a second, then looked away, pretending he hadn't noticed anything out of the ordinary.

Breen looked into the mirror above the sink. The knife wounds on his stomach showed as maroon streaks on his white flesh, cuts made by the man who had killed Helen's sister. He had caught the man, but not before another woman had died. The cuts had healed well, but he didn't like people seeing them. He was ashamed of them; and what they represented.

NINETEEN

On the way to Bobienski's flat that evening he bought a copy of the *Evening News* to pass the time. He had hoped Mrs Caulk would be there to answer the telephone; they would have to manage without her.

Constable Mint was waiting outside.

'Did you find anything? Any address book?' he asked Mint.

'No, Sarge. I think she must have took it.'

Haas answered the door, saying nothing.

On Miss Bobienski's pink sofa, still surrounded by feathers, Breen unwrapped his salt beef sandwiches, bit into one and ate it, slowly, waiting for the phone to ring. He had made the mustard with a little vinegar, in the French way. It gave it just a little tang that he liked.

As he finished, he noticed Mint watching him from the stool he was sitting on. Mint had nothing. He had not known he would be working late. Breen sighed and said, 'Do you want one?'

'Only if you have enough.'

He handed one over and watched Mint mumbling Grace over it before he took his first mouthful.

'It was you who went to the papers, wasn't it?'

Shocked, Mint spat out a crumb of bread. 'How did you know?'

'Well, someone talked, and it wasn't me. And all day you've been looking like you're terrified the sky's going to fall.'

'Does Creamer know then?' Mint reddened.

'No. I told them it could be anyone in CID. I think they actually believed me.'

Mint laid the sandwich on his lap. 'They're trying to cover up the fact that a policeman was one of the prostitute's clients. You said it. It's wrong, isn't it?'

'I was hoping it wasn't you who told them.' Breen picked at a bit of beef that was lodged in his teeth. 'You're lucky,' he said. 'The papers haven't published anything.'

'I wish they had.'

'They won't. Not without calling up the Met first. It's the way things work. And obviously the Met denied it point blank, so they don't have anything to go on. But it was a stupid thing to do,' he said.

'It was the honest thing to do,' said Mint. 'Police are supposed to be honest, aren't they?'

Breen nodded. 'Yes. Supposed to be.'

'Just because I'm not as cynical as you are.'

'If they had printed it, McPhail wouldn't have been so calm about it. You'd lose your job. Like I said, you're lucky.'

Mint's eyes widened, as if he hadn't thought that far ahead.

'It's my fault. I'm sorry,' said Breen.

'What for?'

'Yesterday I thought it was a straight cover-up. I was frustrated. Today, I'm not so sure. I'm beginning to think this may not be as simple as trying to hide one copper's bad behaviour.'

Mint squinted, as if the light was suddenly too bright in the room. 'Did they tell you to tell me this?'

'Who?'

'The people in charge. They did, didn't they?'

'Which people in charge?'

'McPhail. To put me off trying to tell the truth. You saw her flat. You told me.'

'Calm down,' said Breen. Mint was young, idealistic. 'Just listen to me, OK? Thing is, C1 didn't know anything about what had happened there.'

'But someone went there and cleaned the place out. For a reason.'

'Yes.' That was what was worrying him too. If it wasn't C1 who had searched the flat, then who was it? Was it McPhail himself? He watched Mint, chewing on a nail.

'Will they figure out it's me? Who went to the papers.'

'Not necessarily.'

'There are policemen who do far worse. You hear about it every day. There are dishonest people. Coppers who blackmail people into confessing so they can finger someone for a crime. They get away with it. I was trying to be honest.'

'I know you were. But there's no point being right if you can't do anything about it. If Creamer asks if it was you who talked to the press, deny it.'

'That would be lying.'

'Yes. That's right.'

'I can't lie,' he said.

'Of course you can. Think about your children. You'd lose your job, your flat, everything.'

'I can't lie,' Mint said again.

At 6.30 the front doorbell rang. Mint leaped up to answer it, scattering the contents of Breen's sandwich all over the white, feather-strewn carpet. Breen said, 'Too early. It's probably the WPC.'

Florence Caulk had disappeared, so he had put in a request for a woman officer to come and answer the phone instead. The men would be expecting a woman's voice. But when the uniformed policewoman arrived at the flat door panting and exclaimed, 'Bloody lift in't working,' the first thing Mint said was, 'Her accent's all wrong.'

'What's wrong with my accent?' said the WPC. She was an East Ender, somewhere in her forties, one of the tough old women who'd been at the job half their lives.

Mint was right. 'Try and sound a bit less . . . London,' suggested Breen.

'Bloody hell,' she said, looking round at all the feathers. 'What happened here? Someone murdered a chicken?'

They sat looking at the black telephone on Bobienski's small table. When it finally rang twenty minutes later, she picked it up. 'Hello? Can I help you?' she said, all Queen's English.

The caller rang off.

'Any name?'

The WPC shook her head.

'Give it a minute to see if he phones again.'

They waited. The Beatles grinned down from the wall. There were no books; the only magazines were ones for young girls, with stories about horses and pop stars and princes. The adverts were for spot cream and an advice column: 'Dear Cathy and Claire. How do I kiss my boyfriend?'

If he and Helen had a girl, would she want to read things like this?

Eventually Breen picked up the other handset, the ivory-coloured one, and dialled the GPO to find if the operator had had time to discover the number, but the call had been too brief. 'Sorry, mate. Only got to the first couple of switches. Somewhere in Hampstead. You'll have to keep them on the phone for longer.'

The first appointment had been for 7.00. Breen sent Mint downstairs at five to and they waited for the bell to ring.

Mr J rang the doorbell one minute after the hour. Breen whistled down the stairs to Mint, who opened the front door.

Breen could hear them arguing as Mint marched the man upstairs.

'This is a mistake,' said the man. 'I protest.'

He was shocked by the state of the room he entered, and by the presence of another man.

'What's happening? Am I being arrested?'

The man had dark hair, with a high widow's peak and a thin moustache. He was old enough to be Lena Bobienski's father. There was a passable resemblance to Vincent Price.

'Name,' demanded Breen. He said he worked for Cunard, in their accounting department. He told his wife he played poker on Thursday nights.

At nine, the Chartered Surveyor appeared and tried to back out of the front door, but Mint was faster and managed to force the door shut. By the time Breen made it down the stairs, he had him in an armlock, head down on the doormat.

'Dirty bugger,' muttered the WPC, when they brought him back into the flat.

Between appointments, Breen read the newspaper he'd bought. At Headingley, Sobers had bowled Boycott out for 12. In Australia, Mick Jagger's girlfriend, Marianne Faithful, was seriously ill in hospital after a drug overdose. Jagger was there to make a film about a gangster called Ned Kelly. Breen remembered what John had said: *They love all that.*

At eleven one of the residents was just going out, so the new arrival managed to get into the building without ringing the bell and made it all the way up the stairs, Mint tiptoeing behind.

'Julie darling?' he announced himself as he reached the first landing.

The door to the flat was ajar; a man in a pale mackintosh entered the room, looking around. 'Joo-lie?' Mint closed it behind him.

'Police,' said Breen.

'Oh my,' said the man, eyes big.

'You're right. I'm not bloody Joo-lie,' said the WPC.

Bites-His-Nails turned out to be a second violin in the London Philharmonic. He had come from the Albert Hall where he'd been playing Beethoven and Britten and he promised he had never done anything like this ever before. Had he ever seen any other men at Miss Bobienski's flat? Did he have any idea who would have a grudge against her? Did he know anything about the whereabouts of Mrs Caulk? Like both the others, the answers were no.

The musician sat on Miss Bobienski's pink couch weeping into a handkerchief. The shock was genuine, but Breen was not sure if he was crying because he had been caught, or crying because Julie Teenager was dead. He was probably not sure himself.

Breen had asked the other men about the driver. Between sobs, the musician said, 'Yes. Julie said she could send a car to pick me up from the Albert Hall. There was an extra charge. I never used it, though.'

The others were the same. Yes, they had been offered the service but no, they had never used it.

The gold ring was on his finger, as Mrs Caulk had said it would be. 'Do you have children of your own?' asked the WPC.

He stopped crying and began to look scared. Mentally, Breen crossed him off the list, as he had done the last two men. Though it was useful, ruling these men out, Breen was learning little from them.

Helen lay on his bed, hands behind her head. She had woken when he had got home and come in to join him. She was sleeping badly. 'I feel like I'm going to explode,' she said.

Breen's hand was on her belly.

'Boom. Like an H-bomb.'

Helen was becoming a mother; he had never known his own mother; she had died when he was small. He moved his hand to the side, then back again.

'I can't feel it,' he said.

'There. Didn't you feel that? You must be able to. It was a George Best. It's so strange. Like an intruder, poking around inside me.'

She was naked, except for a pair of knickers. The thinness of her legs looked even more absurd now with her swelling belly. She seemed to find it easy, being undressed in front of him. Maybe it was growing up with a sister. Breen was never so at ease with himself, especially now with his scars.

He thought of the ring he had bought, lying in his sock drawer. He told himself that he was waiting for the right moment to give it to her, but he knew he was also putting off giving it to her in case she laughed at him. He wanted more than ever to make some declaration of faithfulness. He would devote himself to her and to the baby. 'This flat's going to feel small,' he said.

She picked his hand off her, and sat up on her elbows. 'So, found any murderers yet?'

'No. This time I think your hippie pal Felix may have been right about something though.'

'Not my pal. About her having some important customer?'

'So you overheard most of what he said then, in the cafe?'

'Yeah, I got the gist of it. That sort are always looking for conspiracies,' said Helen. 'They love them.'

'Like Elfie.'

'I know, I know. But maybe they're right, sometimes. Serious, though.' She shifted, trying to get comfortable. 'Your woman was a kinky prostitute. What are the odds some big shot was doing it with her. Bet you a million. You can imagine it, can't you? Some letch who likes little girls.'

'That's the thing,' said Breen.

'What if the murderer is someone clever enough to make it look like it's just a spur-of-the-moment thing? What about McPhail himself? God there.' She stood and started pacing around his small bedroom.

Breen smiled. 'Seriously? McPhail? I don't think so.'

'What's he like?'

'You know. Ex-army. Stiff back.'

'It's always the stuck-up ones who grab your arse when you're in the lift.'

Breen shook his head.

She crossed her arms in front of her breasts. 'Don't laugh, Cathal. I know you think it's just mucking around, but has anybody ever grabbed your arse in the lift?'

'Of course not.'

'Exactly.'

'This is stupid. It's not going to be McPhail.'

'And you've got no idea of who the policeman is?'

'No. Something else. We're not the only ones. Someone else has been searching her flat.'

'Oh my God. See what you mean. Conspiracy.'

'I'm not joking. I thought it was Scotland Yard, but I'm pretty sure it's not.'

'That's kind of weird. *The Man from U.N.C.L.E.*'

'I know.'

'You think it's whoever killed her? Trying to cover it all up?'

She sat back on the bed, pulling her knees up to her chin. He walked to his sock drawer and pulled it open. The ring box was there, amongst the neat rows of grey socks.

'I'm hungry,' she said, changing the subject, as if she was

bored of it already. And she got up, still naked, and went to the kitchen to put bread under the grill.

When she woke later in the night, he was sitting in the living room with the lights on, on a chair in the middle of the carpet. In a circle, he had arranged pieces of paper around him, labelled from A to L. There were two others. On one was the name Haas, on the other Mrs Caulk. He had put crosses through A, F and J. He had struck out Mr E too, the man who Mrs Caulk had called 'Leonard', who had arrived at the flat on the Friday following Bobienski's murder. On Ronald Russell's he had written 'alibi', but on Mrs Caulk's there was a large question mark.

Breen heard Helen pouring a glass of water in the kitchen, then she padded back out into the living room, squinting in the light before heading back to her room, saying nothing.

One of the men represented by an unknown letter was almost certainly a policeman.

He picked up the papers one by one, and examined them. Then he wrapped them into a large ball and dropped them into the waste basket. Mrs Caulk would turn up tomorrow. Things would start to make sense soon.

TWENTY

On Friday Miss Rasper put through a phone call from a man who wouldn't give his name. 'Very hush-hush.' She winked. She appeared to have forgiven him for yesterday's treatment of Mint.

The moment she connected him, the voice at the other end of the line said, 'I was right, wasn't I?'

It took him a couple of seconds to recognise who it was. 'It's Felix, isn't it? The man from *OZ*.'

'But I was, wasn't I? There was something going on.'

'Why do you think that?'

'Remember how I reckoned there was someone very special on Julie Teenager's list of clients? And I was bloody right. Because I just heard that someone went and slapped a D-Notice on the *Mirror* when they said they were going to print something about Julie Teenager having it off with a copper, only they had to pull it at the last minute.'

Breen pushed his chair back. 'You're wrong. It isn't a D-Notice. They wouldn't slap a D-Notice on something like that.

That's a request not to publish because of an issue of national security. We coppers can't just slap them out because of something we don't like people reading.'

'Just saying what I heard,' said the man on the other end of the phone. 'So there was something going on. Knew it, knew it, knew it. I have a scoop. Who is it?'

'Felix. I really wouldn't if I were you.'

'Why not?'

'Because there will be consequences if you do.' He looked over at Mint. Mint would end up taking the blame if anything did come out.

'Tsk. Are you threatening me?'

'No. Not me personally, but I'm sure Vice Squad will if I ask nicely.'

'Temper, temper. We're the alternative press. We're not part of the D-Notice system.'

'Is that what they're really saying? That it's a D-Notice?'

'Yes.'

'Just don't print anything yet, will you?'

'Why not?'

He couldn't say 'Because if you do, my earnest young colleague will almost certainly be sacked'. Instead, he said, 'Listen. If you hold on to the story, I'll try and find you something good you can publish, OK?'

'*OZ* getting into bed with the fuzz? Not likely. That's not how we work.'

'Just don't print it, please, Felix. I'll see what I can do.'

Breen put down the phone, pulled out his notebook and flicked through it.

When he called the number he'd found, a woman at the *Sunday Times* answered. 'Ronald Russell? I'll see if he's at his desk. Who shall I say is calling?'

'Detective Sergeant Cathal Breen.'

Russell talked quietly, as if he didn't want anyone to overhear his conversation. 'Well, did you speak to my brother-in-law?'

'He confirmed he was with you over that weekend. We're getting him to make a statement.'

'You didn't tell him . . . ?'

'I was discreet.'

'Thank you,' said Russell. 'I very much appreciate that. So I'm in the clear?'

'You have an alibi. I wouldn't say you were in the clear.'

'But—'

'Now I want you to help me,' said Breen. 'Do you have any colleagues who work at the *Mirror*?'

'Naturally.'

Naturally, thought Breen. 'They were going to print an article on Miss Bobienski's clients but they pulled it at the last minute. The Metropolitan Police asked them not to.'

'Thank Christ for that.'

'But I also heard a rumour that someone put a D-Notice on the story.'

'Why the hell . . . ?'

'Exactly. It doesn't seem that likely. But there are other things about this that aren't that likely either. Perhaps you could call your colleagues there and find out for me if it's true or not?'

'Sure. I'll ask around.'

'One more thing. Julie Teenager had a driver to pick up clients. Did you ever use him?'

'A driver? No. I never heard anything about that.' He lowered his voice. 'Why on earth would they put a D-Notice on a story about a prostitute?'

'That's what I want to know.'

The day was a slow one; the investigation was losing its focus. Ruling out suspects was not the same as finding the killer.

'So,' said Creamer, later, as Mint and Breen stood in his office, 'you had one principal witness, who's also a suspect, and somehow she's disappeared.'

'Yes,' said Breen. 'That's right.'

It was Friday. Creamer liked everything tidy before the weekend. He looked from one face to the other, hoping that someone would say something positive. 'I can't say I'm not disappointed,' he said in the end.

But she wasn't missing for much longer. At four Mint picked up the phone. Breen watched his eyes widen, his face whiten.

He scribbled something on a pad, put down the phone and said, 'They found Mrs Caulk.'

'Who's they?'

'River police. They just called.' He stared at his phone.

'Oh Christ. Dead?'

He nodded, looking horrified.

'Where?' Breen remembered how she had asked him for protection. At the time he had thought her overdramatic, self-centred.

'I spoke to her,' said Mint. 'And now she's dead.'

★

East India Docks had been the first of them to shut down. Just two years later, it looked like something left over from the war. Buddleias had sprouted in brick crevices of the warehouses. The windows were black. Moss was sprouting around the old shiny cobbles. Some of the cranes had been removed for scrap, but a few remained, rusting cables dangling in the air. The men who worked here, whose fathers had worked here, were on the dole now. No amount of strikes had saved them. They were planning on closing all the docks eventually and moving the ships downriver to Tilbury. The area which had been so full of noise and smell when he was a boy was silent. St Katharine's, Surrey Docks and London Dock had closed last year. The whole East End was dying. Already it seemed like a place of ghosts.

A group of men were peering over the end of one pier. Breen drove the car towards them. As he approached, a man in overalls ran over, waving his hands for them to halt.

They got out and Breen saw why they had been told to stop. Someone had rigged a cable from an old diesel winch that they'd managed to get working. But the winding-engine was thirty yards away and the steel rope lay in a long line between the engine and the drop into the water. The motor was running, but the cable was still slack. Breen followed it across the dockside to where it disappeared over the end of the pier.

Breen approached the edge, stepping over the line, Mint following behind. When he reached the end, he peered over the worn granite into the dock.

The tide was low, but rising. A small white police launch was bobbing a few feet off, an outsize searchlight on the cabin roof;

next to it a large barge with a crane on it. Leaning over the side of the boat, a policeman was looking into the thick muddy water.

As he watched, a frogman's black-clad head popped up above the water.

Someone shouted, 'Right. Stand clear. Away from the cable.'

A puff of black smoke blew up from the winch. The bystanders who had been gawping at the show moved back. A local copper ran towards Breen. 'Don't want to be there if the bloody thing snaps,' he said, grinning.

'What have they got?' asked Breen.

'Peugeot,' he said. 'They got the body out half an hour ago. Trying to haul the car up but the docks have silted up. Can't drag the bugger out of the mud. Tried twice already an' it slid back in. The silt clutches hold of it, see?'

'Did someone report it going in?'

The copper shook his head. 'Lad saw it at low tide. Just by chance. Apparently you could just make it out under the water.'

The cable tautened, groaned against the dockside, juddering. They could hear the other crane below too, straining at the wreck, sending up a fug of exhaust.

'It's coming,' someone shouted.

The angry tone of the winding engine seemed to calm a little suddenly as the load became lighter. The car must have been sucked from the mud.

'Shut it down, shut it down.'

The moment the operator put the winch into neutral, the cable ran out a little way.

'Whoa!'

Cautiously, Breen approached the edge of the dockside again.

Heated by the afternoon sun, the air was suddenly pungent with the sewerish stench of the dock bottom. The black Peugeot was almost entirely out of the mud, water cascading in arcs around it from cracks between the doors and boot and the bodywork and the driver's open door. The bonnet remained mostly underwater, but what was visible was covered in thick greeny-brown silt.

It was an old model. Below, one of the men wiped the number plate clean with the side of his hand. Breen noted the registration.

'Where was the woman? In the boot?'

'No. Behind the wheel. She must have driven it in there.'

'Suicide, I suppose,' said Mint.

When he heard she was dead, he had assumed someone had killed her. Was it better if it was suicide? He wouldn't feel so responsible for her death, at least. Breen turned to the local constable. 'Where is she?'

'Pathologist took the body away about half an hour ago.'

'It was her then, do you think?' Mint said, uncertainly. 'Killed Miss Bobienski. I mean, you don't drive off the end of a dock on purpose, do you? Guilty conscience?'

The crane on the barge revved again. They were trying to lift the car onto the rusting hulk. The vehicle swung dangerously in the air, creating eddies in the water around it and clanging dully against the barge's side.

On Fridays, it had become part of their routine to go to the Electric Cinema Club in Portobello: he and Helen, Elfie and sometimes John Carmichael too. The Imperial Cinema, where the club took place, was on the wrong side of London, but they showed unusual films; there was nothing like it in the East End. Besides, Amy got them cheap tickets; it was where she worked.

Today in particular, Breen hadn't felt like going. It had been a long week; he felt exhausted. And now his best witness, Florence Caulk, was dead and what if that was his fault?

But Helen felt cooped up at the flat. She looked forward to their one night out. And Mint was taking the shift at Harewood Avenue with a WPC, waiting for Mr B, Mr C and Mr K, who would presumably arrive for the appointments they had booked with Julie Teenager. Breen would rather be there than here and watching a Marx Brothers double bill.

Carmichael had been late. They had taken their seats without him; as Harpo Marx repeatedly pickpocketed a five-dollar note from a policeman, Carmichael finally arrived, squeezing himself down the row until he found a spare seat next to Elfie. Elfie and Helen were giggling. 'God,' said Helen. 'I'm going to wee myself.' Breen wasn't finding any of it funny. Neither was Amy.

'What's wrong with her?' whispered Helen. Now Chico was taking money from Groucho; Breen found it tiresome and childish.

'What do you mean, what's wrong?'

'Amy. The way she's been glaring at John ever since he got here.'

Breen glanced sideways. Amy was sitting on the far side of the aisle. To him, it was hard to say whether she was angry, or just engrossed in the plot.

Afterwards as they waited for a taxi on the street outside, Helen said, 'You didn't laugh once, either, misery man.'

He didn't want to tell her about the case; about McPhail, about the D-Notice, about Florence Caulk. She'd question him, ask him about minute details, when he was still trying to get it all straight in his own head.

'I couldn't concentrate,' he said. 'I've got too much going on. Something I want to ask you, John. I think my prostitute had a driver. Know how I'd track him down?'

'You tried Vice?'

'I was just wondering if you had any ideas.'

'Work, work, work,' complained Elfie.

John shook his head, his arm around Amy, looking embarrassed, uncomfortable. He was so large; she so small next to him. It was clear they had been arguing about something, but what? As the taxi pulled away, Breen looked back and saw Amy wriggling her shoulders and moving away so that John's arm hung there in the air for a second.

'Maybe she's just fed up with him being so unreliable all the time,' Helen said.

It had been a surprise that Amy, young, pretty and hip, had ever gone out with John, a copper, in the first place; but since John and she had started their unlikely romance, Amy had become close to Helen and Elfie. The three of them got on well together.

'We don't argue like that, do we?'

'We?' said Helen.

'Yes. You and me.'

'Only because you're impossible to have a decent argument with.'

Once they had driven a quarter of a mile, Helen was asleep

210

on his shoulder so he had to wake her when the car reached Harewood Avenue.

He handed her and Elfie thirty bob for the fare home.

Helen turned away, pulling her coat tight. 'I'm going to sleep upstairs at Elfie's. That way you won't wake me up when you come in.'

Breen watched the taxi drive away, then rang the bell. Mint came down and opened the door.

'Where's the woman constable?'

'I said she should go home. Didn't seem necessary for both of us to stay on. Nothing happened, the last hour.'

'Did you get them?'

'Only two of them here, but three more on the phone.'

'Good.'

Upstairs, the two punters were both sitting on the same pink sofa, looking miserable. The older of the two held a blue teddy bear he had presumably brought as a present. 'You can't just hold us here. We've done nothing wrong.'

'You've questioned them?'

'Yes. This is Mr C. He is a schoolteacher.' The younger man looked up, ashamed. 'A girls' private school. Do you think we should tell the school?'

Mr C groaned.

'And the other one is Mr K, I take it?' Because of the bear.

'His name's Hardy. He runs a frozen food business.'

'Anything else useful from either of them?'

'Not really, Sarge.'

It was too much to hope that one of them would be the policeman.

'I've got both their addresses. I haven't charged them with anything.'

'It would be a bit difficult, Mint. They haven't committed any offence.'

'Something interesting, though. This gentleman –' he pointed at the schoolteacher – 'was picked up by a car.'

'Oh yes?'

'Only it wasn't a man driving it. It was a woman.'

Breen turned to the man. 'What did she look like?'

'Early twenties. Dark hair, done up on top. A bit Jean Shrimpton, you know?'

'Did she have a name?'

The man shook his head.

'What sort of car?'

'A Cortina. One of the new ones. Car radio and everything.'

'What about a number?'

'Julie's woman dealt with all that.'

Julie's woman: Florence Caulk. Breen held the door open for them both to leave. 'We'll need to get them to account for their movements since Monday too. What about Mr B?'

'Didn't show up, Sarge. Didn't call either.'

'Interesting.' The Slavic man who brought wine.

The phone trace had eliminated two more, both of whom gave names that matched their directory entries and addresses and who could be interviewed further on Monday.

'What jobs did they do?'

'One's the car dealer.'

'Mr L?'

'Yes. And the other's a civil servant. After some discussion he admitted to being the one who favoured corporal punishment, referred to by Mrs Caulk as "Spanky", I believe.'

'Civil servant? Which department?'

'Fisheries.'

Breen had been hoping it would have been something important, like Defence, something that would account for other people being interested in Miss Bobienski – whoever they were. He walked down the stairs into the night. After such a bad day, a good night perhaps, but still no Mr B. And no policeman.

On Saturday morning Breen was in the bath, relaxing with a cigarette, when Helen knocked on the door.

'Let me in,' she said.

'I'm in the bath. I'm naked.'

'I would hope so.'

So he got up, put a towel around him, wrapping it under his armpits so it covered the scars on his belly, and opened the door.

'Get back in the bath. I'll wash your back.'

Naked again, he got into the water, taking a flannel from the rack that lay across the bath and covering his penis.

She was looking at his stomach though. 'Poor Cathal. Is it still sore?' she asked.

He crossed his arms over his belly.

'No. Just itches sometimes.'

'You got in late. I heard you come in.'

'You were upstairs.'

'I couldn't sleep. Elfie snores. I heard you shut the front door.'

'I walked back from Harewood Avenue. Everything's going round in my head. I knew I wouldn't sleep unless I was tired.'

'It must have been gone three you got in. What's wrong?'

'What do you mean?'

'I can tell. You're a million miles away.'

'The prostitute's maid is dead.'

'Oh. How?'

'Looks like suicide. She drove a car into the docks down at Limehouse.'

'Christ. So you think it was her that killed Julie Teenager?'

'I don't know. Wellington said he thought it was a man.'

'He couldn't imagine a woman doing anything other than ironing.'

Breen was unsettled by the death of Florence Caulk and by the uncertainty of whatever it was that McPhail was keeping from him. Large, obscure; a deep disconcerting rumble that wouldn't go away.

Helen sat on the edge of the bath and pushed his arms aside, then moved her hands over his stomach. There was tenderness in Helen's touch, but he just felt awkward, lying there in the soapy, cooling water. There were patches of his skin where, when she ran her fingers over it, he could feel nothing at all.

Saturday was normally a day off, but he caught the bus into town, sitting alongside the shoppers going up to Oxford Street. The papers said the Americans would send a rocket to the moon next week; all the windows on Breen's bus were jammed tight shut and the man crammed into the seat next to him was loudly calling the Irish 'bloody savages'.

When Breen reached his desk there was a note tucked into the cylinder of his typewriter. Breen pulled it out and read it.

Breen read it: 'Mr Russell. Sun. Times. Said thinks you were right about D-Notice.'

Breen looked around to find the constable who had taken the message, but the office was deserted.

That night he sat with a WPC in Julie Teenager's flat, but there was only one call from a first-timer who had found Julie Teenager's advert in an old copy of *Private Eye*. There were no further visitors either.

Breen looked at the list in his notebook. After three days at the flat, only three men remained from Mrs Caulk's list: B, G and I. One of them was a copper; one was a murderer. Maybe one was a copper and a murderer.

TWENTY-ONE

On Sunday afternoon, front door open to keep the flat cool, Breen heard a man shouting in the cul-de-sac.

He walked up the steps to find Klaus, standing at the upstairs front door with a cardboard box full of albums in his arms.

'I don't know where they are,' said Elfie, arms crossed above her bump.

'How can I drive it if I don't have the keys?' He flicked his hair from his eyes. 'They were on the hook in the hallway. They're not there now.' He was tall, fair-haired and wore his flowery shirts open at the collar.

'How do you know? You haven't been here all week. You've been fucking that woman.'

Klaus spotted him hovering on the basement steps.

'Cathal. Come up here. She's stolen the bloody keys to the Magnette,' said Klaus. Klaus's vintage black car sat taking up room in the small cobbled courtyard at the front of their house. 'Tell her I'll call the police if she doesn't give them back.'

'That's my Pentangle album,' said Elfie. 'I bought that with my own money.'

'I'll give it to you if you give me my keys.'

'I don't have your precious keys.'

'What the hell do you think you are doing, Klaus?' demanded Breen.

'I just want to be able to drive my car. Is that too much to ask?'

'She's carrying your baby.'

Other neighbours opened their doors a crack to listen.

'You're a policeman. She's stolen my keys. You should do something.'

'I didn't steal your bloody keys,' protested Elfie.

Because he didn't have the car to carry them in, Klaus left the records in the box by the front door. When he'd gone, Helen went upstairs and sat with Elfie a while as she cried.

On Sunday night, Breen slept badly.

He dreamed he was in a chair, his arms bound tightly. Opposite him, there was a woman dying whom he couldn't reach. When he looked again he saw the woman was pregnant. With a shock, he realised that the dream wasn't right. It wasn't supposed to be Helen there dying. That wasn't the way it had happened. He tried rocking the chair back and forwards to break free, but he was trapped, unable to move. He pushed harder and harder.

Helen woke him, shaking him gently.

'I'll make a mint tea,' she said, quietly.

'You're alive,' he said, damp with sweat.

'I would hope. Do you want to tell me about it?'

'Not really.'

'Poor boy.' Her hand on his forehead.

When he finally closed his eyes again, he slept dreamlessly and missed his alarm clock ringing. Monday morning and he felt sluggish. Mint arrived when he was still shaving.

Helen, dressed only in a nylon dressing gown, invited him in. 'He's late,' she said.

Mint sat awkwardly on the edge of the armchair, drinking coffee.

From the bathroom, Breen could hear them talking. 'Is it too strong?' Helen said. 'Cathal likes it like that. I think it's like drain cleaner.'

'No, it's fine.' A pause. 'When's it due?'

'End of August.'

Breen towelled the shaving foam off his face. 'Soon, then?' Mint was saying.

'I know. Dead scary.'

K Division had towed the Peugeot to a police warehouse in Stepney. Breen drove there, Mint giving directions from a map.

'If she committed suicide, that would be that, wouldn't it?' said Mint.

'Maybe. It's not an admission of guilt, but it would be close.'

'Where did she get the car from?'

'They haven't traced it yet.'

'I just didn't expect it to be her. She seemed, you know, nice, considering.'

'Nice can kill too,' said Breen.

218

The car was sitting in the middle of the warehouse floor, the wooden doors pulled open to let the light in. Yesterday's stink of mud and rot had followed the vehicle.

A few feet away was a trestle table on which they'd placed several items. The car's jack. A soggy newspaper. The victim's shoes and a small brown leather suitcase, lying open, its contents in an untidy pile next to it.

Breen walked over to the table. The clothes that had been in the suitcase were still damp; they smelt musty. There was a dress, a couple of blouses, and several cardigans.

'Like she was going away somewhere,' said Mint.

The local CID officer was called Hope. He was in his forties, dressed in shirtsleeves and tie, a hearty, loud-voiced man whose belly strained over his belt, pushing at his buttons.

'So she was running away?' suggested Mint.

'Perhaps. But what kind of woman packs no underwear?' asked Breen.

Mint leaned forward and started rummaging through the clothes, a puzzled look on his face. Breen left the table and walked towards the car. It was an old Peugeot 203. The bonnet and all four doors were open.

Hope asked, 'Did you get a copy of the preliminary report on the body?'

'Not yet,' said Breen.

'Blow to the head,' he announced, pointing at the front of his own skull and mouthing the word: 'Bang. I'll show you.' And he walked back to the rear of the building where an unmarked police car was parked, opened the door and pulled out a slim, pale brown folder.

In it there was a large black-and-white photograph of the victim's face. Florence Caulk lay on a white slab. One eye was slightly open. She looked much older dead, wet hair flattened against her skull. Her nose was pushed to one side and blood clogged a nostril. Below the hair, across her forehead, was a thick dark bruise.

'Hit her head on the dashboard?'

'She drowned, they reckon. Water in her lungs.'

'But the blow to the head knocked her out . . . and then . . .'

'Could have,' said Hope. 'On the other hand, it wasn't her driving.'

Breen looked up from the photo. 'But I thought her body had been found in the driver's seat?'

'It was.'

Breen frowned. 'And there was no indication that anyone else had been in the car when it went over?'

The detective grinned. 'Nope. And the vehicle was in gear. Looks like the engine had been running when she hit the water. But I doubt she was driving.'

'Why not?'

'Look at the driver's seat.'

Breen put his head into the car. The cracked leather of the seat was still wet. 'What?'

Hope was enjoying himself. 'Go on. Don't you see it?'

Breen looked harder. There was a layer of brown silt on the carpeted floor of the vehicle. There were no signs of any foot-prints there – but then there wouldn't be, would there? The thin mud would have accumulated after she had died.

'I don't understand.'

'Call yourself a detective?'

Taking a step back, Breen examined the car again. He tried to imagine Mrs Caulk sitting behind the wheel. He got out a notebook and did a loose sketch, while the other copper watched him, still smiling.

And then, Breen nodded.

'You got it now?'

He turned to Hope and said, 'When they got her body out of the car, did they have to move the seat back?'

The detective clapped his hands. 'You're getting there.' He grinned delightedly.

'What does he mean?' asked Mint.

'The driver's seat is pushed back as far as it can go.'

'Give the man a medal,' called Hope.

'She couldn't have been driving.'

'That's right. Whoever put her there stuck her in the driver's seat but forgot to change the position. Bet you.'

Breen nodded.

Hope grinned back. 'Look at this, too. This was in the car. In the back seat.' He walked back to the table and lifted a small, muddy piece of 2 × 1 lumber, only about six inches long, up off the trestle table. 'I reckon that was wedged against the accelerator, not so hard as so it's stuck there. Release the clutch and away the car goes. And underwater, the wood floats up and away.'

'Very good. Very clever.'

'Would you have got there on your own?' said the man, rubbing his hands.

'I'm not so sure I would,' said Breen. 'Nice.'

221

'It's what we do, isn't it?'

Mint said what Breen was thinking. 'A blow to the head, then an attempt to conceal the body,' said Mint.

'Yes.'

'Same as Miss Bobienski.'

'Exactly.' For all his awkwardness, he was bright.

'My God.'

'Any idea what she was hit with?'

'Pathologist's report's in tomorrow.' Hope stood there, so pleased with himself.

'She was our key witness in another murder case. She asked me to protect her,' he said. He looked at the photo, into the dead woman's face.

Hope's smile vanished. 'Oh.'

'I didn't take her seriously.' Breen looked away from the picture he was holding. 'I didn't think she'd be in any danger.'

'And you were wrong,' said Hope.

'Yes.'

'That will hurt.'

The other man understood; he did the same job. There were no unwelcome platitudes, no talk of how he wasn't to know. 'I made a mistake.'

'Apparently so.'

In Breen's experience, most murders were almost accidental. The killers rarely intended to kill. Things got out of control. But a person who kills twice knows exactly what they are doing. Breen offered the picture back to Hope, who shook his head.

'I got more.'

Breen tucked it into his briefcase then opened his notebook

to the pages where he had copied down the list of names from the office wall. He added a small 'X' on Haas the caretaker's sheet and a note: 'Killer is a driver? Haas cannot drive.' Unless they were dealing with more than one murderer, whoever had killed Florence Caulk had been able to handle a car. They could cross Mrs Caulk off the list too. Breen pulled out his packet of ten and offered one to Hope as a thank-you. Mint didn't smoke, but he stood with them as they lit their cigarettes in silence, and all three of them looked at the car while bluebottles zigzagged around the room.

At eleven he had a meeting at New Scotland Yard with Vice Squad to see if they could help Breen discover who the mystery driver was.

A sergeant, who must have been five years younger than Breen and who had hair that was long at the back and short at the sides, took him to an office where chairs were ranged around a small table and turned one round to sit on, legs either side of its back.

'Shoot,' he said. His name was Phipps.

'Shoot?'

'Tell us what you want,' said Phipps impatiently. 'It's the Bobienski case, isn't it?'

'You hadn't come across her?'

'Heard of her, yup, pretty sure, but we can't be running round after every girl on the game.'

'Actually, I thought that was your job.'

The man laughed. 'And yours is to wrap up every murder that ever happened. Good luck with that, mate.'

Irritated, Breen hefted his briefcase onto the table and flipped the catches. He yanked two photos out and held one so close to Phipps's face that the man had to jerk his head back.

'Look at it,' Breen demanded.

'Easy, mate,' Phipps said, uneasily. 'No need to get shirty. What are you doing?'

'This woman was murdered last week. Beaten and then left to drown.'

'All right. All right. I get your point.'

'This one.' He swapped the photos. 'She was killed the week before.'

'Oh fuck,' said the man, starting at the eyeless face.

'The first woman was the maid for this prostitute who was called Lena Bobienski. Also known as Julie Teenager. They used a female driver to bring clients to their flat. I need to find out who that woman was.'

'Righto. Calm down. That driver. Was that for outcalls?'

Breen must have looked blank.

'For when she had to go somewhere on the job? Or was it bringing customers?'

'I'm not sure. All I know is that there was a driver who was regularly outside the premises. She was a woman with longish dark hair.'

'Make of car?'

'Black Cortina.'

'No firm involved?'

'Firm' as in 'gang'. 'Not as far as I know.'

Phipps sucked in his teeth. 'Not easy, in that case,' he said.

'Don't you keep a file?'

The man shook his head. 'With us lot, it's all in here,' he said, and he tapped the side of his skull.

'You don't keep records of this sort of thing?'

'No, mate. Paperwork, eh? Who needs it? Besides, the situation changes all the time. Guys move. Girls get put out of business. We'd have our job cut out keeping track. But I'll ask around. Now she's dead, there'll be someone looking for a spot of work, I dare say. Leave it with me. I'll do my best. Swear to God.'

Breen took the shiny metal lift down to the ground floor certain that he would hear nothing from Phipps again. A Chief Superintendent was talking about what was going on in Northern Ireland. 'The RUC got the crap beaten out of them, I gather. Petrol bombs. Flaming tyres. On the plus side, it means we're all going to get some shiny new equipment, bet you.'

He was just leaving the grey office building when he heard a woman calling his name. 'Sergeant Breen?'

He looked around. It took him a second to realise that one of the secretaries from the front desk, a pretty young woman with long straw-coloured hair with dark roots, was beckoning him. 'Sergeant Breen?'

'Yes.'

'I have a call for you.' Across the reception desk she offered him a modern-looking handset, an L-shape of pale cream plastic. Who would know he was here?

'Who is it?'

'I asked, but he wouldn't give his name. He said it was important.'

Breen put the phone to his ear.

'You wanted to speak to me.'

Breen didn't recognise the voice. 'You'll have to excuse me. Who are you?'

'And you'll have to excuse me for not telling you. Your Superintendent said you were keen to know who had searched Lena Bobienski's flat. I think you would like to meet us.'

'Us?'

'The Royal Academy Summer Exhibition. I have not been, this year. Have you? You're an art lover, I believe.'

It was, he realised, a statement intended say more about the caller than it was about Breen, to make him feel uncomfortable. 'How do you know that?' Breen asked.

'If you've been before we could try something else, but the Academy is convenient. Tomorrow morning? Say eleven o'clock?' The voice was self-confident, but oddly classless, neither BBC nor TUC.

'How will I know you?'

'Come to the Reynolds Room, I'm sure you know it. It's on the first floor. I know what you look like. I'll introduce myself there.'

'What's your name?'

But the man had ended the call.

Breen stood at the reception desk looking at the handset as the disconnected tone sang out from it.

'Finished?' The pretty young woman smiled at him and he blinked and handed back the telephone.

One thing he now knew: McPhail was under orders from someone else, someone more powerful. Tomorrow he would find out who. He should be pleased. But the dank musty smell of Florence Caulk's old clothes, hastily stuffed into a suitcase by someone who wanted to make it look like she was running away, lingered in his nostrils.

He walked outside the building, pacing the pavement as the triangular sign that said 'New Scotland Yard' juddered slowly round and round, breathing in and out, but the rotting stink of Thames mud wouldn't leave him.

Amy had come round earlier that day with her Super 8 camera to film Helen and Elfie.

'We were both naked,' said Elfie. 'We had to stand there while she walked round filming us.'

Helen grimaced. 'I felt like Godzilla, King of the Monsters.'

'Beautiful monster,' said Elfie.

'Ugly whale,' said Helen

'No. You were gorgeous monsters,' Amy said. 'Making babies inside you. That's so weird. Isn't it? What if I filmed you when you were having the babies too?'

'Not on your bloody life,' said Helen.

The three girls, Helen, Elfie and Amy, all brought chairs out into the cul-de-sac and sat there laughing in the evening heat.

'Have you spoken to John at all?' asked Amy when Breen pulled up a chair to join them.

'Last time I saw him was Friday. With you, at the cinema,' said Breen.

'We arrange to meet up and then he never shows. And then he's all apologetic about it. And then it happens again. I've just had enough.'

'He probably has work to do.'

'Like last Tuesday. He was supposed to go out with me. He

227

was going to take me for a Chinese. Helen said he was in the pub getting drunk with you.'

'I wasn't drunk,' said Breen.

'You were. You came home reeking. Fell asleep at nine.'

'I think he's getting ready to chuck me,' Amy said. 'It makes me so angry. I don't care if he chucks me anyway.'

'Don't be an idiot. He's mad about you,' said Breen.

'All he ever bloody talks about,' said Helen.

'He never wants to see me. Always not turning up. Saying he's working. It's like he's avoiding me.'

Nobody mentioned Klaus.

'Bloody coppers, eh?' Helen smiled.

'That's daft. He spent so long trying to persuade you to go out with him.'

'I never really wanted a boyfriend in the first place. Ties you down,' said Amy. 'He was the one who kept on at me. I don't even want to talk about him any more. Anyone want to go and see The Soft Machine on Friday? After the cinema.'

Helen wrinkled her nose; Breen took that to mean that she didn't like them much.

'I'll come,' said Elfie. 'Come on, Hel, you need to get out.'

'I'm too tired,' she said. 'I'm tired all the time now.'

Nobody asked if Breen wanted to come; they all assumed he wouldn't want to.

Elfie had cooked a pot roast with chunks of bacon in it.

'Nice, actually,' said Breen. They were sitting in her kitchen.

'Don't sound surprised,' said Helen. 'It's rude.'

They were drinking cider. Elfie had put half a flagon in the casserole, but saved some for a glass with the meal. Amy had had most of it and was a little drunk.

'I know he's your best mate. I just think he's a bastard,' she was saying.

'So I was talking to my friend and she said Brian Jones wasn't murdered in the pool at all,' said Elfie, changing the subject.

'Oh for God's sake,' said Breen.

'I heard that too,' said Amy.

'Seriously?'

'No. Listen. He was killed in the car crash with Tara Browne three years ago.'

'Who's Tara Browne?'

Helen burst out laughing, spraying the table in front of him. 'Sorry.'

'It's not a joke,' said Elfie.

'That Guinness heir who killed himself when he went through a red light in his Lotus in Kensington. You know, The Beatles wrote that song about him,' said Helen. 'Matter of fact, that's the most ridiculous thing I've ever heard, Elfie.'

Elfie was at the head of the table, face reddening. 'No. Seriously. Think about it. After that they replaced him, but they couldn't keep up the fiction. They were being blackmailed by his double so they had to kill him.'

'Is there any more cider?' asked Amy.

Helen was still giggling.

Breen wasn't. 'What's wrong, Cathal?'

'A witness in my case turned up dead,' he said. 'Today I heard she was murdered. The same way as the prostitute. It was my fault, I think. She wanted protection but I never took her seriously.'

Helen stopped laughing. Elfie looked down at the table. In the last few weeks it had been good, coming up here. They were friends. It was carefree and simple; after everything he and Helen had been through in recent months it was good to talk, drink and eat together. But there was a sadness lurking behind everything and that frivolity was so easy to puncture.

Afterwards, Breen stood at the sink, doing the washing-up.

Helen put down the drying-up cloth. 'Oh, Cathal,' she said, and held out her hand towards him. 'I'm sorry.'

But it wasn't just the death of Mrs Caulk. It was listening to Elfie's well-meaning nonsense about conspiracies, when he was beginning to feel like he himself was falling into something dark and bottomless. In the morning he would find out exactly what.

TWENTY-TWO

In the end, there was no time to look at the paintings from the Summer Exhibition.

Burlington House, once a Palladian mansion, now dark with London soot, was set back from the street, as if trying to keep its distance from the commerce of Piccadilly.

Breen climbed the immense staircase; the moment he arrived at the Reynolds Room, an unassuming young man in a dun suit, too fat for his age, approached him.

He was the only other person in the room. 'They have a cafeteria here,' he said. 'The coffee's not bad.'

So they knew he liked coffee too. 'MI6?' said Breen, craning his neck past the man at a painting of a garden from a hotter climate than this. 'Walked across the park from your offices, did you?' The security service's HQ was supposed to be somewhere opposite St James's station.

The man's face was shiny, as if the skin on it were a little too tight. 'People aren't supposed to know where we are. Though I suppose everyone does.'

The cafe was almost empty. There was no one to overhear them.

'No, no, no. My treat,' said the man, putting Breen's coffee on the tray next to his pot of tea. 'So. I appreciated you wanting to communicate, and that the situation must be extremely frustrating for you. I can brief you on what I know. OK?'

'You know my name,' said Breen. 'What's yours?'

'Sand,' said the young man, smiling.

'Though, like Lena Bobienski's customers, that's probably not your name at all.'

'For different reasons, I assure you.'

They found a small table at the back of the room. The man called Sand chose one as far as he could from the only other occupant, an elderly woman with a thinning fox fur, though she didn't look much like a spy to Breen.

'So,' said Sand. 'Obviously my job is to let you know what you need to, while keeping you as much in the dark about everything else. It's just the way things are, I'm afraid.'

'So I can assume that Lena Bobienski was mixed up in espionage?'

'One thing at a time; first, a bit of procedure. I will need you to sign this before we go any further.' He lifted an American-style briefcase, flipped open twin catches, and pulled out a single piece of paper. From what Breen could see, it had been the only thing in the case. He handed it to Breen.

It was a simple statement:

> I, Sergeant Cathal Breen of the Metropolitan Police Force (D
> Division) agree to abide by the restrictions of the Official Secrets
> Act 1920 (10 & 11 Geo 5 c 75).

He looked up. Sand pulled out a fountain pen. 'You may not discuss any of this with your colleagues, you understand? Sign and date please.'

'Quaint,' said Breen.

'Maybe. But personally, I take such things very seriously, and as a policeman I would hope you would, too.'

Breen took his pen and marked the document, then handed it back. 'I'm sure plenty of your colleagues have signed it too. How seriously did they take it?'

Sand put the lid back on the pen and replaced it in his jacket pocket. 'One of the difficulties we face is that many people think all this a daft game. But our freedom in the West depends on it. Intelligence is a delicate network of truths, half-truths and lies. The power in the network is in discovering precisely how much other people know, or think they know. That way you can know where they are in the web of relationships, ergo, you have power over the network itself. As much as anything –' he held up the sheet – 'this is a record of exactly how much you know.'

'Or think I know.'

'Well put,' smiled Sand. 'I will only give you information if I can rely on you to tell no one else about it. I am taking a calculated risk here. I'll be honest. My colleagues have a very low opinion of the Metropolitan Police. If you think our reputation is poor . . .'

Breen had no choice. 'OK. You have my word. This is between the two of us.'

Sand seemed to be scrutinising Breen. 'Don't even tell that girlfriend of yours, Miss Tozer.'

Another reminder of their power. They had investigated him, had been observing him, waited to see if they felt they could trust him. 'Like I said,' Breen repeated, 'between the two of us.'

Sand looked at him a little bit more, as if weighing him up, then spoke. 'You asked about Lena Bobienski. What do you know about her?'

'I know she was a prostitute. I know she was Polish. Her father went back to Poland after the war but disappeared into a Soviet gulag.'

'That's what we know too. She remained here because she was ill. The rest of her family went home.'

'You know what happened to her father?'

'No. Millions disappeared during that time. We are still trying to build a picture of what took place in the gulags, but it appears that his story was not an exceptional one. I would be astonished if he had not died there.'

'So Lena was a spy? For you?'

'One thing at a time,' said Sand. 'According to your superior officer, McPhail, you wished to know which department searched her apartment. We are willing to discuss that. It was, as I'm sure you've guessed by now, our operatives. I would guess you also wish to know whether anything we discovered there might help you in your investigation into who murdered her? The answer is, sadly, no. We did not. We found, I assume, pretty much what you found. I'll admit, we had been hoping for more. Her flat was full of the idiosyncratic tools of her trade as a prostitute, but very few other items of interest. So we couldn't confirm that she was a spy. Or rule it out.'

'Although, presumably, you weren't looking for evidence of who killed her. You were looking for something else.'

A brief hesitation. 'Actually, yes. I suppose we weren't looking for quite the same thing as you. There is a bias involved in any observation. But we were pretty thorough.'

'I saw. Why were you interested in her? What were you looking for?'

'That is complicated.'

'By what?'

'We were keen to find a list of her clients or contacts. Or any information along those lines. Because we were also looking for indications that there may have been more to Miss Bobienski than met the eye.'

'That she was an agent?'

'Possibly. We were looking for equipment that she might have used to communicate with handlers, or cyphers, code books. The usual paraphernalia.'

Breen picked up his coffee and sipped it. It was insipid.

'Did you find any?'

'We don't think so.' He didn't elaborate.

'What made you think she was a spy?'

'A little bird told us.'

Breen looked at him for a while, hoping he would say more, but he didn't.

'There was a loose floorboard in her bedroom where she may have hidden something. Did you find anything there?'

'Again. Possibly. We found some old letters. And a book which may have been used as a crude cypher. Unlikely, but we're not really sure. We're analysing it. You interviewed her maid, I believe. Did you ask her about it?'

Breen paused, looked at him. He didn't appear to know that Florence Caulk was dead.

'No.' Breen raised the cup again and forced himself to drink some coffee, to give him time to think. If Sand knew they had spoken with the maid, somebody, presumably McPhail, was keeping them briefed about the investigation but he was clearly a day or two behind. *The power in the network is in discovering precisely how much other people know, or think they know.*

'One of the clients was possibly Russian,' Breen said. 'We have some information about him. At the moment, he is one of our chief suspects.'

Mrs Caulk had called Mr B, the gentleman who brought wine, 'Slavic', and given that Breen was sitting here opposite a member of MI6, it was worth a guess that he had been a Soviet, or from one of the Eastern Bloc countries.

Interrogation technique was one skill that they probably shared, at least. Breen registered the slightest sideways flicker of his eyes.

'Yes,' said Sand. 'He was actually the reason why we were interested in Miss Bobienski.'

'So he was the little bird?'

Pause. 'Yes. Not that he knew he was.'

'But you weren't going to tell me that?'

Sand looked uncomfortable. 'As you appear to know already, there is no harm, I suppose.'

'And he is . . . ?'

'I can't give too many details, but interestingly we've been employing some modern techniques to identify foreign agents. Instead of waiting for material to drop from the sky by chance, we've been analysing the movements of alien nationals to see if they tell us anything. It's been surprisingly successful. As a result, we recently identified a number of what we believed were dead drops in London.' He stopped. 'You know what a dead drop is?'

'Of course not,' said Breen. 'I'm a humble copper.'

Sand smiled. 'They're places where agents can pass information to their handlers without even meeting them. Or even knowing who they are. If we were right, then this was a golden opportunity for us, so we posted surveillance at every location. And within two days, tra-la, your man turned up at one of our locations, appeared to check it for a drop, and then left. Up until then, we hadn't been aware of him.'

'The Russian? He is KGB?'

'Not entirely sure yet. That or GRU. The Soviet Intelligence Directorate. We'd not had our eyes on him before. Unfortunately, he was the only person who we ever saw using this particular dead drop. We maintained surveillance for over a month, which was an enormous strain on our manpower, but nothing else happened.'

A woman in a pinny came to wipe the tables. Sand raised his voice to say, 'I didn't think so much of the watercolours this year,' as she emptied their ashtray.

When she'd passed on to the next table and was sufficiently out of earshot, Breen said, 'You were wrong? About the sites being dead drops?'

'No. Almost as soon as we learned of the dead drops, they changed all the locations. Which is fairly routine, for security reasons. But at least we spotted the agent. We could have had him expelled, and that would have been that. But we decided not to do anything about it; we want to use him to help us find the new drops. He's the perfect spy. One who's not very good, but is arrogant enough to think that he is. We placed him under round-the-clock observation instead. So far he has done nothing out of the ordinary. He is not a particular danger. His tradecraft is sloppy, which makes him easy to follow. He's a drunk and a womaniser. He visits prostitutes. Miss Bobienski is not the only one.'

Breen considered for a while. 'What if Lena Bobienski's death is connected to all this? What if he feared exposure and panicked?'

'Voice down,' said Sand evenly. Breen looked around, realising he must have been raising his voice as the idea occurred to him, but nobody seemed to be paying them any particular attention.

'What if he killed her because . . . well, maybe he thought she might expose him?'

'Nice theory. But why would she do that?'

'I'm not sure. I'm just thinking aloud . . . So that's why you requested the police to remove patrols from Harewood Avenue. Because you didn't want some inquisitive bobby arresting your man.'

'Correct. Or spotting our own men, for that matter, and wondering why they were there.'

'He has a regular appointment on Fridays. Why didn't you just leave it to that one day?'

'The thing is, he's turned up on several other days and times. He seems to have known her rather more . . . closely than her other customers.'

Breen looked into Sand's grey eyes. 'So they might have been working together? Was he there on Thursday – Thursday the third?'

'The night you believe Miss Bobienski was killed?'

'Yes.'

Sand looked down. 'Well. Thursday is difficult. Unfortunately our operatives lost him that night. Unusually. The man who was following him at that point has been reprimanded, but it does happen, occasionally.'

'Lost him?'

'It's not that easy, you know, following a man in London.'

'Could he have deliberately given your man the slip?'

'Yes. He could. And that's when you think the murder happened?'

'Yes. Thursday evening.'

'We were out of contact for about an hour. He was at Victoria at around ten, but we lost him at the bus stop until about an hour later, when he was spotted drinking in one of his favourite watering holes. One of those decadent night spots where all the fabulous people go,' he said drily.

'It doesn't sound like he's particularly discreet.'

'Not exactly the picture of Stakhanovite rectitude, no. Our man watched him getting drunk there until he was poured into a taxi around two a.m. Let's go for a walk. This place is depressing me now.'

They stood and ambled slowly to Green Park. The grass was

full of deckchairs, the curves of striped canvas in which men and women dozed in the London warmth. 'Where did you pick him up?'

Sand tightened his lips. 'I'd rather not say.'

'Well, how far from Bobienski's flat?'

'I'd say it's a little over half an hour's walk from the prostitute's apartment.'

'A pub? A gentleman's club?'

'A nightclub.'

'A girlie club? Raymond's Revuebar?'

'No.'

'Danny La Rue's in Hanover Square?'

'God, no. Not that indiscreet. And you're not going to get the location out of me by listing every nightclub in London.' Sand smiled.

'So which direction would he have been coming from? The south? Soho? Piccadilly?'

'I know what you're doing. But I am not going to give you information which might lead you to jeopardise our operation.'

'I just need to know if he is a suspect. That's all.'

'He would have been coming from a south-easterly direction, as you policemen might say.'

'Good. So you picked him up again after eleven. He was missing for, what, an hour?'

'Maybe a bit longer. I'll have to check our notes. Sometime after eleven p.m.'

He'd have had to be fast to travel from Victoria to murder Bobienski and make it back to wherever the British agent picked him up again, thought Breen. 'So he could have made it from

Victoria, then to the flat and then back within, say, an hour? Or, as you say, maybe a little longer.'

'Yes. Just about, I suppose.'

'You can't arrange for me to see this man?'

'I know it must be difficult for you but we can't afford to spook him. If you do, he'll know we're on to him. Rather tricky, isn't it?'

'Not being able to interview the suspect in a murder investigation? Yes. Will you tell me where he lives? Or works?'

'Again, no. I'm afraid.' Sand looked apologetic. 'Same reason. Very awkward, I know.'

'Awkward?' said Breen.

'It's just the way I talk. It must be bloody frustrating for you. I'm very sorry. There is a way you could help us, of course.'

'You want me to tell you who Lena Bobienski's other clients were.'

'Exactly.'

Breen walked a little further. 'But I assume you have a direct link into our investigation anyway. So you probably know who our suspects are already.'

'You're an intelligent man. Your insight would be appreciated.'

They had Mrs Caulk's list already, he suspected. In the future, he would have to be careful about what he wrote down, thought Breen.

'There's another suspect you would also be interested in.' Breen scanned Sand's face to try to discern a reaction.

'Who?'

'Ronald Russell. He's a journalist for the *Sunday Times*.'

'Why are you looking into him?'

'Because he was also one of Julie Teenager's customers.'

Sand stopped. 'Well, that is fascinating,' he said.

'Is it? You know him?'

'Yes, of course. He's a pundit on the Soviet Union. Fairly good. We talk to him from time to time ourselves. How long had he been using the prostitute?'

'Three, four month's, he says.'

'I'll look into it. Very interesting. Thank you.'

They were approaching Constitution Hill. A pair of horses ridden by the Queen's Life Guards trotted past. The men looked uncomfortably hot in their uniforms.

'One thing. Quite a big thing, really. One of your men attempted to contact the papers about this case. We had to come down quite hard. You understand it's of national importance that nothing happens to let this Soviet agent know that we are on to him.'

'I assume you were behind the D-Notice.'

'And we know you've been in touch with a member of staff of a pornographic magazine that styles itself as the alternative press.'

'How? How do you know that?' He hadn't told Creamer or McPhail about his meeting with Felix.

'We just do.' Sand smiled apologetically. So it was more than just a paper trail that they had. Was his phone bugged? Or Felix's? That would be equally likely, perhaps. 'You'll understand how important it is not to let a publication like that know any of this. They're loose cannons. They do not share the same interests as us, obviously.'

'Obviously,' said Breen.

'Good.'

'How shall I contact you?' asked Breen.

He handed Breen a business card. 'Calliope Trading Ltd?' said Breen.

Sand shrugged, and gave a small smile, as if he was slightly ashamed of the subterfuge. There was a phone number, but no names.

'Another thing,' said Breen. 'You mentioned Mrs Caulk. How did you know we had interviewed her?'

Sand had the grace to look embarrassed again. 'We are monitoring your progress. You understand, don't you?'

'Spying on us?'

'Observing, that's all. Spying is what we do to our enemies.'

'But you haven't asked anything about her, yet.'

'She's not of interest to us,' he said. Then he looked less certain of himself. 'Should she be?'

'Perhaps she should. She was found dead on Friday.'

Mr Sand looked genuinely shocked. He was right. They hadn't heard. 'I'm very sorry to learn that. Was she killed?'

'Yes.'

'Oh.' Breen could see the concern on his face. By refusing to allow the police to investigate the Russian, there was a possibility Sand might be protecting a murderer.

'I would like to think you have been straight with me,' said Breen. 'But I'm not sure you have been.'

Mr Sand turned away from the trotting horses, looking uncomfortable. 'Look. No hard feelings. It's just the way it is. For us it's about what's best for the whole country. Which, you'll appreciate, we believe is slightly more important than the life of one person.'

'Two people,' corrected Breen.

'Yes. Two, I suppose,' said Sand.

'See,' said Breen. 'That's where we're different. I don't believe that at all.'

'Yes,' said Sand again, looking at his black shiny shoes on the dry summer grass. 'I appreciate that.'

Breen wondered what it was that he was holding back.

He held out his hand with a final smile, then he turned to a mother pushing a pram over the lawns and said, 'I think it's going to rain, don't you?'

Breen left him and walked across the grass and back into Piccadilly's traffic jam, feeling unsettled. Everything he did was being observed, scrutinised.

Mint was eating a pork pie at his desk. 'Is something wrong?' he asked.

'I'm not permitted to say.'

'What?'

'Never mind.'

Mint nodded to the sheets of paper pinned on the wall at the end of his desk. Notes had been added to all but B, G and I, who remained unidentified.

Someone had put a large black cross through Florence Caulk's sheet. Breen looked at it and winced, then leaned forward and added a question mark next to B; the Russian.

'Why's that?'

'I'm beginning to think it may be him,' said Breen. 'But he also might have an alibi. I can't verify it.'

'What do you mean?'

Breen didn't answer.

'But seriously. Just because he has an alibi. Besides, just because they turn up or call up, doesn't mean it's not them, does it? Maybe they're just being clever.'

'Yes.' Methodically crossing letters off the list didn't mean they were necessarily getting closer to the killer. There was something bigger involved; he knew that for certain now. He needed to do something differently; to shake things up, somehow.

He left the office and drove to St John's Wood. Florence Caulk's flat was in a block built in the 1930s. It had the kind of soft-curved, genteel English modernism that dreamed of ocean liners and foreign travel and reminded Breen of Agatha Christie books.

Local coppers were there with detectives from K Division; they had been knocking on the doors with a description of her car, asking if anybody had seen her leave. Sergeant Hope was sitting on a low wall, smoking a cigarette. 'Anything?' Breen asked him.

Hope looked up and shook his head. 'Nothing yet. Sorry, mate.'

Breen walked up to the second floor. The door to Caulk's flat was wide open. He walked down a small corridor lined with oil paintings, into a bright living room lit by sunshine that poured through the metal windows. It was a disorderly room. An Afghan rug, walls crammed with more art; a sofa covered in huge, gaudy cushions and rich Indian cloth; an African stool next to a cool, Danish wooden floor lamp. Propped against one wall was a large colourful Persian backgammon board. The bed was neatly made with an embroidered eiderdown covering it. Above it, there was a portrait of her, painted when she was much younger. She had been beautiful, he realised. It looked as if it was by someone famous, but he couldn't put his finger on who. And he had not taken the trouble to find out who she was, or why she was scared.

TWENTY-THREE

He left St John's Wood and drove west. By the time he reached Russell's house it was after five. The woman who answered was around the same age as he was, tall and thin, dressed plainly but elegantly in a black-and-white-striped dress with a cowl neck, black hair sprayed into place.

'Mrs Russell?'

'And who are you?' She looked him up and down.

'Detective Sergeant Cathal Breen. I'm here to see your husband.'

She narrowed her lips. 'What has he done?'

Breen looked at her. 'Why would he have done anything?'

'You're a policeman. Why are you here then?'

'He's just helping me with some information about a case,' said Breen. 'As a journalist, obviously.'

She crossed her arms and stood in the doorway, not letting him in. 'He didn't tell me anything about it.' She was beautiful in a haughty, high-cheekboned way.

'It's a confidential matter,' said Breen.

'I am his wife.'

'As I said. Confidential. Is Mr Russell in?'

She considered him a second more, then stood to one side. 'He is just changing his clothes. He'll be down presently. Come.'

Breen stepped inside. It was the kind of house that suggested old money. Ancient oil paintings lined the hallway walls. She led him down into a large living room at the back of the house. On the far side of the room, beyond gold-painted Italian furniture and the baby grand piano, there was a sideboard crammed with decanters and bottles.

'Have you been married long?' Breen asked.

'Is this small talk? Or is there a reason you want to know about my marriage?'

Breen heard a voice calling from upstairs. 'Who is it, darling?'

'He swept me off my feet six years ago,' she said, her face smileless. 'What about you? Are you married, officer?'

'Not yet. How did you meet?'

'Darling, do we have guests?' came the voice again. 'Who is it?'

'I was supervising at Cambridge. He was my student. Not one of my best, but at the time I thought him witty and resourceful.'

'Have you changed your mind?'

With no hint of a smile, she said, 'What is this really about, Detective Sergeant? Has there been a misdemeanour of some sort?'

Breen didn't have to answer because Russell was standing at the door. 'I heard voices,' he said.

'A policeman,' said Mrs Russell. 'Apparently you're helping him with his enquiries.'

Breen caught the anxious glance at his wife that Russell made.

She turned. 'What's wrong, darling? You look a little peaky.'

He was wearing a young man's shirt, its flowery cloth cut too tight.

'I've just come to ask you about that case I contacted you about,' Breen intervened. 'You remember? We spoke about it last week.'

'Of course. Yes. Yes. The case.'

Breen approached him. 'Is there somewhere private we can talk?'

'Would the policeman like a drink?' said Mrs Russell. 'A whisky and soda? Or just a cup of tea, perhaps?'

Breen followed her. 'Darling. Sergeant Breen is probably in a hurry. Don't hound him.'

'No particular hurry,' said Breen, smiling at her.

'What are you, by the way?' she asked, frowning. 'Special Branch?'

'CID.'

'I speak Russian too, if it's that you need. I translate. I'm better at it than my husband. I taught him it. He has a poor accent though his grammar is actually not that bad.'

'I'm afraid it's a sensitive situation,' said Breen. 'All I can say is your husband's expertise in Soviet affairs may prove quite useful to us.'

'Affairs?' she said, eyebrow raised.

'Political affairs, obviously.'

'You chose him as your expert?'

Ronald Russell poured himself a large whisky. 'Sergeant. I've a study at the back of the house, if you want to talk in private.'

249

'I'll let you two men alone, then,' she said, not moving.

Breen followed Russell to the study, a small room lined with books, many of which were in Russian. 'You've read all these?'

'A few,' said Russell. 'A lot of them were my father-in-law's.'

'He was Russian?'

'No. Professor of Modern Languages. This used to be his house. The family let us live in it.'

It made sense. It was a rather grand place for a minor journalist to be living in.

'You've made Kate bloody suspicious now,' he said, 'coming here like this.'

'Have I?'

'She's not been well. She sleeps badly. She has to take medication.'

'All your comings and goings in the night, I suppose.'

'You're enjoying this, aren't you?' said Russell.

'I just want to get to the bottom of what was going on.'

Russell switched the wireless on and turned up the volume, presumably for privacy. It was Radio 3. Some concert from the Royal Albert Hall, music that Breen didn't recognise. Russell sat at the desk and held out an Embassy Regal. Breen took one; he had smoked four already today, but the cigarette might make him feel more alert.

'There's no reason to be so superior about this. All men have problems with women. Comes with the territory.'

Breen raised his hands. 'I was just making conversation with your wife.'

Russell poured himself another large whisky. 'So? Well? What is it you want to talk about?'

Breen stood, looking at the Cyrillic script of the titles; the dull binding of the Soviet-printed volumes. 'What did you know about Lena Bobienski that you were not telling me?' he asked.

Russell frowned. 'I don't know what you mean.'

'You're a Soviet expert.'

'Yes. I'm actually not sure what you're driving at?'

Breen sat down in a captain's chair, opposite Russell and asked, 'So why was she under surveillance from the security services?'

The effect on Russell was electric. His mouth fell open. 'She was?'

'You didn't know?'

'Christ, no.' Breen looked into his eyes. The shock seemed genuine enough.

'Why do you think they were keeping tabs on her?'

'Jesus. I don't know. Were they watching her? She was Polish rather than Russian, of course. How did you find this out?'

'I can't say.'

'MI6?'

Breen said nothing.

'Bloody hell. They said she was a Soviet agent? Must have been MI6.'

'It's entirely possible she was more than just a prostitute. Did you know that?'

'But I swear, I had no idea.'

'Was she interested in what you did for a living?'

'Well, yes. But . . .' Russell took a gulp from his glass.

'But?'

'I'm just a bit shocked, that's all.'

'But you didn't know?'

'I bet it was MI6. You think they were watching the flat?'

'Would you be concerned if they had been?'

He lowered his voice. 'Of course I bloody would. You don't understand. If any of this gets back to Kate, she'll divorce me.'

Breen looked around him. 'This is her family's house, not yours.'

'Well, yes. I love her. Obviously. But she'd throw me out.'

'What sort of things did Julie Teenager ask you? Did she talk about your work?'

He seemed flustered. 'Not much. I mean, she was just an innocent girl, really, I assumed. I thought she was just interested, that's all. I find it interesting. I'd expect other people to. I suppose I talked about it a bit. But I talked about my poetry too.'

'You write poetry?'

'I've had a couple of collections. What they call "minor volumes".' He laughed. 'Nobody bought them, of course. My wife is a more successful poet than me, as a matter of fact. There are some of her books in here. Would you like one?'

'I'm not very good at poetry.'

'Nor me, apparently.'

He stood and turned his back to Breen, to scan the shelves behind him, then stopped. 'So you know someone was watching the flat? It was definitely Julie they were interested in?'

'I'm not sure. It might have been a client of hers.'

'Well it wouldn't be me.' He giggled nervously. 'I mean, I'm not that important, am I?'

'Not really,' said Breen.

'It's not funny. Imagine how you'd feel if someone was watching you? It's . . . disturbing, isn't it?'

'Yes. It is.'

Russell's eyes widened. 'They're watching you?'

'Apparently so.'

'Christ. You think they've been watching me? What if they followed you?'

'Why would that concern you, Ronald? You're just a journalist.'

'It's just not a terribly nice feeling. As you're aware, I have been indiscreet. Those kind of people use that against you.'

'And do you say that from personal experience?'

'What do you mean?'

'Did Lena Bobienski ever blackmail you?'

'She asked me to buy a ring. That's all.'

Breen looked at Russell fidgeting in his chair. 'What car do you drive?'

'An Austin. Why?'

He would have hardly expected him to say a Peugeot, but it was worth asking. Could he have killed Mrs Caulk? It was possible, of course.

Breen sat for a while, watching him. You could sometimes learn a lot by just observing, saying nothing. His silence certainly unsettled Russell, who picked up a fountain pen and dotted its nib onto the cover of a jotter, which sucked out ink, creating a circular blue stain.

'So tell me,' said Breen eventually. 'Were there other prostitutes as well?'

'Why do you need to know this?'

'Because you're a suspect.'

'I have an alibi. My brother-in-law said you spoke to him.'

'As alibis go, I've heard better. You're a suspect still.'

'Jesus. What do I have to do? There were one or two others, yes,' Russell answered, watching the blot grow. 'They hadn't meant anything. It was sex. But I suppose I fell for Julie. She was different.'

'Why did you need prostitutes?'

'Lovely girl, Kate. Honestly. But she's frigid, you know. Sort of formal, anyway. Gets headaches. Takes a lot of medicine. Rather old-fashioned, under all that modern clobber. Doesn't think sex is for fun. I suppose I was frustrated.'

'Having a successful wife?'

As if on cue, the audience at the Royal Albert Hall burst into applause. The piece of music on the radio had ended. 'It's not that,' said Russell.

'Isn't it?'

'There's a whole new world out there. People are shagging all the time. Don't you feel frustrated by it? The girls today, they're not all switch-the-lights-out types. I don't see why we should miss out.'

'What would she say if she found out?'

'She'd bloody kill me, I suppose.' Russell looked at him anxiously. 'She doesn't have to know, does she?'

'I'm going to need a record of your movements over the last week.'

'Oh God. Here we go again. What is it this time?'

'I'm afraid I can't say.' There was not yet a time of death for Mrs Caulk; nor had her identity been revealed to the newspapers.

'Well, why don't you go and ask your pals in the security services. I'm sure they'd bloody know,' said Russell darkly.

'If you like.'

'Fine.' Russell reached for a pocket diary.

'Are there many Soviet spies in London?'

'Quite a few. They love it here in the decadent West. The GRU and the KGB. They compete with each other. It's an oddly capitalist model, don't you think? Stalin dreamed it up. One distrusts the other and Brezhnev enjoys playing them off against themselves.'

They went through his diary ticking off times and places. 'The Soviet embassy is full of them,' Russell said as he turned a page. 'And then the trade delegations. And they successfully recruited enough of ours in the past, like Burgess and Maclean and George Blake. And then there are the resident aliens, people like Peter and Helen Kroger. You know, the Portland Spy Ring?'

It had been a huge scandal, Breen remembered: the discovery of a team of foreign residents who had been stealing Britain's nuclear secrets for years. When Special Branch had raided their house in Ruislip, they had found it packed with secret radio equipment that the Krogers had been using to transmit information to the Soviets.

'So, yes, there are always spies.'

'What if one was a client of Lena Bobienski's?'

'You're not serious?'

Breen shrugged. 'It's possible.'

'You think she might have been killed because of something to do with espionage?'

'I haven't any idea.'

255

'Christ. You think it was an assassination of some kind? It might be, of course. How would you ever prove it, anyway?'

'That would be a problem, wouldn't it?' said Breen. 'Of course, it might just have been one of the men who went to her for kicks.'

Russell winced, closed his diary, stubbed out his cigarette. 'I love my wife really,' he said. 'Please don't get me wrong. It's just that she's not sexy. You know? She's serious all the time; she acts like she's so old. I mean. It's almost the Seventies. Women shouldn't be that serious, should they?'

Russell drained his glass and looked at his watch. 'Want one?' he said. 'I'm going to have another.'

Breen shook his head and stood. '

Walking to the gate he turned and looked back at the house. Mrs Russell was at an upstairs window, watching him.

Breen turned right at Regent's Street and drove south. The shops were closed and the pavements looked grubby and grey. A sheet of newspaper hung in the air above the windscreen, caught in an updraught. He slowed, watching it for a second until it drifted over the car, then drove on, not looking behind him to see where it fell. Just before Piccadilly Circus he took a right into a small turning and parked. Swallow Street was one of those places most people walked past without noticing; one of those leftovers from an older, less orderly city. He got out and pressed his thumb onto a polished brass doorbell to the side of a heavy white door.

Sybilla's wasn't open yet; it was too early still for the night-clubs. A tall, big-handed man wearing a pale green pinny opened the door and peered out into the daylight, then smiled. 'Paddy,' he said.

'Hello, Wilco,' said Breen. 'Got a minute?'

The man held the door open wide. 'Let me switch off the Hoover. Barman just broke half a dozen glasses.'

Wilco was one of those men whose arms didn't seem to hang down straight. His chest was too wide for them. At fifty, even in a pinny, he still looked intimidating.

He led him into the club; it was a small room, a plain dance floor in the middle under a low ceiling, a few expensive glass-fibre chairs around the edge. It looked nothing special. There would have been nothing to it if it hadn't been owned by a cousin of Lord Rothermere's, a DJ from Radio 1 and a Beatle.

'Drink?' said Wilco.

He had refused one earlier this evening; this time he nodded. It was summer. He was thirsty. 'Just a half of lager.'

'A half? Don't be a girl.' Wilco took off his pinny and folded it. He was an East Ender. Breen had first known him when he had worked in G Division, when Wilco had been vaguely con-nected to the Krays' gang. His presence in the club had always suggested to Breen that it wasn't only celebrities who had backed the nightclub. If these days the Krays were more or less a spent force, London's cool people liked having them around.

Wilco leaned over the bar and flipped the tap to pour a pint of Harp for himself and another for Breen.

'Well?' he said, sitting down, legs wide apart, on a very white, very modern chair. He nodded to a chair opposite.

'How's business here?' Breen sat.

'So-so. Tourists mainly, this summer. The pop stars are moving on. This ain't their thing so much this year. I don't mind. The tourists spend real money. Fucking pop stars want everything for nothing.' He looked at his watch. 'Get to it, Paddy. Haven't got all day. Open in an hour.'

'I'm looking for a Russian man who comes to places like this. He's a drinker.'

'Russkis? Not many of them to the dollar. What's he look like?'

That was the point. There weren't that many Russians in London – not of an age to go to nightclubs at least. And there weren't that many nightclubs.

'Slim. Good-looking,' said Breen.

'Ain't they all, these days?'

'I just know he was in a nightclub like this on Thursday – a couple of weeks back. He was in a place for about three hours knocking them back. Sounds like he'd be a regular.' MI6 wouldn't have picked him up in a place like this by chance; they'd have known his habits.

'Not here. I know everyone who comes.' He probably did too. 'Maybe the Cromwellian. That's full of dodgy foreigners.'

'Wrong part of London,' said Breen.

'Vile place, anyway. They'd let anyone in. Slip us a Bill-and-Ben and I'll keep my ears out, if you like.'

'Get lost, Wilco. Do it for me for free.'

'Bought you a drink already, didn't I? And it's not even Christmas.'

Wilco would do it anyway, Breen knew. It's how it worked. When it was something easy like making a couple of calls, these clubs always wanted to keep on the right side. It helped them stay discreet for the high-end clientele. So if there was trouble, the police wouldn't make a fuss. Keep it hush-hush for the groovy young people. But just to make sure, Breen leaned closer and said, 'Between you and me, he's a suspect in two murders. Both women.'

'Rape?'

'Can't say,' said Breen.

'Cunt.' Wilco drained his pint. 'I don't like Russians, best of times. Except for the yids. They're not so bad. Enough said, Paddy. I'll ask around.'

In the world Wilco came from, men hurting each other was fine; he just didn't like the idea of men hurting women. Not that way, anyway.

TWENTY-FOUR

'And where were you this time?' asked Creamer.

'Library, sir,' Breen said. 'I'm reading up about the Soviet Union.'

'You can't just disappear without letting people know where you've gone. What on earth's that got to do with . . . ?'

'I'm not entirely sure, sir.' Rasper's phone started ringing.

Breen had spent three hours on Wednesday morning at Westminster Library, leafing through back copies of *The Times* and the *Telegraph*, at least the last two months' worth that hadn't yet been sent away by the library to be bound. Articles warned of the increase in the Russians' stockpiles of intercontinental ballistic missiles. In return, Nixon was using NATO to ramp up pressure on the Soviet Union. After last year's Soviet invasion of Czechoslovakia, there was speculation about what the Soviets were doing to try and tighten their control in Poland.

All of it seemed so far from London's messy streets. In *The*

Times he found only a few short articles by-lined with Russell's name, mostly co-written, generally about Soviet politics or the state of the country's industrial output. 'Russians sign up for new car a year in advance'; or 'Foreign Secretary raises Gerald Brooke spy case'. If he had been hoping for an insight, it had eluded him. All he had to show for it was ink-black fingers.

Creamer was still standing there, hoping for an explanation.

'I have a Sergeant Hope from K Division for you,' said Miss Rasper. 'Do you want to take it at your desk?'

'At my desk,' said Breen.

'Perhaps you can shed some light on what the hell's going on?' Hope demanded, the moment Breen picked up his telephone.

'What do you mean?'

'Somebody upstairs has just requested copies of all our documents on the Florence Caulk case.'

'Same,' Breen said quietly.

'No explanation. Nothing. Why?'

Breen heard a familiar frustration in the detective's voice; he said, 'It turns out, we've got a bit of a situation with this case.'

'A situation? What in hell is that?'

From across the office, Creamer was still glowering at him.

'What are you up to tomorrow morning?'

Sergeant Hope caught on quickly. 'You can't talk now?'

'Yes.' Breen swivelled his chair away from Creamer's gaze. 'Know Joe's All Night Bagel Shop?' he asked.

On Wednesday night, the BBC showed the rocket on the news. The immense tube seemed to take an age to rise from the launch

261

pad, but it soon became a tiny stick riding on top of a flare of flame so bright it burned into the camera lenses, while calm men in American accents talked a jargon of speed and distances.

Breen watched, close to the TV, Elfie on one side of him, Helen on the other. 'According to a man I met,' he said, 'This is just for show, to impress the Soviets.'

'A rocket is like a great big penis,' said Elfie. 'The moon is a woman.'

'Shut up, the pair of you. I think it's amazing,' said Helen. 'I would love to do that. Wouldn't you? Just imagine. Our children will think going to space is like us going to Spain.'

Our children, thought Breen. Though he'd never been outside the country, let alone to Spain, they were living in the future, where anything was possible.

Like everyone watching, he wondered what it would be like to be weightless, free of the world's gravity. Another day had passed. He was no closer to finding the Russian, the driver, or the policeman.

Joe's All Night Bagel Shop was always busy this time of the morning, a queue of workmen snaking out of the door. Joe's daughter made up packed lunches for the single men who had no wives or mothers to make them.

Breen pushed past the line of men, into the small interior of the building, fuggy with heat from the small kitchen. Hope was there already, a mug of tea and a full ashtray in front of him.

'And?' Hope said.

Breen told him everything Sand had; he was not a fan of secrets. Hope sat, slowly shaking his head as Breen spoke. 'But you don't know this. And I never told you. They would bloody hang me to dry if they found out I'd told you.'

'Or just hang you, maybe,' said Hope.

'Exactly.'

'Unbe-fucking-lievable,' said Hope.

'I know.'

Hope leaned closer. 'So what if it's some Russian spy thing? What if that bloke you're on about killed her? How are we ever going to lay our hands on this bastard?'

'Yes.'

Joe's daughter arrived with a coffee for Breen. She looked exhausted, but asked brightly, 'How's Helen? When's the baby due?'

'You're having a baby? And there was I thinking you were in enough shit already,' said Hope when she'd gone. The detective drained his tea. 'Anyway, listen. I might have got something. Not much,' he said.

It was Breen's turn to lean forward.

'Get this. Two days of interviews and it looks like your constable was the last person we know of who saw Mrs Caulk alive. None of Mrs Caulk's neighbours saw her leave her flat on that Tuesday night. But we were also asking if they'd seen anything at all unusual. Turns out, a man in the same block, old guy, didn't even know Mrs Caulk, but said a taxi driver started ringing all the bells about half ten.'

'On the Tuesday night? The day I spoke to her?'

'Right. Apparently someone had called up, ordered a cab to wait outside, but nobody had turned up. So the cabbie started ringing on all the bells. Anyway, as this bloke was talking to the cabbie, saying he didn't know anything about it, some fellow barged right past them both, through the open door.'

'So the murderer may have got in without a key?'

'Exactly.'

'Description?'

'Hat pulled down. Coat pulled up. No chance to see his face. Medium bloody everything. You know what it's like, sometimes. Anyway, the old bloke who was saying this said it was odd, because he hadn't seen the man approach. One minute he wasn't there. Next he was. I reckon he was hiding next to the door. There's a big kind of shrub thing there.'

'Footprints?'

'Checked it. Nothing obvious.'

'You reckon that's how he got in? The man who killed her? Called a cab, then waited for someone to open the door?'

'It's a theory. Sounds like the kind of thing a spy would do? Oh yeah. I got this for you.' Hope reached into his pocket and pulled out a folded sheet of paper, handing it to Breen.

Breen opened up the document. It was a copy of the pathologist's interim report. Breen read through it as the two men sat together, not talking for a while. Men came and went, preparing for the working day.

Reading it, Hope watched Breen grimace. 'Poor old bird,' he said and stood up to leave, holding out his hand to shake.

Creamer had called a morning meeting. Officers sat on desks, pads in their hands.

'Looks very much like the same killer, then,' said Creamer, telling the men what they already knew.

264

For all their faults, Creamer's modern methods were not all bad. These regular meetings seemed to be bringing the department together. They felt more of a team than they had done in the old days, when Carmichael had worked here.

But it was now more than ten days after the first body had been discovered; everyone sensed the inquiry was losing pace. They were still monitoring Bobienski's phones, but nobody had called up since the weekend. The pathologist had confirmed that Caulk was killed by a blow to the front of her skull. 'Must have been bloody hard,' said Breen. 'Probably a metal bar.'

Breen repeated what Hope had told him. Though they now had a theory about how the killer had entered the building, a second day of door-to-doors in St John's Wood had produced nothing; nobody had seen her with anyone on the Tuesday.

'The killer is clearly anxious,' Creamer said. 'I'm guessing he killed Mrs Caulk because he was worried that she knew something that could identify him. So that's our advantage. We need to keep pushing. He'll do something stupid.'

Surprisingly, it was true. If Caulk's death meant anything, it was that the killer felt vulnerable and was acting to cover his tracks. And that he was aware of them closing in, somehow.

'So . . . we know he knew we had tracked down Mrs Caulk,' said Breen. 'How did he know that? Is he an acquaintance of Mrs Caulk's? Or did he get his information from somewhere else?'

Mint said it first, though they had all been thinking it. 'What if he's the copper?'

They all looked at each other. That would be the worst

scenario. One of their own. And someone who knew what they were up to.

And though nobody said it, they all thought: What if it's someone we know?

Later that morning Helen rang him. 'Can you find out about an attempted murder? It happened last night. Somewhere around Chichester. It'll be Sussex Police.'

'What?'

'It's for Elfie.'

'Oh for God's sake. I'm busy, Helen. Things are crazy here. I have two real murders of my own.'

'This is serious too. Take down her name. Kay Fitzpatrick.'

'No,' said Breen.

'Kay Fitzpatrick,' she said again. 'She knew Brian Jones. She was one of his circle. She was one of the people there at his house.'

'The day he died?'

'No. But she'd been there. She knew him well. Someone tried to kill her yesterday.'

'Where does Elfie get this stuff?'

'You know. She has friends who have friends who work for the group's management. The rumour is that Kay Fitzpatrick knew something about Brian Jones's death. Now this woman is in a coma. Apparently it was a violent attack.'

'Rumour,' said Breen.

'Yes. Just a rumour, I know. But still.'

'It's nothing to do with you, Helen. You're not in the police any more.'

Breen could sense others in the CID room pricking up their ears, listening in to the conversation.

'If you don't do it, I'll go there myself,' said Helen.

'She's dragging you into her obsession. She's been acting strangely since her boyfriend told her he was sleeping with another woman. And you're going along with it because . . .'

'Because what, Cathal?'

'Because you can't accept you're not a copper any more.'

'Maybe all that's true. But—'

'It's nuts. Brian Jones drowned because he'd taken too many drugs.'

'Well, Cathal, this woman didn't beat herself up. It might have nothing to do with anything, but someone tried to kill her.'

Breen took a breath. 'You're having a baby. You need to accept that. You don't need this.'

'Please, Cathal.'

He looked up. Men pretended hard to be reading reports that they had been paying no attention to five minutes earlier. Typewriters click-clacked back into life.

Later, in the first-floor kitchen, Mint was making tea. 'Want a cup?'

Breen shook his head.

'What you said just then,' Mint said. 'To your girlfriend. About her needing to accept what she was.'

'It was a private conversation.'

'It's hard for women, sometimes, to understand that they're going to be mothers. My wife was the same. It's, like, a huge change. It's a whole new responsibility. They can't be like they were before.'

Breen stared at him like he was from another planet. 'You don't really know my girlfriend very well, do you?'

Embarrassed, Mint stirred his tea, spilling it onto the counter.

Breen returned to his desk and called the flat.

Helen picked up after the second ring.

'OK,' he said. 'I'll do it.'

'Let me know as soon as you can,' she said.

This time it was him who put down the receiver in anger. He shouldn't be doing this. But he phoned Chichester police station, as she'd asked. The sergeant who took the call promised to get back to him within the hour with whatever details he had managed to find out.

That evening, they argued again.

'I'll go,' he said.

'You can't go running off to Sussex. Creamer would never give you the day off.'

'You can't go either. You're not even a policewoman. You're eight months pregnant. You could have a baby any moment.'

'Course I can,' she said. 'I'm fine. It's just an hour's train journey.'

Sussex Police had said that the woman who had been attacked, Kay Fitzpatrick, was in a hospital in Chichester. She had been discovered, beaten bloody, outside her house, lying in the street. She had been unconscious since the attack; there was a chance she would not wake up.

'It's like you've both gone nuts,' said Breen.

'I'm just curious, that's all.'

Breen wasn't enjoying the food. Helen had cooked bangers and mash with Bisto gravy. The sausages were from the local Fine Fare and were cheap, plain and textureless.

'What's this woman's connection to the Rolling Stones anyway?'

'She works with this bloke who did odd jobs for Brian Jones; goes out with him, though he's married. He's a fixer for the group, like that guy we met in Hyde Park, Tom. He was there at his house the day he died. He was actually in the swimming pool with Brian before he died. It was in the inquest. You read it. Elfie reckons somebody tried to kill this Kay because of something she knew about Brian. I know Elfie's full of mad theories, but what if this is true? You've got to admit, it is a coincidence.'

'You miss being a copper, don't you?'

She looked at him and the anger had vanished. 'Yes. I do.'

He pushed the sausages to one side of the plate. 'You should go then. Though you might find it hard persuading the local plod to talk to you.'

'I already spoke to them on the phone. I charmed the pants off them.'

'You never charmed the pants off anybody, Helen Tozer.'

She had made strawberries-and-cream Angel Delight for pudding. 'It's very modern,' she said.

'It's kids' food isn't it?' He dipped his spoon into it.

'This is what they eat in space,' she said.

'Really?'

'I'll have yours if you don't want it,' she said.

Later, when he was doing the washing-up, she said, 'About Sussex. I wasn't asking your permission, anyway.'

'I know,' he said, and when she took a plate from the rack to dry it, he noticed she was smiling at him.

TWENTY-FIVE

Creamer had had another new idea. Officers who left the office had to log in and out of the CID room, writing in a school exercise book kept by the door, noting where they had gone and why.

Breen had written 'Gone for walk' in its pages.

The CID room had been muggy, full of cigarette smoke and sweat. It was good to get outside. There was something about walking and thinking that went together.

There were too many sides to this case, but no distinct shape; the darkness of Bobienski's trade; the involvement of Russian spies; the presence of a policeman among her customers, and the all-round duplicitousness of the men who paid her. Time was moving on. Unless they could make real progress soon, another murder would come along in their area and then the team would fracture, their concentration waver. The notes would be put into a filing cabinet and they would move on.

He walked east, towards Harewood Avenue. The Marylebone

Road was thick with traffic. Buses blew black smoke. Taxis swerved at likely fares standing by the kerb.

At Warren Street, just outside the tube station, he spotted a man walking back and forward over the same section of pavement. After about thirty yards he would return, passing the front of the station. Anyone who had spent their time as a beat policeman, as he had, developed a knack of spotting people who were up to no good; you never quite lost it. Ordinary people went about their lives, noticing little. Being on the beat made you aware of another world around you.

This man: khaki jacket, black shoes, straggly sideburns. There was definitely something about him, but he wasn't sure what.

It took Breen a minute to work it out. The second he bent down to the ground, Breen realised he was doing the ring scam. He had seen it once or twice before. Breen watched him pretending to scoop it up and hurry after a woman who was standing at the flower stall. 'Excuse me, love. You just dropped this.' He held up the cheap gold ring he had had in his hand all the time.

The woman turned and smiled at him, said something Breen couldn't hear.

She would be saying, 'No, that's not mine.' And her guard would be down.

Quickly Breen moved behind the pickpocket, out of his eyeline, and waited for the moment when his hand dipped into the woman's open handbag, then lurched forward and grabbed him by the wrist.

'Police,' he shouted, yanking the man's arm behind his back and forcing him straight down to the pavement. The man dropped a purse as he fell.

'What are you doing?' screamed the woman.

The throng of people, including her, all stepped back, leaving him a circle of space. The pickpocket was strong and struggled, kicking out his legs.

'This man is a pickpocket. Somebody call a policeman.'

The man was shouting too. 'He attacked me. Help. He's bloody nuts.'

The crowd stood and stared, doing nothing, paralysed by uncertainty about what was happening. Which one to believe: the younger, good-looking man, or the older one, who seemed to have assaulted him? Breen was not as fit as he used to be; he would not be able to hold the man for long.

The woman noticed what the man had dropped. 'That's my purse. Oh my God. That man was trying to nick it.'

At that, the florist stepped forward and grabbed the man's kicking legs. Now others approached to help pin the man down.

It was five minutes, though, before a beat bobby arrived with handcuffs. All the time the man had squirmed and kicked.

Once he was finally subdued, Breen searched for the woman to ask her to make a statement, but as he had lain on the ground struggling, she had simply picked up the purse and had gone without saying anything.

Rubbing his bruises, he turned to the florist and thanked him for helping out. 'Did you see him take anything from her bag?'

'Only thing I saw was you jumping him like a good 'un, mate. Nice piece of work.' He looked around for the woman. 'She didn't even stop to buy you flowers.'

That's when Breen noticed a bucket of yellow roses; he realised where he was.

'My colleague talked to you a couple of weeks ago about those, didn't he?' he said.

'Young guy. Bit nervous?'

'That's him.'

'Younger every bloody day.' The man rubbed his chin. His hands were green with the juice of cut stems. 'Funny thing. That same feller he was on about came back the evening after I spoke to him. He ordered some flowers to be delivered.'

'The man who bought the yellow roses. That would have been Tuesday?' Breen's head was spinning. Mr G. The man who wore flashy clothes and who cried sometimes.

'Yeah. Tuesday. That's right.'

'Why didn't you say anything?'

'Well, I'm telling you now, in't I?' complained the man.

'What was his name?'

'No idea.'

'Where were the flowers to be delivered to? To Harewood Avenue?'

'Hold on a sec.' And he delved behind the upturned milk crates that made his counter and pulled out a tattered notebook. 'What day was it?' he said.

'The eighth of July.'

He flicked over the pages, licking fingers on each turn, until he came to the entry. 'No. Not Harewood Avenue. I got Imperial Cinema, Portobello.'

Breen blinked. 'It was delivered to the cinema?'

'That's what it says.'

Breen frowned at the man's notebook, feeling suddenly dizzy. He was out of shape. 'What about a name?'

'That would have been on the card. We don't write it down here. Just the address, so we can give it to the driver.'

'You must be able to remember. It was a woman's name?'

'Well, bloody obviously, yes, a woman's name. You wouldn't give roses to a feller, would you? But I do deliveries every bloody day. Can't be expected to remember the names and everything. Not at my age.'

'What did he look like?'

'I don't recall. Big bloke, I think.'

When Breen got back to the office, Inspector Creamer was leaning over Miss Rasper's desk, checking his diary with her. He lifted his head and said, 'Productive walk, Paddy?' as archly as he could.

'Perhaps,' said Breen, returning to his desk. Creamer retreated to his room.

Breen sat still for five minutes before he called Scotland Yard, asking to be put through to John Carmichael's extension on the Drug Squad. The phone rang. Carmichael was not picking up.

That night he met Elfie and Helen outside the Imperial Cinema.

'What's wrong, Paddy? You look like you've eaten a wasp,' demanded Elfie. She was dressed for a night on the town in a one-piece orange nylon pantsuit that stretched tightly over her bulge. Breen thought she looked ridiculous.

'Where's Amy?'

Helen had just come on the bus from Victoria. 'I'm exhausted. I'm not sure I want to see this film again anyway.'

'Is something up?'

She looked away. 'Nothing.'

Breen eyed her. 'How were the Sussex Police? Did they have anything to say about that woman?'

'They were fine. It was her bloody acquaintances who were tricky.'

'You were just supposed to be talking to the police.'

'Supposed to be?' she said. 'What does that mean? I talked to them. They told me what they knew, which isn't much. So I thought I'd go along to the hospital and see how she was.'

'And?'

'And she's still in a coma. I spoke to a doctor and he said they weren't sure if she was going to make it.'

'You said acquaintances.'

'There was this man waiting outside the ward. Thing is, they don't let the public in, so the matron kept asking him to leave. There was this room where everybody is supposed to wait. So in he came and I asked him who he was waiting for and he didn't answer. I wasn't sure if he was a relative or anything, but if he was, maybe I could find something out. So I said, is it Kay Fitzpatrick you're here for? And he just looked at me and said, "No." But really abruptly. And I knew something was up then. He looked really rattled. Next thing he just stood up and left.'

'Don't say you followed him.'

'Come on, Cathal. You would have.'

'I'm a policeman. And I'm not eight months pregnant.'

'There was this long corridor. And it can only have been a couple of seconds after he'd left I stuck my head out.'

'Well?'

'Nothing.'

'You lost him.'

'Yes. I don't understand it. The exit was twenty yards away. Either he'd run or he'd gone to hide. I was stupid. I can't shift fast with this.' She put her hand on her belly.

'Man doesn't like being spoken to in a hospital. Walks away. Takes a different corridor to yours.'

'You could be right,' she said.

'Are you joining us?' said Elfie.

'Where's John?' asked Breen. 'Is he coming?'

'He's your friend,' said Helen. 'You should know.'

Amy emerged from the cinema. 'Christ, it's hot in there,' she said.

Somebody in the queue was saying, 'Is it a murder film, *The Killing of Sister George*?'

'You've not heard from John?'

'Not a bloody thing. If he turns up, tell him I don't want anything to do with him any more, anyway.'

'Serious?' said Helen.

'Deadly. I can't put up with his absolute . . . stuff . . . any more.'

Helen wrapped her arms around the smaller girl. 'I know,' she said.

'You're lucky, with Paddy,' said Amy, looking at Breen.

'It's just what John's like,' said Helen. 'He's not been used to having a girlfriend.'

'Well, it's crap,' said Amy. 'All that running after me. I wasn't even interested in him at first. What's wrong with you, Paddy? You look like you're sick or something?'

Inside the cinema they were showing the adverts already.

Breen said, 'Well? Is that all? What did the police say about that woman?'

'Local plod reckon that Kay Fitzpatrick's boyfriend tried to kill her. He's disappeared. But he's their only suspect.'

'See?' said Breen. 'They have a suspect.'

'But they don't know for sure.'

'But they're not looking for any of the Rolling Stones?'

'Course not,' she said.

'Isn't that enough?' The same advert for the orange drink that was on every week came on.

'Aren't you the one who always says you shouldn't jump to conclusions?'

Then the ad for popcorn.

'I was thinking I'd go back tomorrow. You want to come?'

'Don't. Please.'

The film was starting now. 'You think this is just a little game? I've played around a bit and now you want me to stop.' She dropped her voice. 'Maybe Elfie's not right. But a woman was attacked.'

'I know. But . . .'

'I'm interested. I want to find out who did it.'

Someone behind shushed.

'Oh, bollock off,' muttered Helen, taking hold of Breen's arm. He laid his hand over hers. He thought of yellow flowers.

The movie was about two women who lived together. One was older. She was crabby and ugly. The other was sweet and young and beautiful. He sat there, holding Helen's hand. When she tried to move hers away, he reached out and grabbed it again.

'What's wrong?' she asked.

'Everyone keeps asking me that.'

'Because you look strange.'

'I'm just in a bad mood,' he whispered. 'The case isn't going well.'

'Nothing else? Am I pissing you off?'

'No. It's not that.'

'Have a word with John, won't you? He's being an arse.'

'Yes,' he said. 'He is.'

And afterwards, they waited outside for taxis. 'Come on, Hel. Come to the gig.' Elfie tugged at her coat like a schoolgirl.

'I'm shattered,' Helen said. 'I fell asleep in there.'

'I don't know if I want to go,' Amy said.

'Course you do,' said Elfie.

Amy came up to Breen and said, 'When you see your friend, tell him I put his bloody flowers straight into the bin. OK?'

'He sent you flowers,' said Elfie. 'That's nice.'

'No it's fucking not.'

'Yes,' said Breen quietly. 'I'll be sure to tell him that.'

Helen clung on to Breen's arm, as if for support. She looked exhausted. He shouldn't have let her go alone. 'You go,' she said. 'It was so hot in there. I just want my bed.'

'When we've had our babies we'll take them to all the concerts with us,' said Elfie. 'Isle of Wight Free Festival. We'll buy a big tent. Don't look like that, Paddy,' she said.

'Christ sake. My name's Cathal,' he said.

'Grumpy old man.'

He looked out of the window as the cab lurched its way east.

'What's got into you?' said Helen. 'I was supposed to be the moody one.'

He thought of a baby growing inside Helen. He had no idea about babies.

He should be happy. He was about to become a father. But everything was wrong.

Helen went straight to bed in her room. He turned the light off in the hallway and went to bed too but couldn't sleep.

If he had been Helen, maybe he too would have been suspicious about the man in the hospital, but it wasn't their case. And besides, hadn't she said that the Sussex Police already had a suspect?

He had his own worries. Since his father died last year, there was nobody who had been in his life as long as John Carmichael. They had gone through school together, bunked off together. They had blagged their way into basements in Soho to watch Joe Harriott play the sax. He had followed John into the police and they had covered each other's backs at Stoke Newington, before both of them left to join D Division together. For years, his best friend. He turned in his bed, unable to sleep.

He shifted from one side to the other, then lay on his back, eyes refusing to stay closed.

And then Helen was at the door, light blazing behind her.

TWENTY-SIX

'Didn't you hear the phone?' she was saying.

He blinked. 'What phone?' He must have fallen asleep, but he had no sense that he had done so.

'Elfie's in the Hackney Hospital,' Helen was saying. 'Amy just called reverse charges.'

'What's wrong?'

'She's having a bloody baby. We have to go.' She switched on the lamp, and the light burned his eyeballs.

'Won't she be OK?'

'Amy is stuck there with no money.'

He couldn't shake his weariness. It clung to him. It took him a second to understand what she had just said. 'I'll come. Let me go out and hail a cab,' he said, pulling on his trousers.

'That could take ages.'

'What do you expect? It's three in the morning.'

'Yeah, but. What if she's having the baby now? I know a quicker way,' she said.

'What do you mean?'

'It's stealing,' said Breen.

'It's borrowing,' said Helen.

They stood outside looking at Klaus's big old Magnette. 'Besides, big brass bollocks to him. It's his baby she's having.'

Breen looked at the shiny old car. 'So it was you, stole the keys?'

'No wonder you're the detective, Cathal. Stupid thing to do, I know. But I was feeling spiteful.'

He held out his hand. 'Only if I drive.'

'I'm just pregnant, not crippled.'

He stood, holding his arm out until she threw him the keys. Breen got in and turned the key, then pressed the starter button. It was a still night. Hackney was quiet. The old car rattled through dirty, empty streets.

They found Amy sitting on the wooden bench in the reception area, smoking and shivering slightly in the neon glare of the corridor. She stood up and gave Helen a hug.

'Is she OK?'

'They won't say. They won't let me in or anything. They wanted to know who the father was. Sorry I had to call you, only . . .'

'No. I'm glad. What happened?'

'We were just trying to find a taxi after the gig. Then it started. One minute she was fine and then she was wetting herself. I think she's scared.'

'Elfie? Scared?'

'We should call Klaus,' said Breen.

'Stuff Klaus. He doesn't care about her. She doesn't need him here.'

'Maybe she wants him to know.'

'Honestly doubt it,' said Helen. 'They wouldn't let him in anyway,' she said. 'They're not married.'

'I have to go,' said Amy. 'She'll be all right, won't she?'

'We should go home too, Helen. There's nothing we can do.'

'I want to know if she's OK.'

A matron in starched hat and blue uniform burst out of the doors, and stopped, noticing them on the bench. 'Who are you?' she demanded. She was a plump woman in her sixties.

'We're friends of Elfie Silverstein.'

'And who is Elfie Silverstein?'

'She's in there, giving birth.'

'Well, leave her to it. What are you expecting to see, anyway, this time of night? For goodness' sake. Visiting time is three in the afternoon. This is no place for you. Go away. The lot of you. Out.'

And she shooed them out of the door into the night.

'Cow,' said Helen.

'Is that Klaus's car?'

Breen drove the Magnette west across London, the sky in the rear-view mirror lightening behind him. They dropped Amy at her flat on Harrow Road.

'I won't be able to sleep now,' said Helen.

So Breen parked the car outside an all-night cafe near West-bourne Park tube.

'I was supposed to have mine before hers. I'm going to hate that,' said Helen. 'Having the baby.'

283

'Women do it all the time.'

'You don't know anything about it,' she said, opening the car door.

'No,' he said. 'I don't.'

The cafe was dirty and served weak coffee that tasted like dish-water. A couple of truck drivers, hands greasy from their work, smoked hand-rolled cigarettes and argued about the unions.

'I'm not ready to be a mother,' she said.

'You'll be great.'

'You never understand. It's nothing to do with that. I just wanted to do all this stuff with my life, that's all.'

'You're just worried. It'll be fine.'

'Christ, Cathal. Sometimes you're . . .'

Her tea cup had a dark thumbprint on the side of it. He offered to take it back, but she said it was OK and spooned in four sugars. 'Being in hospital is going to drive me mad. I've never been to hospital in my life.'

'It'll only be a few days.'

'Ten days they keep you in? I'm going to go insane.'

Breen had no idea where he had been born. Somewhere in Ireland. He had never imagined his mother going through what would be happening to Elfie now.

'Before all of this,' she said, 'I just wanted to do something, you know. Achieve something. Make something better.'

'You will.'

'Not any more.'

He looked at his watch. It would be gettting light soon. He should have felt tired, but instead he suddenly felt like he had to do something for Helen.

'Why don't we go to Chichester again today? To the hospital.'

'I thought you thought all that was rubbish?'

'We could drive,' he said. 'And be back here again by three in time for visiting Elfie.'

'You're the one who says it's pointless.'

'Maybe it is. I just want to show I'm on your side.'

And she nodded, face serious. 'OK then.'

But when they stepped out of the cafe and saw the first sliver of malevolent-looking violet in the sky between the new tower blocks, he regretted the impulse. He had been tired. She had looked so sad. All he had wanted to do was to show how much he loved her without having to say it.

Helen Tozer slept, head leaning against his shoulder, as the car roared down the empty A3, through small commuter towns. So early on a Saturday morning, there was little in the way of traffic. The car was heavy but the engine was powerful; he watched the old dial on the walnut fascia top 70 m.p.h. on the longer straights. It was looking to be a warm, sunny day, so he drove with the windows down. It was exhilarating, speeding down these empty country roads, and he thought driving had taken his mind off his troubles, but when Helen opened her eyes at Haslemere she said, 'What's wrong?'

'Wrong? Nothing?'

'You look worried. You've looked miserable since yesterday. Is something worrying you? Is it the baby?'

'It's just the thing I'm working on, that's all,' he said evasively.

She leaned into him and slept again. It was almost nine when he pulled the into the hospital car park.

The hospital at the north of the city; a large, old Victorian edifice, its name, Royal West Sussex Hospital, carved into a massive pediment above the front doors.

'You again,' said the nurse sitting at the desk.

'Any improvement?'

'I shall call up,' the nurse said.

'We'd like to go ourselves,' said Helen.

'Told you yesterday. Only relations in visiting hours.'

Breen pulled out his wallet and showed his warrant card.

'I suppose it's OK then.' She glared at Helen, and Breen wondered what Helen had done yesterday to antagonise her so much. 'Albert Ward. Second floor.'

In the large, high-ceilinged ward, other visitors looked round. Fresh flowers sat in glass vases on the bedside cabinets. It took them a few minutes to find a nurse who could tell them where Kay Fitzpatrick was.

Alone, in a side room, curtains half closed against the morning sun, she lay on her back, arms above the sheets and blankets. Her head was held in a metal frame. She was breathing slowly. The clean white bandage that covered nearly all of her face threw the blackness of the bruising into relief in the few parts you could see. There, dark marks faded to purple and yellow at the edge of her face.

'Kay?' said Helen. She reached out and took the woman's hand.

Nothing.

'Can you hear me, Kay?'

'Is this the first time you've seen her?'

'They wouldn't let me in yesterday.'

286

'No copper on her ward?' asked Breen.

Helen shook her head. 'Why would there be?'

'Whoever did this . . . she must know who it was.'

'Right. So you think he's going to come back?'

'Who knows. But. And no other visitors?'

Again, Helen shook her head. 'Not that I've seen. Apart from that bloke yesterday.'

'Poor woman,' said Breen.

A nurse came into the room and, ignoring them, lifted Kay's wrist and, with her other hand, turned the watch pinned to the front of her uniform up to her face and counted quietly to herself.

Breen wished he had bought a newspaper at the station. 'What do you know about her?'

'The police said she worked for a taxi company. Private cars. That's how she got in with the Stones' lot. She was one of their drivers.'

'Don't pop stars know how to drive?'

'Apparently not.'

'You'll have to leave now,' said the nurse. 'I need to wash her.'

'Is she injured anywhere else apart from her face?' asked Breen.

'No. Just the face. Wasn't that enough? She was beaten so badly she'll never see again.'

Helen raised her hand to her mouth, shocked.

'She's probably lost her hearing too, poor girl. The bastard must have really given her some beating.'

'There's no sign she was raped?' said Helen.

'Out, out, out!' The nurse came at them, arms wide, like she was herding animals.

They left the room and returned to the hospital lobby. 'Jesus. I had no idea it was that bad.'

Breen didn't answer.

'What if it's that guy? The one I saw here yesterday?'

'Could have just been anyone. A relative. You know.'

'What do we do now?'

'Wait. Watch. You know. You've done this stuff.'

The bench was like something out of a church: hard and unforgiving.

'Visitors all have to let you know who they're coming to see?' asked Breen.

'That's right,' said the nurse.

'Did you notice a man here, yesterday, at the same time? Did anyone else ask to see Miss Fitzpatrick?'

'No. Why should I? I'm not paid to be nosey,' said the woman.

'Got a shilling?' asked Helen. Breen dug into his pocket and pulled out a coin. Helen stood and went to a public telephone in the reception area. 'I'm going to find out how it's going for Elfie.'

She dialled and pushed the coin into the slot. She stood there waiting for someone to check the news from the maternity hospital. Breen handed over another shilling before a matron was found. 'Poor cow,' said Helen.

'What?' said Breen.

'Still in labour,' said Helen. She looked at her watch and chewed on her lip. 'That's, like, eight hours.'

Breen said nothing. Childbirth was a woman's world, one he had no understanding of.

Leaning against each other, they sat on the bench and watched the visitors come and go, not speaking. When she stood to go to the toilet, he opened his eyes and realised he must have fallen asleep.

'Poor Cathal,' she said. 'You're tired. Lie down. It's OK.'

'Here?'

'Why not?'

So he stretched out on the long dark bench. He was tired; he had slept badly the night before, only a wink last night, and been up since the small hours this morning running around after Elfie. His head ached with fatigue. He could never sleep on benches, but maybe if he shut his eyes for a few minutes he would feel better. So he closed his eyes and listened to the gentle murmur of the activity of the hospital around him.

And then, some time later, she was shaking him, roughly.

'Cathal,' she shouted. 'He was here.' She was excited, alive, eyes wide. 'Just now. He took one look at me and then did a kind of double-take and bloody ran. Wake up, Cathal.'

He blinked, fuzzy-headed and she was gone. By the time he had worked out where he was, Helen had run out of the hospital door into blinding daylight.

TWENTY-SEVEN

Breen ran out of the building, head still fogged with sleep.

Looking around, he caught sight of Helen, already a hundred yards away at the main road, doubled over, as if in pain.

He sprinted past parked cars, over municipal tarmac. By the time he reached her she had straightened.

'Stitch,' she gasped.

'Thank Christ . . . I thought—'

'Did you see him?'

'Who?'

'The man.'

She was panting, looking left and right.

'Did he do something to you? Are you OK?'

She pushed past him looking out of the gate.

'Shit.'

'What happened?'

'He was there. He saw us. Then he scarpered.'

'What did he look like?'

'Your age. Ordinary. Like you.'

'Ordinary?' said Breen, looking around.

'You know. Raincoat. Clean-shaven. Shortish hair. Ordinary.' She paused at the edge of the busy road, scanning the far side. 'He's gone,' she said.

'Who was he?'

'The man I told you about yesterday.'

'The man who had been trying to get to that woman in the hospital?'

She nodded, still panting. They looked around. 'He could have gone that way –' she pointed east – 'or there.' South. 'I'll go that way.' And she set off across the traffic, an open-top sports car honking at her as she strode out in front of it.

Not knowing who he was looking for, he headed south and found himself in an old shopping street, peering inside each shop as he passed. It was Saturday morning. The shops were busy.

He spotted only two men wearing macs; both were elderly. Another man carried one over his right arm, but he was bearded and round-faced, not like him at all. This was pointless.

He retraced his steps. It was a bare street; there were few places in which to conceal yourself and watch from but there was a short terrace of houses just beyond the main hospital and, assuming that Helen's mystery man would be approaching from the north, he tucked in behind the corner on the far side of the road.

Cars passed, but few pedestrians. None of them was a man who looked a bit like him.

He waited, feeling that this was absurd. He was a professional policeman. He wasn't even sure why he was doing this.

After twenty minutes he returned to the hospital. Helen was there, back in the reception area, sitting on the bench, looking pale.

'Anything?'

She shook her head.

When the petrol-pump attendant was topping off the tank, Helen asked, 'Do you have a map?'

The man in blue overalls wiped his hands and returned with a road atlas.

She opened it on the car's bonnet and peered close. Tongue sticking out slightly, she traced the roads until she found what she was looking for. 'How long would it take to drive there?' she asked.

'Couple hours,' said the man.

'Where?' asked Breen. Helen dug out her purse and pulled out two shillings for the map.

It was a village called Hartfield. 'Brian Jones's house,' she said.

'Why?'

'To look at it, obviously. Where he died.'

Breen looked at the route. It was a longer journey, but it was on the way back to London, at least.

'You want to look?' He was interested now, in spite of himself. She had drawn him in, bringing him to see Kay Fitzpatrick; she knew what she was doing.

'We don't have to be at the hospital to see Elfie till three. It's only midday.'

Breen got back in the car. It wouldn't take long. Besides, he was reluctant to go back to London and its problems. He didn't get a chance to drive much; he wouldn't mind going a little further in this car. It would be fun, wouldn't it, him and Helen, side by side? It was summer and the English countryside was green and lush.

But this time the road was slower.

As the car climbed upwards again up the North Downs, she said, 'Sometimes I feel like I'm slowly disappearing. This thing is taking me over.' She put her hand onto the roundness of her belly.

'Aren't you excited, though? Just a bit.'

'Of course I am,' she said, looking away, out of the window, towards brown fields of wheat. 'Talk to me about your case, Cathal. I want to hear about it. Anything.'

So as he rounded corners, engine roaring, he raised his voice above the noise to tell her about Julie Teenager. About the suspects they'd eliminated, about the 'Slavic' man, about the woman who drove clients for the dead prostitute.

'If I'd believed Florence Caulk was in danger . . .' he said. 'That was my fault.'

Like Sergeant Hope, she didn't offer sympathy. She had been a policewoman too. All she said, looking ahead, was: 'Another reason for you to find him.'

The only things he didn't talk about, as they motored through the English countryside, was the florist and the yellow roses.

Cows had escaped from a field near Ditchling, blocking the road. On the twisting road from the South Downs, the queue tailed back for half a mile. On a small lane in the Weald, he had to reverse for what felt like a quarter of a mile to let a lorry through. Tucking into a space next to a stone wall, he scraped a long line of black paint off Helen's side of the car. 'Serve Klaus right,' she said, fanning herself with the map.

Even with the windows down, it was hot in the car, sitting still with the summer sun beating down on it. Looking at the map, Helen tried to find a way round, but the heat was making her irritable and she got lost. They had to flag down a local copper to ask the way.

When they finally reached the village, the house was harder to find than they had imagined.

'Shall we give up and just go home?'

'We're here now, aren't we?' said Helen.

They asked for directions in a pub but it still took them another twenty minutes to find the house. Eventually, they turned down a short lane that opened onto a large expanse of tarmac in front of a large, old red-tiled house.

'I'm so bloody hot I'm going to die,' said Helen.

'You sure this is it?' said Breen.

There were no cars parked by the house. The curtains were closed. Butterflies hovered over dead rose heads in the garden.

'I think so.'

They got out of the car and walked into a courtyard filled with rose bushes. Somebody had left a bunch of wild flowers at the front door, stuffed into a jam jar; a wilting tribute for the dead.

The dead pop star's home was silent, deserted.

Breen said, 'Perhaps we should knock, all the same?' But Helen was already rounding the corner to the left of the court-yard.

'Come on,' she called.

Breen followed her. The pool was behind the house, concealed from view by the house. It was ornately shaped, two rounded ends cut out of the rectangle.

'Coming in?' she said.

'You can't . . .' He looked at the blue pool. It hadn't been cleaned. Dead leaves lay on the bottom. A dying beetle swam slowly in the water.

'Watch me.' And in a single movement, she pulled the light cotton dress she was wearing over her head.

For a second she stood in her mismatched bra and pants, belly shining in the sunlight, grinning, half naked and magnificent.

'Helen. What if somebody . . . ?'

But she raised a leg, stepped forward and fell into the pool. Breen watched her sink to the bottom, sending the dark debris that had fallen into the water swirling upwards around her.

She seemed to be down there an age before her head broke the surface, short hair matted down around her head. 'Fuck. It's cold,' she said, laughing.

'Come out.'

'I thought it would be warm. Aren't you coming in?'

He watched her as she lay back on the surface of the water, bulge upwards, arms extended. The darkness of her pubic hair was visible through her wet knickers. She closed her eyes and floated, and he watched, envying her ease in the water, and her freedom.

Nobody came. The house was empty. Bees buzzed around a small, lichen-covered statue at the far end of the pool.

'It would be so easy,' she said, eyes still closed. 'Wouldn't it? To kill someone in water and make it look like an accident.'

★

They left the old farmhouse too late. Another traffic jam at Sidcup delayed them again. By the time they got there, the maternity ward was quiet, and the lights low. The matron at the front desk crossed her arms. 'Visiting time is over.'

'She's on her own in there. We just want to say hello.'

'She'll have had quite enough to do. The mothers need their rest. You'll be in here soon enough, by the look of things.'

'How was it? The birth.'

The matron opened a book that lay in front of her on the desk. 'Boy. Seven pounds, one ounce. Perfectly normal. Come back tomorrow. Three p.m.' She slapped the ledger shut.

On the short drive home neither spoke. They both felt dirty and tired; they had been in the same clothes since yesterday. Helen's dress was still damp in patches from her swim.

' "Perfectly normal". What does that mean?' asked Helen.

Breen put his hand out and touched her belly.

Leaving her at home in the bath with a packet of cigarettes and an ashtray, he walked to Kingsland Road, where he found a Turkish shop that was still open and sold paprika. On the way back he looked round. A man in a suit, clutching a newspaper, looking out of place in this part of town, was walking about twenty paces behind him, but when he turned towards the cul-de-sac, the man seemed to walk on without hesitating. From behind the corner, Breen watched him, half expecting him to double back, but he didn't.

In the flat, he began browning beef in a frying pan.

'What are you doing?'

'Cooking you something special,' he said.

'What did you say?' The sound of gunfire came from the living room. She was watching a Saturday evening Western on the television.

'Nothing,' he said.

When he'd put the dish into the oven he went to join her in the living room; she was asleep, curled up in the armchair. He turned the volume knob down on the TV, and when he went to remove the dish from the oven she was still asleep, lying in the chair.

He woke her at eight. The table was set and he'd lit candles.

'Why didn't you wake me earlier?' she complained, blinking, then saw the table. 'What is this?'

'Saturday night. I just wanted to do something to make you feel special.'

She looked at him suspiciously; at the candles. 'Just a meal?'

'Yes.'

'OK,' she said, standing stiffly, stretching lanky arms. She leaned over the table and sniffed the casserole. 'What is it?'

'Goulash.'

'Sounds foreign,' she said.

'It is.'

She wrinkled her nose. 'Go on then,' she said. 'I'll try some.'

He ladled a dish for her and she dipped a spoon into the thick sauce and tasted it. 'Nice,' she said and smiled at him.

But just as he ladled a dishful for himself the telephone rang. Breen considered leaving it, but instead, picked up the receiver.

'I think I've found your Russki, Paddy,' said a voice.

'Wilco?'

'I put the word out, like I promised. If it's the same guy, he's at Tramp.'

'What's Tramp?'

'Private club, new place. Jermyn Street. There's a nig-nog called Olly on the door. He's all right. He'll let you in if you tell him I sent you.'

Jermyn Street. Breen did a quick calculation. It was in the right location; close enough to Bobienski's flat. Breen looked at Helen, holding a spoon with a lump of beef in it. She caught his eye.

'It's OK,' she said. 'I understand.'

'Sorry. I wanted this to be special.'

'Don't be stupid. I've got a dish full of stew. I'm OK. Did you say Tramp?'

'You heard of it?'

She scowled. 'Private club. Rich folk. Not my scene. Not yours either. You'll look like a square there. Wear something . . . younger. You going to be long?'

He didn't answer.

She nodded and pushed her bowl away from her.

TWENTY-EIGHT

The taxi dropped him outside the club, but instead of going inside, he looked around. There was a pale Hillman Hunter parked about twenty yards from the door in the direction of St James's Street, just out of the orange pool of street lights. He walked a little way towards it; in the shadows, the car looked innocent enough. Breen strode past the car as if heading away from the club, but when he was about ten paces beyond it he turned the corner into Duke Street and looked back. There had been no one visible behind the wheel when he had approached it, but now, silhouetted against the dim lamplight, there was a man. Whoever it was must have dropped down behind the steering wheel when Breen got nearer. Now he thought he was unobserved, he was sitting up again.

A sign he was in the right place; if the Russian was in the club, he would have a tail.

Olly, the doorman, was expecting him. He was a tall man in a dark jacket with white piping and his face was framed by a globe of frizzy black hair. 'There's not going to be trouble, is there?'

'No. Nothing like that.'

Olly nodded. 'Upstairs. Second booth past the bar,' he said. 'He's been here about an hour. Sign in at the desk first.'

Breen handed him a pound note; the man nodded, pocketed it.

'He's a regular?'

'Once a week maybe.'

'Everyone here signs in?'

'Course.'

'Can you check if he was here on Thursday the third?'

Olly went to the desk, where a heavily made-up young woman was signing in a giggling couple. Olly waited till they'd finished, then leaned over and took the ledger.

'Thursday the third? Yes. He was here.'

'What time?'

'11.55.' Sand had said his men had picked him up at around eleven. In fact they had lost contact with him for almost two hours. Spies turned out to be as unreliable as anyone; they too wanted to cover for their mistakes.

'What name?'

'First name Harry. Second? What do you reckon that is?' The man turned the book round and showed it to Breen.

Breen peered at the scrawl; it seemed to be 'Lyagushin'. He noted down the spelling of the name Sand had refused him.

'Do you have his address?'

'It'll be in our files, yes.'

He was enjoying himself. The secret services were full of men from Oxford and Cambridge who thought they were clever. It seemed easy, tracking down spies.

Tramp was showier than Sybilla's, with coloured flashing lights over a dance floor, where a pair of women danced around a young man with a moustache and long hair, the women's long dresses clinging to their thin bodies.

Breen sat at the bar, ordered a tonic water and affected the role of a single man in a nightclub, looking for company. Helen had been right. He felt conspicuous in his jacket and brogues. Men here wore expensive buckled loafers and wide-cut trousers cut with low waists, shirts with exaggerated lapels and chains around their necks.

If many young people thought these new times were all about a new Eden in which everyone would be equal, not everybody agreed. An older, more English order was reassuring itself. You had to spend money to feel comfortable here.

There were two men in the booth the doorman had told him about, either side of a slightly plump, dark-haired young woman. Both men looked like they were in their early thirties; one had longer hair, carefully parted on one side so it swept across his forehead.

He pretended to glance around the rest of the room in a casually predatory manner while trying to figure out which of the men would be Lyagushin. People drifted onto the dance floor. One woman in crochet hot pants, dancing with another in a gauzy skirt that you could see through as the lights flashed blue, red and white around her. The bra-less one, the two front straps of her polyester dress barely covering her breasts. The sophisticated smoker, hair cropped within an inch of her skull, with giant, round, pink-tinted glasses that Breen guessed were just for show. He was enjoying the excuse to just look.

But then he turned his gaze back to the left, towards the second booth again. One man was drinking a pint; the other spirits. Would the Russian be the one drinking spirits? He was thin, handsome, and dressed stylishly in a Savile Row suit: not Breen's idea of what a KGB agent should look like. Florence Caulk had said Mr B had been a looker.

Abruptly the spirit drinker put his glass down and stood up. The woman was shaking her head, laughing. Now the man was holding out his hand; still she shook her head. No. The thin man reached out and grabbed her arm and yanked, pulling her across the banquette. The woman shrieked. 'Stop it.'

But the man wouldn't take no for an answer. He pulled her out to her feet, then slid his arm round her and marched her to the small dance floor.

There was a slow song playing: a voice breathing '*Je t'aime*'. The woman tried dancing it on her own, hands waving in front of her, but he pushed himself towards her and slid his arms around her waist. She put her head back, laughing again now, as if used to this. She gave up struggling and allowed him to enfold her, possessively. They turned slowly as they danced. When her back was to Breen, he watched the man kneading her buttocks.

The other man who had been sitting at the booth now stood and walked to the toilets, behind where the DJ was spinning records. Breen put down his tonic water and followed him.

When he got there, the toilet appeared to be empty; the man must have gone to a booth. Breen waited at the urinals for him to emerge. After three or four minutes, the man finally came out of the cubicle and went to the mirror. Breen left the urinal and went to wash his hands, next to him, watching the man comb his long blond hair. The man licked his lips. Breen turned to him said, 'Quiet tonight.'

'Early still,' said the man. His accent was clearly English. Breen's first guess seemed right; if he was English, the other man must be the Russian who had signed his name as Lyagushin.

The door opened; a third came in. 'Got any gear, mate?' asked the newcomer.

The long-haired man didn't answer. Ignoring the new arrival, he put his comb in his pocket and pushed past Breen to the exit.

'Moody cunt,' said the man, opening his fly. 'Probably thought you were fuzz or something.'

By the time Breen reached the main room, the Russian had stopped dancing. Another girl had joined them in the booth and there was now a bottle of wine in a silver bucket in front of them. The new girl was smoking cigarettes in a long holder, holding it aloft as if trying to look like Audrey Hepburn in *Breakfast at Tiffany's*. The Russian looked up. Breen turned away, as casually as he could.

The club was gradually filling up. When a man in denim, with cowboy boots on, asked the barman for something called a Sambuca, it gave him the excuse to turn towards him and ask, 'What's that?'

The move put Lyagushin directly into his eyeline again.

The man answered, though Breen wasn't listening; he was watching the booth. The Russian was standing again, this time following the other girl onto the dance floor. This girl was more obviously beautiful. She wore a short dress with delicate shoulder straps and boots with thick soles that made her thin legs look longer. The Russian faced her, but the moment she made it onto the floor, she seemed to be dancing with herself, eyes half closed, running her hands down the side of her own body.

Breen was fascinated. Her display of narcissism seemed utterly appropriate in a place like this. Breen glanced around and everyone else seemed to be watching her, the women with fascination and envy, the men with a kind of hunger. The man at the bar with the glass of whatever-it-was whistled. Together they watched as the Russian placed his hands on her shoulders, as if to claim her, but the girl carried on obliviously, eyes closed.

And then the Russian caught Breen's eye staring at his girl and Lyagushin winked at him and grinned. It was a smile that said: 'Look at me. I have this. What have you got?'

Breen was forced to smile back, angry at himself. He had lulled himself into thinking that he was good at this. He had wanted to be surreptitious, unobserved, to maybe follow him home and learn something about him, but like everyone in the room, he had been drawn in by the sexiness of the young woman. Realising that the best thing to do would be to play the part, Breen carried on staring at the girl, watching her lean body swaying. And as she turned to face them, the denim man sucked in air.

'Look at that. Can see right through the fuckin' dress when she's against the light.'

Breen turned around, facing the bar again. Denim Man left to take his drinks back to his table. When the music stopped he was conscious of someone else sliding onto the seat next to him.

'I saw you looking.'

Breen turned. 'She's beautiful,' he said.

'Are you alone? I have not seen you here before.'

Breen was surprised how good the Russian's English was. The accent was perceptible, but hardly thick.

'I was stood up,' said Breen. 'My date hasn't arrived.'

'That is terrible. So you are here on your own?'

'I'll probably head home soon.'

'No. You must come and meet my friends,' said Lyagushin. 'My name is Harry.' The Russian held out his hand.

'Tom,' said Breen. His father's name. Why had he chosen that?

Lyagushin didn't let go of his hand. 'Another glass for Tom,' he said to the barman, and pulled Breen towards the booth. 'What do you do, Tom?'

'I'm a builder.' It's what his father had done.

Lyagushin paused and frowned, let go of Breen's hand. 'No you're not,' he said. 'You have soft hands.'

Breen wanted to kick himself. 'I tell people I'm a builder. I run a construction company,' he improvised.

Lyagushin relaxed, laughed. 'Sit down, Tom. You are a businessman. The English are the masters of understatement. I am a Russian. We like to oversell ourselves. Would you like wine?' The barman had put down a fresh glass. 'This is Kiki. And Freddie. And I forget this young woman's name.'

'Fuck off, Harry,' said the plumper of the two young women.

'Mr Tom here was stood up by a girl. He's all alone. I don't think he's used to places like this, are you, Tom?'

'Not really.'

'Be nice to him. Where are you from, Tom? Tell me all about yourself.'

'Harry isn't shy,' said the young woman next to Breen. 'He just asks people stuff.'

'I'm not English. Of course I'm not shy.'

'What do you do, Harry?' Breen asked. He had to almost shout above the music. They were playing a rock song now.

'Imports and exports,' he said, brushing his fringe from his face. 'We sell cameras to the West, mostly. Not very good cameras, but they're cheap.'

'And what do you do?' Breen turned to the dark-haired girl next to him. He realised it wouldn't be wise to sound too interested in the Russian. He should at least try to come over more like a man who had come here to pick up girls.

'I'm a model,' she said.

'Really? Would I have seen you in anything?' Breen asked.

'It depends what sort of magazines you look at,' said Lyagushin.

'Leave it out, Harry,' she said. She was pretty, but not pretty enough to be the kind of model that made it into magazines and newspapers. He wondered if, like Bobienski, she was a prostitute.

'What buildings do you build, Tom?'

'Tower blocks.' His father had built them, towards the end of his life.

'It must be a big company,' said Lyagushin, eyebrows raised.

Breen was straying into territory he didn't understand. He hadn't expected to be talking to the Russian; he hadn't prepared a cover story. He was unsettled. Sand had warned him against trying to track down the Russian; he had ignored him.

'Which one?' probed the Russian.

'Oh, it's all very dull,' said Breen.

'On the contrary. I love to see all these big buildings thrusting upwards. It is the future.'

The girl rolled her eyes.

'What constructions exactly are you working on now, Tom?' Lyagushin's smile had vanished. Breen must look out of place here in his plain clothes and sensible haircut. Was he suspicious of him?

The girl saved Breen. 'Fancy a dance?' she said. She seemed more interested in him now he worked for a big company.

'Why not?' He stood, turning his face away from Lyagushin.

'Come back after your dance, Tom. We'll talk some more,' Lyagushin said. 'The next bottle of wine is on you, I think.'

Gratefully, Breen followed the girl to the dance floor, wondering how much a bottle of wine cost in a place like this. Did he have enough in his wallet? The girl was short, only around five foot tall. She fell into a kind of shuffle, shaking her shoulders as she danced, looking at him.

Breen attempted to imitate her, looking down at his feet and moving them uncertainly. The girl said, 'You come here often?'

'Do I look like it?'

She giggled. 'Not really.'

'I'm rubbish.'

'Don't worry. Just don't think about it.'

Breen tried, but ended up feeling even less in control of his limbs.

'What's he like? Harry?'

'Flash Harry. He's all right. Likes to spend money, likes hanging round big people. They'll send him home in a few weeks, so he gets his fun in while he can.'

'Does he treat you OK?'

'What do you mean? I'm not his girlfriend or anything, if that's what you're saying. He just likes having us around him. All the women in Russia look like they drive tractors, he says. Why are you so interested in him, anyway?'

Breen didn't answer; just tried to make his dancing look a little more convincing. How much longer could this record last? The music was loud. It was giving him a headache.

And then, to his surprise, as he sweated away beneath the blue and red lights that flashed around him, he saw a man he knew enter the club room.

Klaus.

He was wearing white trousers, slightly flared, and a white waistcoat with a pink shirt underneath it. Hanging on to his arm was a lanky, straight-coiffed girl with an unimpressed look on her face, as if she wanted everyone to know she came to places like this all the time. Breen felt like an interloper here; Klaus looked instantly at home.

Breen turned his back so that Klaus wouldn't recognise him.

'What's wrong?' asked his partner, moving to face him.

'Nothing.'

'See. You were dancing much better then, when you weren't thinking about it.'

'Really?' Breen felt like he was sweating.

'Do you like my dress?' she asked. 'I don't know if it's right on me.'

Breen didn't answer. He was trying to spin round enough to see where Klaus had gone to. Thankfully the record was fading into another one now. He would make some excuse to the girl,

308

then to Harry about how he was feeling unwell. He didn't want Klaus recognising him and telling people he was a policeman. If Harry heard . . .

To his horror, he saw Lyagushin standing, open-armed, as Klaus approached. They knew each other.

Breen turned his back again just as the woman he was dancing with was about to walk off the floor.

'Another dance?' he said.

'I'm hot.'

'Please. I'm enjoying it.'

'You don't look like you're enjoying it. You don't even make decent conversation. Don't know why I bother.'

'I'm sorry. I'll try harder.' He put on a smile and tried to look like he was having the time of his life.

The girl shrugged and started dancing again. And again he turned his back to Klaus, hoping he wouldn't spot him. If he did, his half-cocked attempt at cover would be done for.

Maybe he should just head for the door; he could disappear out of the club and the Russian would just assume he was a strange Englishman, a little out of his depth in these sophisticated surroundings.

But he didn't have time. 'Tom,' Harry was calling. 'Tom. There's someone I want you to meet.'

Harry was on the dance floor, taking him by the arm. Breen turned and saw Klaus behind Harry, his superior half-smile vanishing as his mouth fell open.

'Klaus,' said Breen.

'You know each other already?'

Breen didn't have time to think. Klaus was about to give voice to his confusion. Everything would be over then.

Breen drew back his fist and punched Klaus as fast and as hard as he could.

On the edge of the dance floor, Klaus dropped like a doll whose strings had been cut. Girls screamed. Breen knelt down on top of him and punched him again. Finally, the awful music stopped.

TWENTY-NINE

After the third punch he stopped, shocked.

He hadn't meant to go so far. He had never been a violent man.

His head began to clear as he looked up. The people around him looked as horrified by the sudden assault as he was. Nobody knew what to do. That would give him time. Klaus was blinking, trying to raise his head off the floor.

'What the hell . . . ?'

Breen leaned his head in close to his ear and whispered, 'Quiet. Listen. You mustn't tell anyone who I am.'

'Why?'

'Because if you do, I'll truly whack you again. Got it?'

The crowd around were starting to murmur.

'You hit me,' Klaus whined.

'Leave him alone,' a girl was sobbing. Somebody had switched on the main lights now. In the glare, the place suddenly looked ordinary.

'Are you mad?' said Klaus.

'Not a word. Not now, not any time. Understand?'

Klaus sat up on his elbows and nodded warily. There was blood seeping from his lip. It dripped onto his white waistcoat. 'I should bloody well sue you,' he muttered.

As Breen stood, the crowd around him took a nervous step backwards. The girl sobbing turned out to be the woman he had been dancing with, not the willowy one Klaus walked in with. She was standing a few paces back, still affecting boredom, while the plumper girl looked horrified at the sudden violence.

Lyagushin was in the crowd, peering at the bleeding man, a wine glass in his hand and a small smile on his face. 'And I thought you were such a nice man. What was that about, Tom the builder?'

'A woman,' said Breen.

'Obviously,' said Lyagushin. 'Though from the way you danced, I was beginning to think you weren't the kind of man who was interested in them. Put your head back, Klaus. You're bleeding all over your lovely trousers.'

The white flares were now streaked with blood.

'Go home, Klaus. Put some ice on it. You'll have a nasty bruise in the morning. Tell me all about it next time.'

From nowhere the bouncer, Olly, appeared and grabbed Breen by the lapel. 'Out.'

'I'm going.' Breen shook him off. 'The other one will need a taxi,' he said. 'Get him home or he'll bleed all over the dance floor.'

The music started up again, like nothing had happened; 'Fly Me to the Moon'.

Olly muttered, 'What the fuck was that about?'

'Sorry,' said Breen. 'I'm sorry . . . I . . .'

'Don't fucking come here again. Ever. Right? If I had known you were going to be a wanker, I'd never have let you in.' Then he took Klaus's arm and said, 'Come with me, sir. We'll get you cleaned up a bit and get you home.'

Lyagushin was already talking to someone else. Breen walked across the dance floor, all eyes on him, and down the stairs, into the still London air.

Outside, the Hillman Hunter had gone, but another car had replaced it, parking at exactly the same place at the shadowed end of the street. It was too dark to see if there was anyone inside. Breen guessed that they changed tails when they could. Would they have recognised him too and reported back to Sand that he had been in the club with Lyagushin? Possibly. He didn't care. He had been stupid, coming here, perhaps, but he now knew who the Russian was, and he had narrowly avoided Lyagushin finding out he was a policeman – or at least he hoped so.

A taxi drew up outside. Breen hesitated, then tapped on the glass. 'Are you here for Klaus?'

'That you?'

'Yes. It is. I'm just waiting for a friend who'll be down in a minute.' Breen got into the back of the taxi and slid down a little in the seat, so he couldn't be seen.

A little while later the door opened and Lyagushin emerged with Klaus on his arm. The advertising man was holding a handkerchief to his face. Breen ducked a little further down. Had Klaus talked?

From his vantage point, low down in the back of the taxi, Breen could see Lyagushin and Klaus's faces clearly. Lyagushin still looked amused.

And then, without moving his head, Lyagushin's eyes darted quickly to the left, looking in the direction of the car parked there. And his amused look remained there.

He knows, realised Breen with a shock. He knows there is a car on his tail.

He had no time to think about what this meant when the car door opened. Klaus was about to get in when he saw Breen. 'Oh.' He stepped back, looking round, frightened, but Lyagushin had already disappeared back inside the club.

Breen leaned forward. 'Get in,' he hissed. 'I'm not going to whack you. I promise.'

The cabbie peered back in his rear-view mirror, suddenly anxious. 'What's going on?'

'Get in. Now,' said Breen.

Klaus did as he was told. 'Why did you hit me?'

'Drive,' he told the taxi driver.

'I think you broke my tooth.'

'Because you were about to say my name. They didn't know I was a policeman. It's important they don't.'

He dabbed his swollen lip. 'Bloody hell. You could have just told me.'

'Maybe I wanted to hit you anyway.'

'Fucking pig. You didn't need to do it so hard.'

'Did you speak to anyone about who I was?'

'I don't remember. I was concussed. I'm bleeding, man.'

'Not in my cab you're not,' said the driver.

'It's OK,' said Breen. 'He's hardly hurt at all.'

'Where to?' asked the cabbie.

Breen turned to Klaus: he gave an address in Ladbroke Grove. 'I'm crashing at a friend's pad,' he explained.

'You know about your baby, then? It's a boy.'

'Really?'

'He was born today. And there you were dancing with some woman in a nightclub.'

'Is that what this bullshit is about?' He wiggled a tooth and winced. 'Do you think I should go to hospital?'

'Only to visit Elfie. You haven't been, have you? You're a coward.'

Klaus looked down and checked the handkerchief for fresh blood. 'I've been busy, obviously.'

'Clearly. Don't you even care?'

'It's not my baby. It's Elfie's baby. She's the one who wanted it. I never wanted to be tied down.'

Breen wished he had hit him harder now. 'Grow up, Klaus.'

'Don't try and guilt-trip me. If she didn't want to go on the Pill, that was her affair. She knew that.'

'You slept with her, Klaus. It's your son.'

The man snorted. 'It's not like that any more. I'm not into that nuclear family patriarchy bullshit. I'm a free man. She's a free woman. We're all free, now.'

'Lucky us.'

The taxi pulled up at a red light, windows rattling as the engine idled.

Klaus said, 'You live your life your way. Let me live mine my way, OK?' He pulled out a cigarette. 'You got a light?'

Breen took a box of matches from his jacket. 'So you know that man at the club, the one called Harry?'

Klaus pushed hair out of his eyes and said, 'Harry the Russian? Oh, I get it. So that's what all this is about? You not wanting Harry to know you were fuzz. Is Harry in trouble?'

'How long have you known him?'

'I don't know. Three months. What's wrong with Harry?'

'Where did you meet him?'

'I don't know. At Aspinall's, maybe. You know, the casino?'

'You never wonder how a Soviet trade attaché could afford to gamble at a casino?'

'Soviet trade attaché? Bullshit. He's just a chancer. Harry never gambles. He just watches.'

'What's he do?'

'He's just a laugh, that's all. He says he has money he can't get out of the country so he has to spend it here. So he has a lot of friends, know what I mean?'

'And that doesn't ever make you suspicious?'

'Why should it? Is he involved in something I should know about?'

'No. And like I told you before. You say nothing more to him about this, OK?'

He held up both hands. In one he grasped the blood-spotted handkerchief. 'Loud and clear, man. Loud and fucking clear.'

'If he asks, my name is Tom and I own a construction company, got it?'

'Are you being serious?'

'Yes. When you were with him, did you ever meet a woman called Julie Teenager?'

'Course, man. She's dead, isn't she?'

'Did you ever meet her with Harry?'

'Sure. Think he introduced me to her. I'm not into that shit, though.'

'Because women give it to you for free?'

'You're just jealous, copper.'

Breen leaned over and opened the door when they got to Ladbroke Grove. 'Give me three pounds,' he said, 'for the taxi.'

'It's only a quid to here,' said Klaus, handing over a single note.

'Go to the hospital. See your baby.'

Klaus closed the door. Breen made the taxi driver wait until he'd gone inside, noting the house number in case he needed to find him again.

When the taxi moved off, he noticed another car pulling out further down the road. Was it the same car that had been parked in Jermyn Street? He was not sure.

At home, Helen took some ice from the freezer compartment of the fridge and wrapped it around his knuckles; they throbbed.

'Surprised you hadn't done it before,' she said and she leaned forward and kissed him on the forehead, rubbing her hands through his hair. 'Hope you broke his nose or something. Ruined his gorgeous looks.'

That night, the pain in his hand stopped him from sleeping. He heard Helen padding around in the corridor outside.

'Indigestion,' she said. 'From the goulash.'

He lay in bed thinking about what he had to do in the morning, and the car that might have followed him earlier this evening, wondering, as an ache travelled up his arm, if it wasn't just Klaus's nose he might have broken. It was years since he had hit a man like that. His own anger had shocked him. He had never liked Klaus much, but it wasn't really even him he was angry about.

THIRTY

It was late on Sunday morning and the midday shift streamed out of the section house off the Bayswater Road. Breen waited outside until the flow of uniformed men died down, then pushed his way through the open doors.

The stairs to the first floor were at the end of the corridor, past the common room. He was about to make his way through the swing door when a man in a worn linen jacket and dustpan in his hand said, 'Who are you?'

'It's OK. I'm a copper,' said Breen.

The man seemed to be a section house sergeant, in charge of the place. 'I don't care if you're a bloody copper or not. You're not a resident here so you're not allowed in. Rules.'

'I need to see John Carmichael.'

The man looked at his watch. 'You'll be bloody lucky, mate. He'll be asleep till gone midday. He was in last night. Bloody steamboats he was. Surprised he made it upstairs.'

Breen pulled out his warrant card. 'I need to see him on business. Will you wake him for me?'

The man clearly didn't like the idea of doing anything for Breen. He scrunched his mouth up, peering at the card. 'Second floor,' he said eventually. 'Room E18. If anyone asks, it wasn't me who said you could go up there.'

Upstairs, the corridor was deserted. He knocked on the chipped brown gloss paint of the door. There was no reply. He knocked again, this time with his whole fist, wincing as the pain travelled up his arm.

'Go away.'

'John. It's me. Cathal.'

There was silence. Breen tried the door, but it was locked.

'I'm not going away, John. I need to talk to you.'

Again, no answer.

Breen thumped louder. Down the corridor, a copper emerged from one of the dormitory rooms, to see what was going on. The man was dressed in trousers and a string vest, blue braces over his bare shoulders.

'Open up, John,' called Breen.

At the other end of the corridor the man stayed, half in, half out of his room, watching. Breen listened for a while. He could hear nothing in the room.

'Come on, John. Otherwise I'm going to start telling you why I'm here. And then everyone's going to know.'

Another door opened and another head appeared. 'What's going on?' he asked the other man.

'Fellow here asking for Big John.'

'Leave him alone, mate. He had a skinful last night. Sling it, OK?'

'Lena Bobienski,' said Breen, through the closed door.

'Did you hear what I just said, pal?' The man in the vest had left his doorway and was walking slowly towards Breen, opening and closing his fists. He was stocky and wide; Breen could see dark hairs on his shoulders.

'Julie Teenager,' said Breen loudly.

Just before the man reached Breen, he heard a bolt shift on the other side of the door. Carmichael opened it, unshaven, red-eyed, and dressed only in a pair of underpants.

'Want me to deal with this, John?' said the man in the vest, squaring up

'He's OK, Squid,' Carmichael mumbled, and pulled Breen into the small room.

Squid stood at the door, chin jutting out, until Carmichael closed the door on him.

Inside, Breen looked around. The bedroom was a mess. Normally Carmichael was a man who took great care of his clothes, but trousers and jacket had been dropped onto the floor. Picking up the discarded jacket, Carmichael lowered himself onto the edge of his small bed and rummaged in the pockets.

'Tell me about Julie Teenager,' said Breen, again.

'Don't know . . .' He found a packet of cigarillos and took one out.

Breen sat down next to him, smelling his sweat, thick with last night's alcohol. 'Don't lie to me, John. Please,' Breen said quietly. 'You're my oldest friend in the bloody world.'

Carmichael lit the small cigar with a lighter. Took a drag and then began coughing. When he stopped, Breen saw tears in his eyes. He wasn't sure, at first, if they were from the smoke or not.

'Yeah,' he said, finally. 'So?'

'So why?'

'For a laugh. That's all. She was a laugh.'

Breen looked straight ahead at the door he had been knocking on. 'A laugh?'

'How did you find out?'

'You bought her flowers. Same place as you sent them to Amy.'

Carmichael giggled. 'Fucking Paddy bloody Breen. Top of the detective charts.'

'You should have told me,' he said.

'I should have, course I should.' Somewhere someone started playing slow brass band music. Breen wasn't sure if it was the radio, or noise drifting across from Regent's Park.

Breen said, 'What about Amy?'

'Did you tell her?'

'No.'

Carmichael took another drag. 'Thanks, mate.'

'*Thanks, mate*? Don't thank me for anything.'

'Like I said. It was just a laugh. I didn't want to hurt anybody.'

'You knew I was investigating her murder. I have spent half this investigation thinking this was a police cover-up. One of my coppers, a good sweet lad who never crossed a wrong line in his life, almost got sacked because he went to the papers. All because you didn't tell me.'

'I know. I was stupid. I'm so, so sorry.'

'You're my friend.'

'Sorry, mate.' But Carmichael didn't turn to look at him.

'We went to school together. I always thought you protected me. Remember the fights?'

'Christ, yes. Those were the days.'

Breen scowled. 'Don't bloody Those-were-the-days me, John. Your mum looked after me. Cooked me dinner.'

'She felt sorry for you because you didn't have a mother yourself.'

'Doesn't that mean anything at all?'

'I said sorry. What more can I say?'

Breen stood. He pulled back the dirty curtains. Sunlight streamed into the room, making Carmichael wince. 'So what was Amy for? All that time you spent chasing after her, but all you want to do is fuck some whore.'

'Shut up now, Paddy. Don't go on about it.'

Breen squatted down in front of him. 'I want to understand.'

'I've got a head like King's Cross bogs, Paddy. Can't we do this another day?' He grinned.

Before he knew what he'd done, Breen had slapped his friend hard across the side of the head. 'Tell me now.'

Carmichael looked stung. Breen saw how he had automatically balled his fists, ready to hit back. John had always had a stronger punch.

'Go on then,' said Breen. If it came to a fight, John would win easily. Besides, his fist was still tender from last night. It was John he'd been wanting to hit, all along.

'Know why I didn't tell you? Because I knew you'd be a sanctimonious little prick about it.'

Meaning it this time, Breen slapped him again with his other hand.

Carmichael was up on his feet, fist pulled back again. Breen smacked him again.

Carmichael rolled his shoulders and Breen waited for the punch to come.

'Come on, hit me, you coward,' shouted Breen. 'Do it.'

But he didn't. Carmichael just flopped backwards onto the bed.

'Amy's chucked me anyway,' he said. 'She told me last night.'

'That's why you got so drunk?'

'I'm glad. She was too good for me.'

Self-pity didn't suit him. 'Yes. Turns out she was.'

'Fuck off, Paddy. Just fuck off. You going to tell her?'

'Why shouldn't I?'

He put his head in his hands. 'Stupid. Like the better it got with me and Amy, the more I had to destroy it, before she found out that I wasn't worth it.'

'That's just being pathetic, now.'

'I'm not ready for this.'

'You're a grown man. Both of us. We're not kids any more. We're grown bloody men, John.' Breen looked around. 'It stinks in here. Let's get out. I need to talk to you about the prostitute.'

'I've got a headache.'

'Good,' said Breen. 'I'll be downstairs. See you in ten minutes.'

'Don't be a cunt, Paddy.'

Breen shouted, 'I'm not the one who withheld evidence for two bloody weeks, John.'

324

Carmichael looked shocked. When he stood, face dark, Breen thought he was going to go for him again. Instead he unhooked his dressing gown off the back of his door and picked up his washing bag.

Breen went downstairs, and he was just about to leave to wait outside on the pavement, when a couple of policemen pushed the front door open. Breen recognised one of them, but it took him a second to remember where from.

'Phipps,' he said as the man passed him.

The man stopped, then looked at Breen, puzzled.

'D Division, CID. I came to you to ask about a woman who was a driver for a murdered prostitute.'

The man from the Vice Squad nodded cautiously. 'Yeah. Right. I know you.'

'You live here?'

'That's right. Oh, sorry, mate. I never got back to you. You know how it is.'

The man was about to open the door at the bottom of the stairs when Breen said, 'One thing . . .'

Phipps stood, hand on the door handle.

'There's a Russian called Lyagushin who visits prostitutes in London. Have you ever heard of him?'

'Lyagushin?' said Phipps, struggling with the name. 'I don't think so.'

'Yes you do,' said his companion. 'He means "Comrade Whip-'em-off". That's what we call him.'

'Oh. Right, yeah. "Whip-'em-off". The dirty delegate.'

'You've heard of him?'

'God, yeah.'

'By mistake?' said Breen.

'He's a trade attaché. Caught him with his pants down at Madame Kiki's in Greek Street. "Diplomatic immunity, diplomatic immunity",' Phipps called out in a phoney Russian accent, waving his hands. 'That's what he said when we found him.' They laughed.

'Better hope that's not the only immunity he has, the way he gets around.'

'So you arrested him?'

'Nah. He's just a john. Besides. We were told to lay off him anyway.'

'Who by?'

'Some tin hat upstairs.' And, laughing, they disappeared up the stairs.

Five minutes later, Carmichael emerged unshaven from the front door of the section house, wearing flares that were too tight around the waist and large dark glasses shading his eyes from the glare of the July light.

'I need a bloody coffee,' he said.

It was a Sunday so their options were limited. 'The Lido,' said Breen.

They crossed the Bayswater Road and walked diagonally across the park towards the Serpentine. A boy on roller skates rattled past them unsteadily as they approached Carriage Drive.

'Was she the first?'

'What if I say she wasn't?'

Breen nodded.

'I don't know why. I didn't even really enjoy them that much. You get hooked. You get drunk. Everyone else goes home to their wives and girlfriends. Even you. Especially you. Next thing you're at some place ringing a doorbell.'

'But you had a girlfriend.'

'I know. I don't know what to say. Once you start it's hard to stop.'

'Bollocks.'

'You don't know me, Paddy. You just think you do.'

'Tell me about Lena Bobienski.'

They turned right at the Serpentine. Though there was only a thin sun, people were sunbathing on the banks of the lake; girls in bikinis lying on towels while their boyfriends smoked and read novels.

'Mostly it was convenience. She ran a good place. Not like the other tarts around King's Cross. There was less chance of getting caught. She was very beautiful, Paddy. You should have seen her. I mean . . .'

'How did you hear about her?'

'When I was in D Division still, last summer. One of the guys in Vice told me about her. She was that close to our station. This woman who was making money pretending to be a teenager.'

'You like that? Young girls? You're thirty-three.'

'It's just a bit of fun, Paddy. Christ's sake. You don't even know what fun is. You're such a boring bastard.'

They found a metal table and a pair of chairs and waited for one of the waiters to see them.

'Did you ever meet any of her other men? Or did she talk

about them?'

He shook his head. 'Course not. Once, maybe. Saw another man going in.'

'What did he look like?'

'You don't actually look, do you? It's kind of an embarrassing situation. It's dark. I don't know. It was outside.'

'There was a woman who picked up clients and drove them to the flat.'

'That's right.'

'Did you ever use her?'

'No. Heard about her. Saw her once. That time I was talking about. He was getting out of the car to come up. His turn next. But he had his back to me, I suppose.'

'What type of car?'

'Cortina. Dark blue or maybe black. 1600E.' The sort of detail that Carmichael would notice.

'What did she look like?'

'Pretty nice, actually. Dark hair. I don't know. Young. Maybe twenty-four, twenty-five.'

'Good.' Breen took out his notebook and wrote down the details.

'Build? Height?'

'Nice. I mean, probably about five-six. Hard to tell when they're sitting down.'

'Did you ever hear Lena say she was under any threat?'

'No. I mean . . .' He looked away. 'She used to ask me to protect her, but that was just a game.'

'Big strong man, protect me?'

He had never seen Carmichael looking this embarrassed

before.

'She played you like an idiot, didn't she?'

Carmichael didn't answer. Breen looked around for a man hiding behind a newspaper. Was he still being followed, observed? Which of the other people sipping tea, reading newspapers, could be the one? The pretty girl in the sage-green minidress? No. What about that man with the khaki hat and a Kodak around his neck? Or the athletic young man in the cricket jumper?

'Did she ever try to blackmail you?'

Carmichael's mouth opened wide. 'Blackmail? Why?'

'It's possible that was one motive for what happened.'

A waiter arrived in a white linen jacket so they ordered large coffees. 'Do you do any breakfasts?'

'Sandwiches and cake.'

Carmichael ordered two ham sandwiches and some chips.

'I mean. She knew I was a copper. She saw my wallet. She thought it was funny. One day she said, "What if I tell your mates on you?" I told her I didn't care if she did. Nobody would be that bothered. Apart from bloody you.'

'Did she ask what you did as a policeman?'

He nodded. From the board, a diver launched himself into the water with a splash.

'I told her. She asked if I had arrested anybody famous. I said that was Pilcher's department. I suppose she was asking, yes. Why?'

'Because one of her clients was a Soviet spy. Another one was a journalist who specialised in Soviet politics. She was Polish. And MI6 were watching her flat.'

Carmichael's mouth dropped wide. 'You're serious?'

329

'Yes. And I think I'm being watched too.'

Carmichael removed his sunglasses and looked around, as if looking for someone amongst the crowd of half-naked sun-worshippers and swimmers. 'MI6?'

'But you had no idea?'

The coffee arrived. Carmichael picked up his cup and drained it, almost in one. 'I mean, she was manipulative. She threw tantrums and everything, like a little child. Wanted me to come back every week. Wanted presents. I just thought it was all part of the act, you know? Spoiled little girl.'

'But you didn't suspect . . . ?'

'No. It doesn't make sense. Are you sure? So she was killed because of this?'

Breen looked at a young boy pulling himself out of the water, shivering. 'I don't know. To be honest, John, I'm not much further along about this than I was when I started. Wasted too much time trying to find a policeman.'

Carmichael nodded. 'You going to tell Helen? She'll tear my bloody eyes out.'

'Good.'

A boy ran past with a balsa-wood model of a plane, shouting, 'Taka-taka-taka-taka!'

Carmichael winced at the noise. 'Are we still mates?'

It was Breen's turn not to answer. He stood and looked around the park. He wanted to be with Helen; for her to put her arms around him and say nothing.

He left Carmichael slowly spooning mustard from a small pot onto his sandwiches.

Buses on Sundays seemed to run to their own timetable; he had promised he would be back in time to visit Elfie in hospital.

Dalston Junction stank of discarded fruit from the early morning market; he walked north from there towards his flat. He put the fact that the police station was quiet down to it being a Sunday, and moved on.

It was when he rounded the corner to the small cul-de-sac that he saw the ambulance and the throng of coppers and broke into a trot. Christ.

There were policemen standing around it, blocking the way. He pushed past. 'Is she having the baby?'

A hand grabbed him. 'Paddy. Don't go in there,' said one of them.

'What?'

The ambulance doors were wide open; he looked inside but it was empty.

'Where is she? Is it the baby?'

Someone took his other arm. 'Don't, Paddy.' He didn't even recognise the man.

'What is it?'

Two coppers, now, holding him back. 'Let me go. Let me go,' he screamed. And the neighbours, out on their front steps, peering round the doorways, sad sympathetic looks on their faces.

THIRTY-ONE

They brought her out, strapped to a stretcher, her face coated in congealing blood, thick, dark, still oozing from a wound somewhere under her hairline.

'She's in and out of consciousness,' said an orderly. 'Get her in. Lift.'

The stillness of Sunday had vanished. Breen shoved forward to get near, almost making one of the coppers lurking around the ambulance tumble to the ground.

'Watch it, mate.'

He struggled closer. He could see her eyes closed, lids swollen, but there was a flickering under the skin.

'Get back, sir,' someone shouted at him and nudged him backwards. Breen was still staggering, trying to regain his balance as they lifted her into the ambulance.

His brain was racing. 'Please. What happened?'

'Assault, mate,' said the copper, letting go of his arm. 'Sorry.'

'Who by?'

'They got a 999 fifteen minutes ago. The operator took a while to understand what she was saying, I heard.' Breen peered past him, standing on his toes to try and see what they were doing in the ambulance. 'When we got here she was on the floor. Somebody had really had a go. That's your place, isn't it?'

'Oh, Christ. Is she going to be OK?'

They were closing the doors of the ambulance.

'Christ, Christ, Christ.'

'Get out the way. It's going to need to turn.'

'I need to go with her. Please.'

A constable he recognised from the Stoke Newington nick put his arm around him. 'Relax, Paddy. We'll take you there. Leave it to us.' A kindly older voice, reassuring, steadying.

He was shaking, he realised. 'Who found her?'

'Constable over there.' He pointed to a pale-faced young copper, holding his helmet under his arm.

Klaus's MG was still parked outside where Breen had left it. 'Let me move the car.'

'You're not doing nothing, Paddy.'

Hurry up, hurry up. He jerked at the arm holding him.

The man gripped him tighter. 'Come on. We need to get you sorted out, Paddy.' The same old constable. Breen couldn't remember his name. He had worked with him years ago when he'd been stationed here.

Oh, Jesus.

'I need to go,' said Breen.

'No. You need to sit down a minute. You've had a bad shock. Come inside. She's in the best hands now. We'll take you down there.'

The ambulance had finally turned 180 degrees and was now driving down the narrow exit to the cul-de-sac, its bell ringing.

Shakily, Breen descended the steps to his flat; the front door was wide open.

'How did he get in?'

'Sit down, mate. Get your breath back.'

It was the blood he saw. The carpet by his dad's old chair was dark with it.

The phone had been yanked off its small table and onto the floor where she had lain; she must have called the ambulance from there.

Helen. Helen. Helen.

'Who?'

'We don't know. But we'll catch him. Don't you worry. And before we do, we'll let you have a little go at him, right, Paddy?'

'A go at him?'

'You know. Fuck him up a bit.'

Breen shook his head. 'He broke in?'

'Squint!' the copper shouted up the stone steps to the street outside. 'Paddy here wants to know about the door.'

The young constable came down the stairs hesitantly, putting his head inside the door, but not crossing the threshold.

'Was the door broken in?'

'No. It was unlocked. We just walked in when we came.'

She left it unlocked all the time, didn't she? He'd told her not to. Oh God.

'She was on the floor, there.' He pointed. 'I held her hand till the ambulance came.'

'Did she say anything?'

'Couldn't really make it out. She was bleeding quite a bit.'

'Hush, man. Bit of fuckin' tact.'

'Sorry.'

'Run back to the station, there's a good lad. Get someone to organise a car to take Paddy here to the hospital.'

Breen looked around. There was no sign of open drawers, that the attacker had been trying to steal anything.

How could he still be observing this? How could he still be thinking like a copper at a time like this? He looked at the blood on the floor. There seemed to be so much of it.

'She was pregnant?' said the constable.

Breen's mind was racing with dark possibilities; he couldn't stop them coming.

The best thing, when you were investigating a case, was for something new to happen so you could see everything you already knew from a fresh angle. The very worst thing was that it would be this.

On a Sunday there was no need for the blue light, but the young copper who was driving put it on anyway, perhaps out of respect for Breen.

The car pulled up right outside the emergency bay, but they had already taken Helen inside. At the open doors, an orderly said: 'Can't go in that way. You have to go round the front.'

He ran to the main entrance. 'A woman has just arrived by ambulance.'

'Name?'

'Helen Tozer.'

'And you are?'

He hesitated. 'Her husband,' he lied.

She looked him up and down, then said: 'Through the door. End of the corridor turn left.'

There was a small seating area with tables with tin ashtrays. A mother sat with a snivelling boy, the front of his shirt wet, presumably from crying, but no one else was here. It was a quiet Sunday; there did not seem to be any staff around.

He walked to the far side of the room, where there were swing doors with round glass windows, and peered through, but could see no one there, either. Pushing the door open, he heard voices.

At a desk cluttered with papers, a West Indian nurse was sitting eating a sandwich, talking to a young man in a white coat. She looked up. 'You can' come in here,' she said, mouth still full.

'Please. I need to know about someone who's just been brought in by ambulance.'

She grunted, put down her sandwich. 'Go sit down, darlin'. I'll go find out what's going on. Patient's name is . . . ?'

He waited with the snuffling boy and his mother until the lad was taken away by a doctor to have something removed from his nose.

'The boy's simple,' the mother said, after the boy had gone. 'It's not his fault.'

The nurse came back.

'What?'

'May have a couple of scars, but she's awake and she can talk.' She sat down next to Breen and put her arm around him. 'Got a few tests but she'll be OK.' With her free hand, she offered him a tissue. 'Doctor's with her now.'

Breen closed his eyes and breathed.

'What about the baby?'

'Too early to tell. But your wife, she's fine, thank the Lord.' And she sat with him for a minute while his chest heaved.

'I'm so sorry,' he said. 'I'm not normally like this.'

'Go on. It's OK.'

'No. It's not.' And he struggled to control himself. He hated this woman, seeing him crying. It wasn't right.

An hour later, another nurse came down and told him Helen was awake.

'Can I see her?'

The nurse led him to the stairs and up to the first floor, into a room with six beds. Five were empty. She was in the sixth. They had cleaned the blood off her, exposing the cuts and bruises. They had shaved her head and there were four bloody stitches on her hairline.

It was as if her face had been reduced to a child's ugly scrawl, careless and disproportionate. Her top lip was enormous, distorting her expression into a cartoon scowl, while her left eye was shut and massively swollen. The eyelid was an even grey-blue. It looked more like an egg laid sideways onto her face; at the bottom of this huge bulge sat a bizarre fringe which Breen realised were her eyelashes.

'S'ry,' she whispered, wincing as she tried to speak.

He looked for a hand to hold, but it was under the covers.

'Who was it?'

'Don't know . . . didn't see.'

'Didn't see?'

The older constable who had been at Breen's flat arrived, pushing his way through the curtain. 'She's talking?'

'She said she didn't see who assaulted her,' said Breen.

'B'stards,' she said.

'There was more than one?' asked Breen.

A tiny sideways motion of her head. 'No. B'stards here. Won't give me painkillers. Headache.'

'So you were in the flat?'

''Es.'

'And someone came in and assaulted you and you didn't see who it was?'

'Too fast. Didn't even hear him.'

A nurse arrived. 'She needs painkillers,' said Breen.

'She's near term with that baby. There's a limit to what we're allowed to give her.'

'Is the baby OK?'

'You'd have to ask a doctor about that.'

'How did the assailant get in?' said the constable.

'Did you leave the door unlocked?'

Helen nodded, winced again.

'She does that,' said Breen. 'She never locks doors.'

'Ca . . .'

'She's trying to say something.'

'Cut,' mumbled Helen.

'What?'

She sighed. Talking was an effort. 'I got 'im. I was on the floor. Cut his leg with . . .' She took a breath. ''Encil.'

'A pencil?' She gave the tiniest of nods as her hand emerged from the blanket. It was bandaged so tightly that only the tops of the fingers showed, but she made small stabbing motions with it.

338

'You cut him?'

Another nod and she closed her open eye, tired out from talking.

'What were his shoes like?'

'Yours.'

'Brogues?'

A tiny nod. 'Old man . . .'

'He was an old man?'

A shake of the head, and a wince. 'Old man shoes,' she whispered. 'Elfie.'

'What's she saying?' asked the copper.

Breen realised it was a question. 'I don't know how Elfie is. I'll go and check after I've spoken to the doctor.'

He beckoned the constable out of the ward. 'What's the news?'

'Done door-to-doors already. Nobody seen anything. Not surprising. It's quiet round your place.'

Breen waited for the doctor, but he didn't arrive for another hour, and when he did, he was an elderly man who wore a pink shirt and said things like 'She had a nasty, nasty knock'.

'Somebody tried to kill her,' said Breen.

'Didn't make a very good job of it, did they?'

'Only because she fought back.'

The doctor raised his eyebrows. 'Well, yes. Good girl, I suppose. We'll keep her under observation. A blow to the head like that could have consequences. It'll take a day or two to know if it's affected the brain, or whether there's any bleeding.'

All this adrenaline going round inside him and nothing to do except wait.

'What about the baby?'

'Seems fine, actually. I think she must have protected him from the worst of it.'

'Him?'

'Or her. Strong woman. We'll take a look at her eye in the morning. Might be some damage there. Good sign is she's alert now.'

Breen left Helen sleeping and went back to the reception area and then, finally, headed to the maternity ward.

A lift took him upstairs, and he found himself in Male Surgical. Men with missing limbs turned and looked as he walked between their beds. 'I was looking for Maternity,' he said.

'Ain't bloody in here, that's for sure.' One old man wheezed with laughter.

Another joined in. 'Eternity, more like it.'

On the floor above, he finally found the ward fifteen minutes before visiting time was over. 'That one,' said the matron, pointing at the row of beds. 'Are you the husband, at long last?'

Breen shook his head. Each bed had a small metal cot next to it; they looked like little hostess trollies. Most were empty, the mothers clutching their children in their arms.

Elfie's baby was still in the cot, crying. Elfie was sitting up in bed, but her eyes were closed.

As another young nurse came by holding a bedpan, Breen turned to ask her, 'Is she OK?'

'A bit weepy. She's not been feeding well. Some of them are trickier than others. She's very . . . difficult.'

Other women had men with them, or families, clustered round. Elfie was on her own. 'Has anyone been to visit her?'

The nurse shook her head. 'Not that I've seen.'

He waited a while by her bedside while the baby continued to cry. Breen looked at the cot. There was a label. 'Born: 20/7/69. Sex: M.' The space after 'Name' had been left blank.

'Elfie?' he said.

She opened her eyes, smiled at Breen. 'Where were you? I've been waiting.'

'Congratulations. On the baby. What's his name?'

'I don't know,' she said.

Breen blinked. 'Is he hungry?' The wailing infant's arms were pumping slowly into the air.

Elfie pulled her blanket up a little higher. 'Where's Hel?'

'She's . . . not well.'

Elfie looked sadder; she looked down at the cot and the whining infant inside it. 'I was waiting for her,' said Elfie.

'She'll come as soon as she can.'

Breen suddenly felt exhausted. He had imagined Elfie would be good at this, confident, but she seemed to be struggling. Around the ward, other mothers had boxes of chocolates and vases of flowers crammed onto their small bedside tables, alongside jugs of squash.

'Have you heard anything from Klaus?'

'He hasn't been to see me,' Elfie said, and pulled her sheet up to wipe her eyes. 'He hasn't even phoned.'

The nurse who had been carrying the bedpan was striding back down between the beds. She paused at Elfie's bed.

'You should be feeding him,' she said. 'Poor little mite is hungry.'

'I've tried,' Elfie snapped. 'It's not working.'

'Just give it another try, love.'

'I can't.' Elfie started to cry. 'I can't. I can't.'

'Are there any relations?'

For the first time, he noticed other people looking disapprovingly. How could this woman be leaving her baby there to cry?

A bell rang. Visiting time was over. People began leaning over, kissing the babies, standing up and putting on coats and cardigans. There was the sound of chairs being pushed back and kisses on cheeks. They were drawing curtains round the beds now. He stood and said, 'I have to go.'

'Tell Helen to come,' she said. 'I want her.'

The corridors were full of families going home, laughing and smiling. Breen took the stairs down, but instead of leaving, turned right, into the corridor that led to Helen's ward.

'Visiting time is over,' said the woman, when he tried to get back in. He pulled out his wallet. 'I'm a policeman.'

'I thought you were her husband?'

The skin around Helen's cheek had the dull blackness of old bananas. 'Elfie?' she said through her swollen lips.

'A boy. He's . . . fine,' he said.

''Ood. She must be happy.' It was still an effort for her to talk. If anything, the swelling was worse, but she looked more relaxed.

''Een thinkin'.'

'What?'

'All the same.'

'Yes. I think it's the same man too. The one who assaulted Kay Fitzpatrick. He must have seen you. Followed you home.'

She shook her head agitatedly. 'But . . .'

'She needs to sleep now,' said the nurse. 'We're turning the lights off in here. The doctor just gave her pethidine. It'll help her.'

'Wait,' Helen said again.

'What are you saying?' said Breen, suddenly puzzled.

'Same man.' Her breaths were shallow and rapid.

'Yes, I understand.'

She shook her head slowly.

'Quite strong, that injection they've given her,' said the nurse.

'J—'

'Kay?'

'No. No. Julie.'

Breen was trying to comprehend what she was saying. In her mind, the drugs must have muddled the two cases.

'It's OK,' said Breen. 'We can talk about it in the morning.' He leaned forward and kissed her, but it must have hurt because she flinched and the last look she gave him before her eyes closed was hostile, angry.

The lights in the room went out.

'Out,' said the nurse.

He walked out into a cool summer evening, down the steps into the car park at the front of the building.

'Is she all right?'

Breen turned. John Carmichael was standing there, unshaven still, looking as rough as he had that morning.

'What are you doing here, John?'

'One of the coppers from Stoke Newington called me. He said something really awful had happened to Helen. He thought you'd be here on your own.'

'And?'

'Just that. You might want a friend around.' His eyes were red, as if he'd been crying.

'A friend?'

'Don't, Paddy,' said Carmichael. 'Come and have a drink.'

'I don't want a bloody drink, John,' said Breen. 'That's your answer to everything, isn't it?'

'Just tell me what happened, will you?'

'She was assaulted. Like you heard.'

Carmichael sniffed. 'Suit yourself. I'm only trying to help.'

'Knight in white bloody armour?'

Carmichael held up his hands. 'OK. OK.' But he didn't leave Breen's side as he turned and walked west down Homerton High Street.

'What are the injuries like?'

'Her face is pretty bad.'

'Permanent?'

'I don't know.'

On a small patch of grass by some council flats, a woman in a blue dress was scolding some boys who were trying to play cricket. 'Any idea who it was?'

'She didn't see him. Just his shoes.'

'What kind of shoes?'

'Like mine, she said.' He stopped and looked down at his feet. ' "Old man shoes" is what she called them. It may be something to do with an assault that was carried out in Sussex last week. She was looking into it.'

'What the hell was she doing that for?'

'It's complicated. It was for a friend. You know her. If she gets a bee in her bonnet about something . . .'

'It was her friend who was beaten up?'

'No. Like I said. It's complicated.'

'And this bloke . . . was trying to frighten her?'

'Or shut her up.'

Carmichael nodded. 'That's good, isn't it, anyway? They have something on him, now.'

'Oh yes. Bloody great,' said Breen, and started walking again.

'You can't be like this, Paddy. I know you're pissed off with me. But you're a fucking policeman. It's what you do.'

'Go away, John. I want to be on my own.'

He left Carmichael standing on the pavement on Homerton High Street as he made his way alone on foot back to the flat, which would be empty now. He spent an hour on his hands and knees trying to soak Helen's blood from the rug on the floor. She must have lost a lot. Each time he wrung the cloth out, the water in the bucket turned pinker.

'Same man,' she had tried to say.

In the end he took the rug up, rolled it up and put it outside the front door. He watched as liquid ran off it, onto the bare concrete. Her blood, still. The violence with which she'd been struck.

'Oh, Christ.'

Same man, he realised, wetness pooling at his feet.

★

He didn't sleep. At six on Monday morning, he called the hospital.

'We can't disturb her.'

'It's urgent.'

'She's asleep anyway.'

At eight, he called Calliope Trading Ltd, but there was no answer. Then he phoned the hospital again. The matron told him to call back after ten, after the doctors had done their rounds. 'But is she all right?'

The matron said, 'She says she's hungry. That's a good sign.'

At nine, at his desk, he called the MI6 number again. Still no answer.

At 9.30 he tried a third time. A fourth, just before ten. The phone rang and rang and rang. Breen imagined an empty office somewhere, the telephone echoing, unattended.

At 10.30 he wrote 'Coffee' in the exercise book, and walked to the 91. It was quiet there. He could think.

'You sick? You don't look good,' said George.

'Tired,' said Breen. 'Sick and tired.'

'Coffee,' said George.

'I'll need more than that.' And as he drank George's coffee, he made up his mind what he had to do. It was what Helen would have done. Normally, he was not such a reckless man.

Back at his desk, he looked around. It was a good time to do it. Jones was out. All the other desks, apart from Mint's and Rasper's, were empty. He picked up the phone and called Felix, the journalist from *OZ* magazine.

Felix sounded half asleep. 'What is it?'

'Did I wake you?'

'Yes.'

He had a plan now. 'You know I promised you a story? I've got a scoop for you,' said Breen. The line clicked and buzzed. In the electric fuzz and static he heard the ghost of his voice, echoing back at him.

THIRTY-TWO

'Why,' demanded Felix, 'would we print what the fuzz feed us?'

'Because you'll find it interesting. It's a story about a Russian trade attaché who's a suspect in the murder of Julie Teenager.'

At the other end of the phone, Breen could hear Felix scrabbling around for a pen and paper.

'Why are you telling me?' he said.

'A Soviet trade attaché. What else do you think he does, besides . . . attaché-ing?' Out of the corner of his eye, he saw Mint, watching him open-mouthed. 'I'd tell the papers,' said Breen, 'only they can't report on stories about national security, can they?'

'Not if they're part of the D-Notice system.'

'But you can, because you're amateurs.'

There was a pause. ' "Alternative press" is what we prefer to call ourselves.'

'Off you go and be alternative, then.'

The moment he'd got off the phone, Mint hissed, 'What do you think you are doing?'

'Let's just say you didn't hear any of that.'

Mint was agitated, scrubbing his hand through his thick hair. 'You said they'd throw me off the police when I spoke to a journalist.'

Miss Rasper looked up.

'Keep your voice down,' said Breen.

'You'll be sacked. Don't you care?'

Breen thought for a second. 'Actually, no. Not any more. I really don't.'

And he picked up the phone again and called the hospital, asked to be put through to the ward. 'No. She's fine,' a woman said. 'Stroppy, though. She's asking for more painkillers, but she just ate scrambled eggs and asked for more.'

He was smiling this time, when he put the receiver down.

'She's in hospital? Is the baby coming?' Mint frowned at him.

'Are you listening to all my calls as well?'

'As well as who?'

'Never mind.'

'No. Just . . .' Mint looked at him. 'Call him. Whoever you spoke to. Tell him you made a mistake. You're about to become a father,' whispered Mint. 'You have responsibilities.'

'Yes, exactly,' said Breen. 'I'm about to become a father. I have responsibilities.' He looked at his watch and stood up.

Breen left Creamer's exercise book blank this time, walking out into sunny, exhaust-filled air. He headed north until he reached the Regent's Canal and descended to the towpath. There were fishermen dotted at regular intervals along the path, lines dipping

349

into the greasy water. They fished to the calls of macaws and parrots and the occasional screeching monkey, the sound drifting over the water from London Zoo.

He arrived back a little after twelve.

'Oh, boy. Are you in the shit,' said Jones with a grin.

Mint looked up, worried. 'You OK?'

'What's happened?'

But before he could answer, Creamer bolted out of his office. 'Upstairs. Superintendent McPhail has been asking to see you. I should warn you. He's in a bit of a temper.'

'I thought he might be,' said Breen. He took a breath and turned to go out of the room again.

'What is going on?' Creamer shouted after him. 'What have you gone and done, Paddy?'

On the next floor, he knocked on the door to McPhail's office. 'Sergeant Breen, sir,' he called.

There were two people in the room when Breen entered, saluting the Superintendent. 'I think you two have already met,' said McPhail.

'Mr Sand.'

'Sergeant Breen.'

The man from MI6 was sitting on the wooden chair in front of McPhail's desk, a small smile on his shiny, round face. He wore a pale summer suit and an ordinary striped tie, presumably some club or school.

'I'm very surprised, an officer of your experience,' said McPhail, tugging on the sleeve of his uniform. 'Surprised and disappointed.'

'Just out of interest, how did you know?' said Sand.

Breen asked him, 'That MI6 were bugging *OZ* magazine? It was pretty bloody obvious. Unless it was someone else in this office?'

'I won't dignify that with an answer,' said McPhail.

Sand looked from McPhail to Breen. 'I wonder if you would let us have a word in private, Superintendent?' said Sand.

McPhail looked at his watch, nodded. 'Of course.'

When he'd gone, Sand pointed towards McPhail's chair. Breen took McPhail's place. 'You see, I thought we understood each other,' said Sand. 'I was mistaken.'

'His name is Harry Lyagushin,' said Breen. 'He is a Soviet trade attaché who claims to be selling cameras to the West. He visits nightclubs and casinos to ingratiate himself with the rich and powerful. Do you want me to go on?'

Sand raised his eyebrows. 'Very clever. I had no idea how much you knew.'

'You think we're all a bit dim on the Met, don't you? We didn't go to nice universities.'

'Believe me, most of our lot who went to nice universities aren't exactly trustworthy.'

'Lyagushin didn't turn up at Julie Teenager's flat at his usual time on Friday. Why? Presumably because he knew she was dead already, because nothing had been reported in the papers. I tried to contact you. You didn't answer.'

'Because you're not playing our game. You can't touch Lyagushin. He's too valuable to us.'

'It's not a fucking game,' said Breen.

351

'I apologise. It's a figure of speech. However, as I said, my priorities are different from yours.'

'I believe he may have killed two women and seriously assaulted two more. My girlfriend was attacked last night. I think it's the same man.'

Sand looked surprised. 'I think you're jumping to the wrong conclusions.'

'Of course you do.'

'Look. Whatever terrible things he may – or may not – have done, we need him to operate freely. It's a golden opportunity for us.'

The desk in front of him was immaculately tidy. A small box of carefully sharpened pencils, a telephone and a clean blotter were the only things on it. 'Is that it?'

'We are constantly reviewing our options. We're not monsters. If circumstances change and I'm able to share more information, obviously I will be happy to.'

'How generous.'

'I don't like sarcasm, Sergeant. I understand your frustration, but I'm unable to do anything. And no reputable paper is going to print the story.'

'That's why I spoke to a disreputable one. Times are changing, Mr Sand.'

'You're being naive, Sergeant Breen. We have our eye on it. We don't like to restrict the freedom of the press, obviously, but that particular publication may not last.'

'You can't just shut papers like that. People won't stand for it.'

'I doubt we'll need to, frankly. I doubt the courts will tolerate it much longer.'

Sand sat, stiff-backed and awkward. 'One thing I will share. I'm sorry to hear about the assault on your . . . woman friend. It's a terrible thing. I'm sure you're under a lot of pressure. I hope your Superintendent will understand how an event like that will have clouded your judgement. I rather doubt it, however. But if you think Lyagushin was involved in the assault on Miss Tozer last night, you are mistaken. We were watching him. He was at home, yesterday evening.'

Breen blinked. 'But you would say that, obviously.'

'I'm not that cynical. It wasn't Lyagushin who assaulted your girlfriend.'

'Why should I believe you? You'd say anything to protect your precious spy.'

'I'm not the monster you think I am, Sergeant Breen. I promise you. Lyagushin was nowhere near your flat.' He stood and picked up an umbrella from the corner, where he'd left it propped up. It was a good one. Robust and hand-made, with a solid stick and a bark handle. Not one of those cheap new American models. Breen wouldn't have been at all surprised if there had been a blade hidden in it.

'If you're working on the assumption that all four assaults were carried out by the same person, he's not your man,' said Sand. 'Goodbye, Sergeant. I wish you well.'

Breen was stunned. 'It's not Lyagushin?'

'No.'

Sand held out his hand to shake. Breen didn't take it. Sand shrugged, then pushed past Breen and out of the door. Breen listened to his footsteps descending the old staircase.

★

He sat for a minute, then leaped up and ran after him down the stairs, passing a startled-looking Superintendent McPhail who was coming the other way. 'Sand,' he shouted.

'Breen. What in God's name . . . ?' exclaimed McPhail.

Breen ignored him. By the front desk he hadn't caught up with the MI6 man. He looked out onto the street, to the left and the right.

A man in a pale suit was about twenty yards away, walking west. Breen ran. 'Sand,' he shouted.

Sand stopped, looked around. 'What now?' he said, irritated.

'I want to make a deal with you.'

'What kind of deal?'

'I have information I think you'd want. If I tell you, will you let me in on what's really going on?'

'We don't work like that, Sergeant.'

'Fine,' said Breen and turned away.

'Wait. What kind of information?'

A passing woman laden with shopping bags paused to light a cigarette. Breen waited till she'd gone and said, 'Lyagushin's on to you.'

Sand's eyes narrowed. 'He can't be.'

'But he is.'

'How do you know that?'

'Talk to me and I'll tell you.'

'You can't just keep stuff like that back, Sergeant. If you know something, it's your duty to share it with us.'

Breen folded his arms across his chest. 'Really?'

Sand hesitated, looking around him, then seemed to make up his mind. 'Let's catch the tube,' he said.

'Where are we going?'

'Nowhere in particular. But I enjoy the underground at this time of day. It's quiet, but not so quiet that anyone can overhear your conversation.'

At Baker Street, they descended to the Bakerloo line and waited on the empty westbound platform. Sand sat on an empty bench beneath a poster for a John Wayne film.

'So. You think he knows we're on to him? How?'

Breen brushed crumbs off the bench and sat down next to him. 'You first. That's the deal.'

Sand seemed to be considering. 'I haven't been able to trust you so far. Why should I now?'

'If you'd trusted me in the first place, I wouldn't be trying to tell *OZ* magazine about Lyagushin.'

Sand nodded. 'Do you know about Gerald Brooke?' Sand said eventually.

'The prisoner? I read about him in the newspaper.'

Sand pulled out a pipe; it was one of those plain ones, a churchwarden, sensible and straight-stemmed. 'Exactly,' he said. 'Sentenced to a labour camp. Silly idiot took some anti-Soviet leaflets to Russia. Propaganda printed by the last of the White Russians. Nostalgia, as much as anything. Totally useless, tactically.'

From down the tunnel came the rumble of a distant tube train.

'What about the Portland spy ring?' Sand asked.

'Of course.' It had been the early Sixties. Breen had still been working at Stoke Newington police station.

'Peter and Helen Kroger?' said Sand.

'The couple from Ruislip.'

'Precisely.'

The train arrived. 'The Russians are good to their spies,' said Sand, getting in. 'They like to have them back so they can celebrate them as heroes of the revolution. They want Peter and Helen Kroger back. They want to swap them. Unfortunately they don't really have much to swap them for. Except for Gerald Brooke. Through diplomatic channels, we've been in negotiation with them for months.'

He packed the pipe from a small pouch, pushing the tobacco down into the bowl with his thumb.

'Of course, we advised the government that it was not a symmetrical exchange. Brooke is a nobody. The Krogers were part of the most sophisticated network of illegal residents we've ever picked up in this country. We would be seen as weak if it goes ahead.'

At Marylebone the doors opened and closed with no one getting into their carriage.

'Unfortunately the PM is very keen.' The PM. Dropped into the conversation as if to suggest how close he was to the Prime Minister, Harold Wilson. 'Parliament has been dead against the deal. The Tories have been having a field day. But here, the Soviets have proved useful. I don't know if you read the *Sunday Times*?'

'When I have time.'

'It turns out your man, Ronald Russell, has been slipping stories into the paper suggesting that Gerald Brooke is not just a naive lecturer caught up in this process, but he's actually a high-powered British spy.'

'Yes. I think I read something like that.'

'Pretending that Gerald Brooke is really a significant pawn in the game makes it easier for Wilson. He doesn't lose face in the exchange.'

'And the articles are written by Ronald Russell?'

'Exactly. From what you told us, useful information as it happens, it's become clear that Lena Bobienski was what the Soviets call a swallow. A honey trapper. Her job was to go out and find men she could compromise. We're fairly sure she was a spy being run by the Polish secret service, the UB.'

'What's this to do with Lyagushin?'

At Edgware Road a woman in a short skirt and yellow sweater got on, her hair wet. It must have started raining.

'Well, I suppose he is important. We would never have known about Lena Bobienski if it hadn't been for Lyagushin. It was him who led us to her. Presumably before he realised he was being followed by us. I assume he was dipping his fingers into the honey jar. He is not a pleasant man.'

'He was there for sex?'

'Possibly. As far as we know, she wasn't GRU or KGB. She was being handled by the Poles, I'm pretty sure. But presumably the UB were working with the Soviets on this one. We've had information from a source in Warsaw that a swallow existed in London for months, but we had no bloody idea at all who she was until Lyagushin conveniently exposed her. He has been very useful like that. We think he was acting as her handler.'

'You knew Lena Bobienski was a Soviet agent all along?'

'A Polish agent. Yes.'

'But her father fought against the Soviets. They killed him. And her mother.'

'Not her mother, we believe. Nor, it seems, her brother.'

'Oh God, yes. She has a brother.'

'Lena was lucky. She stayed behind here in England. We think her brother would have been forced to Siberia with his mother and father. We don't know much about it. But we discovered letters from him in the flat.'

'Under the floorboard? You said you hadn't found anything important.'

'We took the decision that it wouldn't have been any use to you. Besides, we are not inclined to trust the Metropolitan Police with sensitive material. With some justification, as it turns out,' he added, drily. 'We'd been hoping to find cyphers but that's produced nothing of value. In his letters he says he is being held in Mokotów prison in Warsaw. The UB have him locked up there, poor bastard. According to these letters, he'd spent all his life either in the Soviet gulags or the UB dungeons. The Polish secret service seems to have been blackmailing her. If she supplied them with information, her brother says they'll set him free and give him a visa to leave the country.'

'God. How awful.'

'She was doing all this to try and get him released. Yet she was probably too young when they were separated to even know what he looked like.'

'There was a photograph.'

'Yes. But he was just a small boy.' With a bang, one of the ventilation windows slammed open, and the carriage was full of warm air. Sand stood and closed it, smiling at the pretty woman with the wet hair. 'It's a thought, isn't it? Imagine having to live the life she did just on the off-chance she might be saving her

brother. What a powerful thing that is, the need to have a family.'
He looked at Breen's reflection in the train's window.

'Do you think Lyagushin killed her because he knew she had been exposed? If his cover was blown, hers was too?'

'It's possible. It would be a little cruel, after the way they've treated her. But I don't see it. They look after their own. And even if he could have given us the slip on Sunday, which he didn't, why would he have tried to kill your girlfriend? It doesn't make sense.'

'I would have liked to have asked him that. But it seems I won't be given the opportunity. You would be happy to let her killers get off free if it served your purpose.'

'I hope we're not that bad.'

'So, if I understand you, the whole honey trap was simply to get Ronald Russell to print some misinformation about Gerald Brooke, so that they could make it look like Brooke was more valuable than he was? Lena Bobienski had to blackmail him to make up articles saying that Gerald Brooke was a genuine spy?'

'It's what it looks like from where we stand. They were making it easier for Wilson to do the deal. A curious type of cooperation. You provided us with the Ronald Russell connection, for which we're grateful. It was good work. That allowed us to figure it out.'

'Why haven't you arrested Russell, then? I thought you lot were in the business of spy-catching?'

The train stopped in a dark tunnel. The lights flickered. Then the carriage jolted forward again.

'So did I,' he said. There was a touch of darkness in his voice.

'Certain operational reasons?'

The tube train burst into daylight and fresh rain spattered the

359

windows. 'Yes. The Prime Minister wants this exchange to go ahead. He's under public pressure to get Brooke back.'

'Ah.'

'It turns out it's not just the Soviets who gain from portraying Brooke as more than he was. So we do nothing about Ronald Russell. To arrest him would upset that apple cart.'

'So he gets away with being a Soviet stooge.'

'To be fair, it's hardly worth arresting him now Miss Bobienski is dead. And, if we did, they would rumble that we're on to him too. But we'll keep an eye on Russell.'

'It all just seems so pointless,' said Breen.

'That's your judgement. We take a different opinion.' He turned to Breen. 'Right. Your turn. You think Lyagushin knows we know what he is?'

'You had a man parked in Jermyn Street on Saturday night.'

Sand frowned. 'We may have done. I don't have all the oper-ational details.'

'Tramp. That's the nightclub he was in – supposedly at least – the night Lena Bobienski was killed.'

'Like I said earlier, you're better than I thought. I am sorry I underestimated you.'

'He was there again last Saturday. Your men were watching him. They changed shifts some time before eleven.'

'They would have done that, yes.'

'I was with Lyagushin that night. It was clear when he came out of the club he knew exactly where your man was.'

'How?'

'I don't know. But I saw him carefully checking he was there before he stepped out.'

Sand turned and looked directly at Breen. 'Ah,' he said.

'Yes. Exactly. All this time you were watching him . . .'

'He knew.'

'Anything you know is what he wants you to know.'

Sand nodded slowly. 'If what you say is true, we've been outplayed, it seems.'

'So if there's nothing to be gained, we could pull him in for questioning?'

'No.'

'Why not? If he knew where your men were all the time, he probably also knew how to evade them. Think about it. He might have even been making your men his alibis. What if he wasn't in his house on Saturday evening, when Helen was attacked? What if he just let your men think he was?'

Sand looked less certain of himself than Breen had ever seen him. 'That's an absurd hypothesis. You're crediting him with being much too clever.'

'How do you know? He's useless to you now. Why don't we treat him like the murder suspect that he is? If he's not a suspect, he's a witness. We still have a double murderer to find.'

'That's out of the question. This is a sensitive time. If you start pulling in Soviet Embassy staff the whole deal might be off.'

'All I want to do is catch a murderer. You can't get anything from him.'

'Far from it. In fact, you've just given us another interesting piece of information. Before, we thought he didn't know we knew he was a Soviet agent. Now we do. As I told you before, the power in the network is in discovering precisely how much other people know, or think they know. Besides, we can't simply arrest him. Not right now. Maybe in a few weeks.'

Rain streaked the glass.

'It's a very cynical world you operate in,' said Breen.

'I don't see it as cynical at all,' said Sand. 'The opposite, in fact. Much like you, our job is to keep people safe. And in doing so, we keep all that world away from people, so they can continue their lives as normally and peacefully as they can.'

'Our jobs are not the same at all,' said Breen.

'Suit yourself. We both have our principles. Can you make it back to your office from here?' said Sand. The doors opened at Queen's Park. Sand stood clutching his umbrella and held out his other hand to shake.

He ran from Baker Street tube, but still the rain dripped inside his collar; it travelled down his leg into his shoes and soaked the underside of his cotton socks.

By the time he reached the office his pale summer suit was dark with water.

'Miss Rasper?' said Creamer. 'Is there a towel for Sergeant Breen? He's soaking wet. And a cup of something hot, perhaps?'

Miss Rasper stood. 'Very sorry to hear your news, Sergeant Breen. Is Miss Tozer OK?'

'I think so.'

'And the baby?'

'A word in private?' said Creamer.

'I'm praying for them,' said Mint, and he blushed, while other detectives looked away, embarrassed.

362

Breen walked, socks squelching in his shoes.

'So anyway,' said Creamer. 'Obviously you'll be taking some time off.'

'Who will be looking after the case?'

'Miss Bobienski? That is what I wanted to discuss.'

Rasper arrived with a small hand towel, handing it to Breen with a sympathetic smile, then backing out of the room.

'Discuss?' Breen rubbed the towel over his hair and down his neck.

'McPhail tells me the case will be taken over by C1 from now on. Given what has happened to Miss Tozer, I suggest you take a few days to be with her.'

'Sir?'

'Compassionate leave.'

'I thought that was just for bereavement.'

'I'm using my discretion, Paddy. Believe me, it's either that or a suspension. Besides, the case is not ours any longer. It's just come down from above. Look, Paddy, I'm not aware of the reasoning behind this. You may have more insight into the situation. I simply have my orders.'

Breen stood, his feet settling in his shoes with a soft squelch.

'Go home, Paddy. I'll get the boys to make up the folder on the case to pass across. Mint can brief C1. They'll be in touch if they need anything. I'm sure your young woman needs you more than we do right now.'

When he opened the door, everyone was looking at him again.

Creamer emerged behind him. 'Constable Mint? Get a car and drive Sergeant Breen home, will you please.'

'It's safer to walk,' said Breen, and everybody laughed, though a little too heartily.

In the end Mint drove. It had been a long day. Breen was tired now and he just wanted to see Helen, but he needed to change out of his wet clothes first. 'Can we go to my flat first?'

'I don't understand,' said Mint. 'Why are they taking us off the case?'

'Because they think they can do better.'

'Really?'

'No. Not really. Because they don't want anyone to solve this one.'

'You don't actually mean that.'

'No. Of course not.' Though that was exactly what he meant. C1 would sit on the case for a few weeks and then close it.

When they were heading down towards Old Street, Mint said, 'You and your girlfriend . . .'

'Helen?'

'I mean . . . I would prefer it if you were married. It's what I believe in. But it's OK. Jesus forgives everyone.'

'That's very big of him,' said Breen.

'Yes, it is,' said Mint.

They pulled up at the flat. Elfie's windows were dark; the place looked unlived in, unloved. Inside, he changed into dry clothes while Mint waited outside. He was about to leave when he remembered the ring in his sock drawer.

At the hospital, Mint said, 'I'll wait.'

'You don't have to.'

'Not got much else to do, have we?' He saw the box that Breen was fingering. 'Is that a ring?' he said.

Breen got out of the car. As he walked across the tarmac towards the front door, Mint called, 'I'll pray for you both,' from the passenger window.

'You bloody do that,' said Breen and he pushed through the double doors into the hospital.

THIRTY-THREE

She had been put in a surgical ward full of older women, lying asleep in crisp white sheets. Her face was more colourful than it had been on the day before; all blues, purples and yellows. Her breathing was so shallow that once or twice he leaned closer to feel the breath on his cheek, just to reassure himself.

'She's fine,' said a woman's voice.

Breen turned. Behind him, in the neighbouring bed, a woman in her sixties sat knitting. Her long grey hair came down over her shoulders; the sort of hair she'd have normally worn up in a bun.

'Did you do that to her?'

'God, no.'

She shrugged and clicked her needles. 'Mine used to do a bit of that. You her husband?'

'No.'

'Brother?' She didn't wait for an answer. 'Was that her husband just now?'

'There was another man here?'

'Nice man. Just left.' Her lips moved as she knitted, counting rows.

Breen stood and looked up and down the corridor. 'What was he like?'

'I don't see that well. He just wanted to know if she was OK.'

Breen's neck was prickling; his heart started beating. 'What did he look like?'

'Bit like you, I suppose. You a relation then?'

'It's my baby,' he said.

The needles stopped clicking. 'I thought you said you weren't married?'

'Think. Was there anything else about that man?'

'He was nice. He asked me what I was knitting.'

Breen looked at the woollen garment; a children's jumper.

A nurse came by. 'Did Miss Tozer have another visitor?'

'No,' she said. 'You're the first.'

'There was a man here. What did he look like?'

'No need to shout,' said the nurse.

'This woman here said there was a man, visiting my girlfriend. What if it was the man who assaulted her?'

'Girlfriend,' muttered the woman.

'That was the vicar,' said the nurse.

The woman pouted, set her needles clicking again. 'I said he was a nice man.'

Breen laughed, a little too loudly.

Helen Tozer opened her eyes. 'Hello you,' she said. 'I was wondering what all the noise was.'

Relieved, Breen sat down again, this time on the edge of her bed.

'You're meant to bring me chocolates.'

'Right,' he said.

'You look rough,' she said.

'You, on the other hand, look gorgeous.'

'I went to see Elfie,' she said.

'I didn't think you were supposed to get up.'

'It's only my face he messed up, not my legs. I'm bored just sitting here with all these old . . .'

The woman in the next bed with the knitting clacked her needles furiously.

'She's fed up. Poor little lad even looks like Klaus, didn't you notice? She's scared about taking him home on her own, I think. You know, I thought I was the one who wouldn't cope. She was the earth mother, you know? She's falling apart.'

He looked at her and thought of Elfie's baby boy, crying in the cot.

'How's the case?'

'Not so good. I think this time he's getting away with it.'

'No. You'll get him.'

'Maybe not this time.'

Outside, the rain had started again, smearing the windows. He started cautiously. 'What was it you were trying to say, yesterday? You were on some drug.'

'You'll think I'm nuts.'

'So?'

She smiled at him, then winced from the pain of moving her lips. 'I think the man who attacked me was the same one that killed the other two,' she said.

'I heard you saying it yesterday, but at first I didn't understand.

I figured it out last night. You think it's all the same. You, Mrs Caulk, Kay Fitzpatrick, Julie Teenager.'

'He went for my face. Like the others. All of them.'

He nodded. It was true. It was usually husbands or lovers who went for a woman in the face; there was something deliberately vicious about it. Four in a row? It was unusual, but all he said was, 'That could be coincidence.'

'Yes. But what about this? He didn't attack me the first day. He attacked me the second day. When he saw you.'

'I know. The man from the hospital in Chichester.' A bell started ringing far away, down some corridor. It was like the bells were in his head too.

'Yes I think it was him in our flat.'

'Maybe.'

'Something about the height. The way he moved. I don't know.'

'You're sure?'

'And you heard him speak?'

'Just one word.'

'What about his accent? Was it Russian?'

'You couldn't really tell.'

The tea trolley was coming around, pausing by each bed, pouring tea from an urn into pale green cups and saucers.

'He hates women,' she said. 'He wants to disfigure them.'

'Is it a stretch to assume, just because you're all women, that it's the same man?'

'Think about it though. He saw us when you were asleep. I saw him, you didn't. But he saw me and the penny must have dropped that we were together. You and me. He knew I could recognise him. He knew I could identify him to you. That's what changed everything.'

'Right.'

'He's someone who you know. Someone who you've already met in your investigation. That's why he wants to kill me. To stop you making the link.'

'Wants?'

'Yes.'

'Someone I know? But you don't?'

'Exactly.'

Breen nodded. 'Yesterday, before I left you at the flat, I thought I was being watched.' He had assumed it was one of Sand's men. 'But it was you he was waiting for. My God.'

She stared at him, puzzled. 'Why did you think someone was watching you?'

He shook his head. 'I'm off the case,' he said.

'You can't be. What's happened?'

'Can you stand?'

'Of course I can. I'm not a bloody cripple. What's going on?'

'We need to go somewhere private to talk.'

'What about my tea?'

'Take it with you.'

'Three sugars, please,' she said interrupting the woman who was pouring tea for her scowling neighbour.

She was standing now, putting on a dressing gown. Breen took the cup and carried it, rattling in its saucer, through a ward of women who all watched him as he passed.

'This is the father of my child,' she said. 'The one I told you about.'

The women muttered.

She pushed open a door at the end of the corridor and stepped out onto the iron landing of a wet fire escape. Below a group of nurses were on a break, eating sandwiches. The rain had stopped for now, but water still dripped from the poplar trees at the edge of the car park.

'You see, I made a mistake. That's why they've taken the case away. I thought I knew who the man who attacked you was. I tried to expose him.'

'Who?'

Breen paused, then said, 'A Russian spy.'

Helen sprayed tea.

'No. I'm serious. I've stumbled into something I barely understand. It turned out that Julie Teenager worked for Polish intelligence. She was blackmailing Ronald Russell to concoct stories that the Soviets wanted to see in our papers. I thought she may have been killed by her handler. But I can't figure out why or how.'

Her mouth was wide. Standing on the rusty fire escape that looked out over the housing estates towards the treetops of Hackney Marshes, he explained everything that Sand had told him. He didn't care any longer that it was supposed to be a secret. It was because of it all that Helen had been attacked.

'So C1 have taken over the case now?' she asked.

'Yes.'

She stood there, trembling slightly in the cool air. 'Do you still think it's him? The Russian?'

'I can't make it add up. Something's wrong. Something's missing. It's like thrashing around in the dark.'

'So do you think C1 will get him? Whoever he is?'

'Of course bloody not. The case is being mothballed because it's inconvenient. Sand doesn't want anyone to know what actually happened with Lena Bobienski in case it lets the Soviets figure out how much they knew.'

She nodded. 'Fucking hell,' she said. 'This is someone who killed two women.'

'I know.'

She shivered. 'It's July and I'm cold,' she complained. 'They wouldn't really do that, would they? Just let someone get away with all this?'

'I don't know.'

She turned and they walked back to the ward.

'What was he like? The man in Chichester?' Breen asked.

'Ordinary. That's the trouble. Ordinary.' She swung her legs back onto the bed and he pulled the blanket up for her.

'Good-looking?'

'I suppose. Not my type anyway.'

'What if I drew him?' He took out his police notebook and started with a thin face like Lyagushin's, but she said, 'No. Rounder than that.'

'Really?'

He tried again, then again, with different shapes of head. Then adding ears, eyes, hair and nose. 'A bit like that, yeah. Maybe if the ears were bigger.'

'You said they were too big last time.'

'Maybe.'

He sketched.

'I don't know.'

'Try harder.'

'Maybe the eyes were closer together.' She sighed. 'I picked up Elfie's baby. It was . . . terrifying really. He's so small . . . No. Not that close.'

Breen turned the page and started again. Whoever she'd seen at the hospital in Chichester definitely wasn't Lyagushin. He had been wrong.

'I told Elfie about going to see Kay Fitzpatrick. I thought it would be good to get her off thinking about her baby and stuff. Know what she said? Kay's a driver.'

'You said that already.'

'She worked nights.'

Breen stopped drawing.

'That's a bit like him, I think,' she said.

'Hold on. She worked nights?'

'Exactly,' she said.

'How did she know?'

'That guy she knows who works with the Rolling Stones. Remember? We met him at Hyde Park. Tom Keylock. He was in yesterday with chocolates for her. He remembered, anyway.'

'I'll tell C1, I suppose.'

'For all the bloody good it will do.'

He held up the sketch. A man. About thirty. A featureless face. It could be anyone, but at the same time, there was something vaguely familiar about it.

He stared hard at the pencil drawing. When he looked, he saw that Helen was dabbing her eyes with a tissue.

'What's wrong?'

'What you done to her now?' The woman in the next bed was craning over to see what had happened.

'He killed two women, Cathal,' Helen said. She wasn't a woman who cried, usually, but he knew she was thinking of her own sister, the child, murdered and dumped in a ditch close to her family's house.

He fingered the ring box in his jacket pocket. The nurses were coming through the ward now, telling visitors to leave.

'I only just got here,' protested Breen.

'Out,' ordered a sister, tugging at the chair he was sitting in.

'Wait,' said Breen, turning back to Helen. 'I didn't bring chocolates. But I brought this.'

And he reached into his jacket pocket and pulled out the blue velvet box and the ring he had bought from Grima's.

He watched her face for the sign of a smile. 'Cathal?'

'Perhaps you shouldn't look at it now. It's not the time.'

'Please, Cathal,' she said, quietly. 'I don't want this now.'

'Take it. Whatever. If you don't like it you can change it.'

Under the bruises, her skin was white. Tears escaped her eyes again.

'Out,' shouted the nurse.

'Should have done that before he knocked her up,' muttered the woman in the next bed.

'Stupid timing,' said Breen.

Still crying, she opened the ring box.

'Out,' called the nurse again.

He looked back, and she was staring open-mouthed at the ring, a look of horror on her face.

'Just forget it, OK,' he said, and turned away.

374

Fuck. Fuck. Fuck.

'So?' said Mint, grinning at him from the Mini. 'How did it go?'

The flat was dark and miserable. It felt damp and cold, even in July.

He was a fool. He should never have bought the ring, let alone tried to give it to her.

He needed to think, so he put coffee on the stove, but the milk in the fridge had turned, curdling in the bottle. He poured it down the sink and pushed the solids into the drain with a wooden spoon.

With a cup of strong black coffee in his hand, he tore the pages out of the notebook and put them on the kitchen table, staring at them, trying to make them come to life, but the five drawings he had done each looked like different people. She had only seen the man briefly on both occasions. It was not her fault. One looked a little like his own father. Another like Constable Mint.

For all that, there was something about the face she had described that was familiar.

He had an idea. Flicking through his notebook, he found the number for the house at Harewood Avenue. The phone rang for a minute unanswered.

He replaced the receiver, waited a few seconds, then phoned again. This time he heard someone pick it up and hold it to their ear, breathing heavily, as if he had run down the stairs to reach it in time.

'Haas?'

'Who is this?' the voice whispered.

'Detective Sergeant Breen.'

'Oh.' A pause. 'The detective. Have you found the man who killed Lena yet?'

'I'm afraid not. But I wanted to ask you a favour.'

'Me?'

'Is there something wrong, Haas?' There was something anxious about his voice.

'Nothing.'

'OK. Well, I have some drawings I want you to look at. It's possible that one of them might have been a customer of Lena's. I would like to show you them.'

'I told you. I didn't see them.'

'I don't believe you,' said Breen. 'Every time I've been to the house, it was you who answered the door. It was you who picked up the phone just now, when nobody else did, despite the fact you live on the top floor. I think you saw everyone who went in and out. I think that's the kind of man you are.'

Haas sighed. 'Usually, I keep myself . . . under a stone. But maybe I notice some things.'

'I need you to help me.'

'If I can. You are trying to find a man who killed a good woman.'

'Two good women. Florence Caulk was murdered last week.'

'Oh. That is terrible. I did not know.' He could hear Haas on the other end of the phone, sighing. 'I lied to you, Mr Breen,' he said.

'I know.'

'I am sorry. It was not my idea to lie. When the men came to search the house, I said they were police.'

'They weren't. I know.'

'You knew?'

'Yes. Not at the time. But I know now.'

'I am sorry I lied. They told me to.'

'So you knew who they really were?'

'*Natürlich*, yes.' He lowered his voice to a whisper, as if that would stop anyone else hearing what he was saying. 'They were your security service.'

Breen nodded. 'Of course. You were working for them. All along, you were working for them, weren't you?'

'It was not my idea. They told me not to cooperate with you. I am sorry. They ask me to keep a lookout for a man. They showed me a photograph.'

It would be Lyagushin.

'They told me to call every time he visited.'

'So you had to watch all the visitors.'

'Yes.'

Breen took a second. 'We shouldn't talk now,' he said. Every crackle of static on the line was suspicious. 'They may be eaves-dropping. That restaurant you told me about. Do you remember? Don't say the name.'

'You mean—'

'Don't say the name.'

'Oh.'

'Meet me there tomorrow. One o'clock. For lunch.'

'They are listening?'

'I don't know. Maybe.'

That night, Breen slept badly, alone in the flat. At two in the morning, he realised he was awake and that a bird was singing in the cul-de-sac. The middle of the night, yet it was singing as if for dear life.

He got up and looked through the curtains, up the stairs and into the stairwell, wondering if someone had disturbed it. A quarter-moon hung above the police station, to the south. All the way up there, men were walking on it.

He was still awake two hours later when the blackness around him began to thin and so he rose, put on a dressing gown, and started looking again through the pages of his notebooks.

THIRTY-FOUR

It was a modest, two-storey house in Wood Green. Keylock's wife opened the door.

'Tom. It's a policeman,' she said, even before Breen had had a chance to say what he was doing there.

'That obvious?' he asked.

She nodded, unsmiling.

'Is Mr Keylock in?'

The big man replaced her in the doorway, took off his thick glasses, wiped them, and then leaned down to peer at Breen. 'I know you, don't I?'

'About Julie Teenager.'

'What about her?'

'Did you work for her?'

Keylock shook his big square head. 'How did you know I was here?'

'I called Mr Klein's office. He said you were off today.' With Helen and Elfie in hospital, he had called Amy. She had advised him to try the Rolling Stones' manager, an American called Klein.

'Typical,' said Keylock. 'Never a bit of bloody privacy.'

'I thought you didn't get days off.'

'No. Mick and his bird are in Australia making some bloody film. And you know about Brian. I'm no longer needed there. Nothing for me to do, that's all. Couple of days to put my feet up. Is that it?'

'Did you work for Julie Teenager?'

'I work for the Rolling Stones. That's all.'

'What about Kay Fitzpatrick?'

A pause. 'What about her?'

A neighbour walking a Jack Russell down the street paused to let his dog urinate by the gatepost and called, 'Morning, Tom. All right?' looking Breen up and down.

'Kay Fitzpatrick,' said Breen again.

Keylock nodded. 'You better come in, then.' He called into the kitchen, 'Put the kettle on, love.'

For a man who worked for the Rolling Stones, it was an ordinary house. A print of a Chinese-looking woman with a blue face hung in the hallway; a sampler that said 'Welcome Home'. The kind of simple family house he would have wanted to grow up in. In the living room there was a three-piece suite, upholstered in a cosy, reassuring floral pattern. Small wooden tables sat around the room, each with a clean glass ashtray.

'Any news of Kay?' Keylock asked.

'You heard, then?'

'Course I did, poor cow.' He sat down and pointed to the sofa. 'She took a beating. The police say it was her boyfriend.'

'You think it was?'

Keylock looked huge in the armchair, leaning forwards, hands clasped, nodding. 'Could be. There are a lot of nasty cunts.'

Breen sat down opposite him. 'Tell me about Kay.'

He took his big black-framed glasses off, wiped them with a sleeve, then replaced them. 'I'm not paid to go round telling other people's secrets. You know that. My job's to keep my mouth shut. Know what? I once drove Bob Dylan around Britain for three weeks. Big fancy car. You wouldn't believe the shit I've seen. They're kids in the world's biggest sweetshop, these boys. The job is you don't tell no one.'

'What if you know something about a crime?'

'I cooperate fully with the police whenever I'm required to.' And he smiled the smile acquired from cocky young men, ten years younger than him.

'What if it's not her boyfriend? What if the person who beat her up is the same man who killed Julie Teenager?'

Keylock frowned. 'Is that what happened?'

'Yes. I think so.'

'I don't hold with beating women,' said Keylock. 'It's a bad thing. Brian Jones did a bit of that. Didn't like it.'

There was a photo of a young bespectacled soldier in hot weather kit, leaning against what looked like a mud wall. 'Is that you?'

'Palestine. 1947. I was in the Royal Army Service Corps.'

'Did you see action in the war?'

'And some. I was at bloody Arnhem, mate. Jesus. That was something. See this?' He pointed to his nose and face. 'Wounded.

They took the skin from my arse and stuck it on my face. Jagger says maybe that's why I always talk shit.'

Breen laughed, because it was expected. 'Working with a pop group must seem like a picnic after that.'

'Not exactly a picnic,' he said. 'But fewer people die. And the pay's good.'

'I bet you like it, don't you? All the chaos. All the running away from people like us. Trying to cover up for their messes?'

'No comment,' he said, but he gave another little smile.

'I bet you wouldn't mind bending the law a bit, to keep them safe.'

'I don't know what you're trying to imply, officer.'

Breen thought of Zygmunt Wojcik tending his vegetables in his West London garden. The generation who had fought in World War II struggled with ordinary life.

'You were there with Brian Jones the night he died.'

'Nope. You heard wrong. Only afterwards.'

'That's right. You arrived afterwards.'

'I was supposed to be looking after him, but you can't be there round the bloody clock. A mate who was doing some building work for Brian called me up and told me to get down there double quick. The fuzz were already there. I was the one who had to call up Mick and Keith in the recording studio, tell them the news.'

Keylock's wife, a handsome woman, a few years younger than Tom, brought tea, not in a cup and saucer, but in a mug. Breen took his, though he hadn't asked for it. 'Did you see anything strange about his death?'

'Strange? It was just pathetic. Nothing strange about it. I've seen brave men shot to pieces by Nazi artillery. In bits. Brian just died. That's all.'

'I believe you.'

'Look. I liked Brian a lot, especially at the beginning, before he got into the drugs. He was a lost boy. He had his stupid side, dark side, whatever you want to call it. Maybe we all do. I won't deny I gave him a bit of a kicking because he set on his girlfriend, Anita, this one time. Like I said, I don't stand for it. But the Rolling Stones, it had been his group. At the end he was just a sad, fucked-up boy who was afraid of his own shadow, who drank too much and took too many pills. It's a shame. Honest? I don't know what happened that night. I wasn't there. Know what? It doesn't really matter. It doesn't really fucking matter. Brian was going to die anyway. Even if I had been there, maybe it would have been just the same. It's that simple. I heard a couple of the fans saying some shit, but that's all it is. Shit.'

Keylock's wife returned with a plate of ginger nuts. Breen waited until she'd gone, then asked, 'You were there when Jagger and the other one got off their drugs charges.'

'I wasn't at the bust. I wouldn't have let it happen if I had been there, believe me.'

'It doesn't worry you that it's one law for them and another for everybody else?'

'Worry me? This fucking country's always been like that,' said Keylock. 'Sometimes it pretends it's not, but that's the way it is. Don't go kidding yourself. Why fight it?'

Breen remained seated, looking at him.

'You think I'm full of shit, don't you?'

Breen shook his head. 'No.' A vacuum cleaner started whirring in the room next door. 'How well did you know Julie?'

'That bloody noise,' said Keylock, standing. 'Keep it down, love.' The hoover stopped. 'Fancy a vodka?'

Breen looked at his watch; eleven in the morning. 'Not for me.'

Keylock looked disappointed. 'Course I knew her. She was at parties. She liked the music, know what I mean? Did you know she was Polish?'

'Yes. How did you know?'

'Her dad was RAF, wasn't he? She found out I was at Arnhem. I remember she saluted me. Loads of Poles fought there on our side. Say what you like, good fucking men, they were. The Polish Parachute Brigade. Only time I ever seen her get emotional, talking about all that crap. She was a funny girl, Julie was. She was tricky, know what I mean? She flirted with all the boys, but you could tell she didn't mean it. I got the idea she was always looking for some way to take advantage, know what I mean? I wasn't interested, myself. Happily married man. You married, copper?'

'Not yet.'

'Find a nice woman. Get married. Everything else is so much bollocks. You understand? Sure you don't want a little drink?'

'Did you ever work for Julie Teenager?'

'Julie was nothing to do with me, swear to God. I'm paid by the band. Julie was just on the scene. Nice girl. Tougher than a lot of them, you could see that a mile off. Not really friendly with anyone, just there, know what I mean? And maybe the boys liked hanging around with her because they knew what she did.

Made them feel a bit cooler, didn't it? But I ran a car company. That's how I got involved in all this stuff in the first place, driving Mick around and Dylan. So I was always on the lookout for drivers. And some people like a pretty girl at the wheel, know what I mean. And Kay's a looker. Brunette. Lovely legs. Makes you look good if you got a pretty driver. Who wants an ugly mug like mine? So Kay, yeah . . . she was a pal. I got her work.'

'So Kay worked with Julie Teenager?'

Keylock tugged on a long ear lobe. 'Julie wanted a driver to pick up her customers. Thing was, she preferred working with women. She didn't trust men. Maybe she worried about them muscling in. Fair play. I've got a few connections. I put the two of them in touch. That's how Kay ended up with her. That's all. Swear to God. It was just a bit of driving work.'

'How would it work? She'd get a phone call and pick up a client and bring them to Julie's flat?'

'Pretty much. It's simpler all round that way. And safer too. The client knows everything is hush-hush. If you're working with high-end clients, they want discretion. They don't want anything getting into the papers. She did nothing wrong. Is she going to be all right, Kay?'

'I called the hospital at Chichester this morning. She's out of the coma but still confused, apparently. She's blind, you know? There might be brain damage but only time will tell. Sussex Police will be interviewing her in the next couple of days.'

Keylock nodded. 'But you don't reckon it was her boyfriend?'

Breen shrugged. 'Sussex Police say so, but I think they're wrong. There are three people associated with Julie in some way who have been killed or close. All women.'

385

Keylock leaned forward and took a ginger nut from the plate. 'You don't think much of me, working for this lot, do you?'

'I never said that,' said Breen.

'Know what? I fought a fucking war,' said Keylock. 'All I ended up with was a demob suit. This lot ain't having that. That's fine by me.'

'But it's not going to last. It's a fad.'

'You'd think, wouldn't you? But you're wrong,' said Keylock. 'Everything is different now. You lot are stuck in the past. I'm the future.'

He hadn't eaten breakfast; as he stood, Breen took a biscuit and chewed on it thoughtfully.

'Take the whole ruddy plate if you like,' said Keylock, standing too, to let him out.

THIRTY-FIVE

At the Woolworths on Stoke Newington High Street he bought a box of Milk Tray chocolates, then walked on to the bus stop on Rectory Road.

He imagined footsteps behind him, but when he turned, there was no one there. On Brooke Road, he dipped into a newsagent, and as he emerged with a copy of *The Times*, he was sure he saw a man in a light blue mac, collar turned up, standing with his back turned to him, peering hard at the window of the Radio Rentals shop. It was fifty yards away and too far to make out any features.

He stepped back into the newsagent and bought ten No. 6's and a box of matches. When he emerged again, the man was still there, face still turned away.

At the bus stop, he joined a short queue. The buses were quiet, this time of day. Holding the newspaper up, he scanned around for the man in the light blue mac, but couldn't see him.

The double-decker came and Breen boarded it, finding space

downstairs. He sat next to a blind man who opened a purse and spilled pennies onto the floor. He was just leaning down to pick them up for him when the bus pulled off. Someone must have jumped onto the back platform while the bus was moving, because the conductor shouted, 'Oi! Next time, wait. I don't want to be picking you up off the bloody road,' but by the time he had straightened up and turned to look, whoever it was had made it up the stairs to the top floor.

It was a short ride to Aldgate. He paused under the sign: *London's Most Famous Kosher Restaurant*. Haas was not there yet, so he sat on a stool at the window and asked for fried gefilte fish and coffee.

There was an old joke about Bloom's. A customer once complained about his water being brought in a dirty glass. When the waiter returned with fresh water, he called loudly to all the diners, 'Who ordered the water with the clean glass?'

Breen checked his watch; he did not have long. Haas was supposed to be here at one. He would have time to have lunch, then it would be visiting time. He would go and take the ring back, apologise for giving it to her, and hope that they could go back to where they had been before he'd bought it.

The fried gefilte fish came. It lay flat on the plate, with pickled beetroot on the side. He tried a little, but it was dry and hard to eat. He thought of Helen; she would hate this unfamiliar, un-British food. She would be wrinkling her nose; laughing at it, mocking him for ordering it. The coffee was not good: watery and bitter without any flavour. Breen checked his watch.

Out of the corner of his eye, he thought he saw someone looking at him, but when he turned, all he saw was an elderly woman smoking a cigarette in a long holder. Once you know you have been followed, spied on, you cannot get the idea out of your head; you begin to distrust the world around you.

He cut a little more from the fish. It was greasy and cold. Even with the *chrain* – the pickle – it was hard to swallow. He put down his fork and looked at his watch again.

After visiting Keylock, he was more convinced than ever that the two assaults, on Helen and Kay Fitzpatrick, and the two murders, Julie Teenager and Florence Caulk, were all by the same man – as Helen had believed. He had no faith that C1 would be doing anything to find who he was, though. Their job would be to bury it. In his pocket, he had the sketches he had drawn from Helen's description. They weren't much good and he couldn't work out who it was that Helen had seen, but if there was a connection, maybe Haas would recognise someone.

He saw Haas long before Haas saw him. A man in a dark blue workman's jacket, thin, slightly bent. He was standing at the small traffic island at the junction where Commercial Road met Whitechapel High Street.

He looked to the left and right, for a gap in the flow of vehicles. And then, he looked up and he saw Breen waving at him from his table inside the brightly lit restaurant.

The man smiled. It was the plain, open smile of a man who had not let the hardness of his life crush him. A man who, thirty-five years before, had played in orchestras to cheering crowds in gilded rooms but was now just another man in a London crowd.

The traffic was bad here, motorbikes dodging between the vans and cars, taxis lurching between slower vehicles.

And then, behind Haas, Breen saw a man in a light blue mac, collar turned up, who had dodged through the traffic to arrive at the traffic island just behind the caretaker.

Haas smiled at Breen still, staring straight ahead.

Breen's eyes were wide. He had no idea what was about to happen, but was sure it was not good. Behind the glass window, Breen raised both hands: Look out. The man behind you.

Waving his hands, he knocked his plate to the floor where it smashed. Other diners stared at him, the man shouting in the window.

'LOOK OUT!'

Haas can't hear him, of course.

In the second before the lorry obliterates the view, Breen sees Benjamin's smile falter. He is wondering why the policeman is suddenly looking so concerned, why he is gesticulating at him, why he is trying to say something to him? What?

And then there is a screeching of brakes; followed, what seems like ages later, by a kind of stillness.

The busy junction's traffic, so frenetic a few seconds ago, has stopped. Cars are stationary now. Nothing moves.

And then someone starts screaming. And more people join in.

It was strange how everyone had seen it differently.

A woman with a wailing toddler on her arm said she had seen the man trip and fall on the edge of the pavement. The lorry driver said exactly the same, though how he could have seen anything, Breen didn't understand, as Haas had fallen under his rear wheel. A girl with a black bob and too much make-up, who Breen guessed should have been at school, said a man had barged into him, making him stumble, but when Breen asked her to describe the man, she had no idea at all. A Pakistani man said the same. Haas had been jostled.

A pensioner, medals on his grubby jacket, said he'd seen a man in a mac running away from the scene, but when he pointed in one direction, the girl pointed the opposite way. The man said the mac was pale. There was no mention of a colour.

After the lorry had blocked his view, Breen had seen nothing at all. It had taken him long seconds to leave his seat, push out of Bloom's front door, past the crowd at the roadside and round the vehicle.

When a local copper arrived, out of breath, he attempted to shove onlookers away, demanding that the man move his lorry so that the cars could pass.

'I can't drive that,' complained the lorry driver, and he pointed to Benjamin's body.

Benjamin's head was under the large rear wheel, the skull broken like an egg. His body was curled behind it in the gutter, arms by his side. In a single, crooked line, blood ran out over the grey stone and mingled with discarded cigarette packets and chewing gum.

Breen felt the small piece of fish he had eaten rise in his gorge.

Around the body there was a circle of people, staring. Breen nudged a teenage boy out of the way and squatted down. He felt in Benjamin's trouser pockets but there was nothing but loose change and keys.

Haas's old jacket was frayed a little at the sleeve. He felt inside the outer pockets but they too were empty. Unbuttoning it, he found his wallet in the inside pocket.

If Haas had had anything useful to say, it had been obliterated under the wheel of the four-ton truck.

He stood and looked about, staring at the people around him. Was the killer still here, watching him, or had he run away?

THIRTY-SIX

He stood outside the hospital as other visitors gathered. He had been early. Now he had to wait among the gathering crowd, the box of chocolates under his arm.

The normality of it felt ridiculous; obscene. He had just seen a man crushed to death. None of the people waiting here to see their loved ones knew that. It was not their fault that they were carrying on with their lives, chatting, laughing.

He felt alien, distant. An observer.

At three the crowd of visitors began to push through the doors; he made his way up the stairs to Female Surgical. The lifts were already full.

But when he reached the ward, her bed was unoccupied; the sheets were crisp and neatly tucked, as if no one had ever lain there. The bedside table was empty.

He found a nurse. 'Where's Helen Tozer?'

'They for me?' joshed the nurse, holding her hand out for the chocolates.

'Helen Tozer. Where is she?'

'I was just joking around. No need to be so mardy about it.'

'She was in this bed yesterday. Has she been moved?'

The nurse was thin, pretty, with corkscrews of fair hair escaping from under her white cap. 'Young woman. Head wounds? Pregnant? I didn't move her.'

Perhaps she had been admitted to the maternity ward? She returned a minute later saying, 'No. She's not there.'

'Jesus,' he said. 'You can't just lose her. Somebody must know.'

'Keep your voice down, sir. You're disturbing the ward.'

Patients and visitors looked at him, disapproving. He must have been shouting, he realised. He tried to lower his voice. 'You don't understand. She might be in some danger,' he said.

A passing matron, broad-chested and starchy, butted in. 'Miss Tozer? Oh no. She insisted on leaving this morning,' she said.

Breen stopped. 'Leaving?'

'Yes. She went home about two hours ago. Against advice.'

'Home? But . . .'

Had she gone home to find him – surprise him, maybe? But he had not been there. Instead he had been a mile south, watching Haas die. There was a payphone on each floor. He ran to the end of the ward, dug change out of his pocket and called home. The phone rang unanswered for a minute. He rang again. Still no answer.

Of course. He banged his head against the wall. She could not be at home. She would have had no way of getting in. Two days ago she had been brought from home, semi-conscious and she wouldn't have had a key. Had she tried to get in? Was she waiting outside?

Or maybe she hadn't wanted to go back to his flat at all. He remembered the way she had looked at him when he'd given the ring. The look of disgust on her face.

He ran back to the matron. 'What was she like, when she left?'

'When we told her she was in no condition to leave, she was unpleasant. We don't like to hear bad language in our ward,' she said.

She was still angry, then. He thought of Elfie in Maternity and turned on his heels. Helen wouldn't have gone without talking to her, would she?

'No running in the ward,' shouted the matron after him.

Up in Maternity, he pushed open the door. 'I need to speak to Elfie Silverstein,' he said.

'She's feeding. It's not convenient.'

'I'm a policeman. It's urgent.'

The beds were all surrounded by curtains. A reluctant nurse led Breen to Elfie's bed. The baby was tucked under a blanket, stuck to her chest, sucking at the round warm flesh.

Breen turned his head away, embarrassed.

'Helen persuaded me to start,' she said. 'I was afraid I wouldn't be able to. She said it's just like the calves on the farm.' She giggled, then stopped and looked at Breen. 'It's awful, isn't it? What that man did to her? I didn't realise.'

'She was here this morning?'

'No. Yesterday after visiting hours. In the evening. Sit down,' she said. He looked around but there wasn't a chair, so he perched on the edge of her bed. 'She sneaked in last night. We had a long

395

talk. She asked if she could borrow my clothes because the ones she had were covered in blood. Poor girl. Why didn't you tell me about what had happened to her? I was upset.'

'I don't understand. Why didn't she ask me to bring her clothes?'

She wrinkled her nose. 'I don't know. Maybe she was a bit angry with you.'

'Angry?'

'She said you asked her to marry you. Did you?'

'Sort of. I gave her a ring.'

'She showed me it. It was horrible.'

'Did she?'

Elfie pulled the boy out from under the blankets and turned him around, pulling down her nightie on the other side so the baby could lock on to the nipple. 'Maybe I should go outside,' Breen said.

'I don't mind, Paddy.'

'She's checked herself out of the hospital, but she didn't have a key to get in. I'm worried about her. Did she say she was worried about anything?'

Elfie looked down at the boy and said, 'Come on, little man. Come on.' With her new baby, she seemed to be in a world of her own. 'What did you say? Worried?'

'There was a man she'd seen when she was looking for Kay Fitzpatrick. I think it may have been the man who attacked her. He might have come looking for her . . .'

Elfie frowned. 'A man? No. I don't think so. Ow!' she said, looking down. 'Not so greedy.' She giggled. 'Actually, she wanted to find out all about Kay. What I knew about her. I wasn't able to say much. You shouldn't have given her that ring. It was one of those vulgar Andrew Grima things. She'd want something much simpler.'

Breen was puzzled. 'Why did she want to know about Kay?'

'She said she had figured everything out,' said Elfie. 'You know when she gets that look?'

'What do you mean, figured everything out? About Julie Teenager?'

'What? Yes. I think so. She was upset.'

'What do you mean?'

'I don't know. Maybe she was angry with you about giving her the ring. I didn't quite understand what she was saying. My head's like cotton wool.' She tickled the baby's head.

'She didn't want to marry me?'

'No. It wasn't that. She felt bad about it.'

'She did want to marry me?'

'Christ sake let me finish, Paddy. It wasn't that. She was agitated because when she opened it, she saw what it was and she said it was Kay's ring.'

Breen, sitting with the flowers and the chocolates on his lap, was stunned. 'Kay's ring. I don't understand. She said it was Kay's ring?'

'I'm sorry. I was tired. I haven't been able to sleep. There are babies crying in here all the time. I wasn't really listening.'

'That's what she said? That it was Kay's ring?'

'Weird, isn't it? I mean, I don't like that Grima, either, but I thought it was quite sweet of you, too. Do you really want to marry her?'

'Concentrate, Elfie. Kay's ring. You sure she said that?'

'Yes. Ninety-nine per cent. She looked at it like it was poisonous or something.' She reached out her free hand, took his and squeezed it. 'Are you OK?'

Breen sat there on the edge of her bed saying nothing.

She had seen the ring and she had reacted with horror. He had assumed it was because she was revolted by the prospect of marrying him, but it was simply the ring that had made her behave that way.

Something about the ring.

'Paddy?'

It had not been about him, her revulsion; it had been because seeing the ring had allowed her to figure something out.

'What's wrong, Paddy?'

But if seeing the ring had made her understand something, what was it?

'I worry about you, Paddy.'

Slowly he stood. 'I have to go,' he said.

Elfie was staring at him. But it was not him she should be worrying about, it was Ronald Russell. He didn't understand what the ring had signified to Helen, but the rings had originally been bought by Russell. Whatever it was, it was about him. And now he knew where she had gone: to find him.

'Don't you want the chocolates for Hel?'

'You have them.'

Breen took the stairs down, two at a time. In the lobby, a man in a brown coat blocked the door, standing on a chair, putting up a poster with drawing pins. *Life is for living. Live it. Don't be stuck on DRUGS.*

'I need to get past,' said Breen.

'Keep your hair on.'

'It's urgent.'

'Steady,' he shouted as Breen ran past, out into the car park, looking for a taxi.

THIRTY-SEVEN

Strictly speaking, the *Sunday Times* was not a Fleet Street paper. There was a sense of grit about Fleet Street; it was a village within the city, where you could smell ink in the air. In the evenings the streets were full of noise, not just from the pubs where men drank hard; soon the roar and thrum of the machines would rise from the basements of the newspaper offices. Men there strode around with a sense of importance; they were men of words forging them from the news of the day, and then from lead. It was exhilarating being there. If it wasn't the centre of the world, it felt it was.

The *Sunday Times* kept itself a little apart, in a modern building on Gray's Inn Road.

The cab pulled up outside next to a black Rolls-Royce. Over the glass doors the newspaper's name was picked out in large letters. 'I'm looking for Ronald Russell,' he said.

'Where does he work?'

'He's a Soviet correspondent.'

'Foreign desk.' She looked through a directory. 'Mr Russell. Third floor.' She lifted the phone and spoke into it. 'He'll be down,' she said.

Breen stood in the reception area and waited. A young man rode up to the glass doors on a Vespa, camera still around his neck, jumped off the scooter, pushed open the door and ran to the lift behind the desk.

'You can't leave that there,' called a man in a blue uniform, stationed by the door.

'You move it then,' said the photographer, doors already closing on him.

'Cheeky git.'

Breen waited. And waited.

'Has a young woman been here, asking for Mr Russell?' he asked the receptionist. 'She's got short hair and you'd know her because she's pregnant.'

The receptionist shook her head. 'Don't think so.'

A minute later, he was back. 'May I use your phone?'

Again, she shook her head. 'Staff only.' He looked through the glass doors. The nearest box was on the other side of Gray's Inn Road. He wanted to call home again, to see if Helen had somehow made it in there, but he daren't leave the lobby in case Russell appeared.

A couple of men, both in pinstripes that had gone shiny at the knee, walked past, talking loudly. 'Frankly, I'm with what de Gaulle used to say. If they let Britain in the Common Market the whole thing will fall apart.' Journalists returning from lunch full of alcohol and self-importance. Even though he was a few feet away from them, Breen could smell the brandy on their breaths.

He looked around, approached the desk once more. 'Could you call up again?'

'I've got work to do, you know.' Though she didn't seem to be doing anything apart from reading a magazine.

'This is important.'

'They'll be busy, this time of day,' she said, but she called again. After a couple of minutes waiting, she dialled another number. When she put down the phone, she said, 'He's not at his desk. Maybe he's on the way down.'

'If he's not coming down, I need to go up.'

'I'm afraid not, sir.'

'It's a matter of great importance. I'm a policeman.'

The guard who had been on the door approached. 'Sorry, guv. No one goes up unless they're personally invited, copper or not.'

Something was wrong. Had Russell panicked and run from some other exit? He asked the receptionist. 'Was it Russell you spoke to earlier on the phone?'

'Is he causing a nuisance?' said the guard.

'Let her answer,' said Breen.

'No. Some other bloke on the foreign desk.'

'So he may not be upstairs at all?'

'I am just the receptionist,' she complained.

'Who's his boss? I need to speak to him. It's crucial.'

The woman said, 'I'll see if the foreign editor will see you. He's busy though.'

Breen waited again, more anxious by the minute.

A little after four, a woman dressed in a brown jacket, brown skirt and brown shirt appeared at the open lift doors, glasses dangling from a chain around her neck. 'Sergeant Breen?' she said. 'Mr Benson will see you now. Is it something serious?'

'Who's Mr Benson?'

'The foreign editor in charge of Russell's desk. You asked to see him.'

On the second floor there was a large room, glass on three sides so that anyone passing could see inside. 'Is this where Mr Russell works?' asked Breen.

'Obviously.'

Eight desks had been pushed together to form a huge, single table. There were typewriters and telephones dotted around the edge, but for the most part the desk was covered in a sea of papers and books. The piles that spread over almost every inch were huge and precarious; sitting at one side of the desks, you would need to stand to see anyone at the other.

At one end, a small, bald man in a brown suit was squinting at a large sheet of paper that looked like an oversize newspaper page, lips moving as he skimmed across its lines of print.

'I was looking for Ronald Russell,' said Breen.

'Shut up. Can't you see I'm concentrating? Idiot.'

His pen scrawled a line across a column that Breen could see was headed: 'Nixon begins world tour at moment of US indecision'. Breen realised that the idiot was not him, but whoever had written the article. 'Why do they have to mention the moon landing in every bloody piece about America? It's pure sycophancy. I'll be glad when all this space nonsense is over.'

He was looking at a draft of something for next weekend's paper, Breen guessed.

'You asked about Ronald Russell,' said the man, not taking his eyes off the sheet of paper.

'I need to speak to him,' said Breen. 'Urgently.'

'About?'

'I'm afraid I can't tell you, sir.'

'Why not?' The editor folded up the sheet and handed it to the woman in brown. 'The piece about General Franco needs to go to the leader writer's office. Run along.'

'It relates to an investigation. Where is Mr Russell? It's vital that I find him.'

The woman trotted dutifully off and the man swivelled round in his chair to examine Breen.

'Off sick,' said Benson.

Breen was instantly alarmed. 'Nothing serious?'

'Sadly not. Today he should have been reporting on the Kroger spy exchange. He has made himself unavailable at a most inconvenient time.'

'The spies who are being exchanged for Gerald Brooke?'

'The Soviets are getting their spies back. It's obvious it's happening sometime soon. They've moved Brooke from the Potma prison camp to a house in Moscow. They're going to release him any day. It should have been Russell's story. He's been the one who always pestered me to let him write it. And now he's off and I've had to reassign it. There are several MPs who have been on the phone all day. Both sides of the House. They're fuming.'

'About the exchange?'

'They insist Brooke was a nothing. They are demanding a debate about why we are caving into the Soviets.'

'Is he?'

404

'A nothing? Course he is; Russell says he has some intelligence that says he is one of ours, but frankly I doubt it. The Prime Minister's gone soft in the head. Is that all?'

'And this was Russell's story?'

'He's been on it for yonks. And just when it gets interesting, he calls in sick.'

'Have you spoken to him today?'

'No. Why should I? He's sick. Where's that bloody woman?' mumbled the editor.

Breen hesitated. 'Is he good?'

'A journalist is only as good as his sources.'

'Which are?'

The editor took off his glasses and squinted angrily at Breen, then said, 'Bugger off. That's not the kind of information we share. Least of all with the authorities.'

'But you knew who his sources were?'

'It was Russell's job to keep his ear to the ground. Go to parties. Hang around with foreign visitors, embassy staff and so on. See what the talk is. For a long time he was hopeless at it. I thought I'd have to let him go. But recently he seems to have developed more of an instinct for this kind of thing.'

'And he was writing about Gerald Brooke and the Krogers? Anything in particular?'

'I haven't got time for this, I'm afraid, officer. I'm due in an editorial meeting.'

'Can I see what he's written? On the Kroger case. Is that possible?'

The editor stared at Breen for a minute, then screamed, 'Dylis! Show this gentleman the cuttings file. Will that be all?'

The woman in brown returned without a word, went to one of the vacant desks and started poking into the piles of paper, within no time pulling out a bulging green suspension folder.

'I have a meeting with the Americans about the Kennedy trouble,' said the editor. 'Send Mr Breen downstairs when he is finished. Make sure he leaves.'

'This is the file on the Krogers.' Finding no available space on the desk, Breen opened the folder on his lap and started to leaf through the cuttings. Each had been pasted onto a sheet of paper on which there was a small date stamp and, occasionally, additional notes.

They were not all by Russell, 'Early access to Brook denied' was by 'Our Diplomatic Correspondent'. 'Moscow trial closed to West' was by a man who was based in that city. Most were just by 'A *Sunday Times* Reporter' or 'Our Own Correspondent'.

'How do I know which ones are by Russell?'

'I expect that's the one you're looking for,' she said, pulling a single sheet from the pile.

'This one?' Breen looked at the clipping. The article was titled: 'How big a fry is Gerald Brooke?'

'Yes. That was Russell.' She made a face.

'What's wrong?'

'It's not for me to say, but I don't think we should have ever published that.'

'Why?' Breen read it.

Last year, Harold Wilson returned from his trip to Moscow empty-handed. He had been hoping to secure the release of imprisoned lecturer Gerald Brooke, in exchange for the notorious members of the Portland Spy Ring, Peter and Helen Kroger. However, the Foreign Office have consistently scoffed at the suggestion that Brooke himself is a genuine spy and thus a fair exchange for the Krogers. But examination of the trail record printed in Russian seems to confirm that the Soviet court trying Brooke could have pinned espionage charges on him and made them stick. Sources in Moscow suggest that evidence found on Brooke at the time of his arrest included the kind of sophisticated paraphernalia of modern-day espionage, including transmitters and coded materials.

Breen looked up. It was just as Sand had said.

'Finish it,' said the woman.

However inconvenient it is, the question must be asked: was Gerald Brooke simply an ideologue who blundered in the arms of the KGB, or something altogether more embarrassing? If he had been a spy, the Foreign Office would, of course, deny it.

'I have never liked Ronald Russell,' she said. 'The piece was either an unconscionable attempt at controversy or something worse.'

'An attempt to deliberately put misinformation out there?'

'What do you think?'

Ronald Russell; Lyagushin; Lena Bobienski.

'Who spoke to Russell when he called in sick this morning?'

'I did. It wasn't this morning, it was yesterday. Hurt his leg.'

'Hurt his leg?'

'A gardening accident, apparently, at the weekend. He called in this morning. Said the wound became infected.'

'You're sure it was his leg?'

'Absolutely. I hope it drops off. What is this about, Sergeant?'

His leg. Where Helen had got him with her pencil. He had been an idiot, chasing after the Russian; it had been Russell all along. Blood thumping in his ears, Breen stood, picked up a phone and dialled.

'You need to dial 9 for an outside line,' she said.

He dialled again.

'Put me through to Mint.'

'Is that Paddy Breen?'

'Just put me through to Mint.'

Mint came on the phone, voice low. 'What is it?'

'Can you get a car?'

'Why?'

'I need help.'

After the call he stood. The woman said, 'I'm afraid you can't have that file. It's the newspaper's property.'

Breen ignored her, folding it and putting it into his pocket.

'Has he done something wrong?' she said.

'Yes,' he said simply. 'I think he has.'

'Well, I am not the least bit surprised.'

He strode towards the door. 'Don't I get a thank you?' she said. And he waited outside Clerkenwell Road, by the Rolls-Royce, until to the sound of angry horns, the Mini arrived, cutting across the traffic to where he was stood.

THIRTY-EIGHT

'But how would she have known where he lives?' demanded Mint, from the passenger seat.

'She looked at my notebooks.'

The rush-hour traffic was thick and the roads jammed. The bus drivers were on strike, which meant the streets were full of cars and taxis.

'You let her look at them?'

'She used to be a copper.'

Mint said, 'Yes, but . . .'

At the junction with Southampton Row, a lorry had spilled planks onto the road. A traffic policeman was attempting to direct vehicles around the timber while horns honked everywhere.

'Give me a hand, will you, mate?' he called to the Mini, as Breen finally edged the car into a gap between the fallen pieces of wood and a bus.

'Sorry. Can't stop,' Breen shouted back.

The copper swore at him, but Breen wasn't listening. He sped down towards Theobald's Road to where the traffic slowed again.

'So let me get this straight. You think she's gone there already?' Mint peered ahead, trying to see what was holding them up this time. 'But he tried to kill her. Why would she . . . ? Shouldn't we call the police? She could be in trouble.'

'We are the police,' said Breen.

'No, but . . . Can't we just get in touch with the local coppers?'

'No.'

'Why not?'

'Trust me. Please.' Breen didn't want to say it, but if Helen was there . . .

She hadn't told him what she was doing. If she'd known when she saw the ring, then whatever she was planning to do was something she'd meant to keep from him.

He didn't say any more, but Mint's attention was already distracted. Close to the museum, a group of barefoot hippies, dressed in orange, were banging drums and chanting on the pavement, dancing. A crowd had gathered to watch them.

Breen noticed Mint watching the dancers, fascinated and appalled.

'Hare Krishnas,' said Breen. 'Worried about the competition?'

Breen leaned on the horn, disrupting the chant, and they lurched forward towards Oxford Street.

'Delta Mike Six,' the radio crackled. 'Come in.'

'Shall I answer it?' asked Mint.

'Why not?'

'Delta Mike Six. DI Creamer requests your presence at HQ.'

Breen hesitated. 'I can do this alone, if you need to go. Just let me have the car.'

'Delta Mike Six? Can you hear me, over?'

Mint leaned forward and deliberately turned the receiver's volume down.

It was late afternoon by the time they made it to Shepherd's Bush. They parked outside the house, and Breen peered through the gate.

'You think she's in there?'

'Only one way to find out. You stay in the car.'

'No. I should come with you.'

'Please.'

'Why? What are you going to do?'

Breen looked at the house, immaculately white in a row of Georgian facades. He put his hand on the door handle. 'Just stay in the car, will you? Make sure nobody comes in or out.'

A task to keep him out of the way, for at least as long as it took to discover what Helen had done.

It seemed like a long walk to the front door. He rang the bell, then knocked at the door, but no one came. A hollyhock bent drunkenly away from the wall, its flowers pale and its leaves riddled with infection.

He held down the bell button again, but still no one opened the door. If she had not come here, where was she? And where were Russell and his wife? He was about to turn and head back to the car when he thought he heard a noise inside the house.

Squatting down, he pushed open the letter box and peered through. The hallway was empty, quiet.

He knocked this time, loudly, then tugged on the door. 'Helen,' he called, then stepped back.

The house was silent. On either side of the door were large Georgian sash windows. At a guess, the one on the left looked in poorer condition, paint flaking from the sash bars, and putty showing on the panes. Beneath the sill was a small rose bed. He stepped into it, thorns pricking at his legs, and tried the window. Locked, obviously. Pulling out his keys he jumped onto the ledge and, holding on with one hand, forced a key into the space between the sashes and sawed it back and forwards until it moved easily, then wiggled it towards the lock. Every movement seemed to take an age.

The key gave him little leverage, but it was all he had. Luckily the lock shifted. As soon as it was pushed back far enough he dropped back down onto the bed and forced his fingers under the bottom of the frame. It slid upwards.

He looked inside. It was a dining room, shelves along one wall filled with bright, modern Danish crockery. He looked back. Mint was hidden behind the garden wall. Breen pulled himself onto the ledge and tumbled into the empty room.

The door beyond was open.

He tiptoed out of the dining room and into the hallway he had just been looking at. It was then he noticed the light blue coat, hanging on the stand at the back of the passageway.

It was Russell who had killed Haas; not some spook.

His heart thumped. So if Helen had come here she had put herself into extreme danger.

And then, from upstairs came the sound of water. Someone was running a bath. Then there were footsteps.

Urgently, Breen pressed himself back against the wall, in an effort to stay out of sight, but as he did so he caught an oil painting which swung noisily on its hook. Sweating, he wondered if the front door was locked; could he make a run for it to Mint's car?

But, incredibly, nobody had heard him. Surely they must have? The footsteps continued. A door closed. The water carried on running.

He breathed. Placing one foot at the bottom of the dark wood stairs, he began to shift his weight slowly onto the step.

And sensed something move behind him.

He swung round.

Helen stood there, dressed ridiculously in Elfie's fluorescent pantsuit, one finger in front of the lips on her bruised face.

THIRTY-NINE

He smiled.

She took the finger off her lips and beckoned him back into the dining room.

'What the hell . . . ?'

'Shh.'

'You saw the ring. You realised it was him. Why didn't you tell me?'

'That doesn't matter now.'

'You found his address in my notebook?'

They were whispering now, in the living room. 'Sorry,' she said.

Helen: pregnant, bruised, wearing bright, stupid clothes that were too big for her. And she looked great. 'I don't care.' He stood at the door and peered out into the hallway. 'Is he upstairs? We should call the police. We need to get him taken into custody.'

Helen hung back.

'They won't let it come to trial, though,' said Helen. 'You said it yourself. MI6 don't want it out in the open.'

He looked back at her. 'It doesn't mean it doesn't have to come to trial,' said Breen. 'If we work with them, they could try him *in camera*. With reporting restrictions. They won't let him get away with all this.'

'You sure?' she said.

'Well . . . of course. Yes.'

She sat down heavily in a dining chair, looking exhausted.

'Where were you, all this time?'

'I got here a couple of hours ago. I wanted to speak to Mrs Russell. To tell her the truth about her husband. I knew what it was, you see. It was him who attacked me, wasn't it? And I was the lucky one. I got away.'

'That was stupid,' he said. 'Dangerous.'

'He was at work. Or supposed to be. It was fine.'

'But he's here, isn't he?'

'Upstairs. With Kathryn.'

'Kathryn?'

'Mrs Russell. She was in when I called. I thought I was going to have to convince her, but the moment she saw me, she believed me. It was like she must have known about him all along. I told her all about the attack and how I'd stabbed his leg. She knew for sure then. He'd told her it was a gardening accident.'

'So why didn't you call the police?'

'Because he came back unexpectedly. About an hour ago. When Kathryn heard the key in the door she told me to go and hide. That she'd deal with it. That's where I've been . . . downstairs in the cellar, waiting for her to give the all-clear.'

'He wasn't at work,' said Breen. 'He killed Haas. I saw him do it.'

'Oh,' said Helen. 'He's a monster.'

'He's been trying to get rid of anyone who can connect him to killing Lena Bobienski, including you.'

Breen heard footsteps again, this time on the staircase. Looking around fast, he picked up a bronze statuette of a woman with a dog – Diana the Huntress – and held it high.

But the steps didn't come this way. A gentle knocking sound, then: 'Helen? You can come out now. It's safe.'

Breen relaxed. Helen pushed past him and out into the hallway again.

'Oh,' said Mrs Russell, seeing Breen following her. 'It's you. What are you doing here?'

'I was trying to find Helen. And then I realised she would be here.'

'You know, then?'

'Yes.'

'Have you come to take my husband away?'

Breen nodded.

'I understand,' she said.

'You know what he's done?' said Breen.

'Thing is,' said Mrs Russell, 'I knew it was true, the moment this young woman said it. I think I knew, the moment you came here that first time. I've known it all along.'

'What was true?' asked Breen, cautiously.

'He was never really that interested in me, sexually, my husband.' She stood in the hallway, immaculately turned out; make-up neat, wearing another plain chic dress. 'I really thought

416

it was because he was frightened of my intellect. Or maybe my money and background. It took me a while to realise that it was because I was much too old for him.'

'Where is Mr Russell?' said Breen.

'He's upstairs. I gave him a drink when he got in. He seemed upset about something, so he didn't mind having one. And another. He'll be no bother at all, I promise. Would you like a drink, either of you? It's been such an odd day.'

'No.'

'Are you sure?'

'I'm fine.'

'He tried interfering with my niece, once. We sort of hushed it up, of course.'

'Your niece?'

'She was eleven at the time. We didn't believe her. He said she was making it all up, being a dramatic little girl. And naturally, we tended to believe him, because she was hysterical. I'm so sorry.' She raised her hand to her mouth. 'Poor girl. You only realise what you've done later, don't you? I wonder how much else I was turning a blind eye to.'

'All this can be evidence if we get him to trial again.'

'You really think it's possible?' asked Helen.

'Of course it is.'

Helen looked unconvinced.

'I need to take him,' said Breen. 'I have a car outside.'

'And then everything will come out?' said Mrs Russell.

They both looked at her. The public would blame her, of course. Mrs Russell paused. She seemed to be considering something. 'You said you need evidence,' she said.

'Why?'

'There is something you might be interested in. Come with me upstairs.'

'But isn't your husband upstairs?'

'He'll be drunk by now. Don't worry about him. He will have passed out.'

Breen looked at Helen, concerned. A murderer upstairs was one thing; an inebriated one was another.

'Maybe you should go outside,' said Breen. 'Constable Mint is in the car.'

'I'll be OK,' Helen said.

Mrs Russell led the way up the stairs, past a half-landing. 'Excuse me a minute,' she said. 'I just need to turn off the bath. It'll overflow.'

'Where is he?'

'He's in my bedroom.'

'Where?'

'Please don't go in there. You might wake him.' They were on a long landing with several doorways leading off it. It could have been any of the doors, but her eyes gave it away, darting towards a plain door with a white porcelain handle ahead of him.

Breen was becoming suspicious. 'I need to see him.'

'Why? He's not going anywhere.'

'Show me,' he insisted.

She seemed to hesitate again, so Breen moved to the door.

'He's not dressed,' she said.

Breen pushed it open. Ronald Russell was there, as she said he would be. He was naked, save for a pair of white underpants, lying back on a pink flowery eiderdown, mouth open, chest rising and falling. He was a hairy man; his legs seemed too small for his thick frame. There was a large gauze bandage on the side of his right leg, where Helen must have stabbed him.

On the bedside table was a cut-glass tumbler of whisky, still with several inches in it. A dribble of moisture ran from his lips to his chin and dampened the pillow he was lying on.

'See?' she said. 'Dead drunk.'

And then Ronald opened an eye.

'Fuck,' he slurred.

'Go back to sleep, Ronald,' said Mrs Russell.

'Can't walk,' he murmured.

'I'll help you in a minute,' she said. 'A nice bath.' She strode towards him and lifted the glass to his lips. 'Just another sip,' she said.

She turned to Breen as she poured a little of the drink into his mouth. 'You interviewed my brother, didn't you? He was Ronald's alibi. He told me you'd talked to him. We were here together for dinner, he said.'

'Was that true?'

'We were. Ronald wasn't. At least not all of the night. We sleep in separate beds, but I heard him get up and leave. He was away most of the night. When that poor girl was getting killed.'

'Which night?'

'Thursday night. He didn't get back until some ungodly hour on Friday morning. I pretended I hadn't heard him. It's what you do, isn't it?'

'See, Helen?' said Breen. 'New evidence.'

'Ah yes. I wanted to show you something else. If you still need it, come with me.'

'Don't go,' mumbled Ronald, head lolling.

His wife gently pushed his head back down onto the pillow. 'Stay here,' she told him firmly. 'I'll just be a second. Oh, it's fine,' she told Breen. 'I'll lock the bedroom door. He's in no state to go anywhere. We'll only be a minute.'

Breen hesitated.

'Come. You need to see this.'

And she led them out of the room, taking the key from the inside and locking the door from the landing. 'There.'

'What do you want us to see?'

'He keeps them under his mattress,' she said. 'You should come and look.'

'He keeps what?' asked Breen.

'His pictures. You want evidence?'

They walked up the stairs, past the second floor and up to the old servants' quarters at the top of the house, unlocking a door and opening it. Mr Russell's bedroom had a single bed in it, and one shelf piled with books.

'Separate bedrooms?'

'His idea, not mine. He couldn't bear to be in the same bed as me. He likes it here. It's private. He locks the door usually, but I have a spare key he doesn't know about.'

It was a small room. A mirror. A small abstract painting that could have been Soviet. A risqué print by Aubrey Beardsley. The single bed was made up with a tartan blanket on top. 'Here. Help me lift it,' she said.

Under the mattress were three scrapbooks. 'There. It's evidence. Take a look. I always knew they were there. I didn't really know what they meant until Helen here came to tell me about . . .' She pointed to Helen's face. 'And the other women.'

Breen stepped forward.

'People will say it's my fault, I suppose. I should have known, shouldn't I? All those excuses. Working late. The way he looked at young girls. You know what the awful thing is? I realise I did know, in a way. And I never did anything. You really don't believe it. If I had, maybe . . .'

'You can't blame yourself, Mrs Russell,' said Breen. 'He's the one who did it.'

Helen had already opened the first of the scrapbooks. It was full of photographs, cut out from Scandinavian pornographic magazines, carefully pasted onto the blue paper pages. Some of the girls looked very young. They posed in blonde pigtails and dirndls, bare-chested. Others were older, with dark tufts of pubic hair.

'Oh my God,' said Helen, turning a page.

'I can't bear to look at them,' Mrs Russell said.

As for Breen, he found it embarrassing to be looking at these pictures with two women in the room.

She turned the leaf again. And then again. 'Don't you see? The ones that look like little girls . . . And the other ones, the older ones, look what he's done to their faces.'

Breen leaned forward. She was looking at a page with a picture of a naked woman standing on a tennis court, hands on her hips. Her face had been entirely obliterated by biro, so much that the paper it had been on had disintegrated under the repeated, angry circles.

Again, she turned the page. This one showed a young woman, fully clothed, but again, the face had been completely destroyed. 'That's Penelope Tree,' she said. 'You know. She used to be a teenage model.'

Breen started turning pages too. On some older bodies he had pasted the faces of younger girls.

'She found this and she did nothing,' muttered Helen.

He looked round. Mrs Russell had gone. 'What was she supposed to do?'

'What a creep. Murderous, fucking creep.'

The faces of girls left intact; the women's all scrawled out, destroyed.

'Why didn't you tell me? That when you saw the ring, you knew it was him?'

She closed the scrapbook. 'I wasn't sure.'

'Yes, you were. Besides, even if you weren't, you could have told me what you suspected.'

She bit her lip. 'Don't judge me, Cathal. After everything that has happened.'

'Why didn't you trust me?'

'The ring you gave me was the same one he gave to Kay Fitzpatrick. It was in the drawer next to her bed at the hospital. It was just so creepy.'

'Kay was Julie Teenager's driver. I spoke to Tom Keylock. He confirmed it.' The second ring hadn't been for his wife; it had been for Fitzpatrick. He should have figured it out: when he'd asked Russell about the driver, he'd denied even knowing there was one. The others had all admitted they had heard of her, at least.

Russell had known that Kay could identify him; she must have suspected he was the one who had killed Bobienski.

'When I saw the ring and realised it was him, I was just thinking: he had murdered two women and was going to get away with it. It crossed my mind, that if I killed him, everything would be all right, wouldn't it? What would they do to me? A pregnant woman, going a bit mad? I'd be out in a few years.'

'You came here to kill him?'

'Not really. I came here to warn his wife. To tell her what her husband was really like. I was awake all last night, you know. It's not easy to sleep with all the old biddies moaning – Christ, I hope when I'm old I don't smell like they do! I realised how much danger she must be in. And, you know what? I suppose I was angry with her for letting all this happen. So I came here to tell her, instead. To talk to her.'

'How did she take it?'

'I was expecting a row. I was coming to tell her that her husband was a murderer and a pervert. But she just sat me down, made me tea and listened. So I told her everything. She didn't even cry. I think she knew all along. Imagine that, Cathal.'

'We should go back down,' said Breen. 'Mint is outside, with a car.' He picked up the three scrapbooks, went to the door and turned the handle. But when he pulled, the door didn't move. He tugged harder.

'Shit.'

'She's locked us in,' Helen said. She nudged him aside and tried it herself.

'She's going to escape with him, get him away. He's still her husband.'

423

'You think so?'

'We've got to stop her,' said Breen.

He moved back to the door and yanked at it again. Then he tried crashing his shoulder against it, but the door had opened inwards. He would have to break the whole frame to get out that way.

'Help me,' he said, but Helen just stood there.

He looked around for something he could use as a lever, but there were only coat hangers and shoe horns in the closet.

Breen shouted through the door. 'Mrs Russell. There's a police car outside. Don't do anything you'll regret. Please.'

He returned to the door and braced his leg against the wall next to it and pulled as hard as he could. He was sweating now; the damp on his palms made it hard to grip the doorknob. Looking around, he found a cravat and wrapped it round the handle, using it to grip.

Something gave. He shot backwards, landing on the bare floorboards, banging his head against a chair by the bed.

But when he looked up, the door was still closed and the knob was spinning on the floor. All he had done was pull it off.

'It's OK, Cathal. She won't be going anywhere with him. She knows what he did.'

'We can't leave her alone with him. She'll be in danger.'

He ran to the window. It opened onto the back of the house but it was four floors up.

'Can you see anyone?'

'Hello!' he shouted. 'Is there anyone there?' Breen looked down. There was an iron drainpipe just to the left of the window. He tried to reach out to it, but it was too far away.

'Shit.'

When he looked round, Helen was listening at the door.

'What's she doing?'

'Can't tell.'

Breen pushed the bottom sash up as far as it would go, then edged himself onto the sill, clinging on to the frame with both hands.

'Cathal. What the hell are you trying to do?'

'Grab my left hand. So I don't fall.'

'Don't be stupid. Please. There's no need. It'll be OK.'

'Hold it,' he shouted.

She came towards him and took his hand. 'Cathal. Please. No.'

'Tightly,' he said.

Squatting on the window ledge, he swung his right leg at the drainpipe, until his toes could hook around it. There was a bracket about an inch below, so he slowly lowered his shoe until it braced against the rusted metal. The cast iron pipe descended to the ground at the point where two walls met. If it didn't come away from the wall, he could lower himself down on it, bracing himself against the brickwork.

'You're an idiot, Cathal. Please.'

He closed his eyes for a second and breathed to steady himself.

'Stupid bloody wanker,' whispered Helen, but she still held his left hand tightly. 'Don't you want to see this baby?'

He paused. 'Don't say that now,' he said.

He flung his right hand across. It missed the pipe and his right foot slipped.

'Shit.' He scrabbled to raise his foot back up to the bracket, flailing in clear air.

'Fucking fuck,' said Helen. 'This is a stupid idea. I don't want you to do this. I need you, Cathal. Please. I need you.'

Caught there, it would be just as hard to swing his body weight back to the window. There was nothing for it now. Without someone with the strength to pull him back up, his only choice was to climb down – or fall.

A second time he pushed his free arm towards the pipe. This time he got close enough to scrabble his fingernails round the paintwork until they could at last get some kind of grip.

He looked down. Directly below was a small square of concrete with a metal dustbin. If he fell from here he would be lucky just to break his legs.

'Let go.'

'No. I won't.' She gripped his hand more tightly.

'I can't get back in, anyway, now. There's only one way.'

'I can pull you back in. I can.'

'Please. My arm is getting tired. I won't have the strength to do it soon. You have to let go.'

He had seen a man fall from a tower block once. The body had landed next to him, skull flattened like a half-orange on the tarmac.

'Farm girl, remember. I'm strong. Don't, Cathal. Please. You're going to die.'

'No. You have to let go.'

'It'll be my fault if you die, Cathal. Please.'

Breen looked up at her. She was crying now. 'You have to do this. After three. One . . . two . . . th—'

And he felt her loosen her grip on him. It happened fast after that. The moment he felt his hand was in free air, his left leg slipped off the window ledge and he was floundering for a second foothold, his left hand waving in the air.

'Paddy!' she screamed.

Just as his left hand reached the pipe, his feet lost their grip and he began to slide down the pipe. With both hands on the pipe he knew that only his legs could slow his fall, so he pressed his left leg against the rough wall, ripping the cloth from his trousers, and searing his skin.

Miraculously, the ancient pipe held. His body was wedged now, hands on the pipe, knee braced against the rough wall. He stopped falling.

'Cathal?'

'I'm OK.'

He took a breath.

From there, the descent was relatively simple: an ungainly scramble down the back of an old London house. When he reached the bottom, he looked up. Helen was scowling at him.

The kitchen door was open. He ran back upstairs.

The bedroom was empty. Had they run?

Downstairs again. But the front door was locked. Had she escaped through it?

Then he heard the sound of water, splashing from above. Again, he ran back upstairs. He realised the door to the first-floor bathroom, where she had gone to turn off the running bath, was closed now. He turned the handle; locked. Thumped on the door. 'Mrs Russell. Open the door.'

'Just a minute,' a voice answered, as if everything was perfectly normal.

He kicked the door. 'Open it.'

Slightly irritated now: 'Give me a little more time.'

'Cathal,' came a shout from upstairs. 'What's happening?'

Breen raced up the next two flights of stairs to where Helen was still trapped. The key was in the door. He turned it.

'Where is she?'

'In the bathroom.'

'Oh,' she said.

They were too late. By the time they made it downstairs, Mrs Russell was standing at the open doorway to the bathroom, wiping her arms dry with a towel.

'He's gone,' was all she said.

She had unlocked the door herself. Her naked husband was lying in the bath, with only his nose and the backs of his floating hands above the water, very pink and hairy. His white underpants lay crumpled on the mat.

There was an extraordinary stillness to him.

A man drowned.

In the time they were locked in his bedroom, Mrs Russell had dragged the drunken man here, helped him into the bath, and held his head below the water. She would have had to hold it there for two, three minutes, but it would not have been hard.

People die so easily in water.

Breen bent down and grabbed the man's shoulders and lifted them.

'You're too late. He's really dead, you know.'

With his arms under Russell's armpits, splashing water onto himself, he started to drag the warm, flabby body out of the bath.

'Help me.'

428

Helen pushed past Mrs Russell and took the lifeless man's legs. Together they lifted him out of the water and dropped him onto the floor; he fell like a bag of meat.

Breen leaned down, grabbed Russell's nose and forced a breath into his mouth. He tasted the whisky there.

Breen breathed again.

And again.

And again.

He thumped Russel's chest repeatedly, making his body jolt and his flaccid penis flap from side to side, until he heard the ribs crack, but his wife was right. Nothing would bring Ronald Russell back to life again.

There was a doorbell ringing.

When he looked around, Mrs Russell was standing with the Waterford crystal in one hand, an inch of whisky in it, and a bottle of pills in the other.

'Sarge? What's going on?'

It was Mint, calling through the letter box.

'So,' said Mrs Russell, placing the pills and the whisky on the chair by the bath, 'We better get our story straight for the police then.'

'Death by misadventure,' said Helen. 'Like you said, it's easy.'

'Helen?' said Breen.

'They'll believe it, too.'

Breen looked at her, horrified. Whisky, sleeping pills and a warm bath. 'It's not what happened,' he said.

'I'll go and let your policeman in,' said Mrs Russell.

'Not yet,' said Helen. Mint was banging on the door hard now.

'You can't do this.'

'You didn't even know if the courts were going to punish him,' Helen said.

'She's just killed a man. In cold blood.'

'Yes,' Helen said. 'She did.'

And as he peered at her, trying to work out what had happened, Helen leaned forward, took a towel and wiped Mrs Russell's fingerprints off the whisky glass, then, holding it just by the cloth, placed it carefully by the cooling bath and the pale body of Mrs Russell's husband.

FORTY

But Breen said nothing.

When he let Mint in at the door, all he said was, 'There's been an accident. Call for an ambulance.'

'Accident? What kind of accident? How?' Of course, Mint wanted to know everything; to understand what had happened at the house in Upper Addison Gardens. And Breen could not tell him.

'Please, just do as I ask. Call for an ambulance.'

And he sent Mint back to the police car while Helen finished arranging the scene upstairs. A man who had drunk too much, had taken a few of his wife's sleeping tablets, and who had drowned in his own bath.

Now Mint stood on the edge of the garden path as the ambulance men struggled down the steps with the blanket-covered body strapped to its stretcher. Neighbours gaped open-mouthed, shocked. And when he could, Breen sneaked glances at Mint's face, scanning for any flicker of doubt, any suggestion that he would say something to the local coppers who were arriving now. Mint trusted Breen; he was a good, honest copper.

When the stretcher passed, he looked round and saw Breen watching him. In that moment, Breen caught the expression of bewilderment on his face.

Breen, sick at himself, turned to the doorway, where the woman who was having his baby had put her arms around Kathryn Russell, who was weeping, for everyone to see. A grieving widow.

A bystander called to Mint. 'Oi, copper. What happened?'

And he heard Mint answer, 'It was an accident.' But when Breen turned to look at him, Mint glared back with a new look; one of distrust and loathing.

Two days later, on Thursday, when Elfie finally brought the baby home, Klaus sent someone from the agency to pick up his MG Magnette and his stereo.

'Tell him he's a bastard,' said Helen, as the young lad tasked with unplugging the hi-fi pulled up speaker wires from under the carpet.

'Don't say that,' said Elfie. 'He's Jimi's daddy. He's just going through a hard time right now.'

Helen rolled her eyes, but said nothing. In the end, Elfie had named the baby after Jimi Hendrix, though he looked nothing like him. Despite his tubby face and bald head, he still looked the spit of his absent father.

Helen watched from the window as the lad drove the car away. Elfie lay on the living-room floor, with her baby boy next to her on a pink blanket, a gift from her parents. Elfie's mother had turned out to be a writer of romantic novels who lived in a massive mansion in the North-West of England, and had been convinced the baby would be a girl. She was coming to visit at the weekend.

That morning, the news of spy exchange between the Krogers and Gerald Brooke broke in the morning papers. The radio reported that rumours were spreading that Brooke would be released today. In the House of Commons, politicians were tub-thumping, demanding an emergency debate about why the Prime Minister had caved in to Soviet pressure.

'I was thinking. We should all move into a big house in the countryside together. Paddy could paint. Helen and me could look after each other's babies . . .'

'God, no,' said Helen. 'I like it here.'

Elfie put her finger in Jimi's little hand and the fingers closed around it. 'Say what you like, I still think Brian Jones was murdered.'

Helen glanced at Breen, but he said nothing, so she got up and went to Elfie's kitchen to make tea. Breen followed her.

Yesterday, the Shepherd's Bush Police had come to the flat and interviewed them for over an hour; he had found it surprisingly easy to lie to them. He was a copper. Why wouldn't they believe him? Helen had nodded, and told them that everything had happened exactly as Sergeant Breen had said.

'We're going to have to talk about it at some point,' he said quietly. 'Just because you got away with it doesn't mean I don't know.'

'I got away with it?'

'Don't pretend to me it wasn't you who suggested it to Mrs

Russell. I know you did. It was your idea, wasn't it? The whisky, the pills, the bath.'

'You two OK in there?' Elfie called.

'Fine,' Breen shouted back. 'We'll be out in a minute.'

Helen nodded. 'Mrs Russell thinks it's all her fault. At the back of her mind, I think she knew all the time. She has to live with that.'

Helen found a tin of biscuits, took off the lid.

'I won't lie to you, Cathal. This is who I am. I wouldn't have thought twice about doing it myself if I'd had to. He had got away with two murders. No . . . three, with the caretaker. I know what it's like when someone has got away with murder.'

'You didn't know he'd got away with it. I could have proved it. You didn't give me the chance.'

'It was him I didn't give the chance to. Not you.'

She took a biscuit and bit on it, then offered the tin to Breen. He shook his head. From the living room came the sound of cooing.

'So. What now, Cathal?' she asked. 'You and me?'

'I need time, that's all.'

'I know. You're a good man. But sometimes I wonder if you're cut out to be a copper at all. Ow!' she said.

'What's wrong?'

'Nothing. Just a twinge.' She rubbed the bottom of her belly. 'If you want, I'll move out. Whatever you want. I mean it.'

'Doorbell,' shouted Elfie from the other room.

Helen left the kitchen to go and answer the door, leaving Breen on his own. He heard the door opening, closing again.

'Who are they from?' Elfie was saying.

It was a bunch of gladioli for Elfie. The note said: 'Congratulations on the baby. John C.' John Carmichael had sent flowers.

'Flowers?' said Helen. 'Really?'

'What's wrong with flowers?' Elfie stood and took them into the kitchen to put them into the sink. She didn't know what Carmichael had done. 'I think they're lovely.'

'Don't judge everyone by your own standards, Cathal,' said Helen quietly, when Elfie was out of earshot. He had told her all about John Carmichael and Julie Teenager. 'What he did was shit. But he's your oldest friend in the world.'

'What standards exactly?' said Breen. John Carmichael was a policeman who had lied to protect himself; Breen wasn't so different from him, not any more at least. He had no right to judge him now.

'Don't be bitter, Cathal. Please. It doesn't suit you. I'm sorry for what I did to you, but you know, in the circumstances, I'd do it again. It's who I am.'

'Is that your phone?' called Elfie from the kitchen.

From downstairs, through the floorboards, Breen heard a faint trilling.

'Leave it,' said Helen, looking at him sadly. 'Tell me what you want me to do. I'll take that stupid ring and wear it. Or move out. It's your choice, Cathal.'

Breen couldn't just let a telephone ring. He was out of the front door and down the steps, unlocking the door to their flat.

'I didn't expect to ever be saying this to a Met Police officer, but well done,' said a voice, when he picked up the phone.

'Mr Sand? I would have thought you'd have been busy with Gerald Brooke.'

'I'm at the airport now, as it happens. We're expecting the plane from Moscow at any minute. Fortunately for Anglo-Soviet relations, you were wrong. It wasn't Lyagushin after all.'

'Fortunately for you. Unfortunately for Ronald Russell.'

'He was a killer. And he worked for the Soviets, Sergeant Breen. Remember that.' A tannoy announcement obliterated everything for a second. Then Sand was saying, 'Lyagushin is being called home, unsurprisingly. That's the end of that. Anyway, I just wanted you to know. I've called up your Superintendent and asked him to go lightly on you for trying to talk to the press. If he disciplines you, it's not down to us.'

'Why? Why would you do that?'

'We're not bad people, Sergeant. Despite what you think. We just have a job to do. As do you. And I know you were just doing what you thought best.'

'Am I supposed to say thank you?'

'You are. I know you don't think a great deal of us.'

'You got your man back, anyway.'

'Brooke wasn't our man. Never was. Whatever Ronald Russell said. The whole thing was just putting lipstick on a pig. The Soviets outmanoeuvred us on this one.'

Another spy would replace Lyagushin, presumably.

'One other thing you might want to know. Bobienski's brother?'

'Stefan? The one who survived the gulags?'

'Yes, Stefan. Only we believe he didn't survive. Our people in Warsaw say it was all a fiction. The Polish security services, the UB, probably just pretended he was alive in order to blackmail Lena. They sent the photographs and wrote the letters. It's likely they were all forgeries. Of course she'd have never known.

But with her parents dead, she must have so badly wanted him to be alive.'

'That's awful.'

Breen didn't hear Sand's reply. Another tannoy announcement blared down the line.

'What did you say?'

'I said, I like the way you handled yourself. No hard feelings? And one last thing. Your father was Irish, wasn't he?'

'Yes.'

'You see, I only ask because there's quite a bit starting up in Ireland right now. I think it's going to be interesting. Early days yet, but I wouldn't be surprised if it's a fairly big situation. I've been saying that for a while; nobody has been listening so far, but we're going to need men there. Maybe you should come and work for us. I think you'd be a good fit. We need men like you. Resourceful. People who give a damn. None of the old public school queers and poets. They'd stand out a mile over there.'

'I'd rather not,' said Breen. 'If you don't mind.'

'I understand if you're a bit raw right now. But maybe in about six months if things don't settle down there.'

'No,' said Breen again. 'Not ever.'

'Of course. Shame.' Somewhere in the background, a jet roared, taking off for a place far away. 'I sincerely hope our paths cross again, however troublesome you've been,' said Sand. 'Have to go now,' he added.

Breen put down the phone and went back upstairs.

'Who was it?' Helen was in Elfie's living room, still clutching the tin of biscuits.

'No one, really,' said Breen.

And then Breen realised there were biscuits all over the floor, scattering everywhere, breaking into fragments, and Helen had dropped down onto the blankets and throws that covered Elfie's huge sofa.

'Ow!' she said for the second time, hand under her belly, looking up at him, eyes suddenly uncertain. 'Cathal?'

In the ambulance, which smelt of disinfectant and plastic, he sat squeezing her hand as they jostled through the Hackney traffic, thinking how strange it was that she could have ended a life, but now she was bringing one into being. Wondering if he knew her at all.

And, lying on the narrow bed next to where he sat hunched, she looked back at him. He tried to remember if he had ever seen her looking this scared before, in all they'd gone through together. Just the one time, when he was hanging from the window at the back of the house in Upper Addison Gardens. So he squeezed her hand a little harder, and she did the same back, and the ambulance's bell filled the air around them with noise.

THANKS

Numerous theories have been put forward to suggest whether Brian Jones was murdered, and how or why. The finger tends to point at Frank Thorogood, who's mentioned glancingly in this book as the sometime boyfriend of Kay Fitzpatrick and the man who did 'odd jobs for Brian Jones'. I, like Cathal Breen, tend to believe the guitarist's death is more likely to have been, as the initial inquest stated all along, a sad accident. Those who follow the tortuous details of the case might recognise the character of Kay Fitzpatrick as having similarities to Brian Jones's driver Joan Fitzsimons, who was assaulted, blinded and left for dead on a Sussex beach – though they will also spot that I have taken liberties with the date and place of the attack. In the case of the real Joan Fitzsimons, her boyfriend Michael Ziyadeh was convicted of the horrendous attack and sent to Broadmoor before being deported.

In the run-up to the Gerald Brooke spy exchange, the *Sunday Times* did indeed print an article which insinuated, incorrectly, that Brooke may have been a bona fide British spy.

Massive thanks to Christopher Sandford, Paul Trynka and Chris Sansom for their help with background. All errors that remain are my own making. Nick de Somogyi P. D. Viner and Erinna Mettler get thanks too. And love and huge gratitude for being in it for the long haul to Roz Brody, Mike Holmes, Jan King and Chris Sansom; their comments were, as always, invaluable. Thanks to the inspirational Jon Riley and the riverrun team; in particular to Rose Tomaszewska for such great notes. Thanks to Jane McMorrow, obviously. And finally thanks to the amazing community of crime writers who offer their support and advice so freely.